PENGUIN MODERN CLASSICS
Raag Darbari

Shrilal Shukla, 1925–2011, grew up in the village of Atrauli, a few miles from Lucknow. He graduated from Allahabad University and joined the state's administrative service and later became a member of the Indian Administrative Service.

His first novel, *Suni Ghati ka Suraj*, was published in 1957, followed by a collection of satirical short stories and essays in 1958. His major work, *Raag Darbari*, was published in 1968, and received the highly prized Sahitya Akademi Award in 1970. Shukla has written a number of novels, such as *Seemayein Tootati Hain*, *Makaan* and *Pehla Padaav*, a biography of the author Bhagwati Charan Verma, and several collections of short stories, satirical sketches and essays.

~

Gillian Wright is an author, translator and journalist who has lived in India for over forty years. Her travel books include *Introduction to the Hill Stations of India* and an illustrated guide to Sri Lanka. She is co-author, with Mark Tully, of *India in Slow Motion*, a collection of essays on modern India. She has also collaborated with him on three other books—*Amritsar: Mrs Gandhi's Last Battle*, *No Full Stops in India* and *Heart of India*. A scholar of Urdu and Hindi, she has translated several modern classics of Indian literature into English, notably *Raag Darbari* by Shrilal Shukla, *A Village Divided* by Rahi Masoom Reza and *Middle India* by Bhisham Sahni.

SHRILAL SHUKLA

Raag Darbari

Translated from the Hindi by Gillian Wright
With an Introduction by Francesca Orsini

PENGUIN BOOKS

PENGUIN BOOKS
Published by the Penguin Group
Penguin Books India Pvt. Ltd, 11 Community Centre, Panchsheel Park,
New Delhi 110 017, India
Penguin Group (USA) Inc., 375 Hudson Street, New York, New York 10014,
USA
Penguin Group (Canada), 90 Eglinton Avenue East, Suite 700, Toronto,
Ontario, M4P 2Y3, Canada (a division of Pearson Penguin Canada Inc.)
Penguin Books Ltd, 80 Strand, London WC2R 0RL, England
Penguin Ireland, 25 St Stephen's Green, Dublin 2, Ireland (a division of
Penguin Books Ltd)
Penguin Group (Australia), 250 Camberwell Road, Camberwell, Victoria
3124, Australia (a division of Pearson Australia Group Pty Ltd)
Penguin Group (NZ), 67 Apollo Drive, Rosedale, Auckland 0632, New
Zealand (a division of Pearson New Zealand Ltd)
Penguin Group (South Africa) (Pty) Ltd, 24 Sturdee Avenue, Rosebank,
Johannesburg 2196, South Africa

Penguin Books Ltd, Registered Offices: 80 Strand, London WC2R 0RL, England

First published in Hindi by Rajkamal Prakashan Private Ltd, New Delhi 1968
First published in English by Penguin Books India 1992
First published in Penguin Modern Classics 2012

Copyright © Shrilal Shukla 1968, 1992
Translation copyright © Penguin Books India 1992
Introduction copyright © Francesca Orsini 2012

All rights reserved

10 9 8 7 6 5 4 3 2 1

ISBN 9780143418894

Typeset in Goudy Old Style by Eleven Arts, Delhi
Printed at Replika Press Pvt. Ltd, Sonepat

Narrating the Everyday State
Francesca Orsini

The edge of a town. Beyond it the ocean of the Indian countryside.

And there, on the edge of the town, stood a truck. As soon as you saw it you could tell that the sole purpose of its creation had been to rape the roads of India. Like reality, the truck had many aspects. From one point of view, the police could say that it was standing in the middle of the road. Looked at another way, the driver could say that it was on the side . . .

On one side of the road was a petrol station; on the other, shops constructed of bits of rotting thatch, wood, local know-how and various items of assorted junk . . . Nearly all of them offered one of the favourite drinks of the Indian masses which is made from dust, dirt, tea leaves which have already been used several times, boiling water and so forth.

This is surely one of the most memorable beginnings in Hindi literature. It combines utter familiarity—a truck standing in the middle of the road with its side door open, a row of shops and shacks selling super-sweet milk tea and rock-hard snacks—with an ironic attitude that invites us to admire the truck driver's swagger and the tea sellers' impudence in selling inedible food and something that cannot answer to the name of tea. In itself it is a depressing sight, yet irony transforms it into something we can laugh at, just as we can laugh at the nationalist rhetoric of claims such as 'the manual dexterity and scientific expertise of our local working men. [The sweets] showed that even if we don't know how to make a decent razor blade, we're still the only people in the world who can turn rubbish into the tastiest of snacks' (p. 1). Not only does irony give us a little distance from which the dismal sight appears funny, in the context of post-Independence India it also guides us to read this distance as the gap between aspirations and possibilities, between appearances and substance, expectations and outcomes, reality and rhetoric.

Written in the early years of Indira Gandhi's government, when the Congress party ruled uncontested but internally ridden with factions, *Raag Darbari* (1968) traces the distance between Jawaharlal Nehru's grand vision of development planning, democracy and secularization, and the dynamics of an ordinary village. At the same time, *Raag Darbari* reveals the important role the modern Indian state plays in people's daily lives and in their imagination—however ineffective it may be—and describes its distinctively Indian characteristics. In what sounds at first a paradoxical statement but gradually becomes more and more of a truism, Shivpalganj village can and should also be read as a microcosm of wider dynamics playing themselves out on the national stage:

> In just a few days Rangnath began to feel that Shivpalganj was like the great Hindu epic, the Mahabharat—what was to be found nowhere else was there, and what was not there could be found nowhere else. He realized that all Indians are one and that, everywhere, our minds are alike. He observed that the Indian genius for manipulation and manoeuvring existed in an unrefined form in Shivpalganj, in abundance. This was the same genius which was proclaimed by celebrated newspapers in bold type in front-page headlines, and due to which all kinds of great corporations, commissions and administrations were formed, fell and were dragged away. As Rangnath realized this, his faith in Indian cultural unity was reaffirmed. (pp. 48–49)

~

So vast has the perceived gap been between the rhetoric of the newly independent state and its local practices, between the aspirations of working- and middle-class men and women and the realities of their lives, and between the promises of social, gender and economic transformation and the limits and obstacles to almost any kind of personal freedom, that it is little wonder that satirical writing should thrive in Hindi literature. Shrilal Shukla belongs to a rich vein of writing that stretches from Suryakant Tripathi Nirala's autobiographical sketches *Chaturi the Chamar* (*Chaturi Chamar*, 1934), *Kulli Bhat* (1937) and *Billesur the Goatherd* (*Billesur Bakariha*, 1945) to Krishan Chander's sensible donkey in *Autobiography of a Donkey* (*Ek Gadhe ki Sarguzasht*, 1957),[1] from Harishankar Parsai's deft Inspector Matadeen who exports corrupt police practices to the moon to Uday Prakash's wry stories of everyday tragedies, from Vinod Kumar Shukla's almost enchanted contemplation of small-time, small-clerk life in *A Servant's Shirt* (*Naukar ki Kameez*, 1979) to the sardonic performances of cheaters and cheated in the more recent writings of Gyan Chaturvedi and Akhilesh. Indeed, as Shrilal Shukla himself put it in an interview, 'irony is a forceful and fundamental note in every meaningful piece of writing today'.[2]

Yet the status of satirical writing has remained uncertain in the Hindi literary field, uneasily poised between 'timepass' newspaper columns and serious literature that engages in cultural critique and explores the personal as well as the political. Shrilal Shukla himself has suffered as a result. While *Raag Darbari* is recognized as a satirical masterpiece, received the annual prize of India's National Academy of Letters (Sahitya Akademi) in 1970, and has never been out of print since publication, it is yet to be recognized as a *literary* classic. Only one serious volume of criticism exists devoted to Shukla (edited by the writer and editor of the prominent literary journal *Tadbhav*, Akhilesh, in 2000), and only one essay in English (by Rupert Snell), and he is yet to become properly part of the collective understanding of post-Independence Hindi literary history. Yet, as we shall see, not only does *Raag Darbari* deal with the crucial questions of state and politics in postcolonial India, Shrilal Shukla's writing more generally engages in dialogue—and occasionally in polemic—with the main literary trends and cultural attitudes of his time.

~

Shrilal Shukla's background is not unusual among Hindi writers of his generation. He was born in a village of Lucknow district in north India, to a Brahmin family of educated but economically vulnerable small farmers who had one foot in Sanskrit learning and one in modern education and colonial service. Lucknow is famed as the splendid capital of the late Mughal kingdom of Awadh (the old spellings are 'Oudh' or 'Oude'), a city of lavish architectural spectacle and a centre of music, of Urdu and Persian poetry, and of courtesan culture that has loomed large in collective memory far beyond its official demise in 1856, just one year before the great rebellion of 1857. But Shrilal Shukla's Awadh is not that of the Lucknow nawabs. It is the rural Awadh of small tenant farmers who in the late colonial period found themselves increasingly squeezed between the high demands of land tax and free labour to their landlords on the one side and of plummeting grain prices on the other side, and who launched a no-tax campaign in 1920.[3]

Shukla remembered as a child the disastrous effect the slump in grain prices after 1929 had on the holdings of his family and of other farmers.[4] 'Unfortunately,' he writes, 'there is no realistic depiction of the terrible condition of farmers in Hindi literature. Apart from a few works by Premchand, whenever the topic has been written about it has been so tear-jerkingly sentimental that one can hardly recognize the issue.'[5] Here Shukla is referring to the great Hindi–Urdu short story writer and novelist Dhanpat Rai 'Premchand' (1880–1936). Premchand's many stories of village life, his last monumental novel *The Gift of a Cow* (*Godan*, 1936) and an earlier novel that dealt directly with the Awadh peasant movement, *The Abode of Love* (*Premashram*, 1921), give the mistaken impression that Hindi literature at the time was full of peasants. In fact, Premchand was almost an exception. The second point Shukla is referring to, and which comes out in *Raag Darbari* as well, is his strong reaction to the romanticization of the village and of 'happy peasant' life that grew out of Baden-Powell's idea of 'village republics' and M.K. Gandhi's championing of the self-sufficient village community as a counter model to the corruption of urban and Western modernity. The glorification of village life became one of the cornerstones of nationalist rhetoric, and of the statist rhetoric of rural development after Independence. In fact, the first piece Shukla ever sent for publication, in 1953-54, was entitled 'The Golden Village and the Rainy Season' ('Svarg Gram aur Varsha') and was written in angry reaction to a romantic radio play he had heard while stationed in a remote rural area of Uttar Pradesh. In *Raag Darbari* we find a hilarious deconstruction of public speeches on rural development and the public campaign posters that exhort villagers to 'Grow More Grain'—as if they were perversely unwilling to do so—while showing a healthy farmer and his contented, laughing wife (pp. 57-58). What intrigues Shivpalganj villagers, however, is whether the man on the poster is their fellow villager Badri Wrestler, and which of the village girls the woman standing behind him could be.

While Shrilal Shukla's family lived in precarious economic conditions, it was nonetheless cultured and broad-minded. His father enjoyed physical culture and classical music, his village-educated mother was well read and of liberal views, an uncle who was among the first writers in Hindi on psychology and physical culture received the most important Hindi journals of the day, and while still in the village Shrilal Shukla imbibed strong literary tastes, first in the traditional style of versification (*savayya*) and later in modern poetry and fiction.

It is difficult to overestimate the role that Hindi literary journals—miscellanies really—played in the early decades of the twentieth century. They wove together a Hindi-reading public and a community of writers (both male and female) across the wide expanse of north India that stretched for thousands of miles between Rajasthan and Calcutta, and instilled a taste for modern prose and poetry. Practically every writer of the period also owned or edited a journal, and the most successful ones circulated widely and deeply into rural areas thanks to the postal service, to public libraries or to the personal collections of obliging relatives and friends.

The next stage for Shukla after the village was university, first in Allahabad, then famed as the 'Oxford of the East' and host to a vibrant Hindi literary community of student and teachers, and after that briefly in Lucknow. Shukla had to abandon his studies after his father's early death and prepare for the Civil Services Examinations, which he passed in 1948. He later expressed regret at not having taken part in the freedom movement, engrossed as he was in his own personal struggles. At the same time, he objected vigorously to the stereotype of the struggling Hindi writer—a corollary of the idea of 'poor Hindi' vs 'wealthy English'. 'To be poor or unemployed in a country like India is actually no big thing. That's why when a citizen writer offers a pitiful description of his own poverty I feel that he is indirectly offending all those who are living in even greater hardship but do not have the means of self-publication'.[6]

While Shukla did not become a professional littérateur—unlike so many of his contemporaries who viewed government employment as incompatible with creative freedom—already at university in Allahabad, he became friends with some of the most important young Hindi writers of the day, Dharamvir Bharati (1926–97), Sarveshwar Dayal Saxena (1927–83) and Vijay Dev Narayan Sahi. He remained, as he himself put it, on the fringes of the literary circles in Allahabad, where fierce debates raged at the time between Progressive writers and critics (who internally rehearsed the well-known debates between Zhdanov and Lukács) and the so-called experimentalists, modernist poets and fiction writers who placed central emphasis on the creative process. The electric excitement of the students there, who argued over fundamental questions while eyeing their future as leaders and intellectuals of the new nation, and falling in love, is captured in the defining novel of the youth of that generation, Dharamvir Bharati's romantic *The God of Sins* (*Gunahon ka Devta*, 1949).

The 1940s and '50s were a period of enormous creativity in Hindi—in poetry with the path-breaking collections of new poets edited by Sachidanand H. Vatsyayan 'Agyeya' (1911–87), and in novel writing with the very diverse experiments of Bharati, Phanishwarnath 'Renu', Krishna Sobti, Agyeya and so on. Some of them, like Bharati and Agyeya (for example in *Islands in the Stream* [*Nadi ke Dweep*, 1952]), reflected on how personal relationships could grow for modern individuals who craved authenticity and depth while the social institutions of family, neighbourhood and workplace seemed stuck in a conservative mould that prescribed strict gender roles and castigated anyone who broke out of line.

The enormous upheaval of the Partition between India and Pakistan in 1947, with its gory massacres and desperate mass migrations, was refracted in many short stories and in the monumental novel *False Truth* (*Jhutha Sach*, 1958-60) by Yashpal (1903-76). The second part of the novel—which has been recently translated into English as *This Is Not That Dawn*—traces the fate of its characters as refugee-citizens in the new India, mostly in Delhi but also in Lucknow, which took over from Allahabad as the capital of the state of Uttar Pradesh. The refugees' displacement and desperate efforts at survival, especially the women, that are at the emotional heart of Yashpal's novel found an imaginative historical transposition in Krishna Sobti's dazzling first novel, *Separated from the Flock* (*Dar se Bichuri*, 1957, recently translated as *Memory's Daughter*). Set at the time of the Anglo-Sikh Wars of the late 1840s, the novel recounts in her own voice the vicissitudes of a girl separated by circumstances from her family in rural Punjab, her remarkable resilience and refusal to perceive herself as a victim. The novel was first published alongside one of Shukla's early short stories in the book-journal *Nikash*, edited by Dharamvir Bharati.

But the Hindi writer who comes closest to the ironic double vision of the rural India of *Raag Darbari* is Phanishwarnath 'Renu' (1921-77). Also hailed as a masterpiece, Renu's first novel *The Soiled Border* (*Maila Anchal*, 1954) began a new trend in 'regional' writing (*anchalik*; *anchal* means both the border of a sari—here possibly Mother India's—and a region). The term carried connotations of backwardness, quaintness and marginality, and the village it depicted, mired in caste competition, superstition and illiteracy, appeared to be the very opposite of 'modernity'. Yet, if we consider *The Soiled Border*'s use of geography, history, language and society, the novel ironically begins to appear—much like *Raag Darbari*—as a true picture of Indian modernity. The choice of a faraway, self-avowedly backward village, where education, transport and other facilities have yet to arrive, allows for a peculiar offside view on the centre. Nor does the nationalist movement arrive into a vacuum, but to a place where there is already a strong regional identity and a flourishing culture. The story of the village mixes history and myths, both retold orally, and the centrality of the nationalist narrative is displaced already in the novel's structure, which follows rather the rhythm of the agricultural seasons and festivals, of work and leisure. Language could be said to be the main protagonist of *The Soiled Border*, so evident is Renu's pleasure in wordplay, song rhythms, local idioms and the personal language of each character, which carries echoes of religious texts, songs and slogans. The language of the novel is deliberately non-standard, meant to jolt urban readers out of their complacency and catapult them into an almost exclusively oral world.

Village society is presented in *The Soiled Border* with anthropological accuracy—land tenure, caste hierarchy and mobility, group relations, rituals and festivals, and myths and beliefs. Moreover, this is a world of caste competition and in which politics is already crucial for the social and economic mobility of the group. At the same time, as political scientists would discover a few decades later, political divisions tend to retrace pre-existing social divisions, and mobilization is considered easier (even by the socialists) along caste lines. As in *Raag Darbari*, the protagonist of *The Soiled Border* at first appears to be the only young, urban, educated and enlightened male character (a doctor in this case), but he quickly becomes absorbed by the village, which comes to regard him with a mixture of affection and contempt. As in *Raag Darbari*, much of the irony concentrates on the political, though the villagers' imaginative use and misuse of political slogans is here the butt of gentler fun. Far from being marginal, Shrilal Shukla himself argued, anchalik literature like Renu's represents the mainstream of Indian modernity. The same can be said of *Raag Darbari*.

~

The plot of *Raag Darbari* is simple—young MA graduate Rangnath comes to stay with his uncle Vaidyaji in Shivpalganj village in order to regain his health after taxing exams. During the course of his stay he—like many urban Indians—discovers the village to be very different from literary images and depictions through nationalist rhetoric. But what to him appear to be aberrations are to the villagers the normal ways of life: in the college, masters will be more interested in their personal affairs than teaching, and students in warming their seats than studying; rigging elections, exams, and court statements is the norm; the way to get things done is not by protocol but through a judicious choice of either connections or muscle power; rhetoric allows you to say one thing and its opposite in the same breath, depending on what best fits the occasion, and so on and so forth. Occasionally given to pangs of conscience because his relatives are the chief operators (and therefore the chief villains) in the village, Rangnath does not however become the conscience of the novel but himself the butt of irony on such occasions:

> Educated people in India occasionally become afflicted with a certain disease which is known as 'crisis of conscience'. And among them, this disease generally attacks those who consider themselves intellectuals . . .
>
> If Rangnath had been in the town he would have sat in a coffee house with his friends and delivered a long speech on this [college] election . . . he would have said that in a country where such things were done for minor posts, what would people stop at to secure the major ones? Having said all this, and spoken a few sentences in faulty English, he would have drained his coffee cup and felt satisfied that he was an intellectual; and that, having delivered a powerful speech in favour of democracy and unburdened his heart in front of four useless men, he had overcome a 'crisis of faith'.
>
> But he wasn't in the town. He was in the country where, in the words of Ruppan babu, you couldn't trust your own father and where, in the words of Sanichar, no one would piss on your cut finger, let along offer to bandage it.
>
> And so, Rangnath could not overcome his affliction. (pp. 150–51)

Or, as his brawny cousin Badri Wrestler puts it, 'Why worry about what nonsense Rangnath gets up to? He's a town man—like pig shit, no good for plastering the floor or burning' (p. 295). In other words, Shrilal Shukla refuses to champion Rangnath's perspective: 'either I could write it with the attitude of an "angry young man", which I was not, or I could write it as a literate rustic accustomed to the ways of Sanichar, Ruppan babu, Vaidyaji and the others, which I was'.[7] Despite the individual philosophies and idiosyncrasies of Vaidyaji, of Badri Wrestler and his disciple Chhote Wrestler, of the reckless Principal, cautious shopkeeper Gayadin, bhang-loving Sanichar and professional witness Radhelal, much of the strength of the novel comes from the tension between their shared understanding and the urban, middle-class attitudes represented by Rangnath, and from the way all of them are subjected to the author's irony. Shrilal Shukla himself was, in the words of one critic, both a 'true villager' and a 'modern urbanite'.

In thirty-five compact chapters, *Raag Darbari* takes Rangnath and us readers through the significant spaces and critical events in the postcolonial village—with occasional forays into the nearby town. These are the—exclusively male—institutional spaces of the police station, the college, the civil court, the village council or panchayat with its own court, and the cooperative union. At the centre is the informal pivot of power that is Vaidyaji's veranda—this is the modern darbar or court, echoed in the title. And then there are the other significant spaces—the mela or fair, the bus stand, the culverts between fields where people sit and chat, the village pond, the wrestling pit, the Chamrahi or untouchable locality, the shops and trucks by the wayside, the rooftops for secret trysts. Institutional spaces are important because they map the presence of the state in the village, while at the same time they reveal how skilled villagers like Vaidyaji, Ramadhin and the Principal use public institutions as their personal property. Spaces train our look towards how people behave in them, like the Sub-Inspector 'half sitting, half reclining' on his chair in the police station as on a throne (p. 8), and to the importance of gestures, like touching someone's feet. Touching an official's feet, as scholars have pointed out, does not mean that the villagers, like other ordinary Indian citizens, do not grasp the logic of impersonal norms of the modern state. In fact, both the feet toucher and touched know that the gesture undermines the logic of impersonal, bureaucratic norms or of caste equality that, both know, should prevail in an office or in a formal interaction. Vaidyaji will murmur something against the practice while keeping a keen eye on whether a visitor is, in fact, submitting to him by touching his feet.

The unedifying descriptions of the village pond or the bus stop or the fair take us back to Shukla's keenness to counteract urban and nationalist idealizations of the village as a site of beauty and innocence, as well as statist claims about rural development—the beautiful straight lines of a properly developed field carry no seeds. Accused at times of a perverse and Naipaul-esque insistence on depicting defecation and ugliness as characteristic of modern Indians, Shrilal Shukla has nevertheless strongly protested his difference. While appreciative of Naipaul's insights and narrative power in *An Area of Darkness* (1964), what Shukla found missing in Naipaul's account was any interest in trying to understand the humanity behind the dirt, ugliness and poverty he found: 'Actually Naipaul has left untouched that vast pool of humanity which in India constitutes the lower and lower-middle classes and has based his views on the antics of a few hoteliers, servants and guides'.[8] Insights into the often irreverent attitudes of the *ganjahas*—as the villagers of Shivpalganj are called—towards the dignity of public and natural spaces abound in *Raag Darbari*. And what better way of expressing irreverence towards a space than by shitting or pissing on it?

~

Occasional references to the food imports because of food crises, to non-alignment, or to the recent war with China in 1962, or to factionalism within what was still basically a one-party system, or to the villagers' indifference to village council elections (before the 1990s' reforms and lower-caste mobilization turned them into a thriving arena of local politics) anchor *Raag Darbari* to the 1960s. Similarly, women are practically absent from the still patriarchal village—apart from Bela and the veiled, nameless flocks of women who throng the fair or squat to defecate.

In broader terms, however, *Raag Darbari* can be taken as a portrayal of the postcolonial Indian state—and as such deserves to be read by anyone interested in the subject. While the Indian state inherited and preserved colonial institutions, as is obvious from everything from the titles of offices and of civil servants, the architecture of public buildings and the styles of dress of lawyers and policemen, political scientists have convincingly argued that the ethical aspects of the modern state—like sovereignty, citizenship, equal rights and franchise—were imagined by the nationalist intelligentsia as part of the nation-building process. The ideology of the new nation state was thus profoundly different from that of the colonial state. Yet the two-tiered federal system, with a strong centre and strong states, created two distinct levels of political discourse and style, and accommodated different class and group interests within the same party. Political scientists have remarked upon the profound gap that developed between the bureaucratic elite at the centre and lower-level personnel locally in charge of the administration and of implementing central policies of development and planning.

Yet the bottom-up, rural view of *Raag Darbari* suggests that Vaidyaji's manipulations and use of rhetoric are not dissimilar from those of political leaders at the centre. Vaidyaji, who had made his name at the end of the Raj as a recruiter for the army and 'had revered the British', has transitioned successfully after Independence into the role of managing director of the cooperative union and college manager. Not only is he a skilful operator, he is also a master of the Gandhian rhetoric of the political renouncer, practised by many Congress leaders before and after Independence:

> In reality, he didn't want to hold these posts because he had no greed for power. But there was no one else who could carry out such responsible jobs in the locality . . .
>
> [L]ike those hundreds of great men who lived in the capital to serve the country, Vaidyaji was not old despite his age and, like the same great men, he had vowed that he would . . . carry on serving the nation. Like every great Indian politician, he loathed politics . . . Like Gandhi, he took no post in his political party because he wanted to encourage new blood (p. 29)

Fitting with his identity as a Brahmin and a practitioner of the traditional medical system of Ayurveda, his rhetoric also includes references to philosophy and the scriptures. Thus factionalism becomes, according to Vedanta philosophy, 'another name for the ultimate condition of realization that the self "I" and the divine "Thou" are one.' He continues:

In factionalism, every 'I' sees every 'Thou', and every 'Thou' sees every 'I' in a position better than himself. They all want to capture each other's position. 'I' wants to annihilate 'Thou', and 'Thou' to annihilate 'I', so that 'I' becomes 'Thou' and 'Thou' becomes 'I'.

Vedanta is part of our tradition, and because the meaning of factionalism can be drawn from Vedanta, factionalism is also our tradition. (p. 76)

Similarly, renunciation can be a useful political instrument. 'This had also been said in the Upanishads. That's what all reputed leaders did to this day. They enjoyed the fruits of power, renounced them, and then enjoyed the fruits of renunciation' (p. 299). Implied in these statements is that Vaidyaji's vernacular political language is not dissimilar from the language of Congress national leaders other than Nehru. While the irony in the use of these cultural referents is unmistakeable, we also have to admire Vaidyaji's rhetorical skill. Rhetoric is not only a vital skill for the politician who must defend himself from his enemies' accusations but is also the necessary coating for the successful pursuit of one's self-interests within the democratic set-up. Occasionally the veil drops, as when the police Sub-Inspector tells Ruppan, 'But now we have to serve the people. For the citizens . . .' and Ruppan babu touches his arm and says, 'Forget it. Apart from you and me there's no one listening' (p. 12). For Vaidyaji, by contrast, the rhetoric of democracy and development has become second nature.

Vaidyaji's success as the local powerful man is not only due to his rhetorical skills and sangfroid, but also to his mastery of the workings of what has been called the 'everyday state' as discussed by C. J. Fuller and John Harriss.[9] This means that he knows that beyond the state as an impersonal ideal, the state at the local level is embodied in people with whom some kind of social relationship can be established. Knowing personally who is in what post where and having a direct, personal connection is crucial, and in moments of need we see Vaidyaji departing for the town to network with local officials, exchanging their patronage for village ghee, his potency pills or information about powerful astrologers. Vaidyaji knows exactly which official orders are potentially dangerous and which can be easily dismissed, and how to work so as to have state officials transferred away—as the Sub-Inspector learns to his dismay. Vaidyaji, just like his rival Ramadhin Bhikhmakhervi, knows how to extract resources from the state in the form of bogus grant and scheme applications, and how to exercise power by proxy through relatives and hangers-on.

Kalika Prasad, a ganjaha whose profession is spending government grants, reckons he is 'the most modern man in the village because his occupation [is] entirely a product of modern times' (p. 153)—and he may well be right. Vaidyaji's behaviour after the embezzlement of two truckloads of wheat by the supervisor of the cooperative union is exemplary in this regard. First he does nothing to prosecute the culprit, and we suspect that his inaction suggests he was complicit in the act. Then he gets a resolution passed that asks the government to give the union compensation for the money lost. 'What's it got to do with the government?' asks Rangnath, puzzled. But Vaidyaji's logic is flawless—it invokes the ideal state as provider and protector of social welfare and shifts responsibility on to it while appropriating state funds (twice) for personal gain:

> 'Who else will give it? The supervisor is missing. We've informed the police. The rest is the responsibility of the government. We are powerless . . . Whatever happens, if the government wants our union to survive and continue to benefit the people, it will have to pay the compensation. Otherwise, this union will collapse . . .'
>
> Vaidyaji was speaking so reasonably that Rangnath's head began to spin. He mentioned terms like 'the inertia of the administration', 'the welfare of the people', 'responsibility', time and time again. Rangnath became certain that his uncle, despite being of an older generation, was competent at speaking precisely the language understood in modern times. (pp. 73–74)

In this context, Langar's attempt to get a copy of an official paper without bribery (thus alienating the local state clerk) and the honesty of the new cooperative inspector appear ludicrous and incongruous aberrations.

~

Irony and satire—both covered in Hindi by the same term, *vyangya*—form the structuring principle in *Raag Darbari*, rather than plot. In fact the astonishing feat of *Raag Darbari* is that it sustains the ironic mode through its 350-odd pages. This prolonged effort is central to the novel's project. Most satirical writing in Hindi has been short, but Shukla felt that 'until one expresses one's overall reaction to society, short pieces are ineffective, just like pinching . . . that's why I conceived of *Raag Darbari*'.[10] How does irony enable a wide-ranging critique of the postcolonial Indian state and society? First, by setting up correlations between apparently incongruous elements, linking the sublime with the ridiculous. The village pond, despite its filthiness, has its own economic and political value, 'in the same way that any developing country, despite its backwardness, has some economic and political importance' (p. 202). Rangnath is about to give the love letter he has found on the rooftop to Ruppan, 'but the moment he saw Badri he changed his plan, just as, occasionally, we change our economic plans the moment we lay eyes on an American expert' (p. 218). The effect of Sanichar's speech is limited only to himself, 'just as India's claims of leading Asia and Africa are taken seriously only in India' (p. 190). Rangnath reacts strongly to Picasso's name being mentioned in Shivpalganj—the distance between the two worlds is too great. In terms of language, Shukla steadily employs 'pure' (i.e., heavily Sanskritized) Hindi for the language of rhetoric, and to emphasize the ironic contrast between rhetoric and reality he does not hesitate to use a wide range of registers. 'At one extreme is Avadhi [the regional dialect] and at the other extreme are English idioms. Whenever I have used English idioms I have not translated them but tried to incorporate their essence into Hindi'.[11] The Principal often breaks into Awadhi at moments of great tension.

Just like the truck and the roadside sweet shops at the beginning, irony makes us look at a scene with new eyes, while deflating the rhetoric. Watching villagers flocking to the fair, Rangnath reflects that 'if All India Radio had been giving a running commentary, it would certainly have described how, thanks to the prosperity brought by the government's Five-Year Plans, the people, with music and song, were showering each other with love and joy'. But Rangnath knows better by now and notices the hollow enthusiasm of the crowds, how all women are barefoot and no one is wearing a woollen coat despite the cold (p. 114). At other times, statements produce the opposite effect of what one would expect, revealing a deeper truth in the process. The police 'knew perfectly well that it would never come to an exchange of fire and so every constable was armed' (p. 172). Or they 'arrived on the scene as soon as they were thought of, without even waiting for the incident to be over' because they know that 'there was no murder or dacoity going on' (p. 324). Irony makes us read between the lines and come to the opposite conclusion to what is stated: when Jognath resists arrest, a constable's shirt is 'injured'. As a result, 'the minimum necessary force was exercised to control Jognath' and he is later 'found to have twenty contusions and forty abrasions. They were all minor injuries—the result of falling on the ground' (pp. 175–76). Irony also means that, in the context of Shivpalganj, statements of fact that go against the prevailing interests will not be believed and will be easily discarded. In the formal complaint to the education minister that college elections have been rigged,

> this incident was described to such an impossible length that, even if you did manage to finish reading the letter, it was impossible to believe what it said, since it inferred that there was no law and order left in Shivpalganj; that things such as police and police stations did not exist there even in name; and that four hooligans could get together and do exactly as they wanted. There was clearly no need for an inquiry to determine that the complaint was untrue (p. 158)

But irony also points towards one of the ways ganjahas cope with adversities and the mismatch between the system and their expectations, i.e., by laughing at them. Is this ability to laugh in the midst of a crisis—as Langar tries to do—a sign of indomitable strength or of pervasive corruption, one interviewer asked Shrilal Shukla. The answer he gave was—both.

Most of the irony makes use of political rhetoric, and the high-flown language of such rhetoric is one of the main sources and means of comedy in the novel. When the director of the village cooperative union happens to see in the park of the nearby town the supervisor who was rumoured to have fled to Bombay, he does not know what to do. Should he denounce the culprit to the police but risk upsetting the game that is surely at work, or do nothing and pretend not to have seen him? By choosing the latter he behaves like a Hindu saint, immersed in his individual world, and as they part ways they practise 'peaceful cooperation' and the 'principles of Panchsheel', Nehru's famed five principles of international non-alignment (p. 66).

At the end of the novel, Rangnath dreams of escaping from Shivpalganj. The section that follows, entitled 'The Music of Escapism', mocks his dream of escaping the 'mud of humanity' and seeking refuge in the colour pages of Look and Life, in the elite intellectual world of bars and teahouses, of seminars in hill station retreats and in research institutes, or else in dreams of classical India. 'Run, run, run! You're being pursued by reality' (p. 346). Fifty years later, new elite spaces like gated housing communities and air-conditioned malls have joined this list and created a parallel reality to that of the new Shivpalganjes. Meanwhile, the drab and gaudy spaces of the mela, the bus station or the local shops provide 'vernacular' or 'glocal' backdrops for song videos and ads that suggest to the youth of Shivpalganj that they, too, can dream of mobility and modernity from where they are. Like few other novels, Raag Darbari presents rural transformations as both a nightmare and a triumph.

June 2012
London

Notes

1. Translated by H. Bouman as Mr Ass Comes to Town (Delhi: Hind Pocket Books, 1968).

2. Shrilal Shukla, interview by Mamta Kalia, Mere Sakshatkar (New Delhi: Kitab Ghar, 1979), p. 19.

3. See Kapil Kumar, Peasants in Revolt: Tenants, Landlords, Congress and the Raj in Oudh, 1886–1922 (New Delhi: Manohar, 1984).

4. He wrote an article on this subject. See Shrilal Shukla, 'Awadh ke Ve Kisan' [Awadh's peasants], Yeh Ghar Mera Nahin [This house is not mine] (Hapur: Sambhavna Prakashan, 1979), pp. 92–95.

5. 'Apne Bare Mein' [About myself], ibid., p. 125.

6. Ibid., p. 124.

7. Rupert Snell, 'Rural Travesties: Shrilal Shukla's *Raag Darbari*', *Journal of Commonwealth Literature* XXV, no. 1 (1990), p. 176.

8. Shukla, 'Mi. Naipaul aur Andhakar ka Ek Prantar' [Mr Naipaul and *An Area of Darkness*], *Yeh Ghar Mera Nahin* [This house is not mine], p. 104.

9. See Chris Fuller and John Harriss, 'For an Anthropology of the Modern Indian State', in *The Everyday State and Society in Modern India*, eds. C. J. Fuller and V. Bénéï (London: Hurst, 2001).

10. Shrilal Shukla, interview by Akhilesh, *Shrilal Shukla ki Duniya* (New Delhi: Rajkamal Prakashan, 2000), p. 138.

11. Ibid., p. 6.

Translator's Introduction

Raag Darbari is not widely read in Delhi society and you'd be hard-pressed to find anyone who has heard of it or its author at the average dinner party. The latest English novels, on the other hand, are a favourite subject for discussion. But no novel I have ever read in English comes close to capturing life in an ordinary north Indian village, whereas the smell of the earth of Uttar Pradesh emanates from every page of *Raag Darbari*.

Its author, the retired bureaucrat Shrilal Shukla, has spent a lifetime in Uttar Pradesh. His accurate observations of society and keen sense of humour made *Raag Darbari* a bestseller over thirty years ago when it was first published, and are responsible for its continuing popularity wherever Hindi is read and valued. As a bookseller from Lucknow's congested Aminabad area told me, '*Raag Darbari* sells so well because it gives an absolutely correct description of village politics and the working of government machinery.'

Politics and government are the two main themes of the novel.

Uttar Pradesh is India's most politically dominant state and it's often said that politics is the state's main industry. Shrilal Shukla describes politics at the grass roots, but much of the factionalism, nepotism and behind-the-scenes manipulation he portrays is familiar to anyone who follows events through the national press. UP's highly developed bureaucracy, the author's other main target, is satirized for its irrelevance to the common man, inefficiency and close connections with politicians. A senior official in the government of UP sought to explain away the book's appeal by saying, 'You see, it's a sort of Indian *Yes Minister*.' But *Raag Darbari* covers a much wider spectrum than the British television series.

The title itself reveals the political emphasis of the plot. *Raag Darbari* is the name of one of the most difficult raags of Indian classical music, but Shrilal Shukla has taken its meaning literally—the melody of the court. In the novel it refers to the tune sung by the courtiers of a latter-day local raja, that is to say, a village politician. The court of the title is presided over by Vaidyaji, a Brahmin Ayurvedic doctor who is the political mastermind of his village, Shivpalganj. The story, set in the late nineteen-fifties, describes his struggle for political control of Shivpalganj, a fictional village typical of the Raebareli district, south-east of Lucknow. Among the novel's other main characters are Vaidyaji's elder son, the village strongman, Badri Wrestler; his younger son, the student leader Ruppan babu; and his nephew, Rangnath, a graduate from the town. Rangnath comes to his uncle's village of Shivpalganj to recuperate from an illness and the novel covers the period he stays there. During this time Vaidyaji, who controls the local cooperative union and college, launches a bid for power over the village council and faces a stiff challenge to his dominance in the college from a group of dissident teachers backed by his main political rival in the village.

When I met Shrilal Shukla on the lawns of Lucknow's palatial but crumbling Carlton Hotel, I asked him why the cooperative union, the village council and the college were so important for Vaidyaji to control. He replied, 'They are the three key institutions in Shivpalganj because in the late fifties and early sixties, education, cooperatives and panchayats were the three main planks of village development. The fruits of large-scale industrial projects, the "new temples" of the Nehruvian era, had, by and large, not reached the villages. So these three institutions were the three instruments of change and also the institutions which dominant castes in the villages soon learnt to master in order to perpetuate their control of village matters. In *Raag Darbari* the main characters happen to be Brahmins because in much of UP the dominant castes in villages were, and to a large extent still are, Brahmins and Thakurs.'

Shrilal Shukla, besides being a retired member of India's elite IAS cadre, comes from a village not very dissimilar from Shivpalganj and from a conservative Brahmin family. After graduating with a BA from Allahabad University in ancient Indian history, English literature and Sanskrit, he drifted into government service where he was posted mainly in the areas in and around Lucknow, including the *Raebareli* district. At one time he served as director of information of the state government under V.P. Singh who later became prime minister. I naturally drew the conclusion that *Raag Darbari* was a largely autobiographical work.

But the author emphatically denied that. 'It's true I am a Brahmin,' he said, 'but I have never been conscious of my caste when I write, nor is caste particularly important in *Raag Darbari*, as in politics; then, it had not become the dominant force it is today. Similarly Shivpalganj is not my village, and none of the characters are based on individuals I know. Vaidyaji, for example, is a mixture of characteristics from three or four different types of people. And my being in the administration did not mean I had a special insight into the way the government worked or that I wrote as a bureaucrat. In fact I kept my official personality completely detached from my personality as an author. Whatever I describe in the book, for example, the working of the cooperative union, was the kind of thing that was common knowledge. In fact, one of the criticisms of *Raag Darbari* when it first appeared was that it didn't say anything new—it just described what everybody knew already. What I do have is the equipment of any author, a wealth of experiences on which I draw.'

While Shrilal Shukla relied on his experience to create his characters, the novel's episodic plot is clearly the result of the way the book was first conceived back in the sixties. Then, during relaxed lunchtimes spent on the lawns of the same Carlton Hotel, Shukla had related thirty or forty village tales to his friends who were themselves talented writers and journalists. 'The stories seemed good over beer,' he told me, 'but insipid written down.' However, his friends insisted there was something very unusual in these tales. He told me, 'They said the stories had a natural iconoclastic attitude which was the antithesis of contemporary Hindi writing on rural life. That writing either emphasized misery and exploitation or presented an idyllic rustic picture.' So Shrilal Shukla created the loose plot which bound the episodes together. But the environment of rural Shivpalganj remained the element which gave the novel the most cohesion.

Few of the characters at home in this environment are prone to much introspection, although most believe strongly in plain speaking. Some of the most colourful are the wrestlers who repeatedly make their appearance either caked with mud from the wrestling pit or smelling strongly of their latest mustard oil massage. I asked Shrilal Shukla how close they were to reality. He replied, 'That sort of collective exercise of wrestling at an *akhara* is now virtually obsolete, but it was common in villages about fifty years ago and in the fifties and sixties there were still some vestiges of this village institution lingering in central UP. The attitude the wrestlers represent is still very real, but nowadays people don't rely on straight muscle power; there are other sorts of gangsterism in politics, different kinds of wrestlers who rely on illicit firearms for their strength.'

One of the main activites of the wrestlers and other characters is imbibing bhang, the preparation of which Shrilal Shukla has observed since his childhood. As he told me, 'Although Thakurs have always taken liquor, alcohol was taboo for Brahmins and Banias. Bhang was the only sort of socially permitted intoxication and was important as a major source of relaxation and entertainment. When I was a boy in my village, the bhang-making used to start at five every evening. Now norms are changing as a result of closer contact between towns and villages, and other factors, and people are not horrified by drink as they once were.'

Shukla's Shivpalganj is also strangely devoid of women. Apart from the daughter of the local moneylender who climbs over the rooftops to kiss Rangnath, women only appear as passers-by or in bedtime fantasies. I asked the author whether village women were not part of his wealth of experience. Shrilal Shukla replied, 'Society in *Raag Darbari* is a male-dominated society, and politics is still a male-dominated field despite Indira Gandhi having been the prime minister for so long. And all the distortions of values that can attract satire or irony come from men in real life. For example, defections. Very few lady politicians indulge in floor crossing. So male characters are much more attractive if your aim is to satirize distorted values in political life. I don't think a lady would have behaved like Vaidyaji if she'd been in charge of the college.'

Even the distortions Shrilal Shukla sees in traditional social values seem to be male oriented. For example, he debunks the concept of filial devotion, the great respect Indians have for their elders. Two of the characters, Chhote Wrestler and his father, are constantly up in arms against each other, following a family tradition generations old. The author argues that this also represents reality. But perhaps he is unduly cynical about the social system which has given India a remarkably stable society for hundreds of years. When I put this to him, he replied, 'Am I too critical? What else can you be? And then you must bear in mind that I was writing in a mood of high comedy.'

It is the book's lively humour which carries the plot along and makes light of the flaws in the system which Shrilal Shukla highlights. The political and administrative system he describes was inherited from the British who created it to run an empire. It is therefore not surprising that it became strained when asked to run a complex, independent country like India. In fact, many of the systems the British introduced worked far from perfectly even during the Raj. A favourite target of the author is the courts which have been the cause of complaint for the common man ever since the eighteen-fifties when the administrator Sleeman visited villages in what is now UP and found people confounded by the corruption and complications of the newly introduced British legal system. The courtroom scenes in *Raag Darbari*, starring, amongst others, the village's professional witnesses, are some of the funniest episodes in the book.

The author maintains that this humour is not unique to himself and that the people of UP, especially in villages, have a highly developed ability to see the funny side of life. Their humour is reflected in the richness of local dialects. Shrilal Shukla has written *Raag Darbari* using a gamut of literary styles, but he has largely relied on genuinely colloquial Hindi enriched with Hindi translations of expressions drawn from dialect. This technique is unusual. Many writers of village life, for example Premchand, rely heavily on dialect itself to add realism to their writing. Shrilal Shukla's use of translated expressions gives an equally authentic rural flavour to *Raag Darbari*, besides presenting the reader with some startling mental pictures. For example, a person pleased with something that is, in fact, going to prove a nuisance is compared to a man with a tree growing out of his groin who thinks he's going to enjoy the shade.

Shrilal Shukla himself is widely read in English as well as Hindi and Sanskrit, and could easily write in those languages. But he believes that only one's mother tongue will do for creative writing. He remembers the case of his uncle, a brilliant student who wrote a book in 1913 with an English preface and was roundly castigated by his principal for the misuse of the definite article. 'My uncle realized,' he said, 'that it was not his native language, no matter how much he studied it, and he should not write in it.' So Shrilal Shukla continues to write in Hindi, taking long trips to the hills to painstakingly draft and redraft his novels.

His dry humour is still very much intact although he is increasingly disillusioned with the way India has gone since Independence. That's partly because he remembers the days of the Independence movement when he was an idealistic student, and now finds that contemporary realities do not measure up to his hopes. In his opinion, values have degenerated even further since he wrote *Raag Darbari*, rendering his novel outdated.

As he told me on the lawns of the Carlton Hotel, 'In the days when I was writing that novel, we were concerned about mild distortions of the system; now you would have to write a fantasy on the lines of Garcia Marquez to begin to capture what is going on. *Raag Darbari* has become quite irrelevant now.'

He believes that the government's performance since Independence has been 'quite dismal', and points to what he sees as the virtual collapse of the cooperative movement and to the fact that well over half the population is still illiterate as proof of that. He sees money-power, and what's known as the local mafia, playing a much larger role in politics than before, and the administration weakened by excessive political interference. Others share his views. As a Lucknow journalist remarked to me, 'Corruption is now so accepted among politicians that it is no longer an issue, and if an official accepts the set rate of a bribe and doesn't ask for more, he's considered a very good, honest man.'

So Shrilal Shukla appears to be right in saying that distortions in the system have increased. But the system is still the same one inherited from the British Raj and the problems it faces are of a similar nature to those described in *Raag Darbari*. The only difference is that the problems are bigger and will continue to grow until the system is properly adapted to meet Indian needs. Therefore I believe that *Raag Darbari* is still very relevant. Moreover, many of the observations the author makes of everyday life in UP are clearly as accurate as they were twenty-five years ago. Families of domestic pigs still jostle one another as they trot down the roads, truck drivers always park almost in the middle of the road with the vehicle door wide open so that no other vehicle can pass, and groups of village women can still be seen squatting in the fields at dawn and dusk so that they can defecate with some privacy.

Towards the conclusion of the novel, Vaidyaji tries to re-establish his influence by approaching politicians and officials in the town—a thinly disguised Lucknow. Here, too, there's much in the description which is recognizable today. Traffic has increased but a very large proportion of it still consists of government vehicles, the most impressive being the Ambassador cars with flashing red lights and miniature fans which blow air into the faces of the ministers reclining on the rear seats. English, understood by a mere 2.5 per cent of the population, is still the natural language of the elite, and the best schools are still English-medium. English also continues to be the language of shop signs in Hazratganj—the bazaar originally built by and for the British. Paan shops still spring out of every corner, glasses of milky bhang can still be had, and no man ever seems short of a place to pee. Officials and politicians still live in the greenest areas of the city, away from the noise and congestion, and politicians' bungalows are still thronged by favour seekers and representatives of various factions as politics becomes more and more a business of patrons and patronage.

This is not to deny that some things have changed for the better as well as for the worse. While *Raag Darbari* focusses on the negative aspects of the system, there are positive aspects too. For example, sections of society which were traditionally excluded from power are increasingly demanding their due share in government. At the time of writing, the chief minister of UP was a leader belonging to one such backward caste. It's another matter that he was an ex-wrestler and a former teacher at an intermediate college, his brother headed his home district's cooperative federation and a cousin the district board—all proof that even the rising political powers find these local institutions as important to control as they were when *Raag Darbari* was written. Two of the chief minister's main programmes—promoting Hindi and providing latrines for village women—are also as necessary now as they were then.

But the ultimate proof of *Raag Darbari's* continuing relevance is in its expanding readership. A second generation of Hindi readers has discovered the novel, and translations into fifteen different languages have made it accessible to people all over the country. It has also been adapted for stage and television. And now, finally, it has been published in English too. I have tried my best to capture the spirit of the book in this translation, and if I have, I am sure that Shrilal Shukla will win his fair share of acclaim among English readers too.

April 1991
New Delhi

Translator's Acknowledgements

I would particularly like to thank Shrilal Shukla for his patience and comments on the manuscript, Dr Pratibha Arya, who answered my queries during the preparation of the original draft, and Satish Jacob, Onkarnath Srivastava and Shah Ghulam Ahmed Ilmi to whom I also turned for help and advice from time to time. I am also grateful to Mark Tully who encouraged me from the very start of the project, and to my mother whose confidence in me is a great strength.

1

The edge of a town. Beyond it, the ocean of the Indian countryside.

And there, on the edge of the town, stood a truck. As soon as you saw it you could tell that the sole purpose of its creation had been to rape the roads of India. Like reality, the truck had many aspects. From one point of view, the police could say that it was standing in the middle of the road. Looked at another way, the driver could say that it was on the side of the road. According to the dictates of current fashion, the driver had opened the right-hand door so that it hung out like a bird's wing. This enhanced the truck's dimensions and made it impossible for any other vehicle to pass.

On one side of the road there was a petrol station; on the other, shops constructed of bits of rotting thatch, wood, local know-how and various items of assorted junk. At first sight it was clear that the shops were too numerous to count. Nearly all of them offered one of the favourite drinks of the Indian masses which is made from dust, dirt, tea leaves which have already been used several times, boiling water and so forth. The shops also stocked sweets, which battled valiantly day and night against the onslaughts of rain, dust storms, flies and mosquitoes. The sweets demonstrated the manual dexterity and scientific expertise of our local working men. They showed that even if we don't know how to make a decent razor blade, we're still the only people in the world who can turn rubbish into the tastiest of snacks.

The truck driver and the cleaner were standing in front of a shop, drinking tea.

Rangnath spotted the truck from a distance and immediately hastened his step.

Today, the railway had deceived him. He had left home thinking the local passenger train would be two hours late as usual, but it was only

1

an hour and a half late and had left without him. Having contributed
to the literature of the complaints book, and made himself a laughing
stock in the eyes of the railway staff, he left the station. Now, as he
walked down the road towards the truck, he began to smile.

When he reached it, the driver and the cleaner were still sipping
their tea. Glancing around aimlessly and containing his smile,
Rangnath asked the driver in an uninterested way, 'Driver sahib, is
this truck going in the direction of Shivpalganj?'

The driver had his tea to drink and the woman shopkeeper to look
at. Paying little attention to Rangnath, he said, 'It is.'

'Will you take me with you? I'll get out at the fifteenth mile. I have
to go to Shivpalganj.'

The driver assessed all the possibilities of the woman shopkeeper
in one glance and then turned his gaze upon Rangnath. *Oho!* What a
sight! Like the great God Vishnu who stands like a pure lotus flower
from head to toe, so stood Rangnath head to toe, a vision in white
khadi cotton, the homespun cloth popularized by Mahatma Gandhi.
He wore a khadi cap, shirt and pyjamas, and over his shoulder hung
a bag of the kind used by the Gandhian Bhoodan Movement. In his
hand was a leather attaché case. The driver saw him and was amazed.
Then he thought for a moment and said, 'Please take your seat, sir.
We'll leave right away.'

~

The truck shuddered into life and set off. Freeing themselves after a
while from the twisting, chaotic grasp of the town, they came upon
a clear and empty road. Here, the driver was able to get into top gear
for the first time, but the gear lever kept slipping into neutral every
hundred yards, and since the driver had his foot on the accelerator, the
shuddering increased as the speed of the truck decreased. Rangnath
said, 'Driver sahib, your gearbox is exactly like our government.'

The driver accepted this citation of merit with a smile. Rangnath
tried to make his statement more intelligible.

'No matter how often you put it into top gear, it slips every few
yards and goes back into its old rut.'

The driver laughed. 'You've said something very deep, sir.'

Next time he went into top gear, he lifted his leg to an angle of about ninety degrees and held the gear pressed under his thigh. Rangnath wanted to say that the same technique was needed to run the country but, thinking that this would be a still deeper statement, he remained silent.

Meanwhile, the driver returned his thigh to its proper place, put a long stick against the gear and wedged the other end under the dashboard. The truck kept up speed. Terrified at the sight of it, cyclists, pedestrians, horse-drawn carts and all other vehicles for several furlongs ahead drove off the road; judging from the speed at which the vehicles fled, it seemed as if they thought the truck was no truck, but a flame of fire, a typhoon from the Bay of Bengal, some foul-mouthed official unleashed on the public or a gang of wild Pindaris. Rangnath thought that they should have had an announcement made in advance, warning people to keep all their livestock and children at home as a truck had just left the town.

The driver asked, 'Tell me, sir, how are you? It's a long time, is it, since you've been into the country?'

Rangnath smiled, encouraging this attempt at civility.

'What are you doing these days, sir?'

'Digging up grass.'

The driver laughed. He nearly ran over a naked ten-year-old boy. Safe, the boy dropped down on to a small bridge like a wounded house lizard falling from the ceiling.

This had no effect on the driver. Pushing his foot even farther down on the accelerator and laughing, he said, 'What a thing to say! Go on, sir, tell me what you mean.'

'I told you. I'm digging up grass. In English, you call it research. Last year I did my MA. This year I've started research.'

The driver was smiling as if he were listening to *Tales from the Thousand and One Nights*.

'So, sir, why are you going to Shivpalganj?'

'My mother's brother lives there. I've been ill and I'm going to stay in the country for a while to recover.'

The driver laughed for a rather long time.

'What a tale you've made up, sir!'

Rangnath gave him a doubtful look and asked, 'What's made up about it?'

At this innocent question, the driver rocked with mirth.

'What things you're saying! Very well then, forget it. Tell me, how is Mittal sahib? What happened to the murder case in the police lock-up?'

Rangnath was completely unnerved. Choking, he said, 'But how would I know who this Mittal sahib is?'

The driver put a brake on his laughter. The truck too slowed down. He took a close look at Rangnath.

'You don't know Mittal sahib?'

'No.'

'Jain sahib?'

'No.'

The driver spat out of the window and asked in a clear voice, 'You don't work for the CID, then?'

Irritated, Rangnath said, 'CID? What on earth do you mean?'

The driver let out a long sigh and began to examine intently the road ahead. Some bullock carts were travelling along it. In accordance with the popular principle of stretching your legs wherever and whenever you get the chance, the drivers lay on top of their carts, asleep and with their faces covered. The bullocks, not on their own initiative but as a result of long practice, quietly pulled the carts down the road. The scene merited comparison with the bovine public and its lethargic leaders, but Rangnath hadn't the courage to say anything. He had been upset by the remark about the CID. The driver blew, first his rubber horn and then another horn which, despite its three musical tones, was truly terrifying. The bullock carts proceeded on their way. The driver was pushing the truck on at a good speed and seemed to be about to fly over the carts. But as he got closer, he suddenly seemed to realize that he was in a truck, not a helicopter. He braked, the stick which had been wedged against the dashboard fell down, the gear changed and the truck squeezed past the carts, almost touching them.

Further on, the driver spoke to Rangnath with contempt, 'If you're not CID, then how come you're wearing khadi?'

Rangnath had been put in low spirits by these aggressive questions but he treated this one as a normal inquiry and answered simply, 'Everyone wears khadi these days.'

'Come off it, no sensible man does. Only politicians, plain-clothes men and fools.'

He opened the window, spat and changed into top gear. The personality cult surrounding Rangnath had come to an end. For a while he sat quietly. Then he began to whistle. The driver nudged him with his elbow and said, 'Look here, sit quiet. This is no place for hymn singing and such things.'

Rangnath shut up. The driver was annoyed.

'This gear keeps on slipping. It goes into neutral. What are you staring at? Grab hold of it and keep it in place!'

A few minutes later, he said in the same tone, 'Not like that! Like this. Keep the pressure up and hold it properly!'

For some time a horn had been blowing behind the truck. Rangnath had heard it but the driver was paying no attention. After a while, the cleaner, who was travelling in the back, hung round the side of the truck and began to tap on the window by the driver's head. In the language of the truck-wallahs, this action obviously had some dreadful import because the driver slowed down immediately and pulled the truck over to the left-hand side of the road.

The horn belonged to a station wagon—the sort of station wagon which, thanks to foreign aid, is used in hundreds for the progress of the country and which can be seen on any road at any time. The station wagon passed the truck on the right, slowed down, and a khaki-coloured arm stretched out to signal the truck to stop. Both vehicles drew to a halt.

An officer-like peon and a peon-like officer stepped down from the station wagon. Two constables in khaki uniforms also got out. Immediately they began to rob and loot in the style of the old Pindari dacoits. Someone seized the driver's licence; someone else, the registration card; someone began to tap the rear-view mirror; someone else blew the horn. They wobbled the running board, switched on the headlights and rang the bell at the back of the truck. Whatever they looked at was defective. Whatever they touched, they found something wrong with it. In this way, in four minutes those four men had found forty faults with the truck and, standing beneath a tree, they began to discuss the treatment which was to be meted out to the enemy.

Rangnath could only make out that the stories of the principles of karma and poetic justice were true. The truck was being checked and God was taking His revenge on the driver for his insult to Rangnath. He remained where he was. But in the middle of all this discussion, the driver found the opportunity to say, 'Sir, please get down. Where is the need to sit there holding the gear now?'

Rangnath got down and went and stood under another tree. Under the first one, the driver and the checking party were discussing every single point of the truck in detail. As he watched, the discussion shifted from the parts of the truck to the general condition of and the economic chaos facing the country and, in a short time, the individuals present had broken up into small subcommittees. Standing under separate trees, they began to ponder each issue in their capacity as experts. After a lot of discussion, a sort of open session began under one tree and soon it became apparent that the seminar was coming to an end.

Finally, Rangnath heard the nasal voice of the officer.

'Well, Ashfaq miyan, what's your opinion? Should we let him off?'

The peon said, 'What else can you do, sir? How long can we go on drawing up charges? If there were only a couple of faults, we could charge him.'

A constable said, 'It would be tomorrow morning by the time we finish making out the charge sheet.'

After talking around the point, the officer said, 'OK, Banta Singh, you can go. We've let you off.'

The officer had been standing under a tree, watching Rangnath for some time. Lighting a cigarette, he came towards him. When he was close, he asked, 'You too were in the truck?'

'Yes.'

'He didn't take any fare off you, did he?'

'No.'

The officer said, 'I guessed as much by looking at your clothes. But it's my duty to check.'

To annoy him, Rangnath said, 'This isn't real homespun khadi. It's mill cloth.'

The officer replied deferentially, 'Ah, sahib, khadi is khadi. What's the difference between the real and the imitation?'

After the officer left, the driver came up to him with the peon. The driver said, 'Just give us two rupees, will you, sir?'

Turning his face away, Rangnath answered harshly, 'What do you mean? Why should I give you money?'

The driver took the peon's hand and said, 'Please come. Please come with me.'

As he moved off, he said to Rangnath, 'I got checked just *because* of you. And *you* speak to me like this when I'm in trouble. Is this how you've been educated?'

The present education system is like a pariah bitch lying in the road, whom anyone can kick. The driver, as he went on his way, attacked it with a sentence and headed towards the truck with the peon. Rangnath saw that evening was closing in, his attaché case was in the truck, Shivpalganj was still five miles away and he needed people's goodwill. He approached the truck slowly. The driver of the station wagon was blowing his horn repeatedly to call back the peon. Rangnath tried to give the driver two rupees. The driver said, 'If you're giving now, then give to the Orderly sahib. What will I do with your money?'

As he spoke, he began to sound like those religious ascetics who never touch money themselves and tell others that their money is nothing but the dirt of their hands. The peon pocketed the money, took a last puff at his beedi, threw its half-lit stub more or less on to Rangnath's pyjamas and set off towards the station wagon. After he left, the driver started the truck, went into top gear just as before, and gave Rangnath the lever to hold. Then suddenly and without any reason, he puckered up his lips and began to whistle a song from a Hindi film. Rangnath listened in silence.

A little later, he began to distinguish bundle-like objects in the twilight on both sides of the road. They were women sitting in rows, talking contentedly and at the same time relieving themselves. Below the road, there were heaps of rubbish and their stench was making the evening breeze blow with the sluggishness of a pregnant woman.

From some distance away came the sound of barking dogs. A curtain of smoke drifted in front of Rangnath's eyes. All this meant there was no denying that they had come to a village. Shivpalganj.

2

In the Shivpalganj police station, a man was pleading with the Sub-Inspector, his hands folded in supplication: 'Several months have passed while you continually delay matters. Please don't put off charging me any longer.'

The Sub-Inspector was half sitting, half reclining on a seat which must once have been some medieval throne but, now that it was worn out, had been reduced to the status of an armchair. After he heard the request, the Sub-Inspector raised his head and said, 'You will be charged eventually. What's the hurry? What calamity is descending upon you?'

The man sat down on a low stool near the armchair and said, 'For me, it is a calamity. If you charge me, then the trouble will be over.'

The Sub-Inspector started swearing under his breath. It soon became clear that what he meant to say was that the amount of work he had to do was making him thoroughly fed up. There was so much work that he wasn't able to investigate crimes, couldn't charge-sheet cases, couldn't give evidence in court. There was so much work that all work had come to a standstill.

The stool slid towards the armchair. The man said, 'Sir, my enemies have begun to say that there's gambling in Shivpalganj in broad daylight. An anonymous complaint has been sent to the superintendent. And anyway, the agreement is that you charge me once a year. This year, you're late with the charge. If you file it now, then this complaint will also be done with.'

It was not only the armchair—everything was medieval. The raised platform for sitting on, the rag of a rug lying on it, the pen stands, the pots of dried ink, the dusty registers which were turning up at the corners—everything looked several centuries old.

For this police station, the fountain pen hadn't yet been invented; the only progress made in that direction was that the pens were not made out of reeds. For this police station, the telephone was still a thing of the future. By way of weapons there were some ancient rifles which looked as though they had been used in the Revolt of 1857. Anyway, for everyday use, the constables had bamboo staves, about which a poet has written, 'For crossing rivers and canals, for hitting dogs and animals, there's no more useful a thing.' For this police station, jeeps did not exist. In their place, a horse served as a sort of vehicle. It was lovingly cared for by two or three village watchmen, and its ancestors must have performed the same role since the days of the Mughal Empire.

The common people had great expectations of the Sub-Inspector and the police station's dozen or so constables. If there was a burglary in some village eight miles away, in the two hundred and fifty or three hundred villages which came under the jurisdiction of the police station, it was believed that one or the other of the policemen would certainly have witnessed it. If there was a dacoity at night somewhere twelve miles away, it was expected that they would get there ahead of the dacoits. Because of this blind faith, no weapons—other than one- or two-odd rifles—had been given to any village. The fear was that by handing out guns, the uncivilized and savage villagers would learn to use them and set about killing one another. Rivers of blood would flow. As for protection from dacoits, that was left to the magic performed by the Sub-Inspector and his dozen or so men.

In short, the Sub-Inspector and his men were kept there on the understanding that they were no ordinary mortals but genies worthy of being conjured up by Aladdin's lamp. The British had installed them and, in 1947, returned to their homeland. Gradually, people began to find out that the Sub-Inspector and his constables were not genies but men, and the sort of men who themselves rub their lamps day and night in the hope of forcing a genie to come out.

~

After the managing director of the gamblers' union of Shivpalganj left, the Sub-Inspector raised his head once and looked around. Everywhere was peace. The constable in loincloth who had been straining bhang beneath the tamarind tree was now anointing a nearby Shiv lingam with it; a watchman was grooming the horse's haunches; a dacoit sitting in the lock-up was loudly reciting prayers to the monkey god, Lord Hanuman. Just outside the gate, the constable on duty—no doubt in order to be in a position to keep constant watch during the night—was asleep, propped up against a pillar.

The Sub-Inspector wanted to close his eyes and doze but just then he saw Ruppan babu approaching. He grumbled, 'You can't even shut your eyes.' As Ruppan babu came in, he got up from his chair and, despite the fact that 'courtesy week' had long passed, he courteously shook hands. Ruppan babu sat down and immediately said, 'A letter has been received by Ramadhin. The dacoits have asked for five thousand rupees. It says, "On the last night of the dark fortnight, bring five thousand rupees to the southern hill."'

The Sub-Inspector smiled and said, 'Really, sahib, this is too much. In the old days, dacoits used to cross rivers and mountains to collect money from your home, but now they expect you to leave your house and go and deliver the money to them!'

Ruppan babu said, 'Yes, that's what I'm saying. It's not dacoity. It's just bribery.'

The Sub-Inspector continued in the same tone, 'Bribery, theft, dacoity—now they've all become the same. It's communism.'

Ruppan babu said, 'Father says the same thing.'

'What does he say?'

'The same—communism has taken over.'

They both laughed. Ruppan babu said, 'No, I'm not joking. Ramadhin really has received this letter. That's why father has sent me here. He says, so what if Ramadhin is our opponent? He shouldn't be tormented like this.'

'What he says is quite right. And I'll tell it to whomever you want me to tell.'

Ruppan babu narrowed his deep-set eyes and looked at the Sub-Inspector. The Sub-Inspector stared back at him and smiled. He said, 'Don't worry, there'll be no dacoity as long as I'm here.'

Ruppan babu said in a mild tone of voice, 'That I know. The letter is a forgery. Just inquire of your own constables. Perhaps one of them wrote it.'

'No, that couldn't be. My constables are illiterate. Most can't even sign their own names.'

Ruppan babu was about to say something more, but the Sub-Inspector said, 'What's the hurry? For now, let Ramadhin file his complaint. Let him show me the letter.'

For a while both were silent. Then a thought occurred to the Sub-Inspector. 'If you were to ask me the truth, I'd say it seems that this is bound up with the education department.'

'How?'

'And not just the education department—with your college.'

Ruppan babu took this remark badly. 'You're out to get my college.'

'It appears to me that some boy from your college has sent this letter to Ramadhin. What do you think?'

'In your eyes students are responsible for all crime,' Ruppan babu rebuked him. 'If someone took poison in front of you and died, you people wouldn't even admit that was suicide. You'd say that some student had poisoned him.'

'You're right, Ruppan babu, if it were necessary I'd even say that. I am a follower of Bakhtavar Singh. Perhaps you didn't know that.'

After this, they started on the one topic of conversation about government servants—what government servants used to be like and what they were like now. They touched on the subject of Bakhtavar Singh. Sub-Inspector Bakhtavar Singh was returning home alone one evening. Two badmashes called Jhagru and Mangru attacked him in a mango grove and beat him up. The story got out and so Bakhtavar Singh entered a report at the police station about the beating.

The next day, the two badmashes came and clasped his feet. They said, 'Sir, you are our mother and father. If a child gets angry and behaves badly with his parents, they forgive him.'

Bakhtavar Singh fulfilled his duty as a parent and forgave them. They fulfilled their filial duty and made good arrangements for Bakhtavar Singh in his old age. The matter was soon settled.

But the British police officer under whom Bakhtavar Singh served objected to this. 'If you can't conduct a successful investigation into your own case,' he said, 'what hope have you got with anyone else's?

So what if it was dark? If you can't identify anybody, what prevents you from at least suspecting someone?'

Then Bakhtavar Singh picked up three suspects. They were old enemies of Jhagru and Mangru. He prosecuted them. Jhagru and Mangru gave evidence on behalf of Bakhtavar Singh saying that, at the time of the attack, they had both happened to come to the mango grove for a very natural reason—that is, to defecate. All three were sentenced. Seeing the state of Jhagru and Mangru's enemies, several boys of the area began coming to Bakhtavar Singh daily with the request, 'O mother and father! This time, please give us the chance to beat you.'

But Jhagru and Mangru were enough to provide for him in his old age. He refused to increase the number of his offspring.

Ruppan babu laughed for some time. The Sub-Inspector was pleased that Ruppan babu was happy with just one story—he didn't have to tell a second. His second story would come in useful for entertaining another leader. Controlling his laughter, Ruppan babu said, 'So you are a follower of that Bakhtavar Singh!'

'I was. Before Independence. But now we have to serve the people. For the citizens . . .'

Ruppan babu touched his arm and said, 'Forget it. Apart from you and me there's no one listening.'

The Sub-Inspector didn't lose his enthusiasm. 'I am saying that before we got our freedom, I was a follower of Bakhtavar Singh. These days, I am a follower of your father's.'

Ruppan babu said humbly, 'You are most kind. Is my father worthy of such kindness?' He stood up and looked out on to the road. 'It seems Ramadhin is coming. I'm off. Please look into this dacoity letter properly.'

~

Ruppan babu was eighteen. He was in the tenth year at the local college. He loved to study and especially studying in the tenth year—for this reason, he'd been studying in it for the past three years without passing the annual exam which would qualify him to move up a class.

Ruppan babu was a local leader. His personality refuted the claim that, to be a leader in India, your hair had to turn grey in the sun.

His leadership was founded on his view that everyone was equal. The Sub-Inspector in the police station and the thief in the lock-up were one. In the same way, a student who copied in an exam and the college principal were one. He considered them all pitiable; he did favours for all of them and extracted favours from all of them. He was so respected that no capitalist shopkeeper sold him goods, but made an offering of them, and no exploited horse-cart driver took a fare for driving him to the town but only asked for his blessings. The first and last base of his leadership was the local college where, at a sign from him, hundreds of students would make a palm tree out of a sesame seed (or a mountain out of a mole hill) and, if necessary, climb up it.

He was thin and scrawny but no one bandied words with him. He was a long-necked, long-limbed lad. In the belief that a popular leader has to be nattily—if not outlandishly—dressed, he wore a white dhoti and a colourful bush shirt. Round his neck he tied a silk scarf. He kept the loose end of his dhoti on his shoulder. Although he looked like an emaciated calf, he had the presence of a stallion rearing on its hind legs.

He was a born leader because his father was also a leader. His father's name was Vaidyaji.

3

The dak bungalow with two big and two small rooms had been abandoned by the district board. On three sides of it, a thatched roof had been raised on mud walls to make stables. A little away from the stables, a tin roof had been erected on a pukka brick wall and a sort of shop had been created. On one side, there was a one-room guardhouse, of the kind found by railway crossings; on the other, under a large banyan tree, there was a raised platform resembling a tomb. Near the stables, a modern-style building had been constructed, on which was written 'Community Centre, Shivpalganj'. Behind all this lay three or four acres of barren land which had been broken up and sown with fodder plants. Here and there, some had actually grown.

All these buildings were collectively called the Changamal Vidyalaya Intermediate College, Shivpalganj. Merely on the basis of the buildings, the students sitting for their intermediate exams could say, 'We are more advanced than Tagore's university at Shantiniketan. It may try to recapture tradition and hold its classes in models of village architecture, but we are the genuine Indian students. We have no idea what electricity is, what tap water is, what a pukka non-mud floor looks like or what is meant by "a sanitary fitting". We have even had our Western education in an Indian tradition and so, behold, today we are still just as close to nature as ever. Even though we have studied so much, we still pee on tree trunks and find it impossible to relieve ourselves in enclosed spaces.'

Changamal had been the chairman of the district board. With the help of a fake planning proposal, he had transferred the dak bungalow of the board to the managing committee of the college at a time when the college had nothing but a managing committee. The condition for the transfer was that the college be named after Changamal.

Every part of the college had its own story to tell. The community centre had been built with government money taken in the name of the village council, but it housed the Principal's office and classes eleven and twelve. The stables had been constructed with voluntary labour, while the tin shed had been removed in the dead of night from deserted buildings in a military cantonment. The barren land adjoining the college came in useful for agricultural science, and the millet which grew on it here and there came in useful for the Principal's buffalo.

There's a shortage of engineers and doctors in India. The reason is that Indians are traditionally poets. Before comprehending anything they become infatuated and compose poetry. When they look at the huge Bhakra-Nangal dam they say, 'Oho! To reveal His miracle, behold, God has once again chosen the land of India.' When they see a young woman on an operating table they begin reciting romantic verse.

Despite this storm of emotion and other similar hindrances, the country has to produce engineers and doctors. They will truly be engineers and doctors only when they go to America or England, but some initial work—the take-off stage—is to be done here. That was the kind of work being done by the Changamal Vidyalaya Intermediate College.

~

A science class was in progress. Class nine. Master Motiram who, in a way, had passed his BSc exams, was teaching the boys relative density. Outside, sheer beauty enveloped the small village. On the road, bullock carts loaded with sugar cane were heading towards the sugar mill. Some half-starved children were running behind them, pulling out canes to chew. The drivers sitting at the front of the carts were swearing vigorously and at length. The point of fundamental importance while swearing is the volume of the voice. So the oaths and counter oaths entered the classroom through the window and provided background music for the boys who were enjoying the drama and studying science.

One boy said, 'Master sahib, what is relative density?' The master replied by translating the term into English.

Another boy said, 'Master sahib, now look, you're teaching English instead of science.'

The master said, 'How can you learn bloody science without English?'

The boys began to laugh. The reason for their mirth was not the discussion on Hindi and English but the use of 'bloody'.

The master spoke, 'There's no need to laugh.'

The boys were not convinced. They laughed even louder. At this, Master Motiram himself began to laugh with them. They stopped.

Master Motiram forgave the boys. He said, 'If you don't understand relative density in English understand it in Hindi, in a different way. Relative, meaning in comparison with something. Imagine you've opened a flour mill, and next door, your neighbour opens another flour mill. You make five hundred rupees a month from your mill, and your neighbour makes four hundred rupees from his. So, in comparison with him, you've made more profit. In scientific language, we can say that your relative profit is greater. Understood?'

One boy said, 'I understand, Master sahib, but the whole thing is wrong from the start. No one in this village could make five hundred rupees from a flour mill.'

Master Motiram thumped his hand down on the table. 'Why not? A determined man can do anything!'

The remark did not dissuade the boy from answering back. 'He can't. My uncle's mill works non-stop but it's difficult to make two hundred rupees a month.'

'Who is your uncle?' Master Motiram wiped his brow and, looking intently at the boy, he asked, 'You're not Dishonest Munnu's nephew, are you?'

The boy didn't try to conceal his pride. He said in a couldn't-care-less voice, 'So what if I am?'

Dishonest Munnu was an extremely respectable man. Among Englishmen—whose roses have no scent to speak of—there is a saying, 'A rose by any other name would smell as sweet.' Similarly, by whichever name you called him, Dishonest Munnu continued contentedly to run his flour mill, to earn his living and be an honourable man. In fact, Dishonest Munnu hadn't earned his name—he'd inherited it. In childhood, his father had given him the nickname 'Dishonest' out of love, and out of love his mother had called him Munnu. Now, the entire village affectionately called him Dishonest Munnu. He had accepted this name with the same ease as we have accepted the title of 'Acharya' for J.B. Kripalani, 'Pandit' for Jawaharlal Nehru and 'Mahatma' for M.K. Gandhi.

Master Motiram stared at Dishonest Munnu's nephew for a while, then, drawing breath, he said, 'Let it pass.'

He buried himself in the textbook that was open in front of him. When he lifted his eyes he saw the boys had already lifted their eyes and were watching him. 'What is it?' he asked.

One of the boys said, 'So it's settled that you can't earn five hundred rupees from a flour mill in a month?'

'Who says so?' asked Master sahib. 'I myself have earned seven hundred rupees a month from a flour mill many times. But thanks to Dishonest Munnu, everything's being ruined.'

Dishonest Munnu's nephew said politely, 'What is there to be sorry about, Master sahib? It's business. Sometimes you win, sometimes you lose. It happens like that when there's competition.'

'What competition is there between the honest and the dishonest? What nonsense you're talking!' Master Motiram rebuked him. By then, the college *chapraasi* was standing in front of him with a message. Reading the message, the master said, 'Whomever you see seems to be coming to inspect you . . . one teacher to every ten inspectors.'

'It's really dreadful,' said one of the boys.

The master started and looked at the class. 'Who spoke?'

A boy raised his hand and said, 'I did, Master sahib! I was asking how you work out relative density!'

Master Motiram continued, 'In order to work out relative density, you have to know the weight and the volume of an object. After that, you have to know the way of working out the relative density. As far as the way is concerned, there are always two ways—the right way and the wrong way. It's necessary to give you an example to make you understand. Imagine you've set up a flour mill. The mill has fine new machinery, it's shining and it's well greased. The engine is new, the belt is new. You've got everything, but you don't have electricity. So what's the result?'

The boy who had spoken earlier said, 'You'll have to use a diesel engine. Munnu uncle did.'

Master Motiram said, 'Munnu uncle isn't the only one around here with brains. Who was it who first brought a diesel engine into this village? Does anybody know?'

The boys put their hands up and chorused, 'You! You brought it!'

Master sahib looked at Munnu's nephew with satisfaction and said with contempt, 'Did you hear? Dishonest Munnu got a diesel engine only after he saw I had one. But my mill was running before this college was opened. It was at my mill that a full two pounds of flour was taken from every customer as a donation for the college building. That flour—ground in my mill—was taken to the town for sale. It was in my mill that the plans for the college building were made and Manager uncle said, "Moti, you will be called a master in the college, but you'll really be the principal." Everything happened on account of my mill and now, if anyone has a mill, it's Dishonest Munnu! My mill means nothing!'

A boy said, 'How did you say you work out relative density?'

Master sahib said brusquely, 'I'm telling you that.'

He looked out of the window, three feet above the sugar cane carts on the road, and fixed his glance beyond them on to the horizon. He spoke like the poets of yesteryear who wore fixed, romantic expressions. 'She was the only machine of her kind in the whole neighbourhood. She was made of iron but she sparkled like glass . . .'

Suddenly he looked straight at the class and said, 'What did you ask?'

The boy repeated his question, but even before that Master Motiram's attention had drifted off in another direction. The boys pricked up their ears and listened. Outside, above the oaths of the sugar cane stealers and the sugar cane protectors, above the sound of the Principal ticking off the chapraasi, above the *swanv swanv* of a harmonium rising from the music class, a *bak-bak-bak* noise suddenly started up. Master Motiram's mill was working. This was its sound. A genuine sound. Above the people's hue and cry over their lack of food and clothing, above the screams of the rioters, above the arguments that rage over all this, a true leader hears only the voice of his soul and nothing else; in the same way, Master Motiram heard only the sound of his mill. He heard nothing else. Just, *bak-bak-bak*.

He began to run towards the classroom door.

'What's happened to Master sahib?' the boys asked. 'The bell hasn't rung yet.'

Master Motiram said, 'It sounds as if the machine's working again. Let's see how it's running.'

He got to the door, but suddenly turned back. A pained expression spread across his face, as if someone had pinched him hard. He said, 'Read from your textbooks. The chapter on relative density is essential.' Hesitantly, he added, 'It's important.' As he spoke, his face brightened again.

Bak-bak-bak! Duty was summoning him into the complex world of karma outside. The maya of boys and books could not restrain him. He left.

~

At four o'clock in the afternoon, the Principal sahib emerged from his room. Parts of his thin body were covered by khaki shorts and a shirt. He carried a police sergeant's baton pressed under his arm and wore sandals. Altogether, he looked rather sharp and smart, and he considered himself even sharper and smarter than that.

Trailing along after him, as always, was the college clerk. He was a close friend of the Principal sahib's.

They both passed close to Master Motiram's class. The class was being held in the stable-like building. Even from a distance it was clear that no master was present. A boy dressed in pyjamas torn from ankle to thigh was sitting, crying, on the master's desk. He saw the Principal going past and began to cry more loudly. The Principal asked, 'What's going on? Where has the master gone?'

The boy now stood up and went on crying. A second boy said, 'This is Master Motiram's class.'

Then there was no need to say where Master sahib had gone. The clerk said, 'A second-hand machine requires twenty-four-hour supervision. How many times have I told Master Motiram to sell this flour mill! But he doesn't understand. I myself was once prepared to give one thousand and five hundred rupees for it.'

The Principal sahib turned to the clerk. 'Let it be! Go and bring Malaviya from the class over there.'

The clerk told a boy, 'Go and bring Malaviya from the class over there.'

Soon a rather good-looking young man could be seen approaching. As soon as he saw him coming, the Principal shouted out, 'Brother Malaviya, look after this class too!'

Malaviya came up to the Principal, stood holding on to one of the bamboo poles holding up the thatch and said, 'How can I take two classes in one period?'

The boy at the master's desk was still crying. At the back of the class some boys were laughing loudly. The rest of the boys were standing near the members of the staff like a crowd that gathers at a crossroads when there's been an accident.

In a sharp tone, the Principal said, 'Don't start quoting the rules to me! Ever since you've started hanging around with Khanna, every job seems a problem for you.'

Malaviya gazed at the Principal sahib. The clerk said, 'Look at it as the government bus-wallahs do, Malaviya. If a bus breaks down, all the passengers are accommodated in the next bus. Accommodate these boys in your class in the same way.'

Malaviya said sweetly, and with a shade of sarcasm, 'But this is the ninth year; I'm teaching the seventh year over there.'

The Principal sahib turned his head. Those who knew him well knew that now his hands would be thrust into the pockets of his shorts and he would scream. And so it happened. 'I understand it all. You too have begun arguing like Khanna. I know the difference between the seventh and the ninth year. Don't tha' dare try teaching me my job, bhaiya! Just carry out orders, *chuppe*, with no argument. Dost tha' follow me?'

The Principal sahib was from a village nearby. He was renowned far and wide for two qualities. First, for extracting the maximum amount of government money for the college by being imaginative with the accounts, and second, for using the local Awadhi dialect when he was extremely angry. When he falsified the accounts, not even the greatest auditor could find fault with them. When he began to speak Awadhi, not even the greatest sophist could answer his arguments.

Malaviya turned away with a bowed head. Landing his baton on the back of the boy in the torn pyjamas, the Principal said, 'Go. Everyone go and sit quietly in that classroom. If you so much as draw breath I'll flay the hides off you.'

As the boys left, the clerk smiled and said, 'Let's go and take a look at Khanna Master too.'

Khanna Master's real name was Khanna. 'Khanna' is not the name of a caste, just as 'Gandhi' and 'Nehru' are not the names of castes but of individuals. This is a simple way to rid the country of the caste system. If you take the caste name away from a man and convert it into a surname, then nothing remains of caste. It destroys itself.

Khanna Master was a history teacher but at this time he was teaching an intermediate class English. He was grinding his teeth and saying, 'You can write great long love stories in Hindi, but when you have to answer in English you hang your head like a horse!'

A boy was standing up in class hanging his head. Although, due to a shortage of nourishing food and a lack of games and recreation, every average student looks like a half-starved horse, this boy's face was so constructed that with him the name had stuck. His classmates laughed loudly. Khanna Master asked in English, 'Tell me, what does "metaphor" mean?'

The boy stood unmoved. Some time ago, there had been a great hue and cry in India that an illiterate man is like a beast with no horns or tail. In that tumult, the children of many illiterate men and women had left their ploughs and hoes in the fields and launched attacks on the schools. These boys had arrived in thousands, laying siege to schools, colleges and universities. There was turmoil in the field of education. Now, you wouldn't find anyone spreading the word that an illiterate man is a beast. In fact, on the quiet, people had begun to say that only those fit for higher education should take it up and that there should be a screening process. Having come full circle in this way, an opinion was being expressed that village boys should again be made to grasp the handle of the plough and be left in the fields. But even after failing their annual exams year after year, enduring all kinds of reprimands and rebukes, and listening to politicians' outpourings on the greatness of agriculture, those boys were not prepared to return to the world of the plough and the hoe. They stuck to the schools like leeches and were determined to stay stuck to them at any cost.

The boy with the horse-like countenance was one of this group. In a roundabout way he was told every day, 'Go, son, go and milk your buffalo and twist your bullocks' tails; Shelley and Keats are not for you.' But the son had already advanced several centuries ahead of his father and was not prepared to take these hints. Even today, his father was cutting fodder for his bullocks with a blade used commonly in the twelfth century. At the same time, his son was hiding his horse face in a book with a dust-coloured cover and concentrating on the colourful nightlife of twentieth-century Calcutta. He wasn't prepared to suffer any alteration of this state of affairs. And so he couldn't explain the meaning of metaphor and didn't want to argue over the construction of his face.

Like every average student this boy was informal in his attire. At this time he was barefoot, standing clad in dirty pyjamas made of striped material—the kind that town people generally wear to sleep in. He was wearing a thick, catechu-coloured shirt with broken buttons.

His head was covered with stiff, dry hair. His face was unwashed and his eyes had a stupid look about them. As soon as you saw him it was obvious that he had bolted to college, ensnared by the propaganda, like a beast with no horns or tail.

Last year, the boy had copied out a love story from some cheap periodical and had it published in the school magazine under his own name. Khanna Master was besmirching the name he'd earned by this exploit. Changing his tone of voice, he said, 'Respected author, won't you tell us something of what a metaphor is?'

The boy began scratching his thighs. After twisting his mouth a few times, he finally said in Hindi, 'Just as the metaphor of pain appears in the Hindi poetry of Mahadevi . . .'

Khanna Master said sharply, 'Shut up! This is an English class.' The boy stopped scratching his thighs.

The master was wearing khaki trousers and a blue bush shirt and, just to look smart, dark glasses. He got up out of his chair and moved around in front of his desk. He leant a small portion of his rump against it. He was about to say something more to the boy when he noticed the Principal staring at him from the door at the back of the class. He also had a view of the entire shoulder of the clerk who was standing outside on the veranda. Removing his rump from the desk, he stood up straight and said, 'Sir, I was teaching a poem by Shelley.'

The Principal replied quickly, one word tumbling after another, 'But who was listening to you? These boys are looking at pictures!'

He came into the room and poked his cane into the backs of two boys, one after the other. They stood up. One was a greasy boy wearing a dirty bush shirt and pyjamas, his head dripping with hair oil. The second had a shaven head, wore a shirt and pants and was a wrestler type. The Principal sahib asked them, 'What were you being taught?'

He bent down and picked up a magazine from the first boy's chair. This was literature of the cinema. He opened it, held it up and waved it about. The breasts of a white woman flapped before the boys' eyes. The Principal threw the magazine to the floor and screamed in Awadhi, 'Is this what tha' art teaching them?'

The room was so quiet you could hear a pin drop. Seeing his chance, the lover of Mahadevi's poetry quietly slipped back into his seat. Standing at one end of the classroom, the Principal sahib issued a challenge to Khanna Master at the other end.

'This is the level of discipline in your class! The boys are reading film magazines! And on the strength of this, you're getting pressure put on me to make you vice-principal? Is this the way you will conduct yourself as vice-principal? Bhaiya, if tha' goest on like this tha' canst forget vice-principal. Next year I'll damn well see thee out on the street, with no job!'

As he spoke, the spirit of the great Awadhi poet Goswami Tulsidas slipped through his body. He returned to common speech. 'What is there in education? The important thing is discipline! Understand, Master sahib?'

With this, the Principal sahib departed like the hero of Omar Khayyam who came like the water and left like the wind. Behind his back, he heard Khanna Master muttering indignantly.

The Principal and the clerk walked through the college gate. On the side of the road, a man had gathered together a handful of labourers and was losing his temper with them. The Principal went and stood by him. For a few minutes he tried to understand why the man was losing his temper. The labourers were pleading with him. The Principal understood that there was nothing special in it; the labourers and the contractor were just making a display of their daily habit of discussion, and the conversation had reached a stalemate. The Principal went forward and said, 'Go, lads, go and do your work. If you cheat the Contractor sahib, you'll get a shoe-beating.'

The labourers looked gratefully at the Principal sahib. His comments gave them the chance to end the discussion and go back to work. The contractor said to the Principal affectionately, 'They're all thieves. If you so much as shut your eyes for a moment, they'll steal the wax from your ears. They demand one and a half times the going rate and moan if anyone mentions work.'

The Principal sahib said, 'It's the same everywhere. Just look at me . . . No master has any inclination to teach. I'm constantly behind them and so I manage . . .'

The contractor burst out laughing. He said, 'What are you telling me? I do the same. I know everything that goes on.' Pausing, he said, 'Where are you off to?'

The clerk answered, 'To Vaidyaji's house. The cheques have to be signed.'

'Get them signed then.' He motioned the Principal to move on.

When the Principal made to leave, the contractor asked, 'And how are you otherwise?'

The Principal stopped. 'I'm fine. The same old problems with Khanna and his friends. He roams around spreading propaganda against people like you and me.'

The contractor spoke forcefully, 'Don't you worry. You can behave like a king in your college. Tell them that the answer to propaganda is the stick. Tell them this is Shivpalganj. They should watch their step.'

The Principal and the clerk walked on. After a while the clerk said, 'Make the Contractor sahib a member of the college committee too. He'll be useful.'

The Principal sahib was thinking. The clerk continued, 'We'll make him a patron, and write out a receipt for a donation backdated by four years. He should also be on the managing committee. Then, everything will be all right.'

The Principal sahib gave no immediate answer. Hesitating, he said, 'We'll speak to Vaidyaji. These are matters of high politics. Does it matter what we say?'

A man on a bicycle appeared. Motioning him to stop and get down, the Principal sahib said, 'There's a smallpox epidemic in Nandpur and you're standing there with your bag under your arm, composing fancy verses?'

The man joined his hands in greeting and asked, 'Since when? I've had no information.'

Frowning, the Principal said, 'If you could tear yourself away from the town occasionally, then you'd get information. Get over there quietly and start vaccinating. If you don't, there'll be a complaint against you. You'll be out on your ear. And that'll be the end of your Terylene bush shirt.'

Stammering out pleas for forgiveness, the man went on his way. The Principal sahib said to the clerk, 'He's the public health ADO here. Imagine, whoever gets an officer tag on his tail begins to think he's Plato! This one, too. God knows who he thinks he is! He goes by on the road and doesn't even recognize you. I thought to myself, "I'd better teach the boy a lesson."'

'I know. He's just another fool,' said the clerk.

4

Heaps of rubbish, shops worse than rubbish heaps, the tehsil office, the police station, the toddy house, the block development office, the liquor shop, the college—if you went along the street you would see all this. Some way ahead, there was also a mud hut built in a dense mango grove, with its back to the road. Its doorway, which had no door, faced the jungle. In the monsoon, farm labourers retreated from the shade of the trees and held their gambling sessions in the hut; otherwise, it was unoccupied. Although it was empty, people wouldn't let it stay empty and, whenever they had a chance, men and women would put it to their favourite use. The name that Shivpalganj had given the building would have shocked even Henry Miller. Watering it down a bit, one college teacher had dubbed it the 'Love House'. The stretch of road between the heaps of rubbish and the Love House ran along the entire edge of Shivpalganj. Shivpalganj proper was in the other direction, away from the road. Shivpalganj proper was in Vaidyaji's sitting room.

To reach the sitting room, you had to pass through an alley. On both sides there were haphazardly built thatched houses. The raised platforms outside them had been extended over the years and now took up most of the alley. They epitomized the philosophy of encroachment—when you find empty land on your borders, grab a few feet of it when no one's looking.

Suddenly the alley opened out on to an open square. Three or four neem trees grew there. From the way they were flourishing, it was clear that they had been planted before the government had invented 'afforestation festivals'. They had escaped being touched by any leader or official and they had been excused the rituals of transplantation and camera clicking.

In this green and pleasant place, one house had so encroached upon a whole side of the square that it was difficult to get past it. The house was Vaidyaji's. Its front portion was of brick, and quite impressive by rural standards. At the back, the walls were of mud and there was a suspicion that behind them there were heaps of rubbish. The sort of 'symbolic' modernization exemplified by India's gleaming airports and glittering five-star hotels had even had an effect on the architecture of this house, which only goes to prove that, from Delhi to Shivpalganj, the Indian creative genius is more or less the same.

The front half of the house, which included a raised platform outside the door, a veranda and one large room, was graced by the name, 'the sitting room'. But even common construction workers knew that 'the sitting room' was not just the name of a building made of bricks and mortar. Ten Downing Street, the White House, the Kremlin and so forth are not the names merely of buildings, but of power.

~

Returning from the police station, Ruppan babu saw a crowd in the hall of public audience—that is, the veranda. His step quickened and his dhoti began to flap. As soon as he climbed on to the veranda, he found that his cousin Rangnath had come from the town on a truck; on the way, he had been fleeced of two rupees.

A skinny man sat in the room, wearing a dirty vest and striped underpants. It was November and rather cold in the evenings, but he was looking quite comfortable in his vest. His name was Mangal, or Tuesday, an auspicious day, but people called him Sanichar, or Saturday, which comes under Saturn and is the most ill-fated day of the week. His hair had begun to turn grey and his front teeth had fallen out. It was his job to keep sitting in Vaidyaji's sitting room. He generally wore only underpants. Today, seeing him in a vest, Ruppan babu understood that Sanichar wanted to appear formal. In one breath, Sanichar told Ruppan babu of Rangnath's difficulties and, beating out a complicated rhythm on his naked thighs, he said longingly, 'If brother Badri had been here, we'd have seen some fun.'

As soon as he finished greeting Rangnath, Ruppan babu said, 'You did the right thing, brother Rangnath. You cleared up the argument with two rupees. It's not right to shed blood over these small matters.'

Rangnath had not met Ruppan babu for two years. Granting that Ruppan's gravity was the most interesting feature of the day, Rangnath said, 'I was ready to give him a thrashing but then I thought about it and held back.'

Ruppan babu raised his hand in his capacity as an expert on thrashing, and said, 'You did just the right thing. The student community gets a bad name through such incidents.'

Rangnath now looked at him closely. The end of his dhoti flung over his shoulder, his mouth red with fresh betel leaf juice, several litres of oil in his hair—by any standard of local thuggery, he looked a likely lad. Rangnath attempted to change the subject. He asked, 'Where is brother Badri? I haven't seen him.'

Sanichar began to brush his pants as if to get rid of some ants. At the same time he knitted his brows and said, 'I too am missing brother Badri. If he'd been here, by now . . .'

'Where is brother Badri?' Rangnath asked, paying no attention to Sanichar and addressing Ruppan.

Ruppan babu replied unconcernedly, 'Let Sanichar tell you. He didn't ask my permission to go. He's gone somewhere. He must have gone out of the village. He'll come back. Tomorrow, the next day, the day after—he'll be back.'

From his words, it would be difficult to tell that Badri was Ruppan's real brother and lived with him in the same house. Rangnath drew a deep breath.

Sanichar sat on the floor, stretched out his legs and scratched his groin. As he did so, his eyes closed and a glow of pleasure and contentment spread over his face. Gradually, as he rubbed the skin, his mouth opened wide like a wolf's and he yawned. Then, in a drowsy voice, he said, 'Brother Rangnath has come from the town. I can say nothing to him. But if anyone had tried to take a paisa, let alone two rupees, from any *ganjaha* villager, he'd have known it.'

The word 'ganjaha' was not new to Rangnath. This was a technical word which the residents of Shivpalganj used for themselves as a title of respect. On occasion, many apostles of peace in the surrounding villages would also say, 'Don't you bandy words with him; you don't know it, but the bastard's a ganjaha.'

Rangnath asked, 'In which class are you now, Ruppan?'

It appeared from Ruppan's expression that he did not like this question. He said, 'I'm in the tenth year . . . You'll say that I was there two years ago too. But I can't think of any way of getting out of this class in Shivpalganj. You don't know, brother. This country's education system is absolutely useless. Even important leaders say that. I am of the same opinion . . . Besides, you don't know the condition of the college. It's a den of louts and layabouts. The masters have given up teaching and just play politics. They plague father day and night—do this, do that, increase our salaries, massage our necks. Has anyone any chance of passing an exam here? Some do. There are some shameless boys who, sometimes, manage to pass an exam, but because of that . . .'

Inside his room, Vaidyaji was giving medicines to patients. Suddenly he spoke, 'Be still, Ruppan. The end of this maladministration is at hand!'

It seemed as if a voice had spoken from the heavens. In such a voice had Lord Krishna's victory over the evil King Kans been prophesied. Ruppan babu was silent. Rangnath turned towards the room and asked in a loud voice, 'Uncle, what's your connection with the college?'

'Connection?' Vaidyaji's powerful laughter resounded throughout the room. 'You want to know my relation with the college? Ruppan, satisfy Rangnath's curiosity.'

In a very businesslike fashion, Ruppan said, 'Father is the college manager. The appointment of masters is in *his* hands.'

Reading the effect of his words in Rangnath's face he then said, 'You won't find a manager like him in the whole country. With the straight he is perfectly straight, and with the bastards he's a dyed-in-the-wool bastard.'

Rangnath digested this information in silence and, just for the sake of saying something, asked, 'And how is the cooperative union going? Uncle had something to do with that too.'

'Not had, has,' Ruppan said rather sharply. 'He was, is and will remain the managing director.'

~

Vaidyaji was, is and will remain . . .

During the British Raj, he had revered the British. In the days of the Indian government, he began to revere Indian rulers. He was an old servant of the nation. In the last World War, when there was danger from Japan, he had enlisted many soldiers to fight in the Far East. Now, when he needed to, overnight, he could enlist hundreds of members into his political faction. From the first, he had served the people as jury member and assessor in a judge's court, as custodian of disputed property in civil cases, and as a chief among village landowners.

Now, he was the managing director of the cooperative union and the college manager. In reality, he didn't want to hold these posts because he had no greed for power. But there was no one else who could carry out such responsible jobs in the locality, and however many young men there were, like all other young men in the country, they were all useless. So, in his old age, he was forced to take up these positions.

Old age! Only Anno Domini required that these words be used of Vaidyaji. If you wanted to be precise, you could say he was sixty-two. But, like those hundreds of great men who lived in the capital to serve the country, Vaidyaji was not old despite his age and, like the same great men, he had vowed that he would grow old only when he died; and that, until people could convince him that he was dead, he would consider himself alive and he would carry on serving the nation. Like every great Indian politician, he loathed politics and made jokes at the expense of politicians. Like Gandhi, he took no post in his political party because he wanted to encourage new blood; but in the matter of the cooperative and the college, his hand had been forced and he had agreed to its being forced.

One of Vaidyaji's professions was Ayurveda, the traditional Indian medicinal system. In his practice of Ayurvedic medicine, he had two special formulas: 'Free treatment for the poor' and 'Money back if not satisfied'. Leave aside whatever relief these formulas might have brought to other people, they didn't leave Vaidyaji lacking in any comfort.

He had divided diseases into two classes—open and secret. He treated open diseases openly and secret diseases in secret. One of his theories was that all diseases are caused by the loss of chastity. Looking at the lacklustre, half-dead faces of the college boys, he would generally refer to this theory. If any person opined that the boys' health was being ruined by poverty and the absence of a good diet, Vaidyaji would turn this argument around and suggest that the person was denying the importance of chastity; and that, since anyone who denied the importance of chastity was immoral, the person talking of poverty and poor food was immoral, too.

He gave long and terrifying speeches on the consequences of the loss of chastity. Perhaps, Socrates, or someone else, had personally told him that if, after doing it three times, you are going to despoil your virtue a fourth time, you should first dig your own grave. He used to describe this conversation so graphically that it would seem as if Socrates were still his honorary adviser on chastity. In Vaidyaji's opinion, the greatest harm caused by the loss of chastity was that after losing it—even if he had wanted to lose it—a man no longer remained fit to lose it again. In brief, it was his view that in order to remain fit to lose one's chastity, one shouldn't lose one's chastity.

Listening to his speeches, three quarters of the college boys despaired of life. But they did not commit mass suicide because one of the advertisements of Vaidyaji's clinic said, 'A message of hope for young men despairing of life!' If Hope had been the name of some girl, the boys wouldn't have read the advertisement more eagerly. But they knew that the message referred to a tablet which looked like a pellet of goat shit, and which, as soon as it reached the stomach, sent electricity coursing through their veins.

One day, Vaidyaji lectured Rangnath on the benefits of chastity. He described a rather strange physiology from which he calculated that you have to consume several tons of food to produce a few ounces of 'essence'; 'essence' is converted into blood, blood into something else and in this way, finally, one drop of semen is created. He proved that it didn't cost as much to build an atom bomb as it did to produce one drop of semen. Rangnath realized that if there was anything valuable in India, it was semen. Vaidyaji told him that semen had a thousand enemies and all of them were intent on looting it. If anyone contrived to preserve his semen, then he could rest assured, his whole character was saved. From all this, it seemed as if, previously, there had been a great emphasis on semen conservation. On one side flowed rivers of milk and honey; on the other, rivers of semen. Finally, Vaidyaji recited a Sanskrit verse which meant that a man died if he spilled one drop of semen, and if he could raise one drop, life was his.

As soon as he heard the sound of Sanskrit, Sanichar joined his hands and said, 'Praise be to God!' He laid his head on the ground and, in a paroxysm of faith, lifted his rear towards the ceiling. Vaidyaji became more excited and asked Rangnath, 'How can I describe to you the glow of chastity? After some days, see your face in the mirror, then you will know!'

Rangnath stood up to go indoors. He was already acquainted with this side of his uncle's nature. Ruppan babu was standing near the door. Vaidyaji's speech had no effect on him. He whispered to Rangnath, 'Why do you need chastity to bring a glow to your face? Nowadays, you can get it just as well from cream and powder.'

5

The theory of reincarnation was invented in the civil courts so that neither plaintiff nor defendant should die regretting that his case had been left unfinished. Comforted by this theory, both could die in peace knowing they still had the next life in which to hear the judgement.

The man who was sitting on the veranda outside Vaidyaji's sitting room had filed a case in the civil court about seven years ago. So, it was natural that in conversation he regularly referred to the sins of his previous existence, Fate, God and his plans for the next life.

People called him Langar—the Lame One. On his forehead he bore the tilak of the Kabirpanthi ascetics, around his throat hung a necklace of holy tulsi. His face was weathered by dust and thunderstorms, and his thin body was covered with a quilted cotton jacket. One leg had been amputated at the knee and he made up for its loss with a stout stick. His expression resembled that of the early Christian saints who whipped themselves a hundred times daily, to mortify the flesh.

Sanichar pushed a glass of bhang towards him. 'Take this, brother Langar, drink it. There are plenty of fine things in it.'

Langar refused with eyes closed and, for a while, they both discussed such philosophical subjects as the importance of bhang, the benefits of almonds and raisins, the transience of life, material pleasures, and renunciation. Finally, Sanichar freed himself from the debate by wiping his left hand on his underwear and, displaying an indifference to worldly subjects, he growled, 'If you're going to drink it, get it down quickly. If you are not, to hell with you!'

He leapt into the inner sitting room and offered the same glass of bhang to the Principal. Vaidyaji contentedly watched him drink his bhang. Emptying the glass, the Principal said, 'There really is some great stuff in there.'

'Bhang is merely a name,' said Vaidyaji. 'It is and it is not. The real substance is in the almonds, raisins and pistachios. Almonds increase intelligence and potency. Raisins are a purgative. There's also cardamom in it. It has a cooling effect. As a result, semen does not burst out; it remains solid and unmoving. I am also making some small use of this beverage in my treatment of Rangnath.'

The Principal lifted his head and tried to speak but Vaidyaji had already gone on to say, 'Just a few days ago, he began to run a fever. He had become weak. So I have called him here. I have made up a daily programme for him. Almonds are used in the tonics. Two leaves of hemp as well. We'll see what he looks like when he goes back in six months' time.'

The college clerk said, 'He came like a rat, but he'll leave like a rhinoceros, uncle, just you wait and see.'

Whenever the clerk called Vaidyaji 'uncle', the Principal was sorry that he couldn't call Vaidyaji 'father'. His face dropped and he began to leaf through the files in front of him.

By then Langar had appeared in the doorway. He squatted down outside rather like a chicken and greeted Vaidyaji in the way prescribed in the scriptures for a low-caste man meeting a Brahmin.

This showed that in our country the scriptures are still supreme, and all attempts at the eradication of caste, if not fraudulent, are at the least romantic, gestures. Langar whined like a beggar, 'I am leaving, respected father!'

Vaidyaji said, 'Go, brother, you are fighting a righteous battle. Fight on! But how can I help you?'

Langar replied naturally, 'Very well, respected father! In this kind of battle what can you do? When I need someone to speak on my behalf, I will come and rub my head on your doorstep.' Bending forward to touch the floor, he paid his respects and left, hopping away on one leg with the support of his stick.

Vaidyaji laughed loudly. 'His mind is like a child's.'

Vaidyaji seldom laughed. Rangnath was startled to see that when he did, his face softened, gentleness replacing his expression of authority. Instead of a virtuous, great man, he began to look almost debauched.

Rangnath asked, 'What's he fighting for?'

The Principal had begun to gather together the files and cheque books spread out in front of him, under cover of which he used to come for an occasional early-morning glass of bhang. Pausing for a moment, he said, 'He has to get a copy of a document from the tehsil office. He has sworn not to give a bribe and to get a copy by the rules. On the other side, the copy clerk has sworn not to take a bribe and to give the copy by the rules. This is what the fight is all about.'

Rangnath had an MA in history and had studied the causes of countless wars. Alexander attacked India to capture it; Porus resisted—to stop him. Sultan Ala-ud-din said that he would take the beautiful Queen Padmini; her husband the Rana said he would not give her up. So, a war was fought. The root of all battles was the same. One side said, 'I'll take!'; the other, 'I won't give!' This was always the reason for war.

But here was Langar saying that he would take the copy by the rules and the clerk saying that he would give the copy by the rules. And still they were fighting.

Rangnath asked the reason for this historic turnabout. In reply, the Principal quoted a saying in Awadhi which literally meant, 'Elephants come, horses go, but the poor camel lollops along.' Perhaps this saying had its origin in a zoo, but Rangnath managed to comprehend that it had something to do with the length, breadth and depth of government offices. But he still failed to understand the righteous conflict between Langar and the copy clerk. He put his question to the Principal more clearly.

The college clerk replied on his behalf: 'These are ganjaha ways, difficult to understand . . . Langar lives in a village ten miles away. His wife is dead. He fell out with his sons and as far as he's concerned they are dead. He's a religious man. He used to sing bhajans of the saints Kabir and Dadu. He grew tired of singing and, idling around, he went and filed a case in the civil court. He needs a copy of an old judgement for the case. For that, you first have to make an application to the tehsil office. There was something missing from the application, so it was rejected. Then he made a second application. A few days ago, he went to the office to collect the copy. The copy clerk turned out to be a real crook, and asked for a five-rupee bribe. Langar said the fixed rate was two rupees. Then the argument started. Two or three lawyers were standing around. First of all, they told the copy clerk, "Brother, agree to two rupees, the poor man is lame. He'll take the copy and sing your praises." But the clerk refused to budge an inch. Suddenly, he became a man of honour and said, "A man of honour sticks to his word. I'll take exactly what I asked for."

'Then the lawyers reasoned with Langar. "The clerk, too, has family responsibilities. He has to pay for his daughters' weddings. So he's pushed up the rate. Accept what he says and give five rupees." But Langar stuck to his guns. He said, "So now it's come to this. He squanders his salary on liquor and meat curry and takes bribes to get his daughters married."

'The clerk lost his temper. "Get out," he snarled. "I'm not taking any bribe for this. Whatever is to be done will be done by the rules." The lawyers said, "Don't do this. Langar is a devout man, don't take what he says badly." But once the clerk's temper was lost it couldn't be recovered.

'The truth is, Rangnath babu, Langar wasn't wrong. In this country, getting your daughters married has become an excuse for corruption. If one man takes a bribe, another says, "What can he do, poor fellow?

He's got a big family, he's got to pay for dowries." The whole stream of crime is flowing in the name of marriage.

'Anyway, there's been a serious altercation between Langar and the clerk. Nowadays, there are always arguments over the smallest matters concerning bribery. Earlier, the work was done in a regular fashion. In the old days, men used to be true to their word. You put down one rupee, next day the copy was ready. Now you've got a lot of new, young, school-educated boys creeping in and the rates of business are all upset. Seeing what the new boys are up to, the old ones, too, do exactly as they like. Now, the giving and the taking of bribes have both become a big problem.

'Langar was furious. Placing his hand on his necklace of holy tulsi, he said, "Go, clerk! If you can work by the rules, so can I. Now you won't get a single penny from me. I have made my application, sooner or later, my turn will come."

'After this, Langar went to the tehsildar and told him the whole story. The tehsildar laughed and congratulated him on doing the right thing. He said there was no need for him to get involved in bribery. When his turn came, he would get the copy. And he told the clerk of the court, "Look, this man has been driven to distraction for months. Now his work should be done by the rules, no one should harass him." The clerk replied, "Sir, this cripple is a lunatic. Don't get drawn into this mess." Then Langar lost his temper with the clerk. They started yelling at each other until, somehow or the other, the tehsildar managed to restore peace.

'Langar knew that the copy clerk would find some excuse to reject his application. An application, poor thing, has the life of an ant. You need no great strength to kill it. An application can be rejected at any time. Too few fee stamps, an incorrect file number, one column incomplete—any mistake like that is posted on the noticeboard and if it's not corrected by the prescribed date, the application is rejected.

'That's why Langar is now completely prepared. He's locked up his house and left his village. Land, crop, bullocks—he's left them all to the mercy of God. He's camping in a relative's house and, from dawn to dusk, spends his day making rounds to see the tehsil noticeboard. He's scared that some news of the application will appear on the board and he won't know. He doesn't want to miss it and have the application rejected. It's already happened once.

'He has learnt off by heart all the rules about copying documents. He has memorized the fee chart. When a man's fortune is bad, he is fated to see the inside of a court or a police station. Langar's luck is bad. But the way he's attacked the tehsil this time, it looks like he really will get hold of the document.'

Rangnath had not yet committed enough stupidities in life to be considered experienced. Langar's story affected him deeply. He was moved, stirred by the feeling that he should do something to help. But what could he do? He had no answer.

As the feeling within him became intolerable, he blurted out, 'This is all completely wrong . . . Something should be done!'

The clerk pounced on his words like a hound on a hare. 'What can you do, Rangnath babu? What can anyone do? If you have an itch you have to scratch it yourself. People have enough to do coping with their own troubles. Who can carry another's burden? Nowadays it's like this—you scratch your back and I'll scratch mine.'

The clerk stood up to go. The Principal looked about him and said, 'There's no sign of brother Badri.'

Vaidyaji replied, 'Some relative has got involved in a dacoity case. The ways of the police, like those of God, are infinite. You know it well. Badri has gone over there. He should be back today.'

Sanichar was sitting near the doorway. Letting out his breath with a whistle, he said, 'The longer he stays away the better.'

~

By now, the bhang had made the Principal forget the current saying that 'It is wrong to rest'. Pulling a large cushion towards him, he lay back contentedly and asked, 'What's up?'

Sanichar explained softly, 'There's been embezzlement in the cooperative union. If brother Badri hears about it, he'll eat the supervisor alive.'

The Principal was scandalized. He whispered, 'So that's it!'

Vaidyaji thundered, 'What is this whispering like women? So what if there has been embezzlement in the cooperative? Where is the union in which a similar thing hasn't happened?' Pausing, he explained, 'There has never been a case of fraud in our union and people began to suspect something was wrong. Now, we can say we are honest people. There was embezzlement, and we didn't hide it. We admitted it as soon as it happened.' Drawing breath, he concluded, 'Well, it's an ill wind . . . One thorn has been removed from our flesh . . . One worry is over.'

The Principal was propped up motionless on his cushion. He voiced the popular sentiment, 'Nowadays, people have become very dishonest.'

This statement is very efficacious and every decent man can make use of it like a multivitamin tablet, three times a day after meals. But it seemed to the clerk to contain some personal allegation against himself. He replied, 'It depends on the individual. In our college, there's never been any trouble like this.'

Vaidyaji regarded him cordially and smiled. Embezzlement had once taken place when wheat was removed from the seed-grain store. Referring to this, he said, 'How can there be embezzlement like this in the college? You don't have a grain store?'

This was a joke. The Principal laughed and, once he started laughing, he couldn't stop. But the clerk seemed afflicted by the hint of personal criticism. 'No, uncle,' he said, 'but there *are* lots of fodder stores. The minds of everyone there are full of straw.' This caused even more hilarity. Sanichar and Rangnath also laughed. The wave of laughter reached the veranda. A few nameless people sitting there also burst into uncontrolled mirth. The clerk caught the Principal's eye and signalled him to leave.

It is our proud tradition that the real issue surfaces only after three or four hours of conversation. Accordingly, Vaidyaji asked the Principal, 'Anything else you wanted to talk about especially?'

'Nothing . . . the same old problem with Khanna. The day before yesterday, he was teaching a class wearing dark glasses. I gave him a dressing-down right then and there. He was leading the boys astray. I said, "Look here, son, I'll tear you to ribbons on the spot."' The Principal had shown considerable self-control during this speech but as he finished it he began to mumble and only a sort of *fik-fik* noise issued from his lips.

Vaidyaji said seriously, 'You should not do such things. You should treat your opponent with courtesy. Look, every great leader has many enemies. They have all pinned down their opponents through the power of their will. This is a principle of democracy. Our leaders endure their opponents with enormous politeness. The opposition keeps on talking nonsense, and the leadership quietly plays its own game. No one is affected by anyone else. This is model opposition. You, too, should adopt this stance.'

These fundamental principles of politics had no effect on the clerk. He said, 'That doesn't work, uncle! I know Khanna Master. He's an MA in history but he doesn't even know who his father was. He's just an expert in politicking. He keeps calling the boys to his house and teaches them gambling. There's only one way to fix him. Get hold of him sometime and thrash him.'

This made Vaidyaji even more serious, but everyone else became excited. The conversation turned to the method and traditions of administering a shoe-beating. Sanichar chirped up, 'If you're going to thrash Khanna, let me know. It's been a long time since I've given a shoe-beating. I'll come along to land a few blows myself.'

One man remarked that if a shoe is worn out and soaked in water for three days it makes a good noise when it lands on the flesh, and even people at a distance can hear that there's a beating in progress. Another said that if you're going to beat an educated man you should use shoes made out of something other than cow leather, so that he'll be beaten but he won't be disgraced too much. A third man sitting on the veranda said that the correct way to give a shoe-beating was to start counting one hundred blows, and when you reach ninety-nine, you forget where you are and start all over again from one. A fourth man agreed that this was the best method of shoe-beating and that was how even he had begun to learn to count up to a hundred.

6

A cycle rickshaw was coming down the road from the town to the country. The rickshaw-wallah was a long-haired, thin, young man wearing a colourful vest and shorts. His face was running with sweat, a caricature, rather than a picture, of agony.

Riding in the rickshaw, his clenched fists on his thighs, was Badri Wrestler. At his feet, there was a box. Both feet were jammed against the sides of the box to keep it steady. Badri held the box so tightly that even if he fell out of the rickshaw and broke his legs, there was no danger of his letting go of it.

It was the pleasant, pointless hour of evening. The wrestler's village must have still been three miles away. He opened his mouth, yawned like a tiger and, mid-yawn, remarked, 'The crop is looking poor this year.'

The rickshaw-wallah was not in a mood to make pronouncements on agricultural science and economics. He cycled on in silence. The wrestler asked him directly, 'Which district do you come from? What's the crop like in your area?'

The rickshaw-wallah didn't turn round. A lock of hair had fallen into his eyes. He flicked it back with a jerk of his head. 'Crops? I'm not a country man, Thakur sahib, I belong to the town proper.' He swayed his hips from side to side and cycled fast. Seeing another rickshaw ahead, he rang his bell.

The wrestler yawned again and went back to staring at the fields. The rickshaw-wallah was upset to see his passenger so indifferent.

To divert him, he began, 'My principle, Thakur Sahib, is "good wages for good work". I'll not settle for seven annas when I've agreed to eight. I stick to what I say. Once a sahib sat in the back here asking how my family was. He told me the government had given me a bad deal. They should ban cycle rickshaws. What a dreadful thing, he said, that one man should ride on another's back. I said, don't ride. He said, I take rickshaws because, if everyone boycotts them, the rickshaw pullers will starve to death. Then he began bewailing the fate of the rickshaw-wallahs.

'He cried a lot. He went on crying and cursing the government. He kept saying, you should form a union, and demand motor-driven rickshaws. God knows what rubbish he was saying. But, Thakur sahib, I told him, "Son, don't get any ideas. No matter how much you cry, I'll not reduce your eight-anna fare by even a pie."'

The wrestler had closed his eyes. He yawned. 'Do you know any film songs or do you only produce hot air?'

The rickshaw-wallah said, 'There are just two pastimes here, Thakur sahib. Going to the cinema every day, and chain-smoking cigarettes. I would sing you a song too, but at the moment I've got a bad throat.'

The wrestler laughed. 'So what? Are you going to let the name of your town down?'

The rickshaw-wallah swallowed this insult with good grace. Then, after a moment's consideration, he began to sing softly the tune of a popular, old film song. The wrestler paid no attention. The rickshaw-wallah observed his client's declining spirits and spoke again. 'My brother too pulls a rickshaw. But he only takes loads of passengers from certain select localities. He showed some country rickshaw-wallah from Sultanpur a few tricks of the trade and the man began to cry. "I'm an honest man," he said. "Take my life but not my religion. I'm not getting involved in this sort of business." I told my brother, "Stop it. You can't turn a donkey into a horse by making it trot."'

They were approaching Shivpalganj. As if giving the rickshaw-wallah a testimonial, Badri said, 'You are a very good man. You shouldn't allow anyone to take liberties with you. Your way of handling things is right.' He paused. 'But your body is not in good shape. Spend a few months in a gym, and see how you improve.'

'What's the point of that?' asked the rickshaw-wallah. 'You want me to take up wrestling? There's nothing special about wrestling now. In war, when a bomb drops, it kills even the greatest wrestler. As long as you've got a gun in your hand, what difference does it make whether you're a wrestler or not?' Pausing for a moment, he went on contentedly, 'Wrestling is only a country sport now, Thakur sahib! In our locality, knives are the craze.'

At this stage, Badri Wrestler became sensible of being insulted. He stretched out his hand and caught hold of the rickshaw-wallah's vest between his finger and thumb. 'Abeh! You've been calling me "Thakur sahib, Thakur sahib" for the last hour. Don't you know I'm a Brahmin?'

The rickshaw-wallah was startled but assumed an almost Gandhian non-violent expression. 'Let it be, panditji, let it be,' he said and began to observe the natural beauty of the countryside.

~

Ramadhin's full name was Babu Ramadhin Bhikhmakhervi. Bhikhmakhera was a village adjoining Shivpalganj which, like the ancient Greek, Roman and Egyptian civilizations, had been wiped off the face of the earth. That is, it hadn't completely disappeared, it was just that the inhabitants of Shivpalganj, through their own stupidity, thought it had. Bhikhmakhera was still preserved in the form of a few shacks, some records in the revenue department and Ramadhin's old poetry.

When he was a child, Ramadhin Bhikhmakhervi had set out from Shivpalganj and followed the railway tracks to the town. From there, he planned to climb into any train and so, without intending to do so, he landed up in Calcutta. In Calcutta, he first delivered letters for a businessman, then delivered his merchandise and later became his business partner. In the end, he became the owner of the whole business.

The business was opium. Unrefined opium came from west India and he received a commission for delivering it by various ways to big businessmen in Calcutta. He could also have exported opium from Calcutta but he wasn't an ambitious man. He quietly carried on his commission business and spent his spare time enjoying the company of visitors from the western districts. He was fairly well known among the men from that area. They praised his lack of literacy and, seeing his achievements, were able to understand how the great illiterate emperors of old—like the Mughal emperor Akbar—must have run their governments.

There was good money in the opium business and the rivalry between traders was not too great. There was just one small problem with the trade and that was that it was against the law. When his friends mentioned this to Ramadhin, he used to tell them, 'What can I say about this? Nobody asked me before they made the law.'

When Ramadhin was arrested under the opium law and appeared in court before a magistrate, he took the same line. He criticized the

English laws and, referring to the fact that Mahatma Gandhi had found it necessary to break them, tried to explain that these foreign laws were made in an arbitrary fashion and every single little thing was called a 'crime'.

'Your Honour,' he said, 'opium is produced from a plant. When the plant grows, it gets beautiful white flowers. In English, you call them poppies. There is a different sort of poppy which has red flowers. The sahibs grow this in their bungalow gardens. There is another species of this flower called the double poppy. Your Honour, these are the facts about this plant, its leaves and flowers—what have they to do with crime? Later on, from that same white poppy, you get this black stuff. It is used as a medicine. To trade in it cannot be a crime. It's a black law that has made it a crime. It has been made to destroy us!'

Despite this lecture, Babu Ramadhin was sentenced to two years' imprisonment. In those days before Independence, you were always convicted and sentenced, but what mattered was the speech in court before it. Babu Ramadhin knew that hundreds of people—from revolutionaries to disciples of non-violence—had become martyrs by making such speeches, and he was certain that his speech would make it easy for him to become a martyr, too. But after he had served his time and had been released, he realized that, to be a hero, he should have broken the salt laws, not the opium laws. After wandering around Calcutta for a few days he saw that he had been pushed out of the opium market. He sorrowfully recited a few verses of poetry and this time, buying a ticket, travelled back to his village and settled down in Shivpalganj.

He told the villagers this much of the truth—that his commission business had closed down. There was no need to say more. He built a rather small, half-brick, half-mud house, took some land and began to farm it. He taught the village boys to gamble with cards rather than with cowrie shells and, lying on a charpoy at his door, he became an expert at telling tales of his Calcutta days. It was then that the government introduced the new system of village councils called panchayats. And, thanks to the great prestige he'd earned from his sojourn in Calcutta, he managed to have his cousin made head of the new village council. To start with, no one knew what being the head of the village council meant, and so his cousin had a walkover at the polls. Some time later, people found out that there were two heads of the village council—Ramadhin, who handed out ownership deeds for plots of the village common land, and his cousin who, when necessary, would face charges of fraud.

Babu Ramadhin dominated the village for some time. There was a thatched hut in front of his house where the young men of the village gambled. On one side of it, fresh hemp leaves were crushed to make bhang. The atmosphere was very lyrical. He was the first man in the village to grow canna lilies, nasturtiums, larkspur and other English flowers. There were some red flowers, too, about which he occasionally remarked, 'These are poppies, and this bugger is a double poppy.'

His name, Bhikhmakhervi, was a poet's nom de plume, indicating that he was a poet. He no longer wrote but in his good days in Calcutta he had been a poet on a few occasions.

When he went to jail, he had hoped to create a magnum opus while in prison like other great literary figures had done before, which he would present later to the public with a lengthy introduction. But he spent those two years complaining about the jail food, joking with fellow convicts, listening to the warders' insults and daydreaming of his future.

When he returned to Shivpalganj he tagged the title 'Bhikhmakhervi' on to his name again to impress the ganjahas with his exceptional character. Later on, when he fell victim to factional politics—not for any particular reason but just due to the influence of village, or rather, national, culture—he wrote a few couplets and thereby proved that Bhikhmakhervi had a poetical, not only a geographical, meaning.

Some time previously, Badri Wrestler had installed a flour-milling machine in another village ten miles from Shivpalganj. The mill worked splendidly and Vaidyaji's enemies began to say that there was some connection between the mill and the college funds. Ramadhin expressed this popular feeling in the immortal verse:

Oh, Ramadhin Bhikhmakhervi, what a miracle!
He set out to run a college,
And opened a flour mill!

~

Someone hailed Badri Wrestler's rickshaw outside the village. It was rather dark and, from a distance, Badri couldn't make out clearly the face of the person hailing him.

'Who are you, you ass?' he asked.

'Don't call me an ass, wrestler! I'm Ramadhin,' said the figure as he approached the rickshaw. The rickshaw-wallah pulled up suddenly in the middle of the road. The figure was wearing a dhoti and kurta. But in the dim evening light, he was recognizable not by his clothes but by his shaven head. Grasping the handlebars of the rickshaw he said, 'Have you heard? There's going to be a dacoity in my house.'

The wrestler jabbed a finger into the rickshaw-wallah's back and motioned him to go on. To Ramadhin he said, 'So why are you squealing about it now? Call me when the dacoits come to get you.'

The rickshaw-wallah pushed down hard on the pedals, but Ramadhin was holding the handlebars so tightly that the rickshaw didn't move. Badri Wrestler muttered, 'I can't think what calamity can make you stand out in the road, holding a rickshaw and wailing like a widow.'

'I'm not wailing, I'm complaining. You're the one real man in Vaidyaji's house—the rest are all weaklings. That's why I'm telling you. The dacoits sent me a letter demanding five thousand rupees. They said, "On the last day of the dark fortnight of the moon, go to the southern hill and give the money . . ."'

Badri Wrestler slapped his thigh. 'If you want to give the money, go and give it. If you don't, then you don't have to give them a penny. I can't tell you more than this. Get going, rickshaw-wallah!'

Vaidyaji's home was nearby. Outside, the bhang would be ground and ready. Badri would drink it, bathe, tie a good loincloth round his waist, pull on a kurta and settle down in style in the sitting room. People would ask him, 'Wrestler, what have you been doing?' He would sit with his eyes closed, listening to questions and allowing others present to answer them. The intoxication of his physical strength and the bhang would make all the voices of this world seem no more than the whining of mosquitoes.

Badri, who had been sunk in such daydreaming, found it highly displeasing to be stopped on the road at this time. He rebuked the rickshaw-wallah and repeated, 'I'm telling you, get going!'

But how could he move? Ramadhin's hands were still on the handlebars.

'It's not a matter of money,' Ramadhin said. 'Would anyone dare to come and touch my money? I just wanted to tell you to keep Ruppan under control. He's begun to get big-headed. He walks on the ground but thinks he's in the air . . .'

Badri Wrestler flexed his thighs and leapt from the rickshaw. He grabbed hold of Ramadhin and pulled him a short distance away.

'Why are you dirtying your tongue like this? What has Ruppan done?'

'It was Ruppan who had this dacoity letter sent to my house. I can prove it.'

'I can't even leave the house for two or three days,' muttered Badri. 'As soon as my back is turned this nonsense starts up.' He paused and then said, 'If you have proof, what are you worried about?'

He firmly assured Ramadhin of his safety and concluded, 'So then, there will be no dacoity at your house. Go, sleep in peace. Ruppan is no dacoit. He's a young lad. It must be a practical joke.'

Ramadhin replied with some bitterness, 'That I know—Ruppan has played a practical joke. But is this joke at all funny?'

'You're right,' agreed Badri, 'it is a very bad joke.'

A truck was fast approaching. Badri's eyes glittered in the reflection of its headlights as he snarled at the rickshaw-wallah, 'Pull over to the side. The road's not your father's property.'

Ramadhin knew Badri's nature. Hearing his tone of voice, he said, 'There's no need to be annoyed, Wrestler sahib! But think, is this any way to behave?'

Badri walked up to the rickshaw and climbed into it. 'When you're not going to be robbed, there's no point in arguing about it. Get going, rickshaw-wallah.' As the rickshaw moved off, he said, 'I'll have a word with Ruppan. This is not right.'

Ramadhin called after him, 'He has sent me a letter threatening me with dacoity and all you're going to do is have a word with him? This calls for a shoe-beating, not a word!'

The rickshaw was well on its way. Badri Wrestler replied without turning his head, 'If it has upset you so much, send me a threatening letter just like Ruppan's.'

7

There was a room on the flat roof of Vaidyaji's house which, like the holy book in a joint family, always remained open. In one corner, a pair of Indian clubs declared that this room officially belonged to Badri Wrestler. However, the other members of the family also used it whenever it suited them. The women of the house filled mountains of pickle into glass and earthenware pots, left them out on the roof in the sun and, when night fell, picked them up and brought them indoors. The washing met with a similar fate. In the evening, on the rope which hung across the room, you could see loincloths and blouses, towels and petticoats, all swinging to and fro together. Surplus bottles from Vaidyaji's dispensary were also stored in one of the cupboards. Practically all of them were empty. They were labelled with an illustrated advertisement. Under the heading 'Before' was a picture of a semi-human creature, and under 'After' was a picture of a man—naturally in the pink of health—with a curling moustache and a firmly tied loincloth. From these illustrations, you could tell that these were the bottles which made tigers out of thousands of men. It's another matter that they rippled their muscles and paced tiger-like only in the privacy of their bedrooms and bathrooms. Outside, they were still no better than goats.

There is a kind of literature in Hindi called 'secret', which is more dangerous than the literature considered seditious under the British Raj, because it was a crime to publish this literature before 1947, and it is still a crime to publish it. Like many official secrets, this literature doesn't stay secret. It provides a very pleasant literary supplement for those trapped in a tedious routine of food, sleep and fear, and traverses the artificial distinctions between classical and popular literature as it is well established in everyone's heart. In fact, it's nothing very special. It only recounts how a man behaved with another man or a woman or, in a more philosophical language, it is a description of the eternal relationships between human beings. In English, it is called 'pornography'.

The room on the roof was also used for the study of this literature and obviously, as Ruppan was the only student in the house, it was his preserve. Ruppan used the room for other purposes, too. He was drawn to it to experience that elusive joy to discover which others require loaves of bread, the shade of a bough, poetry, flasks of wine, a lover and other items recommended by Omar Khayyam.

This room seemed to raise high the slogan of peaceful coexistence within the family, and could not fail to fill the hearts of those who beheld it with reverence for local culture. With that in view, no sociologist could ever claim that there was the slightest danger to the joint family system in the northern hemisphere.

This was the room which had been allotted to Rangnath. He was to stay for four or five months. Vaidyaji had been right. Studying for his MA had made Rangnath sickly, as it would any normal student. He had begun to run a constant fever. Like any average Indian, he had taken pills from a doctor even though he had no faith in Western medicine. The treatment had not been able to cure him completely. Like the average city dweller, he believed that fresh country air would cure one's ills as effectively as any doctor's pills. So, he came to live in the village. Like any average idiot, he had taken up academic research when he didn't get a job immediately after passing his MA but, like any average man of common sense, he knew that you don't have to stay in a university and sit in the library every day to do research. So he thought he would relax in the village for a while, get well, study and, if necessary, go into town to change his library books. At the same time, his presence provided Vaidyaji with the constant opportunity of remarking politely, 'If only our young people weren't so completely useless, we elders would not have to shoulder all these burdens of responsibility.'

The room on the roof was quite large and, as soon as he arrived, Rangnath stamped it with his own personality. He had it swept and had a charpoy placed there permanently for his use. His bedding took up residence on the charpoy. Rangnath's books were arranged in the cupboard nearby and he banned pocket books of detective stories, and 'secret' literature from infiltrating them. A small desk and chair were also brought for him from the college and put near a window which looked out over orchards and fields.

Ruppan babu had purloined some bricks and stones and had managed to fix them together to make a sort of radio. He had run a long wire over bamboo poles on the roof of the room and into the trees nearby, which made it look like Asia's largest transmitter station. But the radio inside could only be heard over a set of headphones which Rangnath sometimes pressed to his ears to listen to local news reports and the mournful songs of Vaishnavite saints. He could thereby reassure himself that All India Radio was still the same and, despite thousands of complaints and curses from its listeners, had not budged an inch from its old ways.

~

Rangnath's routine was drawn up on Vaidyaji's advice—he got up early and then decided whether the previous day's food had been properly digested, drank cold water from a copper pot, set out for a long walk, did his daily business (because, in this world, that one business is truly daily), strolled back, washed his hands and face, chewed a tooth-cleaning twig, gargled with lukewarm water, exercised, drank milk, studied, ate lunch, rested, studied, went for an evening stroll, returned and did some simple exercises, ate a handful of almonds, raisins and so forth, studied, ate, studied and slept.

Rangnath kept conscientiously to this whole routine. The sole amendment he made was to replace study with enjoying the company of the ganjahas in Vaidyaji's sitting room. As this posed no threat to the preservation of Rangnath's virility and had no overall effect on the entire day's routine, Vaidyaji made no objection to this amendment. In fact, in one way, he was pleased to have an educated man sit next to him and was always ready to introduce him to visitors.

In just a few days Rangnath began to feel that Shivpalganj was like the great Hindu epic, the Mahabharat—what was to be found nowhere else was there, and what was not there could be found nowhere else. He realized that all Indians are one and that, everywhere, our minds are alike. He observed that the Indian genius for manipulation and manoeuvring existed in an unrefined form in Shivpalganj, in abundance. This was the same genius which was proclaimed by celebrated newspapers in bold type in front-page headlines, and due to which all kinds of great corporations, commissions and administrations were formed, fell and were dragged away. As Rangnath realized this, his faith in Indian cultural unity was reaffirmed.

He saw only one weakness in that unity. In towns, he had noticed that there was a growing generation gap between the old and the young. For some days, Rangnath had imagined that the struggle between the generations had not yet arisen in Shivpalganj. But one day his illusion was shattered. He saw that the same struggle was going on in villages and village politics, too.

The argument began over a fourteen-year-old boy. One evening, in the sitting room, a man began to narrate the boy's life story. He explained that the boy's talent for evil was so extraordinary that even the greatest psychologists and sociologists were forced to admit it was miraculous. It was said that several scholars who had qualified abroad had examined the boy's case.

Rangnath was informed that, by the age of ten, the boy could run so fast that a fifteen-year-old couldn't catch him. By the age of eleven he had become expert at ticketless travelling and avoiding the railway ticket inspector. One year later, he began to make passengers' luggage disappear from under their noses just as a clever surgeon administers local anaesthetic and removes a piece of anatomy without the patient on the operating table having the least idea where it went. His fame for this kind of theft grew mainly on the basis that he was never caught. Later on, when he was fourteen, and he was caught, it was discovered that he had become accomplished in the art of breaking the small glass panels above doorways and opening door latches from the inside. He was breaking into bungalows not by climbing through windows, but by opening doors as described and slipping into the house through the correct entrance, like an honest man.

While heaping praise on this boy, one man mentioned Behram the Robber who, at one time, was recognized in the area as a thief of historic proportions. But a youth loudly contradicted the man and, in a speech like those made in the State Assembly—that is, bereft of logic but delivered at shouting pitch—he began to try to prove that Behram the Robber was a nobody.

'By the time Ram Swarup was twelve,' he said, 'he had lifted and got rid of more stuff than Behram the Robber could have moved in a lifetime.'

Rangnath caught a glimpse of the generation gap in the conversation. He asked Sanichar, 'Aren't these modern thieves really just a lot of windbags—talking big but doing nothing? In the old days there really were plenty of robbers, each more dangerous than the last.'

Sanichar was in the age group which the younger generation considered old and the older generation, young. And, because there is no scientific division between generations, both groups considered him an outsider. So he was under no compulsion to support either side. Shaking his head like one of the hundreds of immature literary and art critics in this country, he avoided giving his opinion. 'Brother Rangnath, don't ask me about the good old days. We had Thakur Durbin Singh then. I have seen those days. But don't ask me about these boys today, either.'

~

Some thirty years ago—when today's generation had not been not born and, even if it had been, it would have been singing either 'O Lord Krishna, bestow long life and renown upon our King and Queen', or 'God save our gracious king, George V'—the name of the chief ganjaha of Shivpalganj was Thakur Durbin Singh. His parents had perhaps called him Durbin—telescope—because they wanted their son to do everything in a scientific manner. When he grew up he did just that. He grasped the fundamentals of everything in which he took an interest. He never liked the British laws and so, when Mahatma Gandhi was preparing for the Dandi March merely to break the salt laws, Durbin Singh had begun the fundamental task of breaking every single clause of the Indian Penal Code, one by one.

By nature he was a charitable man. Charity is a matter of individual conscience and every individual has his own concept of it. Some feed flour to ants; some devote themselves to maintaining the health and happiness of spinsters by wearing their hearts on their sleeves, advertising that they are always ready for love; and others prevent people from being forced to take bribes directly—they become go-betweens and run between the two sides, day and night, rain and shine. These are individual notions of charity and Durbin Singh, too, had his own thoughts on the subject. He was ever impatient to protect the weak. So, every time there was any chance of a fight he always turned up—even without being called—and wielded his lathi on behalf of the downtrodden. In those peaceful days, all these things had fixed rates. It was well known throughout the area that Babu Jayramprasad, the lawyer, charged fifty rupees every time he appeared in court to defend a case of assault, and Durbin Singh used to charge fifty rupees for committing the assault in the first place. In major fights which required a gang, the sum increased according to the number of men but still, the rates were fixed and there was never any cheating. You had to give his men meat and liquor but, on those occasions, he himself never touched meat or alcohol. As a result, his stomach remained light and his brain clear, highly desirable qualities in time of war. And since any man who can refuse meat and liquor when they are put in front of him is considered virtuous, he began to be known as a virtuous man.

Durbin Singh had another speciality. He never dug holes in the mud walls of village houses like most traditional thieves. He was a master at wall jumping and could easily have been a world-class pole vault champion. In the beginning, he would occasionally leap over walls when he was short of cash. Later on, he jumped them from time to time just to give his new pupils some practical instruction. Those were the days when thieves were thieves and dacoits were dacoits. Thieves only broke into houses to steal and if they heard even the patter of a five-year-old's feet, they would respectfully leave through the same hole through which they had come. Dacoits were more interested in fighting and less in looting. However, Durbin Singh set the fashion in his area of thrashing any householder who woke up while he was robbing his house—a practice which became extremely popular among his contemporaries. He thereby fundamentally altered the nature of theft by bringing it closer to dacoity, and brought about a radical change in the methodology of both crimes.

But, times change. In his old age, the same Durbin Singh fell off the parapet of a well after a hard slap from his drunken nephew. He broke his spine. For some days, Durbin Singh lay staring at his lathi standing in a corner, and imagined stuffing it into his nephew's face.

Finally, leaving both the lathi and his nephew's face intact, he attained the paradise of courageous warriors and left the earth of Shivpalganj bereft of valour—in other words, he snuffed it.

~

Sanichar related his memories of Durbin Singh. 'Brother Rangnath, it was a dark night and I was walking through the mango grove of the Tiwaris of Bholupur. Then, I was a young man like you, and I would face a panther with as little fear as I would a goat. My body was so full of fight that I would hit out in the air with my lathi and even if the leaves rustled I would scatter them with the foulest abuses. Anyway, it was a dark night and I was striding along with my staff in hand when somebody said from under a tree, "Beware!"

'I thought it was some jinn. You can't fight them with lathis and sticks—it's pointless. I prayed to Lord Hanuman who wears the red loincloth but, brother, Hanuman can help you only when there really are ghosts and spirits and jinns. Then, a muscular young man as black as sin came out from behind a tree and said, "Whatever you've got put it down quietly. Get your clothes off too!"

'When I stretched out my stick to hit him, what did I see but that I was surrounded on all sides by half a dozen men. They all had huge lathis and spears. I said to myself, "Sanichar, you've had it." My stick stayed exactly where it was, I hadn't the strength to hit out.

'One of them then said, "Why have you stopped? Why don't you hit us? Give it a try if you're the real son of your father!"

'I was mad with anger but, brother, I was so angry that when I tried to speak I wept. I said, "Don't kill me. Take whatever I have."

'Another man said, "The bastard's life isn't worth a penny and he's howling for it like a jackal. You're giving us all your stuff. Good. Put it down, all of it."

'But, brother, all I had was a bag with parched gram flour in it. I had a good brass pot from Moradabad—I'd got it from my uncle's house—and a ball of first-class cotton string. The pot was so big it was more like a bucket. It could draw two seers of water from a well. I had some puris fried in real ghee. There was none of this rubbish vegetable oil then! They counted everything and piled it up. Then they made me take off my dhoti and seized the one rupee I had hidden in its folds. When I got up to put my clothes on, one of them said, "Now keep your mouth shut and go home quietly. If you as much as squeak, I'll bury you alive right here in this mango grove."

'When I made to leave, another asked me where I lived.

'I replied, "I'm a ganjaha."

'Don't ask me what happened next, brother! All the robbers stood and stared at me. One of them asked me the name of the headman of Shivpalganj, another the name of the *numberdar*, and a third asked me if I knew Durbin Singh.

'I said, "I have wielded my lathi for Durbin Singh before. When there was a gathering in Rangpur. If peace hadn't been declared, thousands of people would have died there. In the village, I am so close to Durbin Singh I call him uncle!"

'That was it! Ram, Ram, Sita-Ram! It was as if some white army officer had arrived in a crowd of black Indians. There was an uproar. One person brought me my dhoti; another, my kurta; another, my shoes; someone put my bag into my hand. One man stood and pleaded with folded hands, "I have eaten two of your puris. Take the money for them. But don't let Durbin Singh know that we attacked you. If you want, take some money. And if you say so, I'll rip open my stomach and take out the puris. How could we know, brother, that you're a ganjaha?"

'So, brother, I went home and slept. The next morning, as soon as it was light, I went to Durbin Singh, clasped his feet and told him that his name had the power of Hanuman of the red loincloth and that it had saved my life. Durbin Singh drew up his feet. He said, "Go, Sanichar. Don't worry. As long as I'm here you can go wherever you like, day or night. Fear no one. You will have to deal with any snakes or scorpions yourself but leave everybody else to *me*."'

Here, Sanichar drew breath and paused. Rangnath thought that he was adding to the suspense of the story's climax like a cheap thriller writer. 'So the ganjahas must have lived in style as long as Durbin Singh was around,' he remarked.

Then Ruppan babu spoke. For the first time, to Rangnath's knowledge, he made a literary comment. Taking a deep breath he recited:

There is no mightiness in man,
Time it is that's strong.
The forest men stole the milkmaids,
And the once-great Arjun looked on.

'What's the matter, Ruppan babu?' asked Rangnath. 'Has someone looted the milkmaids of Shivpalganj?'

'Sanichar, tell the other story too,' said Ruppan.

Sanichar began another chapter in the history of Durbin Singh.

'Brother, lathi-work is not like being a member of the State Assembly. In the Assembly, the older you get, the more senile you are, the more progress you make. Take Harnam Singh for instance; when he gets up to walk he looks as if he's about to fall down dead. But every day, he gets more influential. Lathi-work depends on the strength of a man's arm. As long as it lasts, he lasts. When it's gone, he's had it.

'It must have been five or six years ago now, I had gone down to the Ganga for the Kartik bathing. It got dark as I was coming back. Night fell near the same Bholupur. There was a full, bright moon. In the mango grove, my spirits rose and I began to sing a verse. At that moment, a lathi landed on my back from the right. No greeting, no warning—a lathi blow from out of nowhere. Now, brother, I finished my song just there, and my bag flew off and fell twenty feet away. I was about to scream when three or four men leapt on top of me. One put his hand over my mouth and gagged me. He said, "Shut up, you miserable bastard, or I'll twist your neck off!" I struggled and tried to get up but, brother, even if a solid wrestler was ambushed and walloped like that he'd be downed, so what hope was there for me?

'For a while I lay there quietly, trying to feel whether I was all in one piece. Then I motioned that I wasn't going to scream. They took the gag out of my mouth. One man asked me where my money was. "Father," I said, "all I have is in this bag." In the bag I had one and a half rupees in small change. One robber picked up the coins and they clinked together in his hand. "Let's see what's in your dhoti," he said. I replied, "Father, don't make me take my dhoti off. I've got nothing on underneath it. I'll be naked."

'Well, brother, he lost his temper. He thought I was joking. Then he made me strip and searched me. The police don't search like that even when they're after drugs. When he didn't find anything, one of the others kicked me from behind and said, "Now get out of here with your mouth shut. Just keep following your nose right back to your pigeon coop."

'By now I had regained my powers of speech. I said, "Father, you people have been wise not to kill me. I don't mind that you've robbed me. But I'm telling you that you are eating your own salt. You may be the king's men, but I am from the royal court."

'They gathered round me and asked who I was, where I came from, whom I was with.

'I said, "I am a ganjaha. I have lived in the company of Durbin Singh."

'You won't believe what happened next, brother Rangnath! They all began to roar with laughter. One of them grabbed my hand and pulled me towards him. I couldn't think what he was going to do. He kicked my legs from under me and I fell flat on my back.

'The robbers were still laughing. One of them said, "I know him. Durbin Singh's days are over now. All those old fogeys used to show off a little lathi-work and put around a lot of tall stories. This Durbin Singh became a hero just by throwing his lathi around and jumping over a couple of walls. Now they teach even schoolchildren to pole-vault."

'Another robber said, "They teach lathi-work at school too. I learned it there myself."

'The first youth spoke again. "So that's the famous Durbin Singh! The bastard hasn't even got a gun, and he thinks he can run our whole area."

'A man who was holding a torch took a gun from his pocket. He said, "Look, son. This is a six-shooter. It doesn't have country-made cartridges but real foreign ones." Saying this, he poked the barrel into my chest. "Go and tell your father there. In those days, the one-eyed man was king in the kingdom of the blind. But not any more. Now those old men should just lie on their string cots and brood. If they ever show their faces outside, they'll get the pulp taken out of their skulls."

'After that, brother, I couldn't stop myself. I was filled with such a passion that I even threw down my stick just there, and ran for it like a gazelle. Behind me, they started guffawing again. One called out, "To hell with that bastard Durbin Singh. Stand still! I'll beat you into a telescope!"

'But, brother, to this day, no one's been able to compete with me at running. Now they blow whistles and teach boys to run in school. Without ever having been taught, I could run so fast that I could leave a hare standing. So, brother, they swore a great deal, but they couldn't catch me. Somehow, I got home. By then, Durbin Singh was not the man he had been. Even the police had begun to turn against him in their heart of hearts. The next day, I felt very perturbed but I didn't tell him what had happened. If I had, uncle Durbin would have dropped dead of shock.'"

Ruppan babu was sitting with a face as long as a wet week. He sighed and said, 'It would have been better to tell him. If he had croaked then, he wouldn't have been killed by his nephew.'

8

Shivpalganj was a village but it was also close to the town and on a main road. Important politicians and officials could have no theoretical objection to going there. Apart from the village wells, some handpumps had been installed; so, when visiting VIPs felt thirsty they could drink the water there without endangering their lives. Food was also conveniently available. There was generally a minor local official who looked sufficiently affluent for the villagers to consider him a complete crook, but whom outsiders would see and exclaim, 'What a gentleman! He comes from a good family. Look, he married Chiko sahib's daughter.' The VIPs could therefore satisfy their hunger at his house without risking their reputation for honesty. Whatever the reason, by this time of the year, a major influx of leaders and servants of the people had already begun. All of them were concerned about the progress of Shivpalganj and as a result they delivered speeches.

These speeches were especially interesting for the ganjahas. From the very start, the speakers would set out with the belief that the audience was a bunch of idiots, and the audience would sit firm in its opinion that the speakers were fools. From the villagers' point of view, these were the perfect conditions for a dialogue. Still, there were so many speeches that, despite their interest, the locals could get indigestion. A speech is really enjoyable only when both sides know that the speaker is talking absolute nonsense. But some speakers took their work so seriously that the audience occasionally felt that they actually believed what they were saying. As soon as this suspicion arose, the speech would begin to seem turgid and insipid, and have a very bad effect on the digestion of the audience. In the light of their experience, the villagers had chosen certain times to listen to speeches depending on their individual constitutions. Some listened to them in the morning before breakfast; others, after lunch. Most people took the largest measure of speechifying during their afternoon nap.

In those days, the main subject under discussion was agriculture but that didn't mean that it had ever been anything else. In fact, for the past few years, the villagers had been cajoled into believing that India was a farming nation. The villagers didn't contest this, but every speaker behaved from the start as if they might. So they used to find one argument after another to prove that India was a farming nation. After this, they would explain that progress in agriculture was progress for the nation. Then, before they could explain anything more, they found it was lunchtime and that the polite young man, who was the offspring of a rich family and had married Chiko sahib's daughter, was tugging at the back of their shirts to let them know that their food was ready. Sometimes, the speakers did continue their speech, and then it became clear that there was no difference between what they had said first and what they went on to say, because, however they framed it, the subject remained the same—India is a farming nation, you are farmers, you should farm well and produce more grain. Every speaker was gripped by the suspicion that farmers did not want to grow more grain.

A publicity campaign made up for anything lacking in the speeches. And in a way, the advertisements stuck or written on the walls gave an accurate introduction to village problems and how to solve them. For example, one problem was that India was a farming nation, but, out of sheer perversity, farmers refused to produce more grain. The solution was to give speeches to farmers and show them all sorts of attractive pictures. These advised them that, if they didn't want to grow more grain for themselves, they should do so for the nation. As a result, posters were stuck in various places to induce farmers to grow grain for the nation. The farmers were greatly influenced by the combined effect of the speeches and the posters, and even the most simple-minded cultivator began to feel that in all likelihood there was some ulterior motive behind the whole campaign.

One advertisement had become especially well known in Shivpalganj. It showed a healthy farmer with a turban wrapped around his head, wearing earrings and a quilted jacket, cutting a tall crop of wheat with a sickle. A woman was standing behind him, very pleased with herself; she was laughing like an official from the department of agriculture.

Below and above the picture was written in Hindi and English— 'Grow More Grain'. Farmers with earrings and quilted jackets who were also scholars of English were expected to be won over by the English slogan, and those who were scholars of Hindi, by the Hindi version. And those who didn't know how to read either language could at least recognize the figures of the man and the laughing woman. The government hoped that as soon as they saw the man and the laughing woman, the farmers would turn away from the poster and start growing more grain like men possessed. This poster had currently become a subject of discussion in several places in Shivpalganj because the local people thought that the man in the picture looked quite like Badri Wrestler. There was a profound difference of opinion about the woman's identity. It had not yet been settled which of the village belles she was.

The most strident advertisements, however, were not about agriculture but malaria. Here and there, written in red ochre on the walls of houses, was the legend, 'Help us to eradicate malaria. Let us exterminate mosquitoes'. This actually assumed that farmers raise mosquitoes with the same enthusiasm with which they raise cattle and that, before you kill the insects, you have to bring about a change of heart in the agricultural community. To effect a change of heart, you need to command their respect, and to do that, you need English. This was the native logic which led to all appeals for the extermination of mosquitoes and the eradication of malaria being generally written in English. As a result, most people had accepted the advertisements not as literature but as visual art and allowed the wall painters to write as much English on the walls as they liked. Walls were painted and mosquitoes died. Dogs barked and people went their way.

One advertisement said simply, 'Save More Money'. Most villagers had been told to save money for generations and practically everyone knew about it. The only innovation in the advertisement was that it mentioned the nation. It hinted that if you can't save for yourself, then save for the nation. The sentiment was just. Moneylenders, important officials, lawyers and doctors were all saving money for themselves, so how could small farmers object to saving for the nation? Everyone basically agreed that money should be saved.

Where and how to deposit your money when you had saved it was also explained clearly in speeches and posters, and no one raised any objection to the methods outlined. The only thing people were not told was how to get money to save, in other words, how much money they should be paid for their labour. The question of savings is linked to income and expenditure. Except for this small point, all aspects of the problem had been considered, and people had accepted the message so readily that the poor posters were left with nothing to say. 'They asked for neither food nor fodder; they neither gave nor took.' So, we should not disturb them.

The advertisements which attracted Rangnath were the contribution of the private, not the public, sector. They revealed the following: 'Ringworm is the most widespread disease in this area. There is one medicine which will bring deep-down relief from ringworm if you rub it on your skin. If you take this medicine, coughs and colds will vanish; and if you mix it with sugary sweets and swallow it with water, it is an effective treatment for cholera. There is no medicine like it anywhere in the world. The man who invented it is still alive and only the malice of the West has prevented him from winning the Nobel Prize.'

In India, there are many other great doctors who have never won the Nobel Prize. One lives in Jahanabad and, as the town has been electrified, he has taken to giving electric shock treatment for impotency. Another doctor who is famous—at least in India—cures hydrocele without an operation. And you can find this fact written in letters of coal tar on any wall in Shivpalganj. Furthermore, a lot of advertisements target dehydration in children, eye disease, diarrhoea and so forth, but there are three main diseases mentioned—ringworm, hydrocele and impotency. The boys of Shivpalganj will find out their cures only when they learn to read and can make out the inscriptions on the walls.

Among the teeming advertisements, Vaidyaji's had its own individuality: 'A Message of Hope for Youth'. It bore no comparison to the obscene scrawl of slogans like, 'Electric shock treatment for impotency'. The message was written in green and red letters on beautiful tin boards and was hung in out-of-the-way corners, on small shops and government buildings, where bill sticking and urinating were forbidden.

It said simply, 'A Message of Hope for Youth', and underneath were Vaidyaji's name and a sentence advising patients to meet him.

One day, Rangnath noticed that a new dimension had been added to the treatment of disease. Early in the morning, several people started painting the word 'Piles!' in huge letters on a wall. This was an indication of the progress that had been made in Shivpalganj. The five, man-sized letters were shouting out, 'The Era of Diarrhoea is passing! The age of soft dispositions, office chairs, comfortable living, round-the-clock food and drink, and light work is gradually infecting the population, and piles, the symbol of modernity, is entering the field to combat the ubiquitous curse of impotency.' By evening, this giant-sized advertisement had made its colourful mark on one wall and begun to announce far and wide, 'A Sure Cure for Piles!'

Before one's very eyes, the world was yielding to piles and its certain cure. The same advertisement started to appear everywhere. Rangnath was most surprised when he saw it in a daily newspaper. This newspaper used to arrive in Shivpalganj from the town by ten o'clock every morning and helped to inform people where a truck had collided with a scooter or where and how a certain bad character by the name of Abbasi had attacked a certain vegetable vendor called Irshad with a certain knife. Rangnath noticed that on this particular day a large portion of the front page had been printed in black and on it shone forth in large white letters, 'Piles!' The letters were written in the same style as was used in the wall advertisements. These letters gave piles a new importance; they dominated the other items on the page. The white letters, standing out on the page against the black background, attracted attention even from a distance. Sanichar, who had innate difficulty in reading just the headlines, was drawn to the paper and buried his eyes in the advertisement. After staring at it for some considerable time, he said to Rangnath, 'It's the same one.'

His voice rang with pride. He felt that the advertisements gleaming on the walls of Shivpalganj were something special. They were published in city newspapers and so, Shivpalganj had everything that the city newspapers had.

~

The truth was that no real dacoit had written the letter to Ramadhin. In those days, the village council and college politics had caused tension between Vaidyaji and Ramadhin Bhikhmakhervi. Had it been the town, and had the politics been of a high standard, then, on such an occasion, some woman would have filed a report with the police to the effect that Ramadhin had attempted to rape her but, as she had resisted, he had failed in his attempt, and she had made her way directly to the police station, her modesty fully intact. But this was a rural area and, as yet, rape had not been accepted as a political hand grenade. They still used the old methods and so the dacoit threat was produced, and Ramadhin was left to stew in his own juice for a few days.

The police, Ramadhin and the whole of Vaidyaji's faction knew that the letter was a forgery. Such letters had been received several times by various people. So, Ramadhin was under no compulsion to climb up the hill with his bag of money on the appointed date and time. Even if the letter had been genuine, Ramadhin may well have preferred to have his house attacked by dacoits rather than quietly hand over the money. But because a case had been registered at the police station, the police were forced to do something about the letter. On the day Ramadhin was meant to deliver the money, the whole area from the village to the hill was surrendered to the police to play Catch the Dacoit. On the hill, there was what looked like a regular police station. The police went over the fallow and the barren land, the woods, the fields and the threshing floors with a fine-tooth comb, but couldn't find any sign of the dacoits. They shook the twigs of the trees near the hill, thrust bayonets into foxholes and, gazing hypnotically at level stretches of ground, satisfied themselves that whatever was out there, it wasn't dacoits but birds, foxes, insects and worms.

That night, when some creature howled at the top of its voice, it was discovered to be not a dacoit, but a jackal; and when some other creature made a noise in the orchard nearby, the conclusion was eventually reached that it was only a bat. The match between Ramadhin Bhikhmakhervi and the dacoits was a draw because neither did the dacoits come for the money nor did Ramadhin deliver it.

The junior sub-inspector of police had been in his post for only a short while. He was entrusted with the job of catching the dacoits on the hill. At about one a.m. he walked down the hill on to the plain and, since it was dark and the weather was turning cold, and he was beginning to miss his girlfriend from the town, and also because he had done a BA in Hindi literature, he started to hum softly and finally to sing, 'Alas, my heart! Alas, my heart!'

'Partridges go in pairs—two behind and two in front.' This lyric from a Hindi film song proved to apply to the police too. Two constables preceded and two followed the junior sub-inspector. The junior sub-inspector went on singing and the constables thought, 'It doesn't matter. He'll get better in a few days.' As they walked across the flat countryside, the junior sub-inspector's singing reached a crescendo and proved that you can very enjoyably sing what is too foolish to be said.

They came near the road. Suddenly, a voice issued from a ditch.

'Whoosh the bashtud?'

The junior sub-inspector's hand travelled to his revolver. The constables hesitated, and then unshouldered their rifles. By then, the voice from the ditch had spoken again. 'Whoosh the bashtud?'

One constable whispered into the junior sub-inspector's ear, 'There could be shooting. We should take cover behind that tree, sir.'

The tree was about five yards away. The junior sub-inspector whispered back, 'You men go behind the tree, I'll investigate.'

He said, 'Who's in the ditch? Come out whoever you are!' Then, remembering a scene he had seen in a Hindi film, he added, 'You people are surrounded. If you don't come out in thirty seconds, I'll give orders to shoot!'

There was silence in the ditch for a few moments, then the voice said, 'Dropsh dead bashtud, rifal shooshter!'

Every Indian, once he steps outside his house, becomes a virtual brick wall where languages are concerned. He hears so many different dialects that, in the end, he admits failure and gives up trying to understand, whether the language is Nepali or Gujarati. But this language made the junior sub-inspector's ears prick up and he wondered what on earth was going on. He managed to follow that the man was swearing; but why couldn't he understand the language? The junior sub-inspector decided to make use of the internationally accepted principle of shooting first and asking questions later. He stretched out the arm holding the revolver and warned, 'Come out of the ditch, or I fire!'

But he didn't have to fire. One constable came out from behind the tree and said, 'Don't shoot, sir. It's Jognath. He's got drunk and fallen into the ditch.'

The other constables came and stood eagerly round the ditch. The junior sub-inspector asked, 'Who's Jognath?'

An old constable said with the voice of experience, 'This is Mr Ramnath's son, Jognath. He's a loner and he drinks too much.'

The policemen picked up Jognath and stood him on his feet, but when someone doesn't want to stand on his own feet how can you make him? So he stumbled and nearly fell over again, but was caught and finally pulled out of the ditch. He sat on the ground with his legs crossed, looking like some great Hindu ascetic. After he had looked everyone in the eyes one by one, shaken his arms, and made some jackal- and bat-like noises in his throat, he became fit to speak on a human level, and repeated, 'Whoosh the bashtud?'

The junior sub-inspector asked, 'What is this language?'

A constable replied, 'We recognized him from his language. It's his own. At the moment, he's not in his senses. That's why he's swearing and talking nonsense.'

Perhaps the junior sub-inspector was impressed by Jognath's attachment to profanity—even when barely conscious, he could swear. He shook Jognath violently by the shoulders and spoke more sternly, 'Come to your senses!'

But Jognath refused to come to his senses. He just said, 'Bashtud!'

The constables laughed. The one who had recognized him first shouted in his ear, 'Jognath, come to your shenshes!'

Jognath didn't react to this either, but the junior sub-inspector suddenly understood his special language. He smiled, 'This bastard is calling us bastards!'

He raised his hand to hit Jognath, but a constable stopped him. 'Let him go, sir.'

The junior sub-inspector was not pleased by the constable's humanitarian attitude. He lowered his hand, but said in a tone which commanded obedience, 'Take him with you and put him in the lock-up. Charge him with Section 109 of the Criminal Procedure Code.'

Another constable spoke up, 'You can't do this, sir. He's a local. He paints advertisements on walls and starts talking this language of his at the drop of a hat. He is a bad character, but at least he does some work for appearances' sake.'

The constables had managed to make Jognath stand up and were making him walk on his own two feet towards the road. 'Maybe he's insulting us because he's drunk,' said the junior sub-inspector, 'but we'll find something to charge him with. Go and lock him up. We'll charge him tomorrow.'

The same constable said, 'Sir, what's the point of getting involved in a lot of senseless trouble? Let's go to the village now and show him into his house. How can we send him to the lock-up? He's Vaidyaji's man.'

The junior sub-inspector was new to the force, but he suddenly realized the reason behind the constables' humanitarian outlook. He said nothing but dropped behind them and tried again to find satisfaction in the darkness, the chill, the thought of his girlfriend in the town and the song, *Alas, my heart.*

9

The embezzlement in the cooperative union had been done in a very straightforward fashion. In comparison with the hundreds of embezzlements which are taking place every day, its charm lay in the fact that it was a pure and simple fraud; there was nothing convoluted about it. There had been no need of forged signatures or false accounts, nor had money been withdrawn against bogus invoices. No technical knowledge was necessary to commit or comprehend this sort of fraud, only willpower.

The cooperative union had a seed godown which was full of wheat. One day, Ram Swarup, the union supervisor, arrived at the godown with two trucks. The trucks were loaded with sacks of wheat and onlookers imagined that this was part of the normal, everyday work of the cooperative.

Ram Swarup himself was sitting beside one of the drivers to take the wheat to the neighbouring godown, and the trucks set off. The trucks would have found the other godown five miles down a mud road which turned off the main highway. But the trucks didn't take the turning—they went straight on. That is where the embezzlement began. The trucks went directly to the town grain market. There, the sacks were unloaded. Both the drivers went on to erase all knowledge of the embezzlement from their memories and began to carry loads of wood and coal to neighbouring districts. Ram Swarup was untraceable for some days and people became convinced that he had sold the grain, filled his pockets with the several thousand rupees he got for it and run off to Bombay. The whole incident was registered in a report at the local police station and, as Vaidyaji put it, 'It's as if a thorn has been removed from the flesh.'

The previous day, a director of the union had seen something which revealed that Ram Swarup had selected a neighbouring town—not Bombay—in which to spend his money. The director had gone to the town simply to have a look at it. On such visits, he had at least one regular item among the others on his programme—to go to a park, sit on a bench under a tree, chew puffed rice and gram, observe the colourful flowers and girls attentively and have his head massaged with oil by some young boy. When he reached the last point of this programme, something happened. He was sitting on a bench underneath a tree; his eyes were closed and the thin, supple fingers of the boy were tapping his head—*tir, tir, tir.* As the boy was joyfully drumming this irregular rhythm on his scalp, the director was thinking with regret that the massage may end too soon. Once he opened his eyes and tried to turn his head to speak to the boy, but he was so much under the commanding influence of the oil massage that his head refused to turn. So he couldn't see the boy and tried to satisfy himself by watching what was in front of him.

In front of him he saw a tree, and on the bench under the tree, he saw Ram Swarup, the supervisor. He, too, was having his head massaged with oil by a young boy and was lost in the blissful sensation of the *tir, tir, tir.* Both parties were immersed in their own individual worlds, like great Hindu saints. These were the ideal circumstances for peaceful coexistence. So they did not interfere in each other's affairs.

For some fifteen minutes they sat on their respective benches like good neighbours and pretended not to see one another. Then they both stretched, stood up, paid their masseurs the appropriate remuneration, told them to meet them again at the same place and, according to the principles of Panchsheel, went their own ways.

As he was returning to Shivpalganj, the director began to wonder whether he hadn't betrayed the cooperative movement for the sake of a head massage. He recalled that Ram Swarup was still on the run and that the police were searching for him. If he had managed to get Ram Swarup caught, the embezzlement case could have been solved. His name would even have been in the papers. These thoughts depressed him. He began to search his soul. Then, for the sake of his peace of mind, he went to see Vaidyaji on his way back and, tossing a dose of asafoetida digestive powder down his throat, told him, 'I saw a man in the park today who looked just like Ram Swarup.'

'Quite possible,' commented Vaidyaji. 'Some people's appearances are very similar.'

The director felt that his conscience would not be satisfied with this. He looked around for a short while and then said, 'I thought to myself, "This must be Ram Swarup."'

Vaidyaji stared at the director.

'It really was Ram Swarup. I wondered what the bastard was doing there. He was having his head massaged.'

'What were you doing there?'

The director replied absently, 'I was tired out and resting under a tree.'

'You should have informed the police at once.'

The director pondered a while and then said carefully, 'I thought that Ram Swarup shouldn't know that anyone had spotted him. That's why I didn't inform the police.'

Vaidyaji was upset by the news that the man accused of embezzlement was not in Bombay but only fifteen miles away, and that his head was still safe on his shoulders—so much so that he could indulge in oil massages. It was essential to call a meeting of the cooperative's directors. Vaidyaji had heard the whole story on an empty stomach. So that it could be retold after a drink of bhang, he called the meeting in the evening.

~

Sanichar was interested in anything from the town and was therefore intrigued by Rangnath. When Rangnath sat near the doorway, Sanichar could always be found nearby. So it was today. Vaidyaji had gone to the cooperative meeting. Only Rangnath and Sanichar were sitting by the door. The sun had begun to set and as the winter evening fell, acrid smoke rose from every home and hung in the air.

Three young men passed down the road in front of the house, roaring with laughter. Their conversation concerned some event in connection with which the words 'noon', 'conman', 'real style', 'cards' and 'cash' were mentioned as frequently as the words 'evaluation', 'coordination' and 'dovetailing' are by officials of the Planning Commission, and 'perspective', 'dimension', 'contemporary perception' and 'context' by the literati. Talking to one another, they passed the sitting room and stopped. Sanichar said, 'Brother Badri teaches these animals wrestling. It's like handing over a rifle to a leopard. As it is, the bastards make it difficult for ordinary people to walk the streets; if they learn wrestling tricks, we'll all have to leave the village.'

Suddenly the young men gave a guffaw.

As soon as he heard their laughter, Sanichar spoke in a commanding tone, 'What are you lot doing, hanging around here? Go your way!'

The young men went on their way with a pocketbook edition of their guffaws. By then a woman had emerged from the darkness, her anklets ringing with each step and, leaving shadows leaping in the dim light of the lantern, she passed on ahead. She was muttering something, the purport of which was that the young boys who only yesterday had been roaming around naked in front of her were now bent on making love to her. Broadcasting to the whole neighbourhood the news that boys were making passes at her, and that she was still worth making a pass at, the woman disappeared into the darkness. Sanichar told Rangnath, 'God knows from where Kana got hold of that bitch. Whenever she sets out of her house someone makes a pass at her.'

'Kana' was the nickname of Pandit Radhelal. One of his eyes was smaller than the other and, because of this, the ganjahas had begun to call him Kana, or One-Eye.

It is an ancient tradition—in fact, all we do is an ancient tradition—that people leave their villages and go and get married for the flimsiest of reasons. This happened to Arjun and to Chitrangada in the Mahabharat. It happened to Dushyant, who begat Bharat, the founding father of the Indian nation; it has happened to Indians who emigrated to Trinidad and Tobago, Burma and Bangkok; it's happening to Indians who go to America and Europe—and it happened to Pandit Radhelal.

He once got the chance of a job in a sugar mill in some eastern district. It was a nightwatchman's job and he went there and stayed with another nightwatchman. At that time, Pandit Radhelal was unmarried and his biggest problem in life was that he didn't get home cooking. For some days, his fellow nightwatchman's wife solved his problem because he ate the food she cooked while he was staying with them. The world-famous saying goes: 'The way to a man's heart is through his stomach.' And so it happened that the nightwatchman's wife tunnelled through Pandit Radhelal's stomach and began to head for his heart. He began to like the food she cooked so much, and she herself became so trapped in her own tunnel that, within the month, he brought her to Shivpalganj to cook for him there. When they left, they took enough with them from her house to keep them in food for a couple of years. At this, their neighbours around the mill came to the conclusion that Pandit Radhelal's fellow nightwatchman was an idiot, while the ganjahas of Shivpalganj thought that Radhelal was a real son of a gun.

Till then, Pandit Radhelal's position had been that of 'an unshakeable witness'. Now, he also became famous as 'a man who never misses'.

As a matter of fact, it was Pandit Radhelal's reputation as an unshakeable witness which earned him his livelihood. He was on the borderline between literacy and illiteracy and, when necessary, could state in court either that he was illiterate or that he could just about sign his name. But he had such an innate knowledge of civil and criminal law that he could give evidence as a witness in any case and, so far, no lawyer had managed to catch him out in a cross-examination. Any judge can decide any case which comes before him, and any lawyer can argue any brief. Similarly, Pandit Radhelal could become an eyewitness to any offence. In short, he too, like the judge, the lawyers and the clerk of the court, formed an essential link in the legal chain. He was bound, like a tyre rod, to the wheels of the motor car of the British justice system in which we ride around proclaiming the 'rule of law' with such great pride, and he turned the wheels whichever way he pleased. The moment he stood up in court and swore to tell the truth by God and the Ganga, everyone, from the opposing side to the magistrate, knew he could only lie. But this knowledge was to no purpose as judgments are reached, not on the basis of knowledge but on the basis of law and, no matter what one might feel about Pandit Radhelal's testimony, the law found it genuine.

Whatever Pandit Radhelal's status might be, that of his beloved was absolutely clear. She had run away from her husband, therefore, she was a bitch. People could joke around with her and always proceed on the assumption that she liked it. It was the good fortune of the young men of Shivpalganj that the bitch never disappointed them. She really did like a joke and, right after a joke, she always swore—a very popular means of self-expression among ganjahas.

Sanichar was relating the story of Pandit Radhelal to Rangnath in a highly dramatic fashion. Then one of the three young men returned and stood at the door of the sitting room. His bare body was smeared with the earth of the wrestling pit. The long, thin end of his loincloth hung down from his waist to his feet like an elephant's trunk. In those days in Shivpalganj, this style was coming into fashion among those who walked around in loincloths. Sanichar asked, 'What's the matter, Chhote Wrestler?'

The wrestler scratched the ringworm on his joints and replied, 'Brother Badri hasn't come to the wrestling pit today. Where has he vanished to?'

'How can he vanish? He must be around somewhere.'

'Where?'

'The union supervisor loaded up some wheat and ran off with it. There's a meeting about it in the union. Badri too must be there.'

The wrestler spat carelessly on the veranda. 'What will brother Badri do in a meeting? Hatch eggs? If he'd got hold of the supervisor and smashed him with a dhobi-slab throw, it would have finished him off. What the hell comes out of any meeting-sheeting?'

Rangnath liked his speech. He said, 'Do people hatch eggs in your meetings?'

The wrestler had not expected any comment from Rangnath's direction. 'If they don't hatch eggs, you think they pull out people's short hairs? Everyone in a meeting just sits there, wailing like a widow. When it's time to do any real work, they grab hold of a peg and refuse to budge.'

Rangnath had no specialized knowledge of this form of the Hindi language. He reflected upon the fact that people were always writing off the language by saying that it lacked a powerful vocabulary. 'If Hindi scholars,' thought Rangnath, 'were put in a wrestling pit for four months with the likes of Chhote Wrestler, then, despite the personal discomfort caused, even the tiny particles of dust there would start to unearth for them a whole new dictionary of words and terms.' Rangnath looked at Chhote Wrestler with respect. In order that he could have a quiet word with him, he invited him to come inside.

'Why?' said the wrestler. 'Am I about to be struck by lightning out here? I am all right where I am.'

After this, Chhote Wrestler displayed some signs of cordiality in his conversation. He asked, 'How are you then, Rangnath guru?'

Rangnath didn't want to say much about himself to the wrestler. The subject of having milk and almonds twice a day and exercising might not awaken the enthusiasm of coffee house intellectuals, but for Chhote Wrestler it would be sufficient for an all-night discussion. Rangnath replied, 'I'm absolutely fit, wrestler. Tell me about yourself. Why did the supervisor need to sell the wheat?'

The wrestler then spat with hatred on to the veranda. He stretched out the end of his loincloth and tightened it, revealing by this unsuccessful attempt to cover himself his wish to prove that he was not naked. Then, coming up to Rangnath, he said, 'Arré, guru! They say, "Not a rag on his back but he'll still eat betel nut." It was the same with the supervisor. He used to wander around doing *phuttpheri* night and day in Lucknow and how can you do phuttpheri without masala? He certainly had to sell the wheat.'

'What is phuttpheri?'

The wrestler laughed. 'You don't know phuttpheri? The bloody wife's father was a big playboy and *lasebazi* trickster. Doing lasebazi is no joke! It takes the kidneys out of the biggest man. Even Jumnapur state went to blazes because of it.'

Boys from Indian universities go to see English films. They can't follow an English conversation, but the poor fellows smile and pretend that they understand everything and that the film is highly enjoyable. Unable to comprehend what he was being told, Rangnath smiled in a similar fashion. The wrestler continued, 'Guru, I've been watching Ram Swarup the supervisor putting it on for a long time. That's why I told Badri Wrestler, "Ustad, this man goes after Lucknow *lasebaz*." Then even Badri Wrestler would tell me, "Don't kick up such a row. If the bastard eats fire, he'll shit sparks." Now he has eaten fire and he's walked off with the wheat. At first, even Vaidya maharaj sat and kept quiet but now, when the shit has surfaced, they are all sitting in the union office playing Chinese whispers. I've heard they're going to pass a resolution. They'll just pass time. Ram Swarup has already taken all the grain from the godown. Now they are going to pass a resolution—as if that will harm a hair of his head.'

Rangnath said, 'It was a waste of time speaking to Badri about this. If you'd only told Vaidyaji about your suspicions, he could have had the man removed from here.'

'*Arré*, guru! Don't force me to open my mouth. Vaidyaji may be your uncle, but he's no father of mine. If I came out with the truth, it would burn your liver, it would.'

Sanichar said, 'Chhote Wrestler, it looks as if you've been straining a lot of bhang before you came here. You're in a very colourful mood.'

'It's nothing to do with being colourful, my son,' remarked the wrestler. 'Every hair on my body is burning. Lift up the tail of anyone round here and you'll see they're all bloody females. Don't force me to talk about Vaidya maharaj. If I open his account, your eyes will be opened wide and you won't be able to close them. The same Ram Swarup used to get together with Vaidyaji every day for private face-to-face talks and tell him all sorts of different stories. And now, for the last two days, Vaidyaji has been writhing around in agony. I too am in the union. He said, "Come for the resolution and raise your hand." I told him, "Don't make me raise my hand, maharaj. Once I raise it, people will be crying in pain." This same Ram Swarup is roaming around the town, up to no good, and he doesn't get him arrested and shut up in the one-lakh government guesthouse; he just wants us to pass a resolution. Badri himself was badly upset, but his own father was involved in the matter. Whatever he does is like opening a woman's thighs. Whichever you open, she loses her modesty.'

By this time they could hear the sounds of people approaching the sitting room. The grand figure of Vaidya maharaj appeared, clad in a homespun dhoti, kurta, jacket, cap and shawl. Several hangers-on attended on him. Badri brought up the rear. His face was as long as a horse's nosebag. As soon as he laid his eyes on Badri, Chhote Wrestler said, 'Ustad, this is a very odd business. I've been standing here for ages waiting to tell you about it.'

Badri Wrestler greeted Chhote with the remark, 'Is the waiting going to make you melt? What's the trouble?' The guru and his disciple then went to the other end of the veranda to talk.

Vaidyaji and four or five men went indoors. One heaved a long sigh of relief which ended in a sob. Another sat on the wooden bed and gave an enormous yawn which concluded with a whistle. Vaidyaji too sat down, leant against a cushion, and flung his cap and kurta to the other end of the bed with the gesture of a classical singer who has just finished a particularly difficult and long-drawn-out note. It was clear that everyone had completed some great work and had come to rid themselves of their fatigue.

Sanichar spoke, 'Maharaj, if you are very tired, should I strain some more bhang?'

Vaidyaji said nothing. One of the union directors said, 'We've already had two glasses at the union meeting. Great stuff. Creamy. Now it's time to go home.'

Vaidyaji sat for a while in silence as before, listening to what was being said. He had adopted this habit since he became convinced that the man who eats less himself leaves more for others to eat; the man who talks less allows others to talk more; and the man who is less of a fool allows others to be more foolish. Then he suddenly spoke, 'Rangnath, what do you make of it?'

Rangnath answered the question without understanding it, in the same way that Vaidyaji had asked it without giving any clue as to what it was about. 'Well, whatever happens happens for the best.'

Vaidyaji smiled into his moustache. He said, 'A very appropriate remark. Badri was against the proposal but later he quietened down. The resolution was passed unanimously. Whatever happened happened for the best.'

It dawned on Rangnath that he had just been robbed of his own opinion. He asked eagerly, 'What resolution did you pass?'

'We passed a resolution that the government should grant us compensation for the eight-thousand-rupee loss the supervisor caused us.'

Rangnath was staggered by this logic. He said, 'What has it got to do with the government? The union supervisor embezzled the wheat, and you want the government to make it up to you?'

'Who else will give it? The supervisor is missing. We've informed the police. The rest is the responsibility of the government. We are powerless. If we weren't, we would get hold of the supervisor and collect the value of the grain from him. Now, whatever has to be done the government will do. Either it will capture the supervisor and bring him before us, or do something else. Whatever happens, if the government wants our union to survive and continue to benefit the people, it will have to pay the compensation. Otherwise, this union will collapse. We have done our job, now it's up to the government. We know, too, that it can be inefficient.'

Vaidyaji was speaking so reasonably that Rangnath's head began to spin. He mentioned terms like 'the inertia of the administration', 'the welfare of the people', 'responsibility', time and time again. Rangnath became certain that his uncle, despite being of an older generation, was competent at speaking precisely the language understood in modern times.

Badri Wrestler had returned after his conversation with Chhote. He said, 'Ramadhin wasn't attacked by dacoits, but there is news of robberies around and about.'

He generally spoke respectfully in his father's presence, and he made this remark, too, as if it were his duty to state it.

Vaidyaji replied, 'Theft! Dacoity! Everywhere, you hear of nothing else. The country's going to hell.'

Badri ignored this and, as if he were a health inspector explaining how to prevent cholera, remarked to the assembly, 'The whole village is talking about robbery. We'll have to sleep with our eyes open from now on.'

Sanichar jumped up, sat down again in a different position and asked, 'How do you sleep with your eyes open, wrestler?'

Badri said cuttingly, 'Don't take the piss out of me. I'm in no mood for jokes.'

He went out to the veranda and stood with Chhote Wrestler.

10

The Changamal Vidyalaya Intermediate College was founded to 'inspire the youthful citizens of the nation with great ideals and, by providing them with the best education, to make them the means of the country's uplift'. Reading the 'Constitution and Regulations' of the college, printed on shiny orange paper, a heart soiled with the dirt of reality would be naturally cleansed and purified, just as it would be after reading the chapter in the Indian Constitution dealing with Fundamental Rights.

The college was established in the national interest and so, naturally, it had its fair share of factionalism, if nothing else. You couldn't say it had an abundant amount of factionalism, but still, considering the progress it had made in a short time span, it seemed as if a good job had been done. In only a couple of years, its factionalism had begun to appear much more solid than that in the surrounding colleges. In fact, in some instances, it had even begun to compete with all-India institutions.

Vaidyaji held sway over the managing committee but Ramadhin Bhikhmakhervi had, by this time, already established a faction of his own. To do this required serious endeavour. For a long time, his faction had consisted only of himself; then he attracted a few members of the committee to his side. Now, after a great deal of hard work, he had managed to split the college employees into two groups, but there was still a lot to be done.

The Principal was entirely reliant on Vaidyaji, but Khanna Master was not dependent on Ramadhin's group to the same extent. He still had to be won over. The boys had not yet been divided into rival groups on the basis of their sympathy for the two factions. They did swear and fight amongst themselves, but these activities had not found a suitable direction. The fights did not further the aim of factionalism, but were carried out for personal reasons and, in this way, the power of the boys' hooliganism was dissipated in individual self-interest and was not employed for the collective good of the nation. The factionalists still had a great deal of work to do on this front, too.

It's true to say that, apart from Vaidyaji, the college factionalists lacked experience. They had neither maturity nor brilliance. On the rare occasions in the year when they managed to pull off a master stroke, it sent waves as far as the town. And they sometimes did pull off a trick which astounded even the greatest, natural-born politicians. The previous year, Ramadhin had caught Vaidyaji out with a trick like that. He hadn't succeeded but his strategy was discussed for miles around and was mentioned in the newspapers. One politician was so affected by the news that he came galloping from the town to the college just to pat both sides on the back. He was a senior factionalist and lived mostly in the capital. For the last forty years, he had devoted twenty-four hours a day to factionalism and was himself factionalism personified. He operated at the all-India level, and his statements were published on front pages every day. They revealed a unique confluence of patriotism and factionalism. Once he visited a college, people were satisfied in the knowledge that even if the college were to close down there would at least be no end to factionalism.

The question is: why factionalism?

This is like asking why rain falls from the heavens, or why you should tell the truth, or what is material and what is God. In fact, this is a socio-psychological, almost a philosophical, question.

According to Vedanta—to which Vaidyaji always referred as a synonym for Ayurveda—factionalism is another name for the ultimate condition of realization that the self 'I' and the divine 'Thou' are one. In factionalism, every 'I' sees every 'Thou', and every 'Thou' sees every 'I' in a position better than himself. They all want to capture each other's position. 'I' wants to annihilate 'Thou', and 'Thou' to annihilate 'I', so that 'I' becomes 'Thou' and 'Thou' becomes 'I'.

Vedanta is part of our tradition and, because the meaning of factionalism can be drawn from Vedanta, factionalism is also our tradition. Both are our cultural heritage. After gaining Independence from the British, we have rediscovered many of our traditions. That is why we travel to Europe by air but first get an astrologer to draw up our programme. We take the blessings of saints to rid ourselves of foreign exchange and income tax problems. We encourage fistulas by drinking Scotch whisky, and then go to yoga ashrams for treatment through deep breathing and by contracting our stomachs. In exactly the same way, we accept the democracy we have learnt from a Western education, and to run it, we rely on our tradition of factionalism. In our history—whether in peace or war—from royal palaces to village threshing floors, we have always had a splendid tradition of turning 'I' into 'Thou' and 'Thou' into 'I' by factionalism. We had forgotten this tradition for a while during the Raj, when we had the bother of running the British out of the country. After we won freedom, we encouraged it, along with many of our other traditions. Now, we are increasing factionalism through arguments and abuse, kicks and shoe-beatings, literature and arts, and all other means. This is our cultural faith. This is the achievement of the country which gave birth to Vedanta.

Apart from these fundamental causes, another reason for the factionalism in the college was the common belief that something should keep happening.

In Shivpalganj, there were no cinemas, restaurants, coffee houses, fights, stabbings, road accidents, fashionable girls, exhibitions or even public meetings ending in abuse. Where could people go? What could they see? What could they listen to?

Therefore, something must keep happening.

Four days ago, a love letter which a boy had written to a girl had been confiscated in college. The boy had been clever; when you read the letter it looked as if it wasn't him approaching the girl, but replying to a letter from her. But his cleverness didn't pay. The boy was reprimanded, beaten, and thrown out of college. Then, on the assurance of the boy's father that the boy wouldn't fall in love again, and on his promise that he would donate fifty thousand bricks for the new college block, his son was readmitted to the college. Whatever impact this had had lasted no more than four days and people were again faced with the same eternal question—what next?

In this mood, people's eyes had turned to the Principal and Vaidyaji. Vaidyaji was sitting contentedly in his usual place with his turban tied in the style worn by the great socialist leader Madan Mohan Malaviya. However, the Principal looked as if he'd shinned up an electricity pylon without any assistance and was screaming out to some person in the far distance: 'Help! Help! They want to do me mischief!' His face too betrayed suspicion, since, like every Indian who is stuck to his chair of office, he feared having it pulled out from under him. People had guessed his weakness and had begun to bait him, and with him, Vaidyaji, too.

From their side, they were prepared to attack as the best means of defence.

One day, about this time, someone told Khanna Master that every college has a principal and a vice-principal. Khanna Master taught history and was the most senior lecturer in the college. Taken in by this tale, he came to Vaidyaji and told him that he should be made vice-principal.

Vaidyaji nodded and replied that this was a novel thought and that young men should always have fresh ideas and that he welcomed every fresh idea, but that this was a question that should be looked into by the managing committee, and if the question arose at its next meeting, it would be considered appropriately. It didn't occur to Khanna Master that the managing committee never did have its next meeting.

He wrote an application for immediate appointment as vice-principal, and gave it to the Principal with an appeal that it should be presented at the next meeting of the managing committee.

The Principal was astounded by Khanna Master's action. He went and asked Vaidyaji if he had advised Khanna Master to submit the application.

Vaidyaji gave a three-word reply, 'He's still young.'

For several days after this, the Principal stated to everyone whom he met on the streets of Shivpalganj the biological fact that, 'No one knows what's got into people nowadays.' He described Khanna Master's action with sayings like: 'God on his lips, and a dagger under his arm'; 'the wolf we nurtured ourselves is now baying at our house' (although wolves don't bay); 'it's a stab in the back'; and 'even the frog has caught a cold.'

On one occasion, standing at the crossroads, he said symbolically, 'One day, a horse was being shod. Seeing it, a frog suddenly developed the desire to have its feet shod too. With great difficulty it persuaded the blacksmith to do it but when the man hammered in the first nail just a little, it was too much for it, and brother frog died on the spot.'

Behind this fable there was a fear: the man who wants to be vice-principal today will want to be principal tomorrow. To achieve this, he will try to get the members of the managing committee on his side.

He'll create a faction among the masters. He'll incite the boys to fight. On top of this, he'll send in complaints. He's a rascal now and a rascal he will remain.

~

False principles cannot truth overpower,
There's never any scent from a paper flower.

Ramadhin Bhikhmakhervi set this couplet at the top of the letter he wrote to Vaidyaji, the purport of which was that the meeting of the managing committee—which had not been held for the last three years—should be held in ten days' time, and an annual general meeting of the college—which had not been held since the college had been established—should be considered at the committee meeting. He also referred to the appointment of a vice-principal as one of the subjects for discussion.

When the Principal put this letter into his pocket and left Vaidyaji's house it felt as though the letter was burning holes in his pocket.

At the college gate, he met Ruppan babu, stopped him and asked, 'Have you seen? Khanna is sitting there holding on to Ramadhin's coat-tail. He fancies himself as vice-principal. Once a frog saw that a horse was being shod, so it too . . .'

Ruppan babu was leaving the college and was in a hurry. He said, 'I know. Everyone here knows the frog story. But I'll tell you one thing straight. I have no sympathy for Khanna, but I think it's necessary to have a vice-principal here. When you're not here, all the masters fight like cats and dogs. I can't describe the hooliganism that goes on in the masters' common room. The same *hain-hain, tain-tain, phain-phain.* It's complete bedlam.' He became grave and said with authority, 'Principal sahib, I believe that we should have a vice-principal here too. Khanna is the most senior. He should be given the job. It's just a nominal thing; you don't have to increase his salary.'

The Principal's heart began to beat so violently that it was in danger of leaping up into his lungs. He said, 'Never make the mistake of saying this, Ruppan babu! This Khanna-vanna will begin to shout that you are on his side. This is Shivpalganj. You should think twice before saying such things, even in jest.'

'I'm telling the truth. Anyway, we'll see what comes of it,' said Ruppan babu as he walked away.

The Principal went quickly to his room. It was cold there but he took off his coat. A calendar from a shop which supplied educational aids hung directly in front of his nose, on the opposite wall. It showed a film actress, with an almost transparent sari wrapped around her naked body, advancing like a huge laddu towards a man. The man had a long, bushy beard. He held one hand over his eyes and, from the expression on his face, it looked as if he had indigestion from eating too many laddus. This was Menaka and Vishwamitra. The Principal looked at them for a while and then, instead of ringing his bell, he shouted loudly for the chapraasi and instructed him to summon Khanna Master.

The chapraasi replied in a discreet tone, 'He's gone off towards the fields. Malaviyaji is with him.'

The Principal wearily pushed away the pen box on the desk in front of him. The pen box, too, had been given away free as a sample by the Education Emporium, and the way the Principal had pushed it seemed to indicate that, this year, there would be no goods bought from that shop for the college.

But this was not the Principal's real intention. He just wanted to let the chapraasi know that, at this precise moment, he was not prepared to listen to his confidential report.

He snapped, 'I'm telling you to call Khanna Master here this minute!'

The chapraasi was wearing a clean kurta of coarse cloth and a reasonably clean dhoti. He wore wooden sandals and had a tilak mark on his forehead. He remarked peaceably, 'I'm on my way. I will call Khanna here. Why are you getting so angry?'

The Principal ground his teeth and gazed through narrowed eyes at a piece of tin on his desk. It had been polished and a red rose had been painted on it. Beneath it, was a calendar showing the date and month. A liquor company had produced this calendar in memory of Pandit Jawaharlal Nehru (who always wore a rose in his buttonhole), and had distributed it freely to all and sundry in the belief that wherever the calendar went, men would never forget the ideals of Pandit Jawaharlal Nehru, or the company's brands of liquor. But at this moment, the calendar had no effect on the Principal. Panditji's red rose gave him no peace; nor was he compelled to close his eyes in contemplation of a foaming glass of beer. He continued to grind his teeth. Suddenly, as the chapraasi's wooden sandals were crossing the veranda, he said, 'Ramadhin will get him made vice-principal! The skunk!'

The chapraasi turned. Standing in the doorway, he said, 'Are you swearing, Principal sahib?'

'All right, all right. Go, get about your work,' he replied.

'I am already doing my work. If you like, I'll stop.'

Scowling, the Principal began to look at another wall calendar. The chapraasi asked in the same tone, 'Would you like me to stop keeping any eye on Khanna?'

The Principal lost his temper. 'Go to hell!'

The chapraasi stood as before with his chest out. He said carelessly, 'Don't think I'm just a Khanna. You can make me work twenty-four hours a day, I can bear it, but I won't put up with any foul language.'

The Principal looked at him in astonishment. The chapraasi said, 'You are a Brahmin and I am a Brahmin. You don't eat salt with salt, and it's no good thinking you can treat me like you treat other people. Ha!'

The Principal tried to placate him. 'You're mistaken. I'm not swearing at you, but at Khanna. He's a skunk. He's got together with Ramadhin and had a notice sent for a meeting.' To convince the chapraasi that this abuse was directed at Khanna, he repeated, 'Skunk!'

'I'll call him just now.' The chapraasi too had calmed down. The Principal listened to the retreating *khat-khat* of his wooden sandals. His glance rested on a third calendar on which two five-year-olds were lying in the snow holding large rifles, apparently waiting for the Chinese army, and at the same time picturesquely advertising a factory that made the very best jute bags.

The Principal fixed his eyes on this calendar and sat waiting for Khanna, thinking how wonderful it would have been if Khanna had never taken a fancy for being vice-principal. He forgot that everyone has their fancies.

Ramadhin Bhikhmakhervi liked to start his letters with Urdu poetry; he himself liked to hang colourful calendars in his room; and the chapraasi who, like the clerk, was a relative of Vaidyaji's, enjoyed putting on airs.

The Principal waited for Khanna. The clerk came and stood on the veranda outside in order to record the forthcoming event for posterity. The drillmaster stood stretching his legs under the window outside the other side of the office and, instead of peeing, lit up a beedi.

There was no longer any danger of the dialogue between the Principal and Khanna being lost in mid-air before it could reach the people.

~

That night, Rangnath and Badri were lying in the room on the roof, and their conversation was wandering as conversation does when one is on the verge of sleep. Concluding whatever he was saying, Rangnath remarked, 'No one knows what went on between the Principal and Khanna. The drillmaster was standing outside. Khanna Master screamed, "This is your humanity!" That was the only thing he heard.'

Badri yawned and said, 'The Principal must have abused him. In reply he must have brought up "humanity". Khanna talks like that. He's a foolish bastard.'

Rangnath commented, 'The answer to abuse is a shoe-beating.'

Badri didn't reply. Rangnath repeated, 'It's a waste of time even to mention humanity in that situation.'

Badri turned over to go to sleep. As if saying goodnight, he said, 'That's right. But here, anyone who knows his ABC starts to spout long Urdu words. At the drop of a hat they start saying "humanity, humanity". When a man doesn't have sufficient strength in his muscles, he pines for humanity.'

He was right. In those days, humanity held sway over Shivpalganj. At midday, young lads gambled in the mango groves. The winners won and the losers complained, 'So this is your humanity? The moment you win, you have to go for a pee. You start looking for excuses to get out of the game.'

Occasionally, the winners too made use of humanity. They would say, 'You call this humanity? You've gone soft in the head just because you've lost a trick? This is the first game I've won in four days, and just for that I have to give up peeing?'

In the toddy shop, labourers were wagging their heads from side to side. In 1962, India was deeply shocked by the treachery of the Chinese and, in the toddy shop, the labourers described a scene just as shocking. 'The old man has built himself a brick house. He's living

in real style, like a big factory-wallah. We told him, "Look, we have
guests. Give us a couple of rupees for toddy." But he didn't give us a
straight answer; he just showed us his backside and walked off. Tell
me, Nageswar, is this humanity?'

This is to say that, in Shivpalganj, humanity was believed to be a
feature of ingenuity and shrewdness, in the same way that leadership is
a feature of politics. It's another matter that Badri considered humanity
the weakness of a man with no muscles. Conveying this thought to
Rangnath, and leaving him to lie awake and apply the principle to
leadership, Badri fell asleep as he spoke.

Rangnath lay wrapped in a blanket, staring at the ceiling. The
door was open and, outside, moonlight spread over the land. For a
while he concentrated on Sophia Loren and Elizabeth Taylor, but then
he realized that this was a sign of low character, and began to think
instead of the town washerman's daughter who, when selecting items
of clothing for herself from the washing, had begun to favour sleeveless
blouses. After some time, he began to think that this too was a sordid
preoccupation, and began to concentrate on film stars again; and this
time, in the name of nationalism and patriotism, he forgot Liz Taylor
etc., and turned for support to Waheeda Rehman and Saira Banu. A
few minutes later, he began to reach the conclusion that it is wrong to
take your inspiration for everything from the West, and that if you put
your heart into it, you can also get a lot of pleasure from patriotism.
Suddenly he began to feel rather sleepy and though he tried hard, his
concentration dwindled even when faced with Saira Banu's full body.
Some tigers and bears began to bounce around in his imagination,
and he made one last great effort to grasp Saira Banu by her waist
and pull her down, but she slipped from his hands, and while he was
engaged in this love play, the bears and the tigers also escaped. It was
then that a picture of Khanna Master began to form and fade in his
mind. It shimmered once or twice and one word began to resound:
'Humanity, humanity'.

At first, it seemed as if someone were whispering it. Then it seemed
as if someone standing on a stage were calling it out in grave tones. Then
it seemed as if a riot had broken out somewhere and from all directions
people were screaming, 'Humanity! Humanity! Humanity!'

He woke up and immediately heard shouts of 'Thief! Thief! Thief! Don't let him get away! Catch him! Thief! Thief! Thief!'

After a few moments, the only thing you could make out was, 'Thief! Thief! Thief!' as if a gramophone record had got stuck.

Rangnath heard the voices heading for the other side of the village. Badri Wrestler had leapt down from his charpoy at the first alarm. Rangnath also sat up. Badri said, 'Chhote told me that there is a gang of thieves hanging around the neighbourhood. It looks like they have come into the village too.'

They both dressed hurriedly and went out on to the roof. 'Getting dressed' didn't mean that Badri had to put on churidar pyjamas and a sherwani; he tightened around his waist the loincloth hanging loosely over his naked body and wrapped a shawl about him. With that, he completed his dressing ritual. Rangnath had not been able to acquire such an ascetic habit; he pulled on a shirt. As they reached the top of the stairs, their steps hastened even more. By then, the cries of 'Thief!' were rising from all directions. The clamour had increased so much as the news was passed from mouth to mouth that, had the British heard it in 1921, they would have left India on the spot and run back to their own country.

They both ran downstairs. Leaving the sitting room, Badri Wrestler said to Rangnath, 'Shut the door and sit here at home. I'll go out and see what's going on.'

Just then Ruppan babu came out from inside the house, flinging the end of his dhoti over his shoulder. He rushed over to where they were standing and said, 'Both of you stay at home. I'll go outside.'

It was as if going outside meant displaying outstanding bravery or facing an impregnable battle formation. Both brothers remained determined to go. Rangnath spoke in a martyred tone, 'If it means so much to you, then both of you go ahead. I'll stay alone at home.'

On the road in front of them three men ran past shouting, 'Thief! Thief!' Two others followed in their wake raising the same cry. Then a lone man passed, also roaring, 'Thief! Thief!' Then, three more men, each one with a lathi. All of them were running; all of them were chasing the thieves.

Badri recognized some of the tail-enders of the procession. He ran off to meet them, calling out, 'Who is it? Chhote! Where's the thief?'

Chhote was breathing heavily as he said, 'Up ahead! They've gone up ahead!' For a while, peace descended.

Ruppan babu and Rangnath shut the door of the sitting room, locked it and went back on to the roof. Below them, Vaidyaji hawked, spat and said, 'Who's there?'

Ruppan babu answered, 'Thieves, Father!'

Vaidyaji was annoyed, and thundered, 'Who's there? Ruppan! Are you on the roof?'

Adding to the general uproar in the village as best he could, Ruppan replied, 'Yes it's me! Why are you asking when you know it's me? Why don't you sleep in peace?'

Hearing his younger son's respectful tones, Vaidyaji became silent. On the roof, Ruppan babu and Rangnath listened to the voices spreading and bursting out over the whole village.

From behind the rear wall of the house someone shouted, 'Murder! They're murdering me!'

More noise. Someone yelled, '*Arré*, no, Chhote! This is Bhagauti!'

'Let go of him! Let him go! Over there! The thieves are over there!'

Someone was weeping. Someone else consoled him, '*Arré*, why are you wailing like a widow? He just hit you once with his stick, and you are making all this noise!'

Sobbing, the answer came, 'I'll get my own back, just wait and see.'

More tumult. 'Over there! Over there! Don't let him get away! Give the bugger one with your lathi! Make him jump! What's wrong, you think the bastard's your father?'

Rangnath began to feel enjoyment as well as enthusiasm and curiosity. What a way of carrying on! Here, you used 'father' as a term of abuse when you were thrashing a man with your lathi. May you prosper India, for your filial devotion!

Ruppan babu said, 'Bhagauti and Chhote had a grudge against one another. It looks like in the middle of all this row, Chhote's gone and done something.'

Rangnath said, 'This means real trouble.'

Ruppan babu disregarded him. 'What trouble? It's a matter of pulling off a wrestling trick. Chhote looks an idiot, but he's really very canny.'

Then both pricked up their ears to listen to the noise and tumult around them. Rangnath said, 'Perhaps the thieves have escaped.'

'They always do, here.'

Rangnath wanted to flatter Ruppan babu's pride in his village. He said, 'It's not possible that any thief could come to Shivpalganj and then get away. Once brother Badri moves out, he can't fail to catch a couple of them.'

Ruppan babu sighed like a leader of a lost generation looking longingly at the past, and said, 'No, brother Rangnath, the old days are over now. That was the time of Thakur Durbin Singh. The greatest thieves trembled at the name of Shivpalganj.'

His eyes shone with the light of hero worship. But his speech stopped there. The last round of uproar had passed and people were shouting, 'Long live Lord Hanuman!' so loudly that they appeared to be trying to split the heavens. Rangnath said, 'It seems they have caught a thief.'

Ruppan babu replied, 'No, I know these ganjahas backwards. They must have chased the thieves out of the village. Isn't it enough that they've not been chased out of the village by the thieves? They're celebrating by shouting to Lord Hanuman.'

In the moonlight people were wandering up and down the streets and alleyways, muttering to one another. Ruppan babu stood by the wall on the edge of the roof and looked down. One group called out from below, 'Keep awake, Ruppan babu! Stay alert the whole night!'

Ruppan babu called down to them with contempt, 'Be off with you! Don't show off to me!'

Rangnath failed to comprehend why Ruppan was disregarding such good advice in this manner. After a short while, similar advice began to resound all around the village—'Keep awake! Keep alert!'

There was still intermittent kerfuffle. Loud whistles could also be heard from all directions. Rangnath asked, 'What are they whistling for?'

Ruppan babu replied, 'Don't the police patrol in the town?'

'Oho! So the police have also turned up for the occasion.'

'Yes, it was the police who faced the dacoits with the help of the villagers. It was the police who beat them up and chased them out of here.'

Rangnath looked at Ruppan babu in astonishment. 'Dacoits?'

'Yes, of course. Who else could they be? Do thieves ever come on moonlit nights? They were certainly dacoits.' Ruppan let out a loud guffaw. 'Brother, these are the ways of the ganjahas. They're difficult to understand. I am just telling you how all this is going to be reported in the papers.'

A whistle rang out from the street immediately below them. Ruppan continued, 'Have you seen Master Motiram or not? He's from the old school. The police inspector really respects him. He really respects the inspector. The Principal respects both of them. None of the bastards does any work; they just keep on respecting each other. The same Master Motiram is the correspondent for the town newspaper. If he doesn't turn the thieves into dacoits, then his name's not Master Motiram.'

Rangnath began to laugh. The whistles and shouts of 'Stay awake!' began to scatter and fade. Outside some houses, people began to shout to be let in. Phrases varying from 'Open up, son!' to 'What's the matter, you bugger, are you dead?' and 'For God's sake, it's me out here, your father!' were brought into use to gain admission.

Someone rattled the chain of the door of Vaidyaji's house, too. A farmer sleeping outside coughed loudly. The chain rattled again. Rangnath said, 'It must be brother Badri. Let's go and open the lock.'

They went downstairs and, as he unlocked the door, Ruppan babu asked, 'Who's there?'

Badri roared, 'Are you opening this door or not? Why the hell are you asking who's there?'

Ruppan stopped unlocking the door. He said, 'What's your name?'

A throat-splitting cry came from the other side of the door. 'Ruppan, I'm telling you, open this door quietly or else!'

'Who is it? Brother Badri?'

'Yes, yes it's me, brother Badri speaking. Open up at once.'

Beginning to open the lock with nervous fingers, Ruppan said, 'Brother Badri, tell me your father's name also.'

Cursing, brother Badri gave Vaidyaji's name. Ruppan asked once more, 'Brother, just tell me your grandfather's name?'

Badri cursed as before and told his grandfather's name. Then he was asked, 'Great-grandfather's name?'

Badri pounded the door with his fist. 'All right, don't open it. I'm going!'

Ruppan babu said, 'Brother, these are dangerous times. I'm asking you all this because there are thieves roaming around out there. If you can't remember your great-grandfather's name, then don't tell me, but there's no point in getting angry. An angry act is a bad act.'

Having tested Badri's identity and expressed his opinion of the worthlessness of anger, Ruppan babu opened the door. Badri Wrestler came in twitching like a scorpion's tail.

Ruppan babu asked, 'What's the matter, brother? All the thieves have run away.'

Badri Wrestler gave no reply. He climbed the stairs in silence. Ruppan babu disappeared into the lower portion of the house. As soon as Rangnath and Badri Wrestler lay down on their respective charpoys in the room upstairs, someone called out from the alley below, 'Ustad! Come down. It's a damn confusing business.'

Badri called down from the doorway of the room, 'What's up, Chhote? Will you let me get some sleep or are you going to stand yoked there all night?'

Chhote answered from below, 'Ustad, forget about sleep! Now they're discussing filing a police report. All the bastards around here were running round the streets shouting "Thief! Thief!" and over there, in the middle of all this hullabaloo, someone struck. Gayadin's been robbed! Come down quickly!'

11

There was a sheet of tin in front of the room on the roof. Rangnath was underneath the tin sheet and a charpoy was underneath Rangnath.

Rangnath's eyes were fixed upon the sunlight on the neem tree but his mind was lost in contemplation of our ancient culture in which, from the earliest times, hundreds of things have been lost, and have only been rediscovered by the efforts of researchers.

Rangnath had chosen one such lost subject for his research. Indians have invented, with British help, a science dealing with their old way of life. Its name is Indology. Rangnath's research was connected with this science—to carry out research in Indology.

Indologists must first research other Indologists and Rangnath was doing just this. Two days earlier, he had gone into town and taken out numerous books from the university library, and now he was studying them by means of staring at the neem tree. To his right was Marshall and to his left, A. Cunningham. Winternitz was right under his nose. He was practically sitting on Keith. V.A. Smith had been shoved to the foot of the charpoy, and Rhys-Davids, too, could be seen there, lying upside down. Percy Brown was hidden under a pillow. In this crowd, Kashi Prasad Jaiswal lay face downwards in the bedclothes, and Bhandarkar was peeping rather nervously from under a sheet. The atmosphere was steeped in Indological study.

So, when Rangnath first heard a 'Hau! Hau!' noise, it was only natural that he thought it was some holy man reciting the Sama Veda. A little while later, the 'Hau! Hau!' came closer and he thought that some Harishen was bursting his lungs proclaiming the victory of Emperor Samudra Gupta. Meanwhile, the 'Hau! Hau!' came from the alley right next to the house and you could hear it interpolated with a few vigorous sentences on the lines of 'I'll murder the bastard!' Then Rangnath realized that this was a purely ganjaha matter.

He went and stood at the edge of the roof. As he glanced down into the alley he saw a young girl. Her head was uncovered, her hair was dry and dishevelled, and her lips were moving constantly. But don't make the mistake of imagining that these were signs of being a city girl or that she was following one of the latest fashions. She was a true country lass, extremely dirty, and her lips were moving, not because she was chewing gum, but because she was saying 'Hale! Hale! Hale!' to the goats accompanying her. Half a dozen or so goats of various sizes were either grazing on a peepul tree growing out of a crack in the wall or, having grazed, were looking for another crack in the wall and another peepul tree.

Rangnath watched this idyllic rustic scene and tried to work out the origin of the 'Hau! Hau!' There was no 'Hau! Hau!' coming from there now, but the sound continued to reverberate in his ears. He left Percy Brown, Cunningham and the others lying as they were on the roof, and he came down to the front door.

At this time, Vaidyaji was conducting surgery. Apart from Sanichar and half a dozen patients, there was no one else there. The '*Hau! Hau!*' sound was now just around the corner.

Rangnath asked Sanichar, 'Can you hear it?'

Sanichar was sitting on the veranda joining an axe head to its shaft. Turning from where he was sitting, and, lifting an ear to the wind, he listened to the '*Hau! Hau!*' for a few moments. Suddenly, the furrows of worry on his brow were smoothed away. He said contentedly, 'Yes, there is some sort of "*Hau! Hau!*" noise. It looks like Chhote Wrestler has fought with Kusahar again.' He said this in the same tone he would have used if a buffalo had rubbed its horn against a wall. He sat back in his original position and began to cut down the axe shaft with an adze.

Suddenly, the '*Hau! Hau!*' appeared before them. It came from a man about sixty years old, with a well-built and naked torso, and a dhoti down to his knees in the fashion worn by wrestlers. There were three wounds on his head and blood was flowing from each in different directions, showing that even blood of the same group preferred not to mix together. The man was wailing '*Hau! Hau!*' and was begging for sympathy with raised hands.

Rangnath was disconcerted by this bloody scene. He asked Sanichar, 'Who . . . who is this? Who has attacked him?'

Sanichar gently laid the shaft of the axe and the adze on the ground. He caught hold of the wounded old man and made him sit down on the veranda. The old man pushed away his hand with a passion of non-cooperation, but did not refuse to sit down. Sanichar narrowed his eyes to examine his wounds, looked towards Vaidyaji and, pursing his lips, indicated that the wounds were not deep.

The old man's '*Hau! Hau!*' became less frantic and moved from allegro to andante and subsequently became stuck in adagio. Such a progression runs opposite to that of our system of music, but its meaning was clear—he was not stirring but staying put where he was. Sanichar heaved a sigh of relief which was not only audible but also visible to all in the vicinity.

Stunned, Rangnath stood up. Sanichar took some cotton wool from a cupboard and said, 'You're asking who has hit him? Is that any question to ask?'

He poured some water into a pot, dropped the cotton wool into it and came up to the old man. He continued, 'Who else would beat him? This is Chhote Wrestler's father. Which bastard but he would dare lay a hand on the old man?'

Perhaps Kusahar—whose full name was Kusahar Prasad—was calmed by this praise of Chhote Wrestler. From where he was sitting, he told Vaidyaji, 'Maharaj, this time young Chhote has murdered me. I can't stand this any more. You have to keep us apart or sometime soon I will kill him with my own hands.'

Vaidyaji got down from the wooden bed and came out to the veranda. Seeing the wounds, he spoke with the voice of experience. 'The wounds don't seem deep. It would be better for you to go to the hospital than be treated here. Go there and get yourself bandaged up.' After this, he addressed all those present with the words, 'Henceforth, Chhote is forbidden to set foot in this house! There's no place here for such infernal people.'

Rangnath's blood began to boil. He said, 'It's surprising that brother Badri mixes with people like him.'

Badri Wrestler came quietly out of the house. He said matter-of-factly, 'Educated men should think carefully before they speak. Who knows who was at fault? This man Kusahar is no angel. When his father Gangadayal died, he even refused to allow people to have a funeral procession. He said he was just going to drag the corpse down to the river and chuck it in.'

With great difficulty Kusahar Prasad managed to emit one more 'Hau! Hau!' which meant that Badri was being excessively cruel to him by making such statements. Then he suddenly stood up and roared, 'Vaidya maharaj, restrain your son! All these boys are determined to say things that set heads rolling! Shut him up, or there'll be nothing short of murder. I will go to the hospital in due course. First, I'm going to the police station. If I don't show young Chhote the inside of a courthouse this time, then don't call me the son of Gangadayal; call me a bastard. I have only come here to show you my wounds. Look at them, Vaid maharaj, my blood is flowing . . . have a good look . . . you're going to have to testify to it!'

Vaidyaji showed no desire to examine the wounds. He began

to look at his patients. At the same time, he began to preach that running feuds were the root cause of grief and advised Kusahar not to get involved in police cases and law courts. Then he began a second sermon on the subject of police stations and law courts also being the root cause of grief.

Kusahar roared, 'Maharaj, keep your knowledge to yourself. A river of blood is flowing here, and you're stuffing Gandhi-isms down my throat. If Badri Wrestler climbs on your chest, I'll see how you comfort yourself by reciting sermons about this world!'

Vaidyaji's moustache trembled, which indicated that he was offended. But a smile suffused his face indicating that he was incapable of taking offence. The faces of the others present hardened, and it became quite clear that from now on Kusahar would get no alms of sympathy here. Badri Wrestler sent him away, saying, 'Off with you! It looks like battling with young Chhote hasn't taken all the fight out of you. Go and get yourself bandaged. Don't come whining around here.'

~

Chhote Wrestler was—as has become obvious by now—a member of an old and respected family. He could even remember his great-grandfather's name and, like any man of good family, he used to relate stories about him. Sometimes, he would tell his friends at the wrestling pit, 'My great-grandfather's name was Bholanath. He had one hell of a temper. All the time, his nostrils would be flaring with rage. Every day, the first thing he would do when he got up was to have a slanging match with his father. Only then would he wash out his mouth and perform his ablutions. If he didn't fight, his stomach would rumble.'

Chhote Wrestler's words dripped with nostalgia and conjured up a picture of a nineteenth-century village in which, at a doorway crowded with cows and oxen, amidst the strong smell of cow's dung and urine, under the shade of a neem tree, brushing off the sticky neem fruit that had dropped on them, two great men with naked torsos sit up on their charpoys and, as soon as they sit up, begin to curse each other for sleeping late. Of these two, one is the father; the other, his son. Then both of them get up from their charpoys, threatening to bury each other alive and, digressing from the original argument and with a few unrestrained remarks, set about their day's work. One heads for his fields twisting his bullocks' tails, and the other heads for other people's fields to graze his buffaloes.

After finishing a story of this sort, Chhote Wrestler used to say, 'When his father died, Baba Bholanath was very grieved.'

Chhote Wrestler didn't tell these stories to boast. They were absolutely true. His family was really like that. There had always been an extremely close relationship between fathers and sons. If they had to be affectionate, they were, and if they decided to wield lathis against each other, they did. They used to test one another for whatever good or bad quality their hands possessed.

Baba Bholanath was genuinely upset by his father's death. There was a void in his life. Now that his father was no longer there, his stomach began to rumble from early morning for someone to fight with. He didn't feel even like washing out his mouth. Despite working day and night in the fields like an ox, he began to complain of constant indigestion. Now his son, Gangadayal, came of use. It's said that a son is the light of one's eyes in old age. So it was that, one day at the age of only seventeen, Gangadayal struck his father Bholanath such a blow with his lathi that Bholanath fell to the ground, his eyes bulging out like cowrie shells and stars raining before them.

After that, the relationship between father and son was settled for good. Bholanath took his father's place and Gangadayal took his. After a few days, his indigestion was cured as a result of constant pain in his arms, legs and back, but his ears began to ring. Perhaps from continually hearing Gangadayal's ear-splitting curses, his ears had developed a permanent echo. Whatever the case, now, Gangadayal's stomach too rumbled in the morning for a fight.

Gangadayal's son, Kusahar Prasad, was Chhote Wrestler's father. Kusahar Prasad was serious by nature, and so did not indulge in Gangadayal's futile curses and insults. He also put an end to the tradition of fighting with one's father every morning before going to the fields.

Kusahar Prasad had two brothers. One was Barakau and the other, Chotakau. Barakau and Chotakau were devotees of peace and non-violence. In their entire lives they had never hit even a dog. Cats crossed their paths as they liked, but they had never had even a clod of earth thrown at them. The brothers had learnt the art of insulting their father and used it to sort out family fights, without recourse to fisticuffs. Every evening, the two brothers and their wives would start yelling and hurling abuse at one another. These sittings would continue until ten o'clock. In this respect, they were rather like important meetings of the Security Council where, to a fair extent, wars are prevented by shouting matches. From this point of view, it would be reactionary to look down on the bedlam that used to break out in Kusahar Prasad's house every evening; but his neighbours' political perceptions were not so progressive. Therefore, in the evening, as soon as Chotakau's and Barakau's curses and screams rose above the barking of the village dogs, the neighbours' criticisms began.

'Now this *kukrahao* clamour will go on half the night.'

'They'll only reform the day you take an old shoe and give them a good beating with it.'

'Their tongues have dysentery. When they start moving, they can't stop.'

Chhote Wrestler's father Kusahar Prasad was unable to comprehend his brothers' eloquence. As has been explained, he was a man of action who spoke little. His special characteristic lay in thrashing people silently and sporadically, and this had nothing in common with the philosophy of life of the other two. Therefore, a few years after his father Gangadayal died, he began to live separately from his brothers—that is, without a word, by the might of his lathi, he drove his brothers out of the house.

Kusahar Prasad's hands had become so accustomed to raising a lathi to his father once every four weeks that, after Gangadayal died, they began to go numb for several days every month. In order to rid himself of the danger of paralysis, one day, Kusahar Prasad raised his lathi again and brought it down at an angle on Chhote's midriff. Chhote had not yet become a wrestler, but there was a railway line near the village. Along its edge ran electric cables and posts. On the posts, there were many white insulators. With constant practice, Chhote had perfected his aim at a very early age. The day Kusahar Prasad hit Chhote on the midriff with his lathi, Chhote had knocked all the insulators off one post with stones from the railway tracks, leaving them scattered along the edge of the line. So, he ran twenty paces and threw a clod of earth at his father's head imagining it to be just another insulator. From that day on, the eternal dharma of the family was established between father and son. Almost every month, one more small scar used to make its appearance on Kusahar's body and, after some years, he became the Rana Sanga of the area.

When Chhote Wrestler reached manhood, father and son ceased to speak to one another. They also began to fight less frequently and violence gradually became something of a ritual which—like the birthdays of great men—was celebrated regularly once a year, whether the general public wanted it or not.

~

After Kusahar Prasad left, a man standing in the road in front of the veranda remarked, 'This is what you call Kali Yug! A son dares to behave like this with his father!'

Lifting his eyes to the sky, shaking off the neem twigs which had fallen on his head, he repeated, 'Oh God, where are you? When will you descend in Kalkin Avatar?'

No voice came from the heavens in reply. Not even a crow cawed. No sparrow so much as shat. The face of the man remembering Kalkin Avatar fell. Sanichar said in a sharp tone, while examining the shaft of his axe, 'Get on with you, go along with Kusahar Prasad too. Go and stand witness. You're bound to get a rupee or so there.'

Badri Wrestler smiled in support of this comment. Rangnath observed that the individual who remembered Kalkin Avatar was a priest-like old man. Sunken cheeks. Salt-and-pepper beard. A buttonless kurta. A Gandhi cap awry on his head, from behind which his topknot stuck out like a conductor protecting his body from celestial lightning. A red sandalwood tika on his forehead. A necklace of sacred *rudraksha* beads around his throat.

This man did indeed follow Kusahar Prasad. Sanichar said, 'That is Radhelal. Till this day, the greatest lawyers have never managed to shake him in cross-examination.'

Near Sanichar, a bystander said respectfully, 'Radhelal maharaj is favoured by a god. He perjures himself with such fluency that the lawyers are left gaping. Even the greatest ones go dumb before him.'

For a while, the praise of Radhelal continued. A discussion began between Sanichar and the bystander. Sanichar's opinion was that Radhelal was very cunning and that the town's lawyers were absolute fools, and that was why they couldn't shake him in cross-examination. On the other side, the bystander was determined to put it down as a miracle and to his being the chosen one of a god. Reason and faith were battling and there's no need to tell you that faith was winning.

Chhote Wrestler came strutting out of an alleyway. Reaching Vaidyaji's door, he began to look around. Then he asked, 'Has he gone?'

Sanichar replied, 'Yes, he's gone. But, wrestler, this policy is against all humanity.'

Chhote ground his teeth. 'To hell with humanity, and you too had better watch out!'

Sanichar stood up with the axe in his hand. He cried out, 'Brother Badri. Look! Your calf is kicking out at me. Control it!'

Vaidyaji leapt to his feet on seeing Chhote. He said to Rangnath, 'It's a sin to lay one's eyes on such a low character. Get him out of here.' With this, he disappeared into the house.

Chhote Wrestler entered the sitting room. The sun was shining. A large flock of parakeets was screaming and flying among the branches of the neem tree opposite. Sanichar was standing on the veranda holding the axe. Badri Wrestler was standing silently in a corner, swinging a pair of Indian clubs. Rangnath was leafing through a book on Ayurvedic medicine. It seemed to Chhote as though a wind of revolt were blowing against him. In response, he stuck out his chest, sat down beside Rangnath with aplomb, and rotating his jaws, began to ruminate on the betel nut which he already held safely inside his mouth.

Chhote looked at Rangnath as if he were some insect flying in front of him. In a depressed tone he said, 'If this is the state of things, I'm going. I came here thinking it was the home of my guru, Badri. Now, it's people like you who are ruling here, and so I won't come here even to piss.'

Rangnath laughed to try and make light of the matter. He said, 'No, no, sit down, wrestler. If your brain's getting overheated, have a drink of cold water.'

Again in the same low spirits, Chhote said, 'Water! I won't take even water from here to clean my arse. Everyone has come together to run me down.'

Badri now regarded Chhote with a dignified look, and weighed an Indian club in his left hand. He smiled as he watched him, and said, 'Anger is for the weak. Why are you getting upset? Are you a man or a pair of pyjamas?'

Chhote Wrestler realized that he was getting support from that corner. He said intractably, 'I don't like it, Badri guru! All those two-paisa bastards are getting at me. They ask, why did you hit your father? Why did I hit my father? It looks like my father is the father of everyone in Shivpalganj! As if I were his only enemy!'

'*Abeh*! Does anyone anywhere beat their father like that?'

Chhote Wrestler became even more intractable. 'Guru, if the bastard was a fatherly father, there would be no cause for complaint.'

For a while all was quiet.

Rangnath gazed at Chhote Wrestler's knitted brows. By now, Sanichar too had entered the sitting room. Advising Chhote, he said, 'You should never utter such things. Keep your feet on the ground. Don't try to open the breast of the heavens. After all, Kusahar sired you, brought you up.'

Chhote growled, 'Did I even make a stamped application asking to be born? To hell with that bastard father of mine!'

Badri was listening quietly to this conversation. He said, 'That's enough now, Chhote, cool down.'

Chhote sat back dejectedly and listened to the parakeets screaming in the neem tree. Finally, he sighed and said, 'You too are putting me down, guru! You don't know, that old man is such a bloody lecher. Because of him, the housemaid had to stop bringing water to our house. Shall I tell you more? How can I? It leaves a bad taste in my mouth.'

12

In the village there lived a man called Gayadin. He was believed to be very able in matters of debit and credit, multiplication and division, because usury was his profession. He had a shop which sold cloth and lent out money. He had a young daughter whose name was Bela, a sister who was a widow, and a wife who was dead. Bela was healthy, beautiful, proficient in housework and educated enough to read the Ramayan and *Maya–Manohar* love stories.

A handsome and worthy groom was being sought for her. Bela was fit to be loved for her body and her temperament, and Ruppan babu loved her, although she didn't know it. Every night before going to sleep, Ruppan babu thought of her, and to maintain his purity of thought he concentrated solely on her body, and not on the clothes upon it. Bela's aunt looked after Gayadin's household and didn't allow Bela to step outside the door. If she needed to go out, she went over the roof, crossing the adjoining rooftops until she arrived at the house of some neighbour. Ruppan babu remained rather stirred up over Bela and he used to write her three or four letters a week—and then tear them up.

These matters are of no immediate importance. The important thing is that Gayadin used to lend money on interest, and he ran a draper's shop. The cooperative union also lent money on interest and ran a draper's shop. Both lived in peaceful coexistence. Gayadin was on good terms with Vaidyaji. He was vice-chairman of the college managing committee. He had money and respect; he had the favour of Vaidyaji, the police, Ruppan, the local MLA and the district board's tax collector.

Despite all this, he was a pessimist. He moved very cautiously. He was very particular in his habits. He wouldn't eat lentils like *urad* dal. Once, when he visited the town, one of his relatives gave him urad dal. Gayadin slowly pushed his plate away, completed the ritual mealtime washing of the hands, and returned to his seat with an empty stomach. After that, he was served different food with a different lentil. This time, he completed his ritual ablutions and then ate. In the evening, his relatives made him tell them why he objected to urad dal. Glancing around him for a few moments, he explained softly that gas forms in the stomach from eating urad dal and that leads to anger.

His host asked, 'Even if you lost your temper, what would it matter? Is anger a tiger or a cheetah? Is there any reason for getting so worried about it?'

The host worked in an office. Gayadin explained that he was right, but that anger did not become everyone. It only became administrators. Even if the government fell, they were still members of a ruling class. But he was a trader. If he started losing his temper, no one would ever make the mistake of coming to his shop. And God knows when a disaster may occur.

There had been a robbery at Gayadin's house. Some jewellery and cloth had been stolen, and the police found it easiest to believe that it was one of the many people who had been chasing thieves that night who had committed the robbery. When the thief jumped from the roof into the courtyard, Gayadin's daughter and sister had not seen him. If they had, they would have seen his face. But when the thief had climbed up the wall, using his lathi as a support, and was about to get on to the roof, they had both seen him, or rather his full back, and the police were highly irritated that this was all they had managed to do. During the last three days, the police had paraded several thieves before them and had shown them their backs as well as their faces. But there was not one of them at whom Bela or her aunt could point and pronounce, 'Inspector, this is the thief of that night.' The police were very annoyed by their behaviour in this respect too, and the Sub-Inspector had begun to grumble that Gayadin's daughter and sister were purposely preventing the thief from being brought to book, and God alone knew what was going on.

Gayadin's pessimism had increased somewhat because there were so many houses in the village but there was only one—his—which had attracted the thief. And when the thief was breaking in, Bela and his sister could have seen him clearly but their eyes had chosen to see only the thief's back. And the Sub-Inspector laughed with everybody; the only person to whom he was unpleasant was Gayadin.

There were several teachers in the village who were fools, one of whom was Khanna Master. Malaviya was another teacher—he too was a fool. Gayadin didn't know the names of the third, fourth, fifth, sixth and seventh teachers, but they were idiots as well, and his pessimism was becoming deeper because all seven masters together were approaching his house, and they were definitely about to express superficial sympathy about the robbery, and then immediately start some nonsense about the college. They did. The masters spent half an hour trying to persuade Gayadin that, since he was vice-chairman of the college managing committee, and since the chairman had been residing in Bombay for several years and was going to continue to reside there, he should act against the malpractices of the manager and the Principal. Gayadin, very coolly, in a supremely civilized fashion, tried to persuade the masters that he was vice-chairman only in name; in reality, it was a nominal position of authority, he had no power and that they should play this game themselves and not drag him into it.

Then the civics master began to explain gravely how great the vice-chairman's power was. In the belief that Gayadin knew nothing of the subject, he began to cite the position of the vice-president of India under the Indian Constitution.

But Gayadin kept drawing a circle in the ground with the toe of his shoe, which didn't mean that he knew geometry but clearly indicated that he was thinking of some trap. Suddenly, he interrupted the master and asked, 'So tell me, Master sahib, who is the vice-president of India?'

When the masters heard this question they were covered in confusion. Some looked this way, some that, but they couldn't find the name of the vice-president of India written anywhere. Finally the civics master said, 'First it was Radhakrishnan, but now he's been transferred.'

Gayadin said softly, 'Now see, Master sahib, how important a vice-president is.'

But the masters didn't agree. One obstinately demanded that Gayadin should have at least one meeting of the managing committee called, but Gayadin just replied, 'Get hold of Ramadhin to call a meeting, Master sahib! He's the right man for the job.'

'We've got hold of him already.'

'Fine, that's enough. Keep on at him. Don't let him slip away.' Saying this, Gayadin began to regard the other people seated around. They were from a neighbouring village and had come to extend their promissory notes, have new ones written but, under no circumstances, to be freed from them.

Khanna Master had decided that the problem would be sorted out with Gayadin that very day. Therefore, he again tried to persuade him. 'Malaviyaji,' he said, 'now, *you* try to make him understand. The Principal is crushing us.'

Gayadin drew a deep breath and thought that perhaps it was written in his fate that these wretched masters would never go away. Shifting, he adopted another position on the charpoy. He said to the villagers, 'So go along, brothers! You go. Just come early tomorrow morning.'

Taking another deep breath, he turned to face Khanna Master and sat down.

Khanna Master said, 'If you permit, I'll tell you the story from the beginning.'

'What are you going to say, Master sahib?' said Gayadin in a bored tone. 'To be a master in a private school is to be crushed. How far can you escape from this?'

Khanna replied, 'The trouble is that the general body of this college hasn't met for five years. Vaidyaji has remained the manager. There have been no new elections whereas they should take place every year.'

Gayadin sat for a while with the emotionless expression of Ram and Lakshman at a Ramlila. Then he said, 'You are an educated man. What can I say? But there are hundreds of institutions where the annual meetings haven't taken place for years. Our own district board! It's been dragging on for ages without an election.' Puffing his cheeks, he said in a choked voice, 'The whole nation is in the same state.' His voice was choked, not with patriotism, but with phlegm.

Malaviya said, 'The Principal spends thousands of rupees as he likes. Every year, the auditors object; every year, he wheedles himself out of it.'

Gayadin said very innocently, 'Are you in charge of the audit?'

Raising his voice, Malaviya riposted, 'No, that is not the point, but I can't bear to watch public money being squandered in this way. After all . . .'

Here, Gayadin interrupted him and said in the same gentle tone, 'Then how would you like to see public money being squandered? In building huge buildings? In holding assemblies? In having banquets thrown?'

Malaviya bowed before this wisdom. Gayadin magnanimously expanded: 'Master sahib, I am not well educated, but in good times I've seen Bombay and Calcutta. Even I understand a little. It's not right to get so upset over public money. In any case, it's bound to be wasted.'

Gayadin's stream of thought seemed very deep to Malaviya. He spoke, 'Gayadinji, I know that all this is none of our business. Even if Vaidyaji installs a flour mill instead of looking after the school, even if the Principal arranges his daughter's wedding . . . But still, if this institution belongs to anyone, it belongs to you people! So many inadmissible things are going on in broad daylight! There's no morality left even in name!'

Meanwhile, for the first time, some kind of worry clouded Gayadin's face. But when he spoke, his voice had the same weary tone as before. 'Don't mention morality, Master sahib! If anyone hears it he'll file a case against you.'

They were all silent. Then Gayadin excelled himself. He looked into a corner. In it lay a broken wooden bed of his daughter's. Pointing to it, he said, 'Morality—consider it to be like this seat. Lying in a corner. At the time of council and society meetings, it is covered with a sheet. Then it looks very fine. Speakers stand on it to deliver lectures and rebukes. It is for that purpose.'

This point silenced the masters completely. Comforting them, he said, 'And so, tell me, Master sahib, what difficulties are you up against? Up till now, you've just been relating the troubles of the public.'

Khanna Master became excited. 'It's a waste of time telling you any of our problems. You don't accept that anything is a problem.'

'Why shouldn't I accept your problems?' asked Gayadin indulgently. 'Of course I'll accept them. Come on, tell me.'

Malaviya said, 'The Principal has taken responsibilities away from all of us. He hasn't made Khanna hostel in-charge, and he's taken games from me. Ray sahib has always been exam superintendent. He too has been shifted. He's giving all these jobs to his own people.'

Gayadin found himself in a dilemma. He spoke again, 'If I say anything to you, you'll lose your tempers. But if the Principal has the authority to choose in-charges as he wishes, how can you complain?' When the masters began to fidget, he added, 'Surely in this world, not all things are going to be done according to your liking, Master sahib? Remember what happened the year before last? The Governor made that Lal sahib of Baijegaon a vice chancellor, didn't he? People leapt and danced around the place, but did anyone manage to do anything about it? Afterwards they shut up. You too shut up. Screaming gets you nowhere. People will just call you scoundrels.'

A master stood on tiptoe at the back and said, 'But what can we do about this? The Principal is instigating the boys against us. He uses four-letter words to us. He writes false reports. If we hand in any letter or memo to him, he loses it purposely. Then he demands that we explain why we didn't give it to him.'

Gayadin moved slightly, and looked slightly surprised at the creak which the charpoy made. He remarked pensively, 'You are describing to me how an office works. Things like this happen in offices all the time.'

The master on tiptoe was enraged. 'When a dozen or so people are killed, you'll understand what's special about this situation.' Gayadin regarded his rage with pity, realizing he must have eaten urad dal that day. Then he replied gently, 'What would be special about that? People are dropping dead all around us every day.'

Khanna Master controlled the situation. 'Don't mind his anger; we are all at our wits' end. It's very difficult. See for yourself: he appointed three of his relations as masters this July. He's made them senior to us and is giving them all the responsibilities. Nepotism rules. Tell me, shouldn't we feel bad?'

'Why should you feel bad?' Gayadin began to cough. 'You yourselves say that nepotism rules. He couldn't have found any relations of Vaidyaji's for the posts, so the poor man has appointed his own.'

A few of the masters started to laugh. Gayadin continued in the same tone, 'It's not a laughing matter. This is the dharma of the age. The Principal is doing what everyone does. What do you expect him to do with his relatives?' Addressing Khanna Master, he said, 'You read history, don't you, Master sahib? How was the Sinhagarh Fort captured?'

Khanna Master began to search for an answer.

'I'll tell you myself. What did Tanaji take with him? A hill iguana. He tied a rope to it and threw it up on to the wall of the fort. Now the iguana stayed put where it crouched, stuck to the wall.

The soldiers climbed up the rope in quick succession and reached the ramparts.'

Perhaps he had grown weary of speaking. In the hope that the masters had somewhat understood, he looked at their faces, but they were without expression. Gayadin explained his point: 'Our country is in the same position, Master sahib! Wherever anyone is, he sticks to his place like an iguana. He won't budge an inch. However much you goad him, however much you try to drive him off, he will sit tight, and all his relatives—as many as he has—will climb up his tail, one after another, and get to the top. Why are you defaming the college? It's the same everywhere!'

Then, drawing breath, he asked, 'Well, now, Master sahib, where doesn't it happen like this?'

~

The group of masters passed near Chamrahi. Their faces were so long they looked as if they were about to drop down to their feet.

Chamrahi was the name of one quarter of the village where the Chamars, or cobblers, lived. Chamar is the name of a caste which is considered untouchable. An untouchable is a kind of biped which, before the enforcement of the Indian Constitution, people used to not touch. The Constitution is a poem, in Clause 17 of which, untouchability stands abolished. Because, in this country, people depend on religion and not on poetry, and because untouchability is an article of faith in this country, in Shivpalganj too—as in other villages—there were separate quarters for untouchables, of which the main one was Chamrahi. At one time, the big landowners of the village had established it with great enthusiasm. This enthusiasm was not due to the landowners' desire to develop the leather industry but because the Chamars who came to live there were very good with their lathis and the landowners could use their strength.

After the Constitution was brought into effect, a piece of good work was done between Chamrahi and the other parts of Shivpalganj—a platform which was called the Gandhi platform was constructed there. Gandhi, as some people will still remember today, was born in India itself and, after his bones and ashes—as well as his principles—had been immersed in the holy confluence of the Ganga, it was settled that, from then on, only brick and concrete buildings would be erected in his memory and, in this tumultuous activity, the platform in Shivpalganj was constructed. The platform was most useful for sunbathing in the winter months, and mostly dogs sunbathed here. And since no bathrooms are made for them, while sunbathing, they would pee on one corner of it. When the men saw this, sometimes they, too, used the platform for the same purpose.

The group of masters saw that, today, Langar had lit a fire on the platform and was sitting in front of it roasting something over the flames. Coming closer, they saw that the object being roasted was a round, solid chapatti, which he was certainly not warming for the dogs encircling him. As soon as they caught sight of Langar, the masters' hearts rose. They stopped and began to talk to him, and in two minutes had discovered that he was just about to get the copy for which he had applied from the tehsil office, absolutely in accordance with the rules and without having spent a cowrie in bribes.

The masters couldn't believe it. 'So, when will you get the copy?'

'Consider that I've already got it, father—only another fifteen to twenty days. The file has gone to the main office. Now, the application too will go there. The copy will be made there; then it will come back here; then it will be entered in the register . . .'

Langar continued to relate his plan to get the copy. He didn't even notice that the masters had wandered away, bored with his conversation and the smell which hovered around the Gandhi platform.

When he raised his head, he saw near him only the familiar dogs, pigs and piles of rubbish, in whose company he had set out to fight a righteous war against officialdom.

13

Despite being a tehsil headquarters, Shivpalganj was not a sufficiently big enough village to be entitled urban area status. There was a village council in Shivpalganj, and the villagers wanted to keep it just that, so that they wouldn't have to pay the extra urban area tax. The head of the village council, or pradhan, was Ramadhin Bhikhmakhervi's brother, whose greatest quality was never to have been to a lunatic asylum or jail, although he had been pradhan for so many years. Among the ganjahas, he was famous for his stupidity to which he had owed his universal popularity before he became pradhan.

The village council elections were due in January, and November had already begun. The question was who should be made pradhan this time? Vaidyaji had taken no interest in the last elections because he had considered village council work extremely demeaning. And, in one way, it was because village council officials are practically powerless. They had neither the stick of the police, nor the status of the tehsildar, and having one's work subjected to their scrutiny, day after day, lowered one's self-respect.

The pradhan had to file legal suits over village council land and property and, in the town court, the officials and lawyers did not treat him at all with the honour due to one thief from another. In litigation, the pradhan made an enormous number of enemies and, when he landed in trouble, the police just smiled and ignored him and, occasionally addressing him with deliberate sarcasm as 'Respected Pradhanji', conveyed to him just how little he mattered.

But for some time now, Vaidyaji had begun to show an interest in the village council, because he had read a speech by the prime minister in some newspaper. In that speech, the PM had said that 'village uplift' was only possible on the basis of schools, cooperative committees and village panchayats, and suddenly Vaidyaji realized that he had been working for the village uplift only through the cooperative union and the college, and the village panchayat was completely out of his hands. 'Aha!' he must have thought. 'That's why Shivpalganj is not being properly uplifted. Why didn't I realize it earlier?'

As soon as he took an interest, several things came to his notice: for instance, that Ramadhin's brother had ruined the village council. Some people had just grabbed the village wasteland, and the pradhan had definitely taken bribes. The council had no money and the pradhan had definitely embezzled it. The village had become filthy, and the pradhan was definitely the son of a pig. The police had prosecuted several people on complaints from the pradhan, from which one could only conclude that he had now become a police agent. The pradhan had been granted a licence for a shotgun, which had definitely been loaned out to dacoits. And last year, in the village, Bajrangi had been murdered, and you can guess why that happened.

~

For bhang drinkers, grinding bhang is an art, a poem, a great work, a craft, a ritual. Even if you chew half an anna's worth of the leaf and then have a drink of water, you get fairly high, but this is cheap inebriation. Ideally, almonds, pistachios, rose-petal conserve, milk, cream and so on, should all be used with the leaf. The bhang should be ground to the point where the grinding stones stick together and become one. Before it is drunk, verses in praise of Lord Shiva should be recited; and the whole exercise should be a community—not an individual—event.

In Vaidyaji's sitting room, it was Sanichar's job to bring to the fore the social aspect of bhang. Now, as he did every day, he was grinding bhang. A voice called out to him, 'Sanichar!'

Sanichar drew in his breath with a hiss and raised his head.

Vaidyaji said, as if he were a prime minister demanding a minister's resignation, 'Hand the bhang work over to someone else, and come inside.'

Sanichar began to grumble, 'To whom should I hand it? Is there anyone at all who can do this work? What do the young boys of today know about these things? They'll just grind it as if it were no more than turmeric and chilli.' But he put a young man in charge of the grinding stone, washed his hands, wiped them on the back of his underpants and went and stood by Vaidyaji.

On the wooden bed sat Vaidyaji, Rangnath, Badri Wrestler and the Principal sahib. Edging to one corner, the Principal said, 'Please do take a seat, Sanicharji.'

The courtesy of this remark put Sanichar on the alert. So he stuck out his broken teeth and began to scratch the hairs on his chest. He made himself look rather stupid as he knew it was the best way to counter a cunning attack.

He said, '*Arré*, Principal sahib, now don't make me sit on the same level as yourself. It'd be a sin and you'd be sending me to hell.'

Badri Wrestler laughed. He said, 'Bastard! Don't try to be clever! Are you going to go to hell for sitting with the Principal sahib?' Then, changing his tone, he said, 'Sit down over there.'

Vaidyaji said, as if voicing an eternal truth, 'Don't speak in that fashion, Badri. You haven't the slightest idea what fate has in store for Mr Mangal Das.'

For the first time in years, Sanichar heard his real name. He sat down and said importantly, 'Now, don't disgrace the wrestler too much, maharaj. After all, what's his age? When the time comes, he'll understand.'

Vaidyaji remarked, 'So, Principal sahib, say whatever you have to say.'

The Principal began in Awadhi, 'Should I make so bold as to speak? You all know the matter.' Then, impaling himself on the spike of common Hindi, he said, 'The village council elections are being held; the pradhan here is an important man. He also sits on the college committee—so, in a way, he's also my superior.'

Suddenly, Vaidyaji came out with, 'Listen, Mangal Das, this time, we want to make you the head of the village council.'

Sanichar's face contorted. He folded his hands in supplication, his body thrilled, tears sprang to his eyes. He was like a neglected, third-grade, village-level party worker with venereal disease who receives an order appointing him the chairman of a medical council. Then he pulled himself together and said, 'Arré, no, maharaj! It is enough that you have considered this unworthy creature worthy of such a thing! But I do not deserve this honour!'

Sanichar was amazed at his own erudition. Then Badri Wrestler spoke, 'Abeh, don't start blabbering now. People talk like that only after they become pradhan. Until then, just keep your mouth shut.'

At this point, Rangnath entered the conversation. Tapping Sanichar on the shoulder he said, 'It's nothing to do with your worth or lack of it, Sanichar! We agree that you aren't fit for the job, but what does that matter? It's not as if you were making yourself pradhan. It's the people who are making you pradhan. The people will do as they please. Who are you to interfere?'

The Principal sahib explained in the manner of an educated man, 'Yes, brother, it's democracy. Everywhere, things work like this in a democracy.' To encourage Sanichar, he remarked, 'Good man, Sanichar, get ready for it,' and gave him a look as if to say, 'Go on, son, go and crucify yourself.' Giving Sanichar the last push, he continued, 'The pradhan can't be any ordinary, stupid human being. It's a weighty office. The owner of the whole of the village property! If he likes, in one day he can make decisions worth lakhs. He's the local boss. If he wants, he can charge the whole village with Article 107 and have all of us locked up. All sorts of important officials come and sit at his door! Anyone against whom he complains finds it difficult to keep his job. He just puts his stamp on a paper, and takes out oil and sugar from the government shop at will. Without his permission, no one in the village can so much as throw rubbish on their rubbish heap. Everyone has to follow his advice. He holds everyone's keys. He is everyone's guardian. Well, what do you say?'

To Rangnath, these words seemed somewhat lacking in idealism. He said, 'Master sahib, you're making pradhans out to be complete dacoits.'

'Heh, heh, heh,' laughed the Principal, indicating that he was purposely making such foolish statements. This was his way of showing his listeners that he was well acquainted with the stupidity of his remarks and was, therefore, not stupid himself. 'Heh, heh, heh, Rangnath babu! What must you be thinking? I was talking about the way the present pradhan behaves.'

Meanwhile, Sanichar was saying, 'But, brother Badri, so many important officials come to the door of the pradhan . . . And I don't even have a door; you've seen my broken-down hut!'

Badri Wrestler always felt it was humiliating to have to say much to Sanichar. He suspected that, now that Sanichar had the opportunity, he was getting impudent. So, Badri stood up. Retying his lungi, which was falling down from his waist, he said, 'Don't worry. I'll even have a matchstick put to your broken-down hut. I'll get rid of that problem right now.'

Saying this, he went indoors. Thinking this was a joke, first, the Principal laughed, then Sanichar too. As Rangnath was still trying to see the point of it, the conversation changed course. Vaidyaji said, 'What's the problem? After all, my house is available. With great pleasure you can sit here. Welcome all the officials here. After a while, a pukka panchayat building will be put up, then you can go and stay there. From there, you can serve on the village council.'

Once more, Sanichar humbly joined his hands. He just had this to say: 'What should I do? The whole world will say that, when such people as you were there, in Shivpalganj, a loafer has been made . . .'

Making use of his familiar 'heh, heh, heh' and his Awadhi, the Principal told Sanicharji that he had started blabbering again. 'Where I hail from in Rajapur, the Babu sahib made his own ploughman pradhan. The *dhakapel* free-for-all tha' finds in village councils is not for the likes of decent, respectable folk.'

The Principal continued with unabated enthusiasm, 'And, Manager sahib, that ploughman put up some performance as head of the council. There's a famous story about the time there was a meeting at the tehsil office. Deputy sahib had come. All the pradhans were sitting there. They had been made to sit on a mat which was spread out on the floor. Deputy sahib was sitting on a chair.

'Then, our man, the ploughman, said, "What sort of justice is this? We have been called here and made to sit on the floor and Deputy sahib himself sits on a chair." Deputy sahib, too, was wet behind the ears. He got on a high horse. Then it became a matter of honour on both sides. All the pradhans were with our man the ploughman. They began to shout, "Long live the revolution!" Deputy sahib stuck to his seat screaming, "Peace! Peace!" But where was the peace and where was the tranquillity? The pradhans refused to attend the meeting and the ploughman of Rajapur ended up as leader of the tehsil area. The very next day, three political parties sent him requests to join their ranks. But Babu sahib refused to let him join any of them saying, "Don't you dare do anything yet. You join the party I tell you to when I tell you to."'

The slogan 'Long live the revolution!' was resounding in Sanichar's ears. He was imagining a man completely naked but for a pair of underpants, backed by a couple of hundred men raising their arms again and again, and shouting. Vaidyaji spoke, 'That was bad manners. If I had been pradhan, I would have come away. Then, two months later, I would have held a function in the village. I would have invited Deputy sahib. I would have made him sit on the ground, and then sat myself on a chair and delivered a speech saying, "Brothers! By nature, I find it difficult to sit on a chair, but Deputy sahib taught us this rule of hospitality on such-and-such a date when he called us to the tehsil office. Therefore, because of the lesson he taught us, I have been compelled to accept *this* inconvenience."' Vaidyaji guffawed with self-satisfaction. To win Rangnath's support, he said, 'Well then, son, this would have been the proper thing to do, wouldn't it?'

Rangnath replied, 'Yes, fine. I myself was taught this trick through the fable of the fox and the crane.'

This led to inquiries about what the fox and the crane actually did. It is a simple fable in which a fox invites a crane to dinner and serves food in a plate from which the crane can't eat due to its long beak. Then the crane, Rangnath informed the audience, gets its own back on the fox by inviting it to dinner and serving food at the bottom of a jar so tall that the fox's tongue can't reach.

As Rangnath concluded his story, Vaidyaji decided it was time to bring the discussions about the pradhan's post to an end. He said to Sanichar, 'Then it's settled. Go and make sure that that fool hasn't really ground the bhang like turmeric and chilli. Go. There's no pleasure in bhang if it's not made by your hand.'

Badri Wrestler smiled from the doorway and said, 'Go on, you old fool, go and mash the same bhang again!'

For some time, there was silence. Then the Principal said softly, 'If you permit, may I say a word about Khanna Master?'

Vaidyaji raised his eyebrows. Permission was granted. The Principal said, 'There was an incident. The evening before last, an object fell into Gayadin's courtyard. At that time, he had gone out to the fields to relieve himself. In the house, Bela's aunt saw the object and picked it up. It was a folded envelope. The aunt wanted Bela to read out the contents to her, but Bela was unable to do so . . .'

Rangnath was listening attentively. He asked, 'Was it written in English?'

'Who's going to write anything in English? It was written in Hindi, but how could an unmarried girl have read it? It was a love letter.'

Vaidyaji listened in silence. Rangnath didn't have the courage to ask who had written it.

The Principal spoke, 'There's no knowing who wrote it. It looks to me like the mischief of one of Khanna Master's group. The bastards are all thugs, absolute thugs. But Khanna Master is spreading tales against you. He says that the letter was sent by Ruppan babu. Look at his cheek! He dares to cast a slur on your home.'

Vaidyaji seemed unaffected by all this, except that he sat silently for a minute. Then he said, 'How on earth is he casting a slur on my home? He is defaming Gayadin's house. After all, the girl is his.'

The Principal looked hard at Vaidyaji, but his expression was inscrutable. In agitation, the Principal rolled down on to the floor of Awadhi. Turning towards the door, he said, 'Sanichar, be quick and bring me some *thandai-fandai* bhang. It's near time for the college labour t' leave.'

14

Every year, on the full moon day of Kartik, the eighth month of the Hindu calendar, a fair, or mela, is held at a place about five miles away from Shivpalganj. There is some jungle and a small hill on which there is a temple of the goddess, with bricks from some old building scattered around in all directions. In the jungle, which is spread over undulating ground, there are bushes of corinda, makoy and jujube. In this jungle, anything—from a rabbit to a wolf and from a maize pilferer to a dacoit—can easily find a place to hide in. Love affairs, which are initiated on a spiritual level in the villages nearby, are consummated on a physical level here. Sometimes, picnicking couples from the town, too, come to wander, and display their practical knowledge of each other. Occasionally, they also visit the temple and take their contracting bodies and swelling hearts back home again.

The inhabitants of this area are extremely proud of their hill because it is their Ajanta, Ellora, Khajuraho and Mahabalipuram. They are convinced that the temple was made by the gods with their own hands, as a residence for the goddess after the battle between the gods and the demons. They believe that a very big treasure is buried underneath the hill. So the hill has great historical, religious and economic importance.

Because of his knowledge of history and archaeology, Rangnath was very keen to survey this hill. He had been told that the images there belonged to the Gupta period and that there were many terracotta potsherds of the Maurya period.

~

The late Awadhi poet Parhis composed a verse which translates into common speech as:

> In the fair you go with open face
> To offer all and sundry sweets,
> But when your father-in-law you see
> You hide your face so shyly
> With a veil a metre long.

The same was true of all the women going to this fair. They were proceeding briskly, without veils on their faces or reins on their tongues. They were screaming—lung-, cheek- and throat-rending screams, producing the kind of shrieking which urban scholars and broadcasters call folk songs. Whole flocks of women were coming forward in this fashion.

Ruppan babu, Rangnath, Sanichar and Jognath were following a narrow path off the main road to the mela. After watching several relays of women go past them, Chhote Wrestler said, 'They are all squealing like stuck pigs.'

Sanichar explained, 'It's a mela.'

Among the groups of women were children and men. All of them were walking fast, all kicking up clouds of dust. Bullock carts were racing against one another, clearing a way for themselves in the most amazing fashion. In an even more amazing fashion, pedestrians were managing to get out of their striking range.

The same survival instinct, which saves hares from carnivorous beasts or, in towns, keeps pedestrians alive despite all attempts to the contrary by truck drivers, was protecting the people on their way to the mela from the wheels of the bullock carts.

The excitement generated by the mela was reaching its peak, and if All India Radio had been giving a running commentary, it would certainly have described how, thanks to the prosperity brought by the government's Five-Year Plans, the people, with music and song, were showering each other with love and joy. But Rangnath had been in the village for about one and a half months. He had seen enough to know that just because Sanichar—in his vest and underpants—was able to laugh heartily, it did not make him rich like a Birla or a Dalmia. He began to watch the mela crowds carefully, and he quickly saw the hollowness of all the enthusiasm. Even though the cold weather had set in, he noticed that no one was wearing a woollen coat. Certainly, there were a few children in torn sweaters. The women were wrapped in colourful but cheap saris; practically all were barefoot. And what could one say about the men? Typical Indian dandies—half clean, half filthy. 'Studying archaeology is a much more comfortable occupation than having to witness and understand all this,' thought Rangnath with some self-mockery as he turned to Ruppan babu.

Ruppan babu had called out to three cyclists who stopped and dismounted. They stood on the edge of the path, out of the way of the crowd, supporting their bicycles. One man, who appeared to be the leader of the three, took a discoloured hat from his head and began to fan himself with it. It was cool, but there was sweat on his brow. He was wearing shorts, a shirt and an open-necked jacket. He had tied a belt quite tightly round his middle so that his shorts didn't fall down over his pot belly, and his stomach area was thereby divided more or less into two equal parts. Both his companions wore dhoti–kurtas and caps and, despite appearing uncouth, were behaving very politely towards their leader.

'There'll be plenty of money floating about in the mela today, sahib!' laughed Ruppan babu, as if issuing a challenge. The man closed his eyes, nodded his head and said wisely, 'There must be. But now money has lost its value, Ruppan babu!'

Ruppan babu and the man exchanged some remarks about sweets and especially about *khoya*. Suddenly the man stopped paying attention to Ruppan and said, 'Wait, Ruppan babu!' He handed his bicycle to one of his companions, gave his hat to the other and waddled off on his fat legs to a nearby field of *arhar*. Disregarding the several people who were making their way along the path through the middle of the field, and the fact that the growth of arhar plants was rather thin, he started to undress in enormous haste. With great difficulty he managed to undo the buttons of his jacket and shirt, and pull out his sacred thread from inside. When he couldn't pull enough of it out, he bent his head down to one side and, somehow or the other, managed to hook a part of the thread over one ear. Then, struggling with his shorts, he began to pour a stream of liquid on to the arhar crop.

By now, Rangnath had understood that the man's name was Singh sahib. He was the local sanitary inspector. He had also found out that the man standing holding Singh sahib's bicycle was a member of the district board, and the man holding his hat was the board's tax collector.

When the inspector returned, the conversation continued. However, the subject of the conversation was no longer sweets but the chairman of the district board, the Inspector sahib's retirement and the fact that 'times are bad'. When the three men rode away, Ruppan told Rangnath quite a few things about the Inspector sahib.

He had been cut out for great things but, after becoming sanitary inspector, he had adopted an attitude of contentment with his lot. Shivpalganj was the only developed part of the area where he was posted; the rest was backward. All the inhabitants there knew that if they were deprived of their backwardness, they would have nothing left. Generally, whenever they met someone, they would immediately and proudly state that they came from a backward area. Similarly, they were proud of the Inspector sahib who had been posted in the area for over forty years, and he was still needed as much as he had been forty years earlier.

~

Today, Jognath had come to the mela with Ruppan babu. He was afraid that if he were left alone, the police would tease him and, in their affection, might suddenly make a grab for him.

They had all come dressed up for the mela. Ruppan babu had tied a brand-new silk scarf underneath his shirt collar and, to enhance his good looks, he had slipped on a pair of dark glasses. In addition to his underpants, Sanichar had put on a cotton string vest which came to a halt one and a half inches above the top of the pants. Today, Chhote Wrestler did not permit the end of his loincloth to dangle down like an elephant's trunk. He had tied it behind him so tightly that it would stick to him like a tail even if the rest of the loincloth were torn to shreds. Not only that, he was also wearing a transparent kurta—without a vest—and round his waist as a lungi, a short cotton cloth, also thin enough to be transparent. Jognath was sticking closely to Ruppan babu.

Since the day the thieves came, the people had begun to see Jognath in a different light. As soon as he arrived in the mango groves where graziers habitually gambled with cowrie shells, they avoided his eyes, tied their money up in knots in their dhotis, and then invited him to sit down. At the bhang parties outside Ramadhin's house, innumerable joyful hands would pat him on the back.

Then, just a few days earlier, the police Sub-Inspector had called him over to the station. Jognath took Ruppan babu along with him. The Sub-Inspector said, 'Ruppan babu, nothing can be achieved without the public's cooperation.'

He explained gravely, 'We are unable to find any clues to the robbery in Gayadin's house. Unless you people cooperate it will be difficult to find out anything.'

Ruppan babu said, 'You have our full cooperation. If you don't believe me, go and see what happens if you arrest any student from the college.'

The Sub-Inspector paced up and down a bit, and then said, 'The British way of dealing with these matters is the best. Eighty per cent of criminals confess their crimes. However, in this country . . .' Here, he paused and gave Jognath a straight look. Jognath looked back at the Sub-Inspector with the same steady gaze he used when bluffing in a game of flush.

The reply came from Ruppan babu. 'Don't start these British habits here. If 80 per cent of the people began to confess their crimes, by tomorrow, you'd only have two out of your ten constables left to go on duty. The rest would be in the lock-up.'

It so happened that the matter had been laughed off and the meeting had ended there. It still wasn't clear why the Sub-Inspector had summoned Jognath. Referring to the incident, Ruppan babu said with authority, 'Eh, Jognath, what's the point of hanging around with a face like a dead bat? Enjoy yourself. The Sub-Inspector isn't a hyena that's going to eat you!'

Then Chhote Wrestler remarked grumpily, 'We have a saying that if you eat fire you'll shit sparks. Jognath hadn't asked for Vaidyaji's advice before he jumped into Gayadin's house. So, why is he hanging on to him for help now?'

Jognath said nothing to counter this, for at that moment a bullock cart came rumbling past. Rangnath began to wipe the dust from his face; Chhote Wrestler didn't so much as blink. He confronted the cloud of dust sent up by the bullock cart with the same style with which Arjun had endured the dust of battle for eighteen days at Kurukshetra after listening to the exposition of the Bhagavad Gita. Then he said in a bored tone, 'There aren't many who can accept a home truth or a kick from a donkey. I've just spoken out loud what the whole village is whispering about Jognath. What's there to argue about in that?'

Sanichar attempted to restore peace. In the anticipation of becoming pradhan, he'd already begun to practise Vaidyaji's style of speaking as if pronouncing eternal truths. He said, 'It's not right to yap at one another. No matter what the whole world may say about Jognath, since I have once called him a good man, then that's what he is. Does a man stand by his word, or doesn't he?'

Chhote Wrestler remarked contemptuously, 'So you think you're a man?'

On their way they saw Langar. Rangnath said, 'He's even turned up here!'

Langar was relaxing on a piece of cheap cotton cloth spread out under a makoy bush and muttering to himself. Sanichar said, 'Langar's the kind of man who drops anchor wherever he feels like it. He's a happy-go-lucky sort.'

As they passed by, Ruppan taunted him, 'Tell us, Langar Master, what's the latest? Have you got the copy?'

Langar stopped muttering. Shading his eyes with one hand, he discerned Ruppan babu standing in the sunlight. He said, 'How am I going to get it, father? From here, the application for the copy was sent to the headquarters and then, by the same route, it was sent back again. Now the whole matter will be held up for another fortnight.'

Chhote Wrestler looked at him with loathing and then addressed a remark to the trees and shrubs. 'Why go on beating about the bush? Why doesn't the old fool just go and stick five rupees on the copy clerk?'

'You won't understand, Chhote Wrestler! This is a matter of principle,' explained Rangnath.

Chhote Wrestler cast an idle glance over his strong shoulders, and said, 'If that is the problem, let him keep going round in circles.' With this, like hundreds of other visitors to the fair, he went off to a bush to pee but, seeing another man relieving himself in the open, cursed him and turned away.

15

Chhote Wrestler said, 'I don't want any darshan-varshan. I am a slave only to Hanuman, the god of the red loincloth and, as far as I am concerned, all the other gods and goddesses are so much straw!'

They were discussing whether to go to have a darshan of the goddess in the temple. No one countered Chhote Wrestler's statement. No one tried to persuade him. They all knew that there was only one way to persuade Chhote Wrestler and that was to knock him down, climb on to his chest and break his bones. To show that he wasn't an atheist, Chhote stood up and began drumming a rhythm on his thigh. When he felt that his faith had not been adequately proved by this, he began to sing, 'Bajrangbali, row my boat with the oar of your grace!'

Pointing to a sweet shop he said, 'I'll go there and put something in my stomach in the meantime. Meet me there.' Then he remarked to himself, 'I've been wandering round with a tied mouth all morning. The bloody stomach is rumbling.'

Rangnath had been told that the temple was built in the Sat Yug, millions of years ago. At first, he had imagined himself deciphering letters of the ancient Brahmi script from some lump of rock. But when he saw the temple in the distance, he was immediately convinced that his compatriots correctly understood only two terms concerning time—*anadi* and *anant*—time without beginning and time without end. If this were not the case, how could they so easily attribute a seventy-five-year-old temple to the Gupta or the Maurya period?

Through the vines and verdure which decorated the exterior of the temple could be seen inscribed: 'The temple platform, dedicated to Mahishasurmardini, was constructed by Iqbal Bahadur Singh, son of Narendra Bahadur Singh of the throne of Bhikapur, on the tenth day of the dark half of the lunar month of Kartik in the year 1950 of the Vikram era.'

Reading this, Rangnath's archaeological aspirations vanished into thin air.

Don't imagine that the seat of Bhikapur was like the thrones of Satara or Pune. In the homes of lakhs of landowning families of the former kingdom of Awadh lie goodness knows how many broken-down seats, which the landowners occupy to receive the respects of their subjects—that is to say, one or two ploughmen—at the Holi and Dussehra festivals. Estimating what had been spent on the temple, Rangnath realized that the throne of Bhikapur, too, was one of those lakhs of seats of Awadh.

The temple itself wasn't much bigger than a seat. It had one room, which had just one entrance. Against the inside walls, a number of wardrobe-like cupboards had been built, in which there were arrangements for several different gods to take up their abode.

As one squeezed through the doorway, among the images in the wardrobe immediately facing one was the main image of the goddess. As soon as Jognath entered the temple, he prostrated himself completely, like a soldier on the battlefield when he hears an explosion. Then, crouching with his weight on his toes, he began to sing a bhajan with great passion. No one could understand the words, but they could make out that he was singing, not crying. Jognath's devotion was not the product of a pipe of hashish or of a bottle of booze, but solely the result of his terror of the police. Whatever the reason, his devotion was so obvious that several people forgot their own bhajans and became engrossed in his.

Sanichar was aspiring to become pradhan. Therefore he, too, somehow managed to kneel down right in the centre of the temple, and began to raise the slogan, 'Jagadambike! Consort of Shiva!'

There was a terrific crowd on the platform outside the main shrine and no one was paying attention to anyone else, but which ganjaha worth his salt could fail to impose his rustic presence on the local population the moment he arrived? People stood aside for Sanichar. Ruppan babu also closed his eyes, immediately demanded a boon, and immediately opened them again. Then he began to watch the mela. A girl next to him, murmuring a prayer, was kneeling in front of an image. In Ruppan babu's opinion, she represented the real entertainment of the fair.

Rangnath joined his hands and went right up to the main image. He took one look at it and was rooted to the spot. All that he had read about ancient sculpture suddenly seemed totally meaningless. He thought, 'If this is the statue of a goddess, what were the ones I saw in Khajuraho, Bhubaneshwar or in the Kailash Temple at Ellora?'

Shutting his eyes again, he tried with all his might to forget all that he had learnt. In his heart of hearts he began to scream, 'Help! Help! My faith is being attacked by reason! Help me!' But when he opened his eyes he felt that all his devotion had disappeared, and that he was being violently shaken by all the history he had learnt parrot-fashion.

The fact was that the iconography of the statue was somewhat novel. It wore a sort of military headgear, and beneath its neck was a broad and flat chest. The area below the chest was missing. Those who came to the temple not out of devotion, but out of academic curiosity born of reading books by historians writing in the English language, could only state that this was the statue of a soldier dating approximately to the twelfth century.

Whatever else you may say about our country's sculpture, you cannot criticize it on the grounds of any confusion over sex. Even if we can be deceived about the sex of some women who wear their hair short and walk around golf courses in shirts and trousers, there is no possibility of our making the same mistake when it comes to our ancient statues of female figures.

Rangnath asked the priest, 'Of which god is this a statue?'

The priest was very busy. He shouted, 'Get some money out of your pocket and make an offering, then you'll find out which god it is!'

Rangnath's curiosity led him to step forward and touch the statue's neck. The priest looked at him suspiciously and then said like an educated man, 'Touching the idol is strictly forbidden.'

The girl whom Ruppan babu had been watching had left the temple. As far as he was concerned, the mela was over. He tugged Rangnath by the hand and said, 'We've taken darshan; now let's go. Come on.'

History is the greatest iconoclast. It now overwhelmed Rangnath and made him say, 'What sort of darshan is this? This isn't even the image of a goddess!'

As soon as they heard this, the three ganjahas with Rangnath blenched. Several people gave a start and began to look in his direction. Then Rangnath explained to Ruppan babu like an assistant curator in a museum, 'Don't you see? This is undoubtedly the statue of a soldier. Look, this is his helmet and, look here, this is a quiver sticking out at the back, and look, the chest is absolutely flat . . .'

Rangnath was unable to complete his description of the soldier's thorax because the priest leapt up and shoved him so hard that he cut through the crowds effortlessly, like an arrow, and came to rest near the door.

The priest stopped his business of conducting pujas and collecting money, and began to curse Rangnath with all his heart. The priest's mouth was small, but some very substantial curses came tumbling out brokenly. Very soon, the temple resounded with shouts and curses because the pilgrims, too, began assisting the priest in his abuse of Rangnath.

The ganjahas went out of the temple completely flabbergasted. The priest came to the door of the temple and began to scream, 'As soon as I saw your face I knew it! You're Christian! Spawn of the British! You learn a bit of their *git-pit git-pit* language and then dare to say that this isn't a goddess! After four days you'll be saying that your father is not your father!'

Sanichar and Jognath could not comprehend exactly what was going on. Still, they flailed around and started to kick up a fuss. By then Ruppan had recovered his ability to handle the situation. He caught hold of Rangnath's hand and said, 'Let's go, brother.' Then, turning to the priest he remarked loudly, but in a cool tone, 'Look here, maharaj, don't go smoking too much hash on mela days. You're getting old and it goes to your head.'

The priest had opened his mouth to say something, but Ruppan stalled him. 'Enough, enough. Don't try to talk back to me. We belong to Shivpalganj. Put your tongue back in its snake hole.'

After walking for some time, Rangnath said, 'I was wrong. I shouldn't have said anything.'

Ruppan babu consoled him. 'You're right. But it's not your fault, it's the fault of your education.'

Sanichar too piped up, 'When a man studies, he begins to talk like educated people. He forgets the real way to speak. Isn't that so, Jognath?'

Jognath didn't reply because by then he had slipped in among the waves of pilgrims and was busy nudging young women and, from the expression on his face, it looked as though it was something he wanted to keep on doing.

~

Sanichar too caught the mela mood. With long strides he made his way over to the sweet shop where Chhote Wrestler was sitting. He pushed aside hundreds of elderly people, lovingly laid his hands on the shoulders of several women, groped them to check the size and shape of their breasts, and all with such detachment that you'd think it was a man's bounden duty to do so while thrusting his way through a crowd. To achieve this, the puny man suddenly developed such agility that any American tonic manufacturer would have proudly employed him to advertise 'pep'.

Rangnath was thoroughly annoyed. Once he pushed away Sanichar's hand as it was moving towards a young girl's cheek and said, 'What sort of behaviour is this?'

Sanichar's eyes opened wide. He replied, 'This isn't behaviour, guru; it's a mela.' Then suddenly becoming humble, he stuck out his teeth and continued, 'Guru, it's a country mela matter. These dodges, guru, are the wonders of the mela.'

There was quite a crowd in front of the sweet and chaat shops. Pile upon pile of *barfi*, the empress of Indian sweets, was stacked up, and every young boy was well aware that in a street fight they could be used just like brickbats. To make these sweets, the confectioners and the food inspectors had to carry out an enormous amount of scientific research. After a great deal of hard work, they had discovered that, instead of condensed milk, they could use arum, potato and rice flour, soil or even cow's dung. They were all believers of harmony, expertly balancing ingredients, and they had taken an oath never to make or sell anything which was not adulterated.

Chhote Wrestler could be seen beside one shop. He was sitting on a stool a little removed from the crowd, eating pieces of potato that he was spearing with a neem twig out of a leaf cup. Sanichar and Jognath left Ruppan babu and went off towards Chhote. Sanichar said, 'Guru, if you allow us, we'll eat a few pieces of barfi.'

Chhote looked at Sanichar and smiled benignly. As if he were conferring a boon, he said, 'Eat, son. Get some for Jognath too.'

Rangnath's stomach turned at the sight of the dust, the flies and other substances which were adding to the weight of the barfi and the chaat. He asked Ruppan, 'Will you have anything?'

Ruppan replied uninterestedly, 'Why on earth should I?' With this, he surveyed the crowds. Some way off he spotted Singh sahib, whom he had met earlier. The sola hat planted firmly on his head at the moment gave him the appearance of a senior police officer rather than a sanitary inspector. Several people were surrounding Singh sahib. Ruppan babu said, 'While these gluttons are stuck into the sweets, we'll go and see how that old fool is getting on.'

He went up to Singh sahib. Singh's face was covered with four or five days' growth of beard, and tobacco juice was just about to drip from the corners of his mouth but, despite all this, his sola hat managed to make him look reasonably smart.

Ruppan babu spoke, 'So, Singh sahib, what's up?'

'Nothing's up, it's down, brother! I've had to charge ten vendors with adulteration. Now, Ruppan babu, to have come to this at my age! I'm going to wear the skin off my soles doing the rounds of the courts to give evidence.'

Overriding the general clamour by raising his voice, Ruppan babu replied, 'What's in a charge, Singh sahib? Take five or ten rupees from each of them and the whole matter is settled.'

Raising his voice to a similar pitch, Singh sahib said, 'Which bastard is giving me five or ten rupees? All the vendors I have charged over here, all the bastards, they're only willing to part with two rupees. I told them, "If all you want is the charge, then take it, I'll make it out for you right now."'

Ruppan babu raised his hand and asked, 'Where on earth do these vendors come from? They're complete ignoramuses.'

A tall, strong man walked up to them. He looked quite awe-inspiring, but when he spoke he was like a big, fat, rotten watermelon. 'We are from Rohupur, sahib,' he whined. 'We've been waiting so long to please the 'Nispictor sahib, but he won't bring down his rate below ten rupees a stall.'

Ruppan babu said, 'Settle up, Singh sahib. Even with a rate of two rupees, you'll get twenty rupees. What's wrong with that? It's not as if you've sold them a pile of wheat or anything valuable.'

Singh sahib nearly split his throat as he roared, 'Two rupees!' He laughed. 'Don't do me so much dishonour, Ruppan babu.'

Encouraged by Ruppan's support, the fat man said, 'Now, Babu sahib, just consider our predicament. We've put up stalls here after a full year. If we lose ten rupees to him, what will we have left?'

Ruppan had started this discussion in jest, but now he was beginning to enjoy taking the vendors' side. He said in a voice which matched Singh sahib's in volume, 'He's right you know. What will he have left? Now settle, Singh sahib, let it come down to two and a half rupees—then both sides will have given ground.' He addressed the fat man. 'Go this moment and hand over twenty-five rupees to Singh sahib . . . and some sweets, too.'

Singh sahib shouted after his retreating figure, 'Don't bring any sweets!' He explained his request to the general public in a reasoned fashion. 'God knows whether the bloody stuff's made in castor oil or mahua oil. It stinks like goat droppings.'

Ruppan babu came up closer still. They began to talk of domestic matters. Ruppan asked, 'How's the mansion?'

Singh sahib replied regretfully, 'No longer a mansion; you can only call it a house now.' He fell silent, and then added in a lifeless tone, 'It's lying half finished. I'm thinking of auctioning it off just as it is.'

Inwardly, Rangnath was seething. After the insult in the temple, he was longing for a fight. He remarked, 'Even after taking so many bribes you haven't managed to build yourself a mansion?'

Singh sahib wasn't annoyed by this comment. He looked at Ruppan and raised his eyebrows as if to say, 'Who's this?' Ruppan explained that Rangnath was his dada, and that Singh sahib shouldn't take anything he said to heart; his dada was a bit too well educated and so, occasionally, put the cart before the horse. He assured the official, 'But it doesn't matter; after all, whatever he may be like, he is one of us.'

Rangnath bit his lip and heaved a deep sigh. Singh sahib began to explain to him, 'The good old days are over, brother! That was the age of mansions. Nowadays, no one can build himself a mansion out of bribes. If you can keep your roof thatched, that's a lot to be thankful for. Haven't you seen the sort of rates we're getting? My hands are worn out writing ten charges and what do I get for it? It's like going to kill a heron and ending up with no more than a handful of feathers.'

The fat man returned. He pressed twenty-five one-rupee notes into Singh sahib's hand. Leaving his speech unfinished, Singh sahib carefully counted the notes, twice. One note was particularly grubby, so he had it changed. Then he slowly put the money into a pocket in his vest.

Rangnath was watching his face. Singh sahib said, 'Have you seen what things have come to? Earlier, when people found out that an official was ready to take bribes, they would surround him in thousands. They used to give money and be grateful to you for taking it. Now no one comes near you. If anyone does, then they bring someone with them like Ruppan babu, and because of my regard for him the whole business is spoilt.

'These days, taking bribes is a very humiliating business. There's no charm left in it. There's really no difference left between a man who takes bribes and one who doesn't. Both of them are in a bad way.'

The conversation was interrupted by an uproar at a nearby shop. Someone said, 'It's started, it's started,' which meant that people had started beating each other with lathis.

'What's the matter? What's up?' asked a number of people converging on the shop. One man behaved as if the whole matter was concealed somewhere in a tray of barfi. He grabbed a fistful of the sweets and shouted, 'What's the matter?' For some time, the matter was investigated in a similar way. One man found it was hidden in a pile of laddus, another man found it in the sugar cake. There was a fair old free-for-all.

Suddenly two or three constables appeared on the scene, brandishing batons. They were generous rather than discreet in their wielding of them and so, very soon, you could say that the situation was under control. The crowd scattered. At the shop where the main incident had taken place, the proprietor was lying on his back sobbing and rubbing the spot where he had been hit by a baton. On one side stood Chhote Wrestler, Jognath and Sanichar. Ruppan and Rangnath came and joined them. The stage was set.

One constable asked, 'Let's hear what happened then! You're rubbing your back so hard you'd think someone had dropped an atom bomb on you.'

The shopkeeper stopped sobbing and addressed the public, 'Whatever happened happened, and I've nothing more to say.'

Chhote Wrestler was standing rubbing the dirt on his elbows into small rolls. Looking at the shopkeeper he said, 'No one can swindle ganjahas like this. There's still the matter of our money.'

Ruppan babu now entered the field. Tossing back the locks which had fallen forward on to his brow, he impressed the constable with his learning. He said, 'This wrestler is with us. Don't think these people are orphans and you can do what you like with them. If you handle the matter properly you will have our fullest cooperation. But if you do anything crooked there'll be seven hundred college students out here tomorrow.'

One of the constables replied, 'Don't say anything just now, brother. We know who you are. Whatever is to be done will be done properly.'

Then he turned to the shopkeeper and asked, 'What statement do you have to make?'

The shopkeeper became immediately alert. His hands automatically stopped rubbing his back. He said, 'Statement? I will not make a statement now, sir! I shall only do so in the presence of my lawyer.'

The constable barked, '*Abeh*! Who the hell's taking your statement? I'm asking you what happened.'

The shopkeeper said, 'It was like this, O Embodiment of Justice! First, that wrestler came and sat on the stool at the back. He ate two plates of spinach and two plates of arum. When he was eating the second plate of arum, these two ganjahas here arrived.' Looking askance at Sanichar and Jognath, he continued, 'These two asked for one hundred and fifty grams of barfi each. I gave it to them.'

The constable turned to Chhote Wrestler and asked, 'Is all this true?'

Chhote, making his reply sound like a curse, uttered the words, 'Yes, it is.'

'Then, both these ganjahas ate their barfi and started to walk away,' went on the shopkeeper. 'I said, "You owe me half a rupee." They turned on me and said, "We've already given you half a rupee, how many times do you want to be paid?" Here, I feed hundreds of customers at a time. How could I dare to try and cheat them? I kept on asking for my money and they kept on saying that they had already given it. I got a bit short with them and they started cursing and swearing at me.'

Sanichar interrupted, 'Just stick to the truth, Lala Chiranjimal! You say we ate half a rupee's worth of barfi and so do we. You say that we didn't give the money, and we say we did.'

Rangnath interjected, 'So what's the trouble then? If he hasn't got the money already, they'll give it to him.'

Sanichar said, 'Listen to this brother here! If we begin paying for things twice like this, we'll soon be reduced to begging in the streets.'

'The real trouble is not over half a rupee,' said the shopkeeper. 'It's over that wrestler there. When these two ganjahas were kicking up a row over their half-rupee, he told me not to get so busy arguing with them so as to forget the rupee he had given me. Now *he* hadn't paid even a quarter of a paisa, and here he was, telling me not to forget the rupee he had given me! What is the world coming to?'

The wrestler did not react to this accusation. He was still rubbing little rolls of dirt off his body.

The constable said, 'What do you have to say, wrestler?'

Chhote replied, 'What do I have to say? I am not one to make too much fuss. All I want is my half-rupee change and have nothing more to do with all this.'

The discussion continued for some considerable time. People in the surrounding crowd also began to talk amongst themselves, the general theme of these conversations being that there was a fight like this at the mela every year, that it was always the ganjahas who started it, that the ganjahas were all rogues, but who could talk back to them? And the fact was that, if truth be told, every village had the same problem; all the young lads were just as wild and . . .

It still wasn't settled as to who should give how much and to whom. Finally, a constable suggested the simple solution that the simple solution would be for both sides to call it quits. If the wrestler had given a rupee, he should forget about the change, and if the shopkeeper hadn't been paid, he should forget about the payment.

Both sides were very dissatisfied with this suggestion, but after a lot of hue and cry they both accepted it. Then, a similar uproar broke out in the direction of the country liquor shop, and the police hurried off there. The crowd thinned out.

Suddenly, Rangnath said severely, 'I did not know that I was in the company of looters. What a bunch of characters!'

Ruppan babu stared at him in surprise, 'Who? The shopkeepers? *Hunh*, they are born looters.'

Rangnath's face began to turn red. He went up to the shopkeeper. Taking a five-rupee note from his pocket he offered it to him and said, 'Cut the price of three people's sweets and snacks out of this. Forget it happened.'

He turned towards his companions. Ruppan pulled a face as if to say that this boy is set on displaying all his stupidity in one day. Chhote said softly, 'Let him get it off his chest. He's an educated man. He's *Aym May* pass; who's going to argue with him?'

Chhote began to look around as if the whole business had nothing to do with him, and the problem was only that some man with an MA degree had embarked on a course of idiocy.

But Ruppan spoke up, 'The decision's been reached, brother! Now, you have no right to speak. If you wanted to do anything, you should have done it in front of the police; then there would have been a point to it.'

Rangnath threw down the note in front of the shopkeeper. Ignoring Ruppan, he said, 'Quick, give me back the change.'

A crowd had begun to gather again. The shopkeeper took a hasty look around and returned the note, saying, 'You're an outsider here, babuji. I have to live here.'

~

The group now divided into three. Jognath headed off to the liquor shop, and Sanichar and Chhote Wrestler went to the far side of the mela where a few of their acquaintances were straining bhang. Rangnath and Ruppan babu went on together.

Rangnath had become rather grave, and he was also tired. He sat down to rest on the wall surrounding a well. Ruppan babu remained standing and began to watch the preparations for a partridge fight which was about to start nearby.

At a short distance from the well, there was a ruined building. Next to a pillar sat a girl—a young girl with a wheaten complexion, in a brightly coloured sari, a gold ring in her nose. After the dirt of the mela, this scene appealed to Rangnath. He gazed in her direction.

A man in a dirty lungi and a clean, shiny, imitation silk kurta was standing some distance from the girl, puffing at a beedi. Behind his ear was a ball of lime; oil dripped from his hair. Slowly he approached the girl and sat down about a yard from her. He said something and the girl smiled. Rangnath was pleased by her smile. He wished she would look in his direction, and the girl did indeed look at him. He wished that she would smile at him. She did smile. The man with the dripping hair lit another beedi.

A man wearing a dhoti, kurta and cap came up to Rangnath. By country standards he looked quite respectable. Rangnath glanced at him, and then looked back towards the girl. She had stopped smiling. Her face had assumed something of the tender expression which the faces of Hindi film heroines assume before breaking into a love song.

The man near Rangnath asked softly, 'You come from around these parts?'

Rangnath shook his head and said, 'No.'

The man came and sat down confidently by Rangnath. He said, 'These rustics don't understand anything. Sing this film song, sing that film song . . . !'

Rangnath listened to his remarks with interest, but couldn't follow his meaning. The man continued, 'But if you ask her to sing a *tillana*, a *dadra* or even a *thumri*, anything at all classical, she will sing her heart out.'

Musing, he said, dreamy-eyed and romantically, 'She went to Rohupur. Now she's off to Baijegaon.'

In the town, Rangnath had once heard a similar remark being made of Ravi Shankar. An announcer had said, 'He has just returned from Edinburgh; now, in the winter months, he's going to New York.'

Rangnath nodded encouragingly, and the man began to give him a complete picture of the girl's qualities. Hesitating at first, he said, 'Her art isn't the sort you can appreciate by the roadside. Come to her room and listen to her there. Then you'll be able to tell a real performer from an impostor.'

Rangnath was still watching the girl. The man with the dripping hair was now sitting right next to her. Both were talking, smiling and occasionally looking towards Rangnath. He finally realized that these people had great hopes of him.

Seeing the man in the dhoti–kurta and cap and Rangnath from a distance, anyone would have thought that two serious-minded men were in profound contemplation of the problems facing the nation. His brows drawn together, the man was saying, 'The new laws have ruined everything. All kinds of aristocrats are longing to hear her songs. But now the police, too, have given permission, and music has started in the houses of joy.'

Rangnath stood up. So did the man, saying, 'I have pushed myself to my limits in training her the last ten years. Now, she has developed a voice like a peacock's. After all this practice, she's become one in a thousand.'

Rangnath looked towards Ruppan babu. He had slipped away to watch the partridge fight.

Rangnath called out, 'Ruppan!'

The man thought for a while and then said, 'She's a girl of your own religion, a Hindu, and very simple.'

Then, pulling a long face, he continued with pride, 'She only sings. She's been with people of quality. She's not a prostitute.'

Rangnath told the man, 'A very good thing, too. If singers become prostitutes, their music suffers. Music requires mental harmony. Make sure she stays the way she is.'

The man was taken aback. He said, 'You know everything. I don't have to explain. One day come to her room . . .'

Catching sight of Ruppan babu, he stopped. Ruppan had suddenly come up from behind. He thundered, 'Certainly he'll come to her room. But who do you think you're talking to? Turn round and recognize your father!'

The man joined his hands, his demeanour changed. He smiled roguishly and said, 'Sir, my father is money!'

Rangnath smiled. Darting a glance at the girl, he saw that she was grinning.

~

Ruppan and Rangnath walked on in silence. Finally, Ruppan said, 'What was he telling you? Did he say she had started taking men or not?'

Rangnath didn't reply.

'We're surrounded by frauds. I've been seeing this bloody whore since I was a child,' remarked Ruppan like a senior citizen. 'For years she's been roaming round with a ring in her nose, and he's been beating out praise for her dadras and thumris. She's got a voice like a buffalo's, pretends to be a master musician, and is actually the rottenest whore in the whole area. No one would pay even a cowrie for her.'

Rangnath was proceeding rather wearily. Ruppan told him, 'If I hadn't come when I did there's no way he'd have shut up. He had practically hooked you.'

He continued in the same mode. Suddenly Rangnath asked, 'Ruppan, why did you write a love letter to Bela?'

Ruppan babu's speech faltered but, recovering himself, he said, 'You've been in the town all this time and you still don't know why people write love letters!'

Rangnath had an answer to this. He merely said, 'Uncle will be very annoyed.'

Ruppan babu drew himself up to his full height and stiffened. 'What right has he to get angry? Tell him to talk to me face-to-face. He married when he was fourteen. My mother died, and so he married again at the age of seventeen. He couldn't do without it for even a year . . . That's what he's done legally. And what he's done on the side, if you want to hear about that too . . .'

'No,' said Rangnath, 'I don't want to.'

16

The ground under a thatched roof where buffaloes were tethered at night was being wiped dry with paddy straw and ash. When the smell of buffalo urine had been subdued by the ash, the man who was wiping the ground was assured it was clean. On top of the ash he spread a large piece of sacking, and on the sacking a colourful cotton rug, on one corner of which was written, 'Village Judicial Council, Bhikhmakhera'.

He fetched a wooden box and placed it in the centre of the rug. Then, going up to the brick platform nearby, he spat out as much spittle as he could in two spits and lit a beedi.

The jurisdiction of the judicial council of Bhikhmakhera also extended over the Shivpalganj village council area. Kusahar Prasad had filed a case of assault against his son, Chhote Wrestler. Today was the third hearing. The only decision taken at the previous two hearings was that the case could not be taken up as Kusahar and Chhote were present, but the *panches*, or members of the council, were not.

Sitting on the platform was the beedi-smoking chapraasi of the judicial council. After finishing his beedi, he spat again; then, bending to one side, he stretched, gave an enormous yawn and said to himself, 'Where the hell have these people got to?' When there was no answer, he lit another beedi.

Five men appeared, walking together. One was Kusahar Prasad and another was Chhote Wrestler. The other three were the sarpanch and the two panches. There were two rather faint scars on Kusahar's head. He had shaved his head so that they might be displayed more prominently. On the map of his bald pate, the two plateaus of the wounds were clearly visible.

A file was opened. The sarpanch asked one of the panches, 'Please read out Kusahar's prosecution case to the defendant.'

The panch looked at the file rather uncertainly, flipping the pages back and forth. In the same way that a man who knows Hindi is stupefied by the sight of Tamil, Telugu, Kannada and Malayalam scripts, the panch said in a rather faraway voice, 'When a senior man like you is present, how can I read the case? Do please read it out yourself and proceed with it.'

The file became something of a hot potato. The first panch turned it around and handed it back to the sarpanch. The sarpanch took it with one hand and, with the other, gave it to the second panch. The second panch examined rather closely a round stamp on the last page and, suddenly, passed the file back to panch number one. The file passed through so many hands that it seemed impossible that their job was not complete.

Finally, Kusahar Prasad said, 'Sarpanchji, the secretary hasn't come today. How long will you go on troubling yourself with all this botheration of reading and writing? Set another date. The case can be heard later.'

The sarpanch replied heroically, 'What are you saying, Kusahar Prasad? The soldier who fears the bullet and the sarpanch who fears reading and writing, they are both . . .'

Chhote Wrestler yawned and stretched so hard that a cracking sound came from his ribs. In a bored tone, he commented, 'You people have been messing around for a whole hour. Are you going to start the hearing or just keep on twiddling your thumbs?'

Immediately, the sarpanch opened the proceedings. He tried again to read the file. He held one of its pages up to his mouth. Spittle oozed out to the corners of his lips. He screwed up his eyes, making the crow's feet around them stand out. It looked as though this was one of the most exceptional moments of his life.

The file was now almost touching his mouth. He clicked his tongue, drew in his breath and, without consuming even a morsel of it, put it down again. After this ritual, he said formally, 'I have read the prosecution case of Mr Kusahar Prasad. Kusahar Prasad says that the son of Kusahar Prasad, Chhote—father's name Kusahar Prasad—has beaten Kusahar Prasad with a lathi without reason. The prosecution is being made under Section 323 of the Indian Penal Code.'

Chhote Wrestler sat there as if he had no connection with the proceedings. The sarpanch's forehead clouded. He asked, 'What do you have to say, Kusahar? This is the problem, isn't it? The defendant, Chhote, beat you?'

'Yes, sarpanchji, in front of thousands of people. He beat all my ribs and bones to chaff.'

The sarpanch said gravely, 'Think twice before you say that, Kusahar! If your bones were broken, the charge becomes serious. Then you will have to go to the town court. Here, we only deal with Section 323. If it turns into a 325, you will not be done with it until you've tasted the water of the town tap.'

Kusahar pondered for a moment. 'Then, sarpanchji, my bones were really only a little broken! It was just a manner of speech. But he beat me badly. He thrashed me like paddy straw. Look at the wounds on my head. He's no son to me; he's an enemy.'

One panch was sitting on the edge of the sackcloth, quietly telling his prayer beads. On his brow was a white tilak, around his neck, a string of sacred rudraksha beads. He was an elderly, respectable man. He looked an expert at calculating auspicious dates and times, and at performing rituals, and was an experienced practitioner of Ayurvedic medicine as well. These skills were enough for him to make a comfortable country living. But this was not all. When he had the chance, he would also show off his talents in the town. There, he would meet all kinds of senior officials, reveal the end of the seven and a half years of Saturn's influence on them, predict their promotion or a foreign trip and, thereby, extract from them handsome remunerations, as well as even handsomer government grants. When he heard Kusahar say that Chhote was not his son but his enemy, he cut short his prayers and uttered the words, 'Oh God!'

Chhote cleared his throat. The sarpanch said, 'You are coughing a lot.'

The wrestler replied, 'My father is wailing like a widow. Listen to him. Take my cough into consideration later.'

The sarpanch asked Kusahar, 'So your bones were not broken. If that is the case, the matter is one of Section 323.'

Slowly he repeated, 'Then this remains a case of Section 323. No spears or daggers were involved? If they were, say so. Because, then it becomes a matter of Section 324.'

Kusahar said nervously, 'No, sarpanchji, what use would we have for spears and daggers? For seven generations we people have been using lathis.'

'Good!' said the sarpanch. He turned over a few pages in the file and asked, 'Kusahar, tell me then, why did Chhote beat you?'

Chhote answered, 'How can he tell you? Shall I give you the reason?'

The sarpanch smiled and said, 'In law, too, people have to wait for their turn, wrestler. First, the plaintiff; then, the defendant. Your turn will come, don't worry.'

'Who's worrying? And don't you worry, either. When God wills it, your number, too, will come up.'

The sarpanch ignored this. Instead, he asked Kusahar, 'So tell me, brother, why did Chhote beat you?'

'How can I say why he hit me? Why does a savage bullock attack people? He's young, he's a wrestler. No one in the whole village can do him down. His body longs to fight. His hands were itching and, to stop them, he went and had a go at me . . .'

'Not true!' interjected the sarpanch. 'It takes two hands to clap! You must have done something to provoke him!'

Kusahar pretended innocence. 'What could I have done, sarpanchji? How can I stand up against Chhote?'

The sarpanch looked down as if deep in thought. After a while he went on, 'Don't pretend to be so simple, Kusahar Prasad. The court here knows every vein in your body. Our investigations have uncovered the whole story. Running after women at your age? You're trying to make fools of us, maharaj! You're no less a rascal than anyone else!'

Kusahar's voice faltered, 'Sarpanchji, in my house I was beaten with a lathi, and here, you are beating me with words. What sort of justice is this?'

The prayer-bead-telling panch said, 'Let's leave what's covered up, covered up. But just don't try raking things up too much, Kusahar maharaj! We all know you're no great saint.'

The other panch said, 'Let the case continue! Whatever Kusahar may have got up to, the case before us is one of Section 323, so let's keep it at that.'

But the intoxication of the case had gone to the sarpanch's head. Stubbornly he said, 'What do you know of what's going on anywhere? I have just come back from the tehsil office. On the way I talked to some people. Old Sanichar, too, was there. What I heard made my ears burn. This Kusahar is no better than he should be. There is as much of him sunk below the ground as there is above it. The village's . . .'

This insult knocked Kusahar sideways. He began glancing around meekly. In his day he'd been quite fierce but only where fighting was concerned. Faced with the law, he had always behaved humbly. At that moment he was making a silent appeal to all those present; tears were practically dripping from his eyes. However, the panches and the sarpanch were sitting contentedly observing his discomfiture.

Kusahar slowly raised his head to look at Chhote and suddenly appeared apprehensive.

Chhote was frowning. His lips were compressed. He stood up and told the sarpanch, 'Eh, you fool, don't kick up such a row! If I give you one clout round the ear you'll sink into the ground—you and your cases-vases. For the last two hours I have been listening to you calling my father a bastard. If my father is a bastard, then what do you think your father is?' As he said this, Chhote's voice began to tremble. 'I haven't died yet,' he went on. 'Now, if there is anyone here who is the real son of his father, let him try to insult my father and see how far he gets.'

There was pin-drop silence. The chapraasi quietly bounded over to the far corner of the thatched area like a cat, and hid. The sarpanch was dumbfounded. Kusahar breathed a sigh of relief. The prayer-bead-telling panch closed his eyes and muttered, 'God!'

Chhote growled like a tiger, 'Eh, God! I'll stuff your prayer beads down your throat and take them out through your stomach. I'll have this God-act out of you in a moment!'

Kusahar now spoke up, 'Oh, Chhotua! That's enough. Now be quiet! It's a legal matter. The case will take its course.'

'You sit there and take it, father. I know what's going on. Tomorrow, I'll go to the town in person and lodge a complaint against them. They have called you God knows what in a public meeting. If I don't have every one of them doing hard labour in the one-and-a-quarter-lakh jailhouse, then you'll know I wasn't born of your urine.'

With this, he caught hold of Kusahar's arm and dragged him out from under the thatch.

17

In the early hours of the morning, Vaidyaji began to feel the cold and woke up. The cold broke down the combined defences provided by doses of Ayurvedic tonics like Chyavanprash, Swambhasm and Badam Pak. It crept under his skin, pierced the thick layers of his flesh and chilled him to the marrow. He tried to wrap the quilt around him properly, remembering that a bed is always colder when there is no one to share it. This thought triggered off a succession of memories, the practical effect of which was to lull him into a doze. Explosions of wind began to erupt from the upper and lower portions of his body. He pressed the quilt closely around him and turned over. Finally, as he was listening to one last explosion from this internal revolution, he drifted off again. Immediately, the wind of revolution was tamed and began merely to flow in and out of his nostrils in snores. Vaidyaji slept and it was then that he dreamed of Democracy.

He saw Democracy squatting on the ground next to his wooden bed, his hands folded in supplication. His face looked like a ploughman's, and he couldn't even speak good Hindi, let alone English. Still, he was pleading with Vaidyaji and Vaidyaji was listening to his pleas. Time and time again, Vaidyaji tried to persuade him to come and sit on the wooden bed beside him, telling him that he might be poor, but he was, after all, Vaidyaji's own relative. But again and again, Democracy addressed him as 'Sir' and 'Master'. After a lot of persuasion, Democracy did get up and sit on the corner of the wooden bed and, when he had been sufficiently consoled to be able to talk sense, he appealed to Vaidyaji, saying, 'My clothes are in rags, and I'll soon be naked. I'm ashamed to face anyone in this state, therefore, oh, Vaidya Maharaj, give me a clean new dhoti to wear!'

Vaidyaji was about to ask Badri Wrestler to fetch a dhoti from inside the house when Democracy shook his head and said, 'I am the Democracy of your college and the annual meeting hasn't been held there for years. The election for the post of manager hasn't been held since the day the college opened. These days, everything in the college is flourishing—only I am left to rot in a corner. Please hold a proper election just once! That will give me new clothes for my body. My shame will be covered.'

Saying this, Democracy left the sitting room and Vaidyaji's sleep was interrupted a second time. As he woke up, he heard a fresh explosion from the internal revolution coming from under the quilt in the direction of the foot of the bed, and immediately decided that no matter how dull-witted Democracy looked, he was a good man and one of his own men, too, and that he should be helped. At the very least, he should be given new clothes so that he would be fit to sit in the company of gentlemen.

~

The next day, the Principal was instructed by Vaidyaji to call the annual meeting of the college and to hold elections for the post of the manager as well as those of the other office-bearers. The Principal tried hard to persuade Vaidyaji that it was neither necessary nor appropriate to hold fresh elections. But Vaidyaji told him to keep quiet as this was a matter of principle. Even then the Principal went on to point out that, so far, there had been no adverse criticism of the college in the newspapers, nor had there been any complaint made to the higher authorities, nor had anyone taken out a protest demonstration, nor gone on a hunger strike. Everyone was quiet. No one as much as mentioned the annual meeting; and the people who did, after all, who were they? The same Khanna Master, the same Ramadhin Bhikhmakhervi and a few of his hangers-on. It would not be wise, he argued, to be tricked by them into holding the annual meeting.

Vaidyaji listened to all he had to say and then replied, 'You are right. But this matter is beyond your understanding because it's a matter of principle. So go and prepare for the meeting.'

That very evening, Rangnath and Ruppan babu were dispatched to find out Gayadin's opinion on the election. As vice-president of the college committee, he was at that moment a rather important man, and it was essential to discover whom he wanted to see as the manager. And if he wasn't on Vaidyaji's side, it was also essential somehow or the other to bring about a change of heart. Ruppan babu and Rangnath went to him with the intention of opening preliminary discussions.

But from the very start, Gayadin made their task easy. He politely invited them to sit down on a charpoy, asked Rangnath a few questions about education in the town, fed them savoury cakes and laddus made with pure ghee, and as soon as the matter of the elections was mentioned, he stated clearly, 'Everything should be done after due consideration. You shouldn't get carried away by whichever wind happens to be blowing. There is no harm in holding an election for the manager's post, but Vaidya maharaj should remain the manager because the college belongs to Vaidya maharaj. How could anyone else become manager? This point should be well understood.'

He made it sound as if Rangnath and Ruppan babu were about to vote against Vaidyaji while he was the one running Vaidyaji's election campaign. Rangnath was amused. He said, 'You are one of the old school. You think out everything properly. But Ramadhin

Bhikhmakhervi and a few other people want to put someone else in uncle's place. I can't think of what's possessed them.'

Gayadin cleared his throat and said softly, 'They are inexperienced. They think if someone else becomes manager he will be able to achieve something, but nothing ever happens like that.' He paused, and then completed his point. 'The cobra is no different from the viper.'

Rangnath was none too happy with this comment as it cast aspersions on Vaidyaji's standing. He said, 'That's all very well but how can you compare uncle with these other people?'

'I have already told you how,' explained Gayadin. 'The college is Vaidya maharaj's and should stay in his hands. The village council is Ramadhin's and should stay with him. Everyone should be happy in their own place. There is nothing to be gained from this show of elections. If you choose a new man, he, too, will turn out to be fifth-rate. They are all the same. That is why I said choose the man who is already there. Let him stay where he is. What is the point of turning everything upside down?'

Ruppan babu was wondering whether or not to eat the last remaining laddu. As soon as he heard that Gayadin wanted to keep Vaidyaji as the manager he had lost interest in the conversation. He knew that from now on it would all be nonsense. But to Rangnath, Gayadin's views were rather novel. Here, he'd heard a new opinion of democracy—that, since the people who stand for election are generally fifth-rate, you had better not exchange the devil you know for one whom you don't. Designating this as the Gayadin Theory of Democracy, Rangnath listened to him go on to say, 'Even if a new man wants to achieve something, what can he do? You can achieve something only when other people let you. In these times, does anyone let anyone do anything? The only thing left nowadays is . . .'

~

The boys of the Changamal Vidyalaya Intermediate College were quite well acquainted with the sports world since, every month, their ears were twisted until they deposited their sports fees. It was quite another matter that there were no playing fields in the vicinity of the college. No one, however, minded this. In fact, all parties were content. Thanks to sports, the games master had so much free time that he could infiltrate both factions of masters and win their confidence.

The Principal, too, was saved a lot of bother. There were never any fights between hockey teams (because there were no hockey teams) and so, no problem of discipline ever arose in the college on that score. The boys' fathers were happy that the nuisance of sports could be put off just by paying the fees, and that the boys were saved from becoming real sportsmen. The boys were happy too. They knew that in the same time as it would take to run like a lunatic from one goal to another holding a stick and chasing after a ball the size of a clod of earth, they could swallow a whole pitcher of toddy, or, if their luck was in, win five or six rupees at cards.

But today, these same boys were clutching hockey sticks and cricket bats with as much arrogance as if they'd been rifles. About fifty of them were roaming around in front of the college gate.

Seeing them thus equipped, Rangnath asked, 'What's the matter? Is there also going to be a college inspection today?'

Chhote Wrestler prepared to answer—that is, he gathered his falling lungi around him before saying, 'With all this hullabaloo, who's going to hold an inspection? These are the preparations for the annual meeting.'

Chhote Wrestler was also a member of the college committee. The boys let out a whoop of joy at the sight of him. At the gate itself, the Principal sahib welcomed him saying, 'Please come in, Chhotelalji, we were just waiting for you.'

'After coming all the way here I'm hardly likely to go away again. Go on, after you,' said Chhote in a gentlemanly fashion. When a dog gets drenched in the rain it sneezes in a particular way. When the Principal laughed shyly he made the same sort of noise. He began to walk ahead, saying, 'Ramadhin's faction has put in a lot of effort. With the help of Lal sahib of Baijegaon they have managed to win over quite a few people. God knows why Lal sahib has got involved in this business. He lives in the town but he sticks his nose into everything that goes on in the village. Ramadhin's head is swollen. You can't tell how many men are on our side and how many on his.'

Chhote Wrestler gazed at the flower beds in front of the college building as the Principal continued, 'What can I say? The things Vaidyaji does sometimes. Where was the need for this election . . .?' Chhote recited a verse from a hymn popular at the time: 'What have I to do with the world? Sri Krishna alone is dear to me.'

Inside the gate, the Principal told Rangnath too, 'Please do come in, Rangnath babu, there's no restriction on you.'

He nodded to indicate that he would follow them, but he didn't go inside.

Slowly, the other members of the general committee arrived in several ways by various routes. A director of the cooperative came on foot, walking so fast and entering the building with such speed that people looked at each other in astonishment. A few minutes later, Contractor sahib could be seen coming from the opposite direction, trampling over the crops in the college fields. Halting where the labourers were at work, with dramatic gestures he seemed to lift something up to the sky and then throw it down again, before suddenly disappearing from view. A little later, Babu Gayadin came slowly up to the college gate and sat on the low wall of the small bridge which crossed the ditch running in front of it. He gazed unhappily at the sticks and bats in the boys' hands and then stared at a ball that a boy was holding tightly, as if to mesmerize it. From the gate, the Principal sahib said, 'Do come in, Member sahib. Everyone else has arrived.'

As if he had been arrested for dacoity and was being summoned to be identified by the witnesses, he replied dispiritedly, 'Let's go.' Walking with his legs splayed out like a penguin, slowly, inconspicuously, he entered the college building.

A little later, a horseman could be discerned riding up the road. He was wearing a brilliantly coloured turban, and it seemed as if he had just stepped out of the twelfth century. One boy said, 'Now, no one can touch a hair on Vaidyaji's head. Thakur Balram Singh has come!'

As soon as he dismounted, Balram Singh gave the reins of his horse to one of the boys. Without the horse, he began to look more like a man of the eighteenth century.

He rushed on to the bridge hastily, as if entering Agra Fort mounted on a camel to deliver news of a rebellion to a Mughal emperor, and asked one boy, 'There has been no fighting yet, has there?'

The boy replied, 'Fighting? We are all on the Principal's side and are followers of non-violence.'

Balram Singh stroked his moustache. Smiling, he remarked, 'You lads are no less rascals than anyone else. You're wandering around brandishing hockey sticks and pretending to be sons of Mahatma Gandhi at the same time.'

The boy said, 'Mahatma Gandhi, too, used to walk with a stick. We aren't armed. These are hockey sticks; we can't even hit the bloody ball with them, let alone a man.'

The Principal sahib came out again. 'Please do come in, Member sahib. A quorum has been reached. The meeting is about to start.'

Balram Singh wiped his forehead with the end of his turban. 'Tell one of your pupils to give my horse food and water. What have I got to do with the meeting inside? I've got my own quorum out here.'

The Principal nodded happily. Balram Singh grasped the pocket of his kurta and said, 'If you don't believe me, feel it. My pocket's full. This is the real quorum.'

The Principal sahib did not touch his pocket, but said, 'I don't need to feel it. Do you ever speak empty words?'

Balram Singh went on, 'It's a real foreign piece—a six-shooter—not one of those country pistols which blow up if you fire them once. If this starts firing, six members of Ramadhin's faction will roll over like hen-sparrows.'

'What words! What words!' exclaimed the Principal as if great poetry were dropping from Balram Singh's lips into his ears. As he walked away he said, 'I'm going to the meeting. Please take care of things outside.' Then, sounding like Mahatma Vidura trying to prevent the Mahabharat war, he appealed, 'Let the job be done in peace, with shanti.'

'It's all shanti here. I've got fifty shantis under my thigh.'

The Principal sahib left.

~

Balram Singh sat on the bridge. For a while he occupied himself with rolling tobacco-induced saliva around his mouth and spitting it out. Then he said to the boy who considered himself a bigger follower of non-violence than Mahatma Gandhi, 'Son, just go and take a round of the college compound and see if our men have blockaded the place properly or not. And tell that bastard Ramesera not to start any altercations. He's to send anyone who won't listen to reason round here to the gate.'

The boy went off to reconnoitre like a Boy Scout upon whose success rests his country's victory in war. The chatter among the boys who were strolling around increased. Balram Singh said, 'You can take a long walk, my sons, no need to worry about anything. As long as I'm here on the bridge, no enemy can come near.'

It was three o'clock. Trucks and bullock carts were passing along the road. Balram Singh sat cross-legged on the bridge and watched their comings and goings dreamily. Once his horse whinnied and he called out, 'Good boy, Chetak, be patient! You'll get your grain and water on time!' Chetak was patient and, to prove it, began to let forth a stream of urine. A circle of boys stood round the horse observing its reactions before and after urination, and joking intimately with one another.

Suddenly a truck drove up in front of the college. A man in a clean kurta–pyjama and cap, and armed with a cane, jumped down and walked briskly in the direction of the college. As soon as they saw the truck stop, the students came running towards the bridge from all directions. Balram Singh interrupted the man's progress with the words, 'Panditji, I touch your feet.'

The man mumbled something under his breath and headed towards the gate. Balram Singh said, 'Pandit, just slow down. No one's after you.'

The pandit gave an embarrassed laugh and replied, 'The meeting has started, hasn't it?'

Balram Singh stood up and went slowly across to the pandit. The boys encircling them closed in. Balram Singh rebuked them, 'Run away, boys; go and play somewhere else!'

Then, coming close to the pandit he said, 'Your presence in the meeting has already been registered. Now go back!'

The pandit attempted to speak, but pushing even closer to him, Balram Singh repeated, 'I'm saying this with reason. Go back!'

The pandit felt something hard pressing into his thigh. He glanced down at Balram Singh's kurta pocket and took two steps backwards in astonishment.

Bidding him farewell, Balram Singh said again, 'I touch your feet, panditji.'

The pandit returned in silence. There was no vehicle on the road. The truck had driven off. He went off hurriedly on foot. A boy said, 'Gone.'

Balram Singh remarked, 'The pandit is a very sensible man. He understood.'

'He may have understood, but why did he have to run away like that?' asked a student.

'You're still only a boy, son!' replied Balram Singh. 'On such occasions a man moves exactly like that.'

Another student had begun feeding his horse. It whinnied. This time, Balram Singh scolded it, 'Quiet, Chetak!'

The Boy Scout had returned. Without changing his tone, Balram Singh snapped, 'Well, what is it then? What news have you got?'

The scout grinned with fear like any average scared student and replied, 'Thakur sahib! Everything is all right.'

'How many men came on that side?'

'Five.'

'Did they all understand, or was any of them foolish?'

'They all understood.' By now the scout had recovered his courage. Gesturing towards the receding figure of the pandit, he said, 'Like him, they all turned tail and ran.' He laughed loudly.

Balram Singh said, 'This sort of thing would be the death of even a sensible man.'

~

There were joyous shouts in the college. One person raised the cry, 'Say, "Victory to Ram Chandra, spouse of Sita!"' When it comes to hailing someone's—or some god's—victory, can anyone beat the Indians? The shouts started with Ram Chandra, spouse of Sita, followed by 'Hail,

Hanuman, son of the wind!' Then, God knows why, they suddenly pounced on Mahatma Gandhi.

'Say, "Victory to the Mahatma!"' Then it was as if they had been given the green signal. There was one call for the victory of Jawaharlal Nehru, one each for the state leaders, one each for the district leaders and, finally, the real cry of triumph, 'Say, "Victory to Vaidya maharaj!"'

The Principal sahib walked out of the building squealing like a pig stuck with a dagger, and he too screamed, 'Say, "Victory to . . ."'

'Vaidya maharaj!' came the ready shouts of the younger generation outside the gate. It was like a mela. The Principal sahib began to explain to Rangnath, 'Well then, once again, Vaidya maharaj has been elected unanimously. You will see the progress the college will make now. *Dhakadhak, dhakadhak, dhakadhak!* It'll run like the Toofan Mail!' He was jubilant, and his face was turning red.

Chhote Wrestler said, 'Eh, Principal, don't be so hasty. Listen to what I have to say. You had better give those boys who are running around with sticks in their hands, a ball each as well, so that they can get in some target practice. There's not one of them who could hit a ball. They all just thrash the dust as if they were killing a snake.'

'Certainly, Member sahib, certainly. There will also be sports facilities. We have got over this problem, now . . .'

'That you have, but let me finish what I was saying. You say yes to everything, but on your own you couldn't even pull up a radish if you tried. I was talking about sports. The boys just hang around brandishing those hockey sticks. Today, if they'd needed to, they wouldn't have been able to do more than whirl them in the air. If they had tried to land them on anyone's back, they would have hit their own knees instead. When the time comes, their aim should be good.'

Vaidyaji said from behind, 'Sports are also important, Principal sahib! Chhote's words are not out of place.'

'Heh, heh,' said the Principal admiring the wrestler's body with a loving look. 'Is this man a wrestler, or isn't he? Could he ever say anything out of place?'

18

'It's a very old story. There was a nawab and he had a son. You people were talking about the judicial council. That's what reminded me of this story. It's good that Chhote challenged the sarpanch there and then. The justice of the village court is not for people of the likes of Chhotelal. He's a very important man. Such a great wrestler! A member of our college committee. That sort of justice is for peasants. "Kaurilla-brand" justice. Heh, heh, heh! Do you know what kaurilla is? It's a weed that grows on barren land. You must have seen it in the summer—it has white flowers. But then, you're from the town, where would you have seen it? Anyway, all these village judicial councils do kaurilla-brand justice. And that sarpanch? He spouts the same nonsense to everybody. But this time, he fell into the hands of Chhote Wrestler. That's what finished off the man. He got twice as much as he had bargained for.

'Right from the start, I told Kusahar Prasad not to go to the village court. But he wouldn't listen. Now he has realized that I was right. The sarpanch taking him to task straightened him out. He made peace with Chhotelalji on the spot . . . and that was right, too. How can you have a father and a son fighting?

'So . . . he had a son, the Nawab sahib. Yes, yes, I'm telling that story. One day, the poor prince fell ill. He had a fever which wouldn't get better. It went on for months. He was given all kinds of very expensive medicines. All the vaids, hakims and doctors were at their wits' ends. Crores of rupees were poured down the drain to try and cure him, but the prince was still in exactly the same condition.

'The nawab began to beat his head in despair. He had announcements made everywhere that whoever cured the prince could have half his kingdom and marry his daughter. Then hakims began to arrive from great distances. They tried their very best, but the prince didn't even open his eyes.

'Finally, an elderly hakim arrived. He examined the prince and said, "Refuge of the World, half the kingdom and your daughter's hand won't do for me. I have no need for such a life of luxury. If only one small request of mine is granted, the responsibility of curing the prince is mine. To submit my request, I need to talk to you alone."

'When all the courtiers had been sent away, the hakim said, "Protector of Men, I request that now your Begum sahiba should come speak to me, and that she should answer truthfully whatever I ask."

'The nawab too went out of the room. The queen presented herself before the hakim. The hakim looked at her sternly and said, "Look here, Begum sahiba, if your son's life is dear to you, tell me honestly who is the prince's father? From whose seed was he born?"

'The queen began to cry. She sobbed, "Please do not reveal this to anyone. But the truth is this that the prince is the son of one of the palace water carriers. The poor wretch had come fresh from the countryside, and I don't know how it happened but . . ."

'Hearing this, the hakim said, "Thank you! Now there's no need to say any more." He clicked his fingers and said confidently, "I'll restore the prince to health this instant."

'Then the hakim had all the medicines that had been prescribed for the prince thrown away. Each one was more expensive than the last: compounds made of diamonds and pearls, gold and silver. All kinds of rare essences. They all went down the drain. After that, the hakim sprinkled water on the prince's eyelids and said, "*Abeh*, get up, Spawn of a Water Carrier!"

'That was all. The prince opened his eyes with a start. After that, the hakim went into the fields and pulled some kaurilla plants, ground them in water and made the prince drink it. After three days of drinking the kaurilla, the prince was well.'

The Principal was relating this tale in Vaidyaji's sitting room. The main listener was Rangnath. The main subject was the village court, and the main inspiration for the storyteller was bhang. He continued, 'So, Rangnath Babu, that's what you call kaurilla-brand justice. That's the justice peasants understand. What else do these lowbred types need? They go off to the village court and come back with their kaurilla-brand justice.

'And for bigger men—aristocrats-varistocrats, officials-vofficials, well-bred people—there is expensive justice. No grass-cutting sarpanch but a judge who speaks English like the English and wears thick spectacles on his nose. So, for the important people, there are the big courts of the district. Whichever kind of court you require, you can find.

'For even bigger people, there are great, big high courts and, for the highest class of all, the Supreme Court. If anyone so much as casts an admonishing glance at them they go straight to Delhi to file a writ petition.

'If a kaurilla-brand, lowbred man once gets caught there, it's like him lying down never to get up again. He's left completely destitute.

'I ask you, has everybody got resources to go to the high court and the Supreme Court? You could maintain a hundred whores on what it costs to employ just one lawyer.

'That's why, for peasants, there's this arrangement of kaurilla-brand justice. They invest nothing and gain everything. They take just one dose of it, and their temperature goes down. Our legal system is very solid—a court to suit everyone.'

He suddenly descended into Awadhi, 'A harness t' suit the beast.'

~

Outside the village, there was a wide, open plain which was gradually becoming barren. Now, not even grass grew on it. It looked like ideal land to give away to Vinoba Bhave's Bhoodan Movement. And indeed it had been. Two years earlier, this land had been donated for the betterment of the landless as part of the Bhoodan Movement. Then it had been taken back as a gift by the village council. Then the village council had gifted it to the pradhan. The pradhan had gifted it first to his friends and relations and, on a straight cash-sale basis, disposed of the remaining part to some of the poor and landless. Afterwards it turned out that the plots which had been distributed to the poor and landless were not part of this land, but in fact, fell within the boundaries of someone's farm. Litigation started over this, it was still continuing, and was expected to continue for some time.

In one corner of this land, several forest-protection and tree-plantation schemes had been started. Whether they had been successful or not was a moot point. Looking at them, you could see that at least some trenches had been dug, and it was said that babul seeds had been sown in them. It was also said that if the ganjahas had not been ganjahas, and had been as industrious as the people in the neighbouring villages, there would have been a forest of babuls waving in the breeze on this barren land. But the babuls had just not sprouted from the trenches because of the poor quality of the soil, and the only thing Shivpalganj had gained from the entire programme was that the trenches were being used as public conveniences, meaning that the forestry scheme had been transformed into a household one.

On the opposite corner of the land, there was a banyan tree, which stood as if raping the whole wilderness. Next to it was a well, and on the wall of the well sat Rangnath.

Educated people in India occasionally become afflicted with a certain disease which is known as 'crisis of conscience'. And among them, this disease generally attacks those who consider themselves intellectuals. The day he witnessed the election for the post of college manager, Rangnath began to suspect that he had contracted this disease. Whenever he set eyes on Vaidyaji, he would suddenly recall the moment when the Principal sahib had come out of the college after the election squealing like a pig stuck with a dagger and hailing Vaidyaji's victory. It seemed to him that living with Vaidyaji had made him a member of a gang of dacoits. Whenever the Principal sahib was in front of him relating some interesting story—and he had no shortage of such tales—Rangnath would feel that he might at any moment pounce and grab someone by the throat.

If Rangnath had been in the town he would have sat in a coffee house with his friends and delivered a long speech on this election. He would have told them how the managership of the Changamal Vidyalaya Intermediate College had been won by the power of the gun and, thumping his fist on the table, he would have said that in a country where such things were done for minor posts, what would people stop at to secure the major ones? Having said all this, and spoken a few sentences in faulty English, he would have drained his coffee cup and felt satisfied that he was an intellectual; and that, having delivered a powerful speech in favour of democracy and unburdened his heart in front of four useless men, he had overcome a 'crisis of faith'.

But he wasn't in the town. He was in the country where, in the words of Ruppan babu, you couldn't trust your own father and where, in the words of Sanichar, no one would piss on your cut finger, let alone offer to bandage it.

And so, Rangnath could not overcome his affliction. Day by day, he became increasingly convinced that he had fallen among dacoits who, after raiding and looting the college, were now preparing to attack somewhere else. He longed to abuse Vaidyaji, and longed even more to find someone in front of whom he could freely abuse Vaidyaji.

Where could he find such a companion? Khanna Master was a gossip. If he said anything to him, the next day, it would go all round the village and everyone would start saying that Vaidyaji's own nephew was abusing him, and that it just went to show what sort of manners educated people had nowadays! He could talk to Malaviya Master but, although he belonged to a faction, he was a simple man and there would be no fun in telling him.

So who? Ruppan babu?

Rangnath had some confidence in Ruppan because he sometimes abused the Principal and spoke about the misfortunes of the college. Ruppan's complaint was that, academically, the Principal was an ignoramus, but that when it came to worldly wisdom, he was a master, a thorough operator. He had tricked Ruppan's own father into doing everything he wanted, while the latter imagined that he was doing everything according to his own wishes. Also, the Principal had, Ruppan argued, behaved very high-handedly with Khanna Master. Khanna Master might be a complete idiot, but still he shouldn't have treated him so unjustly, because it wasn't right that one idiot should misuse Vaidyaji's support to beat another idiot . . .

Under the banyan tree, sitting on the edge of the wall of the well, Rangnath breathed a deep sigh of relief because today, for the first time in a long time, his illness was not troubling him. As it happened, he had summoned up his courage and laid his crisis of conscience before Ruppan. He had told him frankly that his uncle should not have done what he did, and had asked him what the point was in winning the manager's post at gunpoint, if it meant that his name would be sullied throughout the whole area.

Ruppan babu replied in his own hard-hitting style, 'Look here, dada, this is politics. A lot of even worse things happen. This is nothing. You have to go even farther than this when you take the path that my father has. You have to finish your enemies by whichever means you can. If you can't, you'll be finished yourself and will be left sitting filling packets of digestive powder with no one giving a damn about you.

'But improvements are needed in the college. The Principal's a bastard. Day and night, he's busy playing the factionalism card. Khanna Master himself is the son of an ass, but he's not a bastard. This bastard, the Principal, has really kept him down; now, Khanna Master should come up. I have spoken to father about this too, but he doesn't want to uproot the Principal.

'I've decided that we shouldn't say anything more to father for some days, but just gently bring up Khanna Master. That will finish the Principal. The bastard has got so puffed up that he needs to have some air taken out of him. Once he's deflated, father will also see that he wasn't such a great operator.'

Rangnath sighed with relief because this much had become clear—he could now mention this subject to Ruppan babu. It was also clear that in Ruppan's presence he could show sympathy for Khanna Master, bring up the downtrodden, deflate the inflated and, in short, stand up against injustice, if not openly at least privately, and so regain his lost health.

~

To become pradhan, Sanichar needed to announce to the electorate, 'See here, brothers, I am as big an operator as the next man, so, don't go and refuse to vote for me because you think I'm honest.' He wanted to do something to show them the stuff of which he was made. He'd heard from Rangnath that all big political leaders visit their constituencies before elections, taking barrow-loads of money that they have somehow managed to collect, and wasting it in the name of the welfare of the people. Sanichar too wanted to perform a similar feat without consulting Vaidyaji. To do this, he chose as partner a ganjaha called Kalika Prasad.

Kalika Prasad's profession was spending government grants and loans. He lived on government money, for government money. He had three helpmates in this—the local MLA, khadi cotton clothes and a catchphrase, which he used whenever the time came to repay a loan: 'Please don't mention the repayment yet. I've already put in a request to the higher authorities so that you'll have no trouble in preventing action being taken against me.'

By Kalika Prasad's own calculation, he was the most modern man in the village because his occupation was entirely a product of modern times.

When a rule was passed providing grants for raising poultry, he announced he was going to become a poultry farmer. One day, he stated that caste was completely meaningless, and that Brahmins like him were no different from Chamars. This was because a grant for curing leather was about to be distributed. The Chamars were dumbfounded. He took the grant and spent it on making his own skin sleeker. Kalika Prasad had taken grants for making brick-lined fertilizer pits, for fitting a smokeless stove in his house and for installing a new design of lavatory.

He applied for loans under every government scheme; every official supported his applications; every time, he got the loan; and every time he didn't make the repayments, he took action to stop action being taken against him.

His knowledge was labyrinthine. By the time the Central Planning Committee worked out any new scheme, he had already found out everything about it. Despite his rustic manners, he was cleverer than the businessmen who manage to get hold of the details of new tax proposals before the budget is announced. Several times, he had reached the district offices with his application even before the funds had been sanctioned by the higher authorities, and had informed the officials about new schemes in the pipeline.

It was this Kalika Prasad whom Sanichar chose as his aide.

There was one part of the land previously described which had not been offered as a sacrifice to the Bhoodan Movement; it was mainly rough and uneven—the rest of it was barren, though it was shown as an orchard in the documents of the village record-keeper. Because of its multifaceted character, over the last few years, this land had been used in various ways. Every year, the village held its forest festival here, the aim of which was not to have a picnic, but to plant trees in fallow land. Occasionally, the Tehsildar sahib and, every year by compulsion, the Block Development Officer sahib came with great fanfare to plant saplings. By adopting this land as college property, the intermediate college had been able to start its classes in agricultural science. By declaring it their sports field, the young men of the village who had formed a youth association, called the Yuvak Mangal Dal, were able to draw a sports grant every year under its name. It was this piece of land which Sanichar made his field of action.

There was still a month left before the election for the pradhan's post. One day Chhote Wrestler said in Vaidyaji's sitting room, 'Sanichar has been going round the town for three days with Kalika Prasad. Today, I found out that the thing's been settled.'

Vaidyaji was sitting on his wooden bed. Hearing this, he was overcome with curiosity. But, speaking directly to Chhote Wrestler or expressing curiosity, both would have lowered his dignity. So he said to Rangnath, 'Have Sanichar called here.'

Chhote Wrestler stood up and yelled, 'SANICHAR, SANICHAR, OOOOH SANICHAR!'

This style of summoning people who were out of sight or reach was peculiar to Shivpalganj. To practise it, all you needed was a hardened throat, strong lungs and unadulterated rusticity. It was used with the understanding that wherever the sought-for person might happen to be, he would hear his name at least once. If he didn't, he would hear it if he were called a second time because, the second time, he would be called like this: 'WHERE HAVE YOU DROPPED DEAD, OOOOOOH SANICHARRRRRR, SANICHARRRRR!'

The moment he heard his name, Sanichar entered the sitting room as unceremoniously as he had been summoned by Chhote Wrestler. He was naked but for his underpants which were torn in some important places, but mustard oil was dripping from his head and he appeared joyous. It was difficult to tell which was bigger—his grin or the holes in his underpants. Seeing him thus proved the point that if we are happy not even poverty can make us unhappy, and the real way to remove poverty was to remain constantly happy.

Vaidyaji asked Sanichar, 'What news have you brought? I hear you showed yourself to be very capable in the town.'

Sanichar replied humbly, 'Yes, maharaj, I had to show myself as very capable. When capability was thrust from all sides, everything fell into place.'

This conversation was getting to be more than Rangnath could bear. He asked, '*Aji*, why are you talking in riddles? What happened?'

Sanichar drew in his breath through his teeth and said, 'Rangnath babu, these are ganjaha riddles. They won't come to you that quickly.'

But after this, he gabbled out his sentences one after the other like an All India Radio newsreader, relating the whole story without a pause.

'Guru maharaj, this man, Kalika Prasad, he is a real bastard.' Sanichar said this as if Kalika Prasad were being awarded the Padma Shri.

'*Arré*, Guru maharaj, what words can describe his operations! Heh, heh, heh! In the government offices, from the chapraasis up to the clerks and the clerks to the officials, he's got his contacts everywhere. He's a woodworm, a real woodworm. He'll worm his way through to the bottom of any case file you like. He's done Shivpalganj proud.

'But, guruji, I have something up there too. In fact, the truth is that the real brains were mine. So I found out that nowadays there's a great emphasis on cooperatives. One ADO came from the block office and said, "Don't just say your fields are yours, say everyone's fields are yours, and say your fields belong to everyone. Then you will have cooperative farming and your grain production will boom." I told him the idea was excellent and if I became pradhan I would give all the fields to the government for cooperative farms. The ADO said, "What will the government do with your land? Are fields some sort of machinery or factory that the government can run? The fields will remain yours. You will do the farming. Merely by filling the stomach of a small farm you become a cooperative. A cooperative farm will open in the village. Shivpalganj is already ahead in every way—now it will be ahead in this way, too."

'Guru maharaj, I thought that whether Shivpalganj is ahead or behind, I have to obey the orders of Guru maharaj. When I stood for the pradhan's post, I got to become pradhan. So I said to the ADO, "ADO sahib, what do you take Shivpalganj for? Our piss is as thick as anyone else's. We are ahead in every way, and will remain so." Then and there, I wheedled out of the ADO whether there was any money in it or not. He admitted there was.

'Then, guruji, I remembered Kalika Prasad. I prayed to Bajrangbali, Lord Hanuman, saying, "You've filled Kalika Prasad's bowl a hundred times, so, just for once, do some good for this monkey of yours, too. Why should money always only run in the direction of Kalika Prasad's house? Just once, please put it in my way, too."

'That was all. Then concentrating on Lord Hanuman, and tying a red loincloth around me, I went off to Kalika Prasad's house. On the spot, the two of us worked out such a scheme that the Block ADO, FDO—all of them—would get their cut. The ADO sahib slapped me on the back and told me that I was a ganjaha. We spoke about it only yesterday, and today the scheme is ready.

'Guruji, it's like this. Now, a cooperative farm will open in the village. There won't be another like it in the whole area. The farm will flourish on the barren ground over on the west. There's no harm in its being barren. The block-development-wallahs will look after the paperwork. In these matters, they make even the tehsil officials and the police look like amateurs. If you ask them, they'll set up a cooperative in heaven, and here we are, only asking for one on earth.

'We have gone to the town and fixed everything. I thought, Guru maharaj, that just as you had caught hold of a minister, last year, to come to the college, I could rope one in for this, too. But that can't be done without your touch. Kalika Prasad said that if you want to get the job done, what do you need a minister for? Get round an official.

'The rest of the job was done thanks to Kalika Prasad's efforts. He went round the whole town, sometimes spitting fire and other times as meek as a maggot. There I saw what a fine grasp he has of everything! "Officials are everything," he says, and he's right too. He got hold of one official who's very fond of wearing garlands and making speeches. Until his admirers have garlanded him ten times, he won't even clean his teeth in the morning. He sits there with an unwashed face. That was the official we caught.

'Now, guruji, we have put a lot of pressure on our heads. In just three days' time, there will be a meeting here to discuss the farm. You will have to take the lead. After all, the block-wallahs are there only to organize the band and music, garlands and tents, photo-shots, but there are also a lot of arrangements we will have to make. Pea curry cooked in butter will do for food. The official said that when among farmers he eats like a farmer. I knew very well that despite what he ate he'd never agree to come if we didn't feed him. We'll have to bring peas from the town. There are none here.'

When Sanichar began talking about the preparations for the meeting, Chhote Wrestler asked him sharply, 'Now stop all this pea-shee nonsense. Let's get to the point. How much did you get?'

Sanichar, turning altruistic, said carelessly, 'What am I going to get, wrestler? The society which is to be formed will receive five hundred rupees to set up the farm—that is the standard rate. Whatever money comes will go to the society.'

Chhote Wrestler roared with laughter. 'Well done, Mangal Das, my son! What an achievement! You started from nowhere and look where you have landed.'

Vaidyaji was listening happily. From his expression it seemed as if the future was bright. He related a story rather like an Aesop's Fable and, praising Sanichar, he said, 'When the tiger's cub went out on his first hunt, he killed a twelve-horn stag with his very first leap.'

19

January was nearly halfway through; after it would come February, when the village council elections were due; then March, when the high school and intermediate exams were scheduled to start. In the service of democracy, the elections had, on one side, Badri Wrestler and the men of his wrestling pit and, on the other, Ramadhin Bhikhmakhervi and his gambler-warriors. So far, the main form of service that both parties were rendering was screaming abuse about each other behind each other's back. It was hoped that, in February, they would start doing this face-to-face. As for the March examinations, they hadn't been able to catch anyone's interest yet. The students, the teachers and, especially, the Principal sahib, were still totally unconcerned.

But the Principal was involved in another matter. A few days after the annual general meeting of the college committee, when Vaidyaji had again been unanimously elected manager, some members had sent a letter of complaint about this to the education minister. They claimed that the members who were going to oppose Vaidyaji had been prevented from attending the meeting and had been threatened at gunpoint. In the complaint, this incident was described to such an impossible length that, even if you did manage to finish reading the letter, it was impossible to believe what it said, since it inferred that there was no law and order left in Shivpalganj; that things such as police and police stations did not exist there even in name; and that four hooligans could get together and do exactly as they wanted. There was clearly no need for an inquiry to determine that the complaint was untrue but still, some opposing members had gone to the town and given copies of the complaint to senior officials in the education department.

Then they had come back and started spreading the news around the whole area that an official called the deputy director of education was going to hold an inquiry. According to them, he was as meek as a cow but, this time, even Vaidyaji's father wouldn't be able to milk him as orders had come from high up that the inquiry should be impartial.

This was enough to engage the Principal's attention. He knew that Vaidyaji himself would take care of the inquiry, but he would have to look after the officials who came there on visits in connection with it. What would the officials look at when they came to the college? The Principal himself provided the answer—buildings!

So, now, he was determined to improve the appearance of the buildings.

In the town, he had noticed that if a little plant were surrounded by bricks on four sides and those bricks were painted red, yellow and white, for no reason, the untouched piece of land would begin to look like a park. He decided that a row of gulmohar and laburnum trees should be planted in front of the college building, and that colourful brick surrounds should be constructed for them before the officials' arrival. If, on their arrival, they were presented with a clean, smart and colourful building, and when they left, they had first-class tea and snacks in their stomachs, how could they write anything against him? The Principal sahib had made up his mind; disregarding the cold January weather and proceeding on the scientific assumption that all seasons are good for planting trees, he got to work.

The Principal was standing near the college walls getting some holes dug. In his hand was a thick and shiny book which looked very expensive. He was wearing his work clothes—that is, shorts and shoes without socks—and thought himself (no matter what others may think) to be very smart and clever. He was holding the book lovingly like a pet cat.

One labourer put down his mattock and asked the Principal, 'See, Master, you want the hole this deep, don't you?'

The Principal sahib shook his head and said, '*Hunh*! You call that a hole? If a bird shat in it once it would overflow. Keep digging, son, keep digging.'

He looked with pride at a master standing nearby. He had known this master for a very long time because he was his first cousin. The master looked around to see if the field was clear of enemies—that is, the other masters—and said fraternally, 'Brother, in this college you've become an expert even in gardening.'

The Principal pressed the book to his bosom and said, 'It's all thanks to this. But the bastard has written really difficult English. If a man of average understanding were to read it, it would make him dizzy.'

'You're a man of iron,' said the cousin. 'You do so much work in the college. Politics alone would make one's head spin in any case but, on top of that, you also manage to read books. Myself, I'd rather have someone beat me ten times with a shoe than ask me to read. I am sick of books.'

The Principal commented, half as an elder brother and half as a principal, 'Be quiet. You shouldn't say such things. You should keep your books with you even when you travel. If you don't, what would only wearing a jacket and trousers prove? It certainly wouldn't prove you're a teacher. Even greengrocers can wear jackets and trousers.'

The cousin replied, 'You are right. I'm not contradicting you. But is there really any difference between us and greengrocers? Those bloody textbooks with which we keep filling the boys' stomachs are just like rotten fruit. Some boys can digest them; others vomit them up.'

The Principal began to laugh. 'You've stretched the point a bit. All this would be the death of a sensible man.'

He began to peep down into a hole as if it was just where he would bury the sensible man when he died.

At that moment, Khanna Master came hurrying along and, handing a sheet of paper to the Principal, said, 'Please take this.'

The Principal looked to his cousin for support. Then, standing next to the hole, he suddenly stiffened and said officiously, 'What is this?'

'What is it? It's a sheet of paper.'

The Principal, his chest stuck out, gave Khanna Master a penetrating stare.

The Principal's cousin was standing with his eyes fixed on Khanna's face, like an Alsatian, from inside his master's bungalow, watching a pariah dog on the street. The Principal turned his gaze on the paper. If he had been one of the rishis of ancient times, the paper would have burnt to ashes. Then he handed it back to Khanna Master.

Irritated, Khanna asked, 'What's this?'

'What is it? It's a sheet of paper,' said the Principal walking over to inspect another hole.

Khanna Master bit his lip. Containing himself, he said, 'Whatever happens, you have to give a written order in reply to a written request.'

The Principal had begun talking to a labourer. He was saying, 'All right, all right, stop digging now. *Abeh*, you're digging a hole, not a well. That's enough.'

Khanna Master stood mute for a while. Then he said, 'I have to go out of Shivpalganj for four days. I want leave. I have written to you and you have to give a reply.'

The Principal suddenly squatted on the earth dug out of the hole to prove to onlookers that he wouldn't hesitate to roll in the gutter for the well-being of the college, and began to issue detailed instructions to the labourers about the ridges of earth around the holes.

Khanna's voice now rose to become more than just background music. He, too, squatted down on the edge of the hole opposite the

Principal, and said, 'Answer my question first, please, and then go and jump down the hole.'

The Principal finally looked him straight in the eye. 'I will certainly jump into the hole but only after I've pushed you down first and can jump on top of you. Do you understand, Khanna Master?' He turned towards his cousin. The cousin immediately said in a humble and subservient tone, 'I will go and call the chapraasis. It seems there may be a fight. But, Principal sahib, I appeal to you not to say anything until help comes.'

'What can I say, brother? I go on suffering everything in silence. The day this man's pitcher is full, it will break all of its own accord.'

It was as if the Principal were laying a curse on Khanna Master with these words. Khanna began to panic. He was afraid that the Principal might go and start screaming that he was beating him. He might get embroiled in a court case. He quietly rose from the edge of the hole and went to stand some way off next to another master. From there, he said loudly enough for the whole world to hear: 'Don't threaten me, Principal sahib, the days of the nawabs are over. You can't finish me off that easily. I'm warning you, if you lay a hand on me, blood will flow. I'm telling you! Yes!'

Khanna Master hadn't wanted to shout but, while thinking about someone else making a scene, he himself had made one. Some masters came and gathered around him.

Suddenly, he screamed again, 'Well hit me! Why don't you hit me then? Call the chapraasis. Disgrace me by making them beat me. Why have you stopped?'

Gathering correctly that some sort of spectacle was going on, masters from both factions arrived on the scene. The boys had still not come out in any great numbers. The ones who had turned up had been scolded and sent off by the chapraasi. They stood on the veranda of the college watching the action. On the spot, it was an 'adults only' show.

The Principal was at first badly upset by this uncontrolled display but then reined in his anger and went up to Khanna Master. He pulled the leave request from his hand and said coolly, 'Don't scream, Master sahib! You are mistaken. Here, I'll write an instruction on your application.'

At his signal, his cousin handed him a fountain pen. Resting the request letter on his gardening book he began to write. As he wrote, he said, 'We people disagree on principles. Where does the question of fisticuffs arise? Things should be settled peacefully.'

Khanna Master was getting fed up with his own performance. He said, 'First, write an order on this paper and then we'll talk about other things.'

'That's what I'm doing,' replied the Principal, smiling. 'There!' He had crossed out several words, and drawn circles over others. At the bottom he had written in English—'Refused'.

Before Khanna Master could say anything, the Principal pushed the application into his hands with the words, 'Your spelling is very weak. You have spelt holiday with a "y" after the "l". I don't know whether Khanna has been spelt with a capital letter or a small one. You should pay attention to all these things.'

Khanna was stunned for a while. Then, opening his mouth like a rhinoceros, he gave an ear-splitting cry, 'Come out of the college right now. Then I'll show you how to spell!'

The battle had begun.

This happened in the morning. By lunchtime, both sides had filed reports at the police station. From the reports it was clear that the teachers had rioted and attempted to kill one another. Seeing that there had been no one there to stop them from killing each other, it was not clear why, in fact, they had not done so. Picking on this point, the police began their investigation absolutely the wrong way around.

The same day, at lunchtime, in Vaidyaji's sitting room, there was an exchange of views on the incident. The main reaction of the common citizens was that the incident should have been rather more serious. That is to say, there was no harm in anyone from their side not having his bones broken, but at least someone should have been hurt sufficiently for some blood to flow. Sanichar, thinking that he might achieve one more feat of political leadership before becoming pradhan, offered his services free of charge and said that nothing was lost, and if the Principal liked, he could stab him in the hand with a spear, and that the Principal could add that injury to the charges against Khanna Master. Chhote Wrestler snarled at him to shut up.

Rangnath and Ruppan babu listened in silence to all that was said which, in Shivpalganj, is considered a sign of being an idiot, but, in fact, they were burning inside with anger against the Principal. After some considerable time, Ruppan walked out and said, 'Now this bastard Principal is leading my father to court, and then he'll not leave him till he's had him sent to jail.'

During lunchtime, Vaidyaji listened gravely to the story about Khanna Master as told by the Principal and, after hearing the whole tale, made a comment which had no connection with the day's incident. His comment was very righteous and expressed the kind of sentiment which could make a sick man well.

He said, 'I was astounded to see the faith of the district inspector of schools. I saw a man lying prostrate before Lord Hanuman's temple. When he got up, I was left speechless. It was the honourable inspector. A hundred tears of devotion were dripping from his eyes. I greeted him and, in reply, he closed his eyes, and emitted a sort of "haun, haun" sound.

'Half a dozen seers of the best ghee should be taken to him. Such a religious man is ruining his religion by eating low-grade vegetable oil every day.

'The games that Fate plays!'

~

An ancient Sanskrit verse explains a point of geography—that the sun doesn't rise depending on where the east is, rather where the east is depends on where the sun rises. In the same way, senior officials do not go on tour depending on their work but, whenever they go anywhere, it automatically becomes an official tour.

In accordance with this novel solar principle, that same day, at about four o'clock in the afternoon, a great man came speeding in a motor car, from the town into the country. Casting glances over the fields on either side of the road, he congratulated himself that, thanks to the speeches he had made last year, the winter crop this year was going to be good. The farmers were cultivating the land according to his instructions. They had realized that land should be ploughed, and that not only fertilizer but seeds, too, should be put into it. They had begun to understand all they were told, and they had lost their apprehensions about new ideas. The farmers were becoming progressive and, in short, the only backward thing about them was that they were still farmers.

The car passed in front of the Changamal Vidyalaya Intermediate College. Several boys were sitting on the bridge in front of it wearing underpants and bush shirts, or striped pyjama trousers and kurtas with no vests underneath, and making noises like partridge calls. From the boys' absurd dress, it took the great man just a fraction of a second to recognize that they were students.

The car had gone on about a furlong more when it suddenly occurred to the great man that he hadn't delivered a speech to young men for the past forty-eight hours. All at once he recalled the sufferings he had undergone for the country's youth. For their sake he had left his home in the village and taken a bungalow in the town. He had forsaken his place on the banks of the village pond and had become used to sitting cooped up in a small toilet. How much he had changed himself! As soon as it occurred to him that he hadn't spoken to those dear youths for forty-eight hours, he began to think, 'Hai! I haven't given a lecture for so long! I had so many elevated thoughts, and I have selfishly kept them to myself. Hai! I am so mean! May I be cursed for keeping my mouth shut for so long, despite being born in India.'

'Forty-eight hours!' he thought in astonishment. 'Two thousand eight hundred and eighty minutes, and if you multiply that by sixty, that many seconds! So many seconds! And in all this time I have not given one speech to encourage the youth! What can have happened to me? Have I died of paralysis?'

He thought all this in as little time as it took to blink, and then ordered his driver, 'Turn the car around. I'm going to give the college a surprise inspection.'

As soon as he entered the college, a holiday was declared. Boys began to pour out of the classrooms and sit down in the field outside. Local officials, men who gambled for cowries in the mango groves, layabouts from the country liquor shop, all assembled in an instant. There was a fair crowd. But if there hadn't been, there would still have been a meeting. If a speaker is sufficiently shameless, a lamp post is enough of an audience for him. He'll hold a meeting on his own. But here, there was a real meeting. The obvious advantage in having so many boys was that if you put them indoors they would become a college, and if you put them outdoors they would become a meeting.

The great man told the boys that they were the nation's future, and the teachers, that they were the builders of the nation's future. Both the boys and the masters already knew this. Then he upbraided the masters for not teaching self-restraint. He complained that the boys knew nothing about the national flag, the national anthem and so on, and that, even though the masters did know these things, they still demanded allowances and salary increases. The masters and the boys hadn't had the time to consider their faults before he launched into the one subject about which every person giving a speech in an educational institution speaks.

He said that our education system was bad and that those who went through it only aspired to be clerks. He suggested to the boys that there was a need for a fundamental reform in the education system. He referred to the hundreds of scholars and thousands of committees which had established that our education system was bad.

He quoted Vinoba on the subject, and even Gandhi. Vaidyaji, the college manager, nodded his head to say that our education system was indeed bad. This was then supported by the Principal, the teachers and the louts and layabouts of the bazaar. His speech fully succeeded in assuring even the toddy drinkers and gamblers.

The great man then went on to tell them a number of things which they could equally well have told him—that they should farm their fields, drink milk, look after their health and keep themselves prepared to be the next Nehrus and Gandhis. Then he spoke the mandatory sentence about harmony, unity and love for the national language, made his annual promise to consider the college problems and, after eating the dried fruits and nuts and drinking the tea which were served to him immediately after he had served the students, he set off again at seventy miles an hour.

The boys and the masters wended their way home imitating the way he'd kept saying, 'Brothers and Sisters'.

The gardener, the chapraasi and the labourers were left in the college to take action on the proposal to fundamentally change the education system.

The college clerk looked at the plate of dried fruit and at first thought of eating the leftover cashew nuts, but then, after some consideration, threw them into the gutter.

20

Badri Wrestler had gone to bail out a young man from a neighbouring district who was facing charges of rape and assault. Before he left, he remarked to Rangnath, 'He's a thug. Wherever he goes, he lands himself in some trouble or the other.'

He had taken one thousand five hundred rupees from Vaidyaji and stuffed them into the inside pocket of his Nehru jacket. Rangnath asked him why he needed to take so much cash.

Badri replied, 'Thugs don't only come under the law, they also run the courts. The magistrates announce bail after a little hesitation and then hand over the paperwork to the clerks. That's where dozens of problems arise. Make out the bail papers. Show a plan of the property you are offering as surety. Then a rough estimate of its value, then the confirmed value, and all along you have to keep on shelling out the rupees.

'Dealing in hard cash is much easier. As soon as the magistrate says he'll put him on a thousand-rupee bail, I'll throw down ten bank notes on the table and say, "Take it and put it where you like!"'

Rangnath took the conversation further by asking, 'Brother Badri, if he's a thug why do you help him? Let the bastard rot in the lock-up.'

'Tell me who isn't a thug, Rangnath babu? After all, thugs don't have horns and a tail,' said Badri slowly. 'I know this much—he was a student in my wrestling pit. However big a thug he may be in the eyes of the world, I still remember him hitting the ground whenever I used to fell him with a leg trick.'

~

As Badri was out of the village, Rangnath was alone on the roof. The cold weather was at its peak and to enjoy it fully, Badri had moved his charpoy out of the room and on to the veranda. Rangnath continued to sleep in the room.

It was about eleven o'clock at night. He couldn't sleep.

Darkness! The winter night revealed itself in all its grandeur. At such times, even if a man doesn't believe in God he begins to believe in ghosts. Rangnath didn't suddenly feel scared, but he did feel a 'strange sensation' which, if the truth were told, is another name for fear. But fear in all its sharpness could not overcome him because, at that moment, he began to think about Ruppan babu; and the moment he began to think about Ruppan, he remembered a girl called Bela whom he had never seen but to whom, so he had heard, Ruppan babu had written a love letter.

Rangnath didn't know the contents of the love letter but, according to the rumours floating around, it seemed that it was made up of phrases from Hindi film songs, joined together in sentences. It was well known that Bela's aunt had first found the letter lying in a corner of Gayadin's house. Later, she read it out to Gayadin. For the first two or three sentences, he wasn't able to understand what it was about, but then his sister read, 'Embrace me, come, my fellow wayfarer!' As he studied this sentence, the doors of comprehension burst open, and he understood that this invitation was directed to Bela. By the time he came to the end of the last line, the truth about the document became crystal clear. It ended with, 'After reading my love letter, please do not be angry, but you are my life, I worship you.' The writer had signed himself 'Mr R'.

Rangnath had heard that other than Gayadin, only the Principal sahib had been given the opportunity to see the letter and that was, perhaps, because Gayadin somehow linked him with Ruppan's moral decline and fall.

The Principal had tried to explain to him that it was not a love letter but a compilation of poems of considerable quality and that its literary significance was not diminished by its being signed by a 'Mr R'. But despite this attempt to set his mind at rest, Gayadin still believed that these writings were proof of immoral conduct, and when the Principal quoted lines from several poems to explain that this sort of sentiment abounds in literature, Gayadin replied that the Principal's idea of literature only served to prove his own immoral conduct. In the end, both of them agreed that nothing more should be said about the letter.

The very next day, several rumours spread in Shivpalganj. One was that a boy from Khanna Master's faction had written a love letter to Bela and had falsely signed Ruppan's name to it. The second was that Bela had written Ruppan a love letter, and Ruppan had replied to it but that his letter had fallen into Gayadin's hands, and he had been thoroughly disgraced. The third rumour—and the most widely circulated—was that Bela was a girl of low morals.

It was the wonderful effect of the third rumour that now stopped Rangnath from feeling scared and made him start thinking about Bela. Since the day when he had talked to Ruppan about the love letter, he had not had sufficient courage to raise the subject again. Now, in solitude, he had only his imagination, his frustration and masturbation to satisfy his curiosity about Bela and since, to a large extent, these are the forces which inspire Indian art, Rangnath was for these few minutes living his life as an artist.

What must she be like? Like Vyjayanthimala in *Madhumati*? Shubha Khote in *Godan*? Waheeda Rehman in *Abhijan*? All these actresses had become old—like Mother India—but Bela must still be fresh. What could she be like? He didn't know more than that, but whatever she was like, she must be 'by God, without compare'. This fragment from a Hindi film song stuck in Rangnath's throat like a bone, but he smiled. In that darkness, he smiled a beautiful, one-and-a-half-inch smile.

He thought a lot about Bela. So much so, in fact, that hundreds of breasts and buttocks of all different shapes and sizes began to rise and fall in his mind. They came in pairs, swelled in bunches and ran away jostling each other. Rangnath really wanted to create a picture of one whole girl but he couldn't.

His imagination did grasp the body of a whole woman once, but that wasn't any good because her face was missing. After a while, only a few circles of disconnected breasts were left in his mind. Finally, he tensed once, relaxed his body and dozed off underneath the quilt.

~

The next night when Rangnath was lying in bed in the room on the roof, he did not think of Bela. He was recalling Vaidyaji's manly face flushed with rage.

That day, the cooperative farm which had been created through the efforts of Sanichar and Kalika Prasad had been inaugurated. Vaidyaji had mentioned the embezzlement in his cooperative union to the official who had come for the inauguration, and had referred to the suggestion that the government should be asked to give a sum equal to the embezzled sum, to the cooperative union in the form of a grant. Vaidyaji had explained to the official in a reasonable tone that if the government did not give the grant, it could only be concluded that government officials did not want the cooperative movement to progress.

The official must have definitely read Dale Carnegie's books, and that was why he replied to each point that Vaidyaji made with, 'What you say is right, but . . .' He repeated this sentence seven times. When he opened his mouth to speak for the eighth time, it was not to say the melodious words, 'You will get the grant', but the same old, 'What you say is right, but . . .'

As soon as he heard this, Vaidyaji fell on the official with the ire of the sage Durvasa, the tyranny of Hitler and the storminess of Nehru, combined.

'This is the way you people are going to uplift the country? What are all these ifs and buts and howevers? What are they? Sir, this is the language of eunuchs! This is the way idle individuals bring themselves and their country down! Your decision should be clear! But! If! *Thoo!*' He spat.

After this, Vaidyaji delivered a speech on the miserable state of the country, and after that, he began to grumble. The official, too, despite his humility, grumbled. Then other people began to grumble as well. Sanichar's meeting was already over and this grumbling did not affect its success. But in the end, the grumbling came out on top.

Rangnath lay on his charpoy. He had heard this sort of grumbling everywhere in the town, all the time. He knew that his country was a country of grumblers. In offices and shops, factories and workshops, parks and restaurants, newspapers, fiction and non-fiction, everywhere, people were grumbling. This was the mentality of the age and he was very familiar with it. Here in the village, too, he heard the same grumbling. The farmers grumbled against government officials and clerks. The officials distanced themselves from the general public and complained about them. Then, in the next breath, they distanced themselves from the government and complained about it. Practically everybody had some trouble or the other and no one went to the root of the matter. They grabbed hold of whichever reason came immediately to hand and grumbled about it.

Vaidyaji's speciality was that he did not grumble. Today, by doing so, he had shattered Rangnath's illusions. Rangnath had hoped that he would thunder and then roar, but he thundered and sat down to grumble and that too when the official, wagging his tail and grumbling at the same time, had indicated that it would be necessary to hold a special audit of the cooperative union's accounts.

'This is not a nation of thunderers but of grumblers,' thought Rangnath.

Breaking the stillness of the night, a coarse shout fell on Rangnath's ears like a slap. Kusahar Prasad was sitting in his doorway, cursing someone. The wise old leader of the grumblers. As he wasn't crying, it was obvious that his curses were not meant for Chhote Wrestler but for someone else. It was difficult to tell who because, when Kusahar was swearing at somebody else, his curses had no particular meaning but were simply instinctive—just like a peacock dancing in the jungle or a leader making a speech at an inaugural function.

~

In an atmosphere of faint voices and darkness, at some point, Rangnath drifted off to sleep. While he slept, he dreamed that he was standing in a lift and was going down several floors. Suddenly the lift shot up, passing three or four floors together. Rangnath stirred.

The scent of coconut oil and some cheap perfume filled his nostrils. It was neither a pleasant nor an unpleasant smell; it was just a smell. The tinkling of glass bangles jolted his slumber, and he suddenly felt something which a lifetime's study of the erotic sculpture at Khajuraho and Konark could never give him.

She was sitting on the edge of his charpoy. One of her arms was flung across his body and on his chest he felt the intense pressure of two breasts. Between his chest and the breasts, besides the clothes covering them, there was also a thick quilt. But the warmth and firmness of the breasts could not be disguised.

Rangnath's breath stopped.

The quilt had been pulled from his face, but in the darkness they could not see one another. The warmth and explosive pressure on his chest seemed to increase. Then a silky smooth cheek pressed against his, and with a deep, long, drawn-out sob a voice said, '*Hai!* Have you gone to sleep?'

Rangnath was suddenly fully awake. He shook his head and said unnaturally, 'Who? Who's there?'

For a moment, the heartbeat in the two breasts pressing into him seemed to stop. Then suddenly, the girl leapt up from the charpoy and, standing some way off, said in a subdued voice, 'Oh, mother!'

Respect for one's mother is a fine thing but, at this time, these words only indicated her agitation. Rangnath flung off the quilt and leapt to his feet but by then she had climbed from the roof on to another roof and from that roof on to yet another one.

Rangnath came out of the open door and stood on the veranda roof. It was chilly. He listened carefully for a while but heard nothing more than the sighing of the wind. After the pure-hearted enunciation of her mother's name the visitor had no more messages for him.

When he had locked the door from inside and lain down again on his charpoy, he realized several things. Firstly, that if the swelling female statues of Konark, Bhubaneshwar and Khajuraho were to come to life, they would be enough to drive a man crazy. Secondly, that everything which he had learnt about archaeology and Indian art was incomplete and foolish, and that it was more of an achievement to win the support of two live breasts posing like ancient goddesses than to get a doctorate in Indian art.

Pushing these lighter thoughts aside, he came to the real thought which was churning him up inside. He told himself, 'Young man, you are an idiot. Why did you have to say anything? Why did you get nervous? Why didn't you give her the chance to do something more?

'Young man, you are not an idiot, you're an ass. You've added another line to the list of your life's missed opportunities, haven't you? You're just another of those Indian students who are never fated to enjoy a real woman.'

He tried to go back to sleep, but how could he? His hand moved towards his breast of its own volition and he accepted regretfully that there was nothing more there than his own rough chest.

Who was she? He couldn't think too much about this because the path of his thought was blocked by two mountains.

21

The next morning, news spread round the village that the police had arrested Jognath. Like every arrest, this one, too, took place in dramatic circumstances. At 4.30 a.m., the police surrounded his house. They all knew perfectly well that it would never come to an exchange of fire and so every constable was armed.

Tight security arrangements were enforced. The constables all sat like statues for a full half-hour without spitting tobacco or smoking beedis. No one laughed or tried to make anyone else laugh. One constable took off his shoes and tiptoed like a thief from one man to another, whispering, 'Keep calm. There's no danger,' as if it were a great strength-inspiring charm. The Sub-Inspector with his pistol, and the head constable with his rifle, stood at Jognath's door.

A man came down the lane. He saw them and was about to turn back when the head constable beckoned to him. He came forward confidently. The head constable said in his ear, 'Trying to run away?'

'Run away?' the man replied unhesitatingly. 'I just want to avoid having to see you first thing in the morning.'

The Sub-Inspector put a finger to his lips and made a shushing sound. The head constable said softly into the man's ear, 'Sit down on the veranda. We'll need you as a witness.'

The man replied, 'So why do you need me to sit down? Just call me whenever you need me—tomorrow, the next day, the day after—and I'll stand witness. You can always count on me.'

He tried to slip away. The head constable whispered, 'Then it's all right; go, but be careful; don't let anyone know about our presence here.'

Poking his nose into the head constable's ear, the man replied in a similarly hushed tone, 'Who is there to tell? The whole village knows.'

He left. The men posted at the back of the house began to long for their tobacco and beedis. By then, dawn was breaking and they were able to make out each other's faces even from a distance.

Suddenly there was a creaking noise. Perhaps the front door had been opened. They heard a hasty conversation, and they realized that the time had come to enter the field of duty and action. They fixed bayonets and stood up.

The conversation coming from the direction of the front door was growing louder and moving away quickly. The constables became uneasy, and they coughed, at the same time expelling air from every orifice. Shortly afterwards, a policeman's whistle sounded the warning signal and they all ran round to the front door. From there, they ran about fifty yards to a spot next to a mango grove. The moment they arrived there, matters took a dramatic turn.

They saw Jognath sitting on the ground and the Sub-Inspector standing with a pistol pointing at his chest. On the other side, the head constable stood threatening Jognath with a bayonet. It was a very theatrical scene and the curtain was not about to fall. The constables immediately surrounded the players and pointed their weapons at the parts of Jognath's body not covered by the pistol and the bayonet.

A short distance from Jognath, there was a lota lying on the ground, water spilled around it. The Sub-Inspector told a constable, 'Seize that pot. It can be used as evidence.'

The constable picked up the pot, inspected it closely and said in admiration, 'It's a real Moradabadi one.' After a few moments' consideration, he said, 'Should I seal it, sir?'

'That will be done, but later.'

The constable thought again and, pointing to the water-soaked earth, asked, 'Should I also seize some soil?'

The head constable reprimanded him sharply, 'Don't try to be clever. Just do what you're told.'

The Sub-Inspector made Jognath get to his feet and had him searched. Then the bayonets were unfixed and the pistol put back into its leather holster. The constables began to chat amongst themselves.

One said, 'He must have been going out for his morning shit.' Another suggested, 'Who knows, maybe there is a gang hiding around here and he was going to give them food and water!' A third said, 'Now Vaidyaji is going to kick up a fuss,' and a fourth remarked quietly that Vaidyaji had the Sub-Inspector in his pocket and that the arrest had been made on the order of the senior superintendent of police. A fifth said, 'Quiet! Quiet! Just look at what's going on!'

Jognath was in the same place posing like a folk dancer, but from his face it was clear that he was not about to dance. Suddenly the Sub-Inspector slapped him hard on the cheek and asked, 'Where were you off to with that lota?'

Jognath rubbed his eyes to reduce the effect of the blow, looked the Sub-Inspector straight in the eye and said, 'You can cut me up into pieces but even then I won't say anything unless my lawyer tells me to.'

The Sub-Inspector ordered the head constable to handcuff him and take him away as they now had to search his house.

'We have to give him a going-over, too,' said the head constable.

~

If anyone were to ask the Sub-Inspector to describe the whole incident he would have said:

'Some days ago, some thieves came to the village. With the help of the village protection committee, the police tried to apprehend them. But, as generally happens on such occasions, the thieves used extreme cunning to disappear into the darkness, leaving behind a member of the gang who was a local man. Due to the vigilance of the police and the village protection committee, even though they were not apprehended, their criminal intentions were foiled. But the local member of the gang, while the entry of the thieves was causing a commotion, took unfair advantage of the villagers' panic and entered Gayadin's house with the intention of committing a theft. Due to the shouts of alarm raised by the village protection committee, the residents of Gayadin's house awoke, and they saw a man climbing a ladder on to the roof. That instant, the police arrived like the wind, but by that time the man had disappeared. At the scene of the crime, Gayadin handed a list to the police, saying it was a list of the jewellery which had just been stolen. Having examined the scene of the crime, the police returned and for approximately fifteen days made detailed and thorough inquiries.

'From those inquiries, the police reached the conclusion that Gayadin's house had been burgled that night. Not only that but that the man who was discovered hastily climbing from a ladder up on to the roof could be said with certainty to have been the thief himself.

'After this, the police discovered through an informer that, at the house of Jognath, son of Ramnath, resident of Village Shivpalganj, there were several ornaments which might belong to Gayadin. After the investigations were complete, this morning at dawn, a raid was made on his house. At that time, Jognath was going out somewhere with a lota. In front of the police, he confessed his crime and he himself permitted the police to search his house in his presence. The search, as required by law, was carried out in the presence of a respectable citizen of the locality. It's also necessary to say that in this village you can't find men easily, and if you do find one, it's very difficult to believe he's respectable. Anyway, this search was carried out in the presence of Chhote Wrestler, son of Kusahar Prasad, and Baijnath, son of Triveni Sahai. Baijnath is not a resident of this village. This respectable man was called from a neighbouring village.

'A hole was excavated in a room at a spot indicated by Jognath. From it, a pot was taken out, and from the pot were recovered four ornaments—one girdle of silver wire, value about fifty rupees; one pair of toe rings, value about three rupees; one necklace of silver coins, value about twenty-five rupees; and one gold nose pin, value about thirty rupees. A list of the recovered items was prepared and signed by the witnesses. The items and the pot were tied in a cloth and sealed. This action was carried out at the scene—that is, within the house.

'Jognath resisted arrest. In the course of apprehending him, the head constable's shirt was torn and he sustained an injury to his arm. The minimum necessary force was exercised to control Jognath. Afterwards, both Jognath and the injured constable were presented for a medical examination. The constable went home after taking permission for two weeks' sick leave, and Jognath was found to have twenty contusions and forty abrasions. They were all minor injuries—the result of falling on the ground.'

~

That day, for the first time, Vaidyaji doubted the eternal wisdom of the belief that whatever the police do is right.

Vaidyaji did not have a very good opinion of Jognath, but he lived in a world where a man was respected, not for his goodness but for his usefulness. Among his men, Jognath was the only heavy drinker, and whether it was him or someone else paying made no difference to the quantity of liquor he drank. Altogether, he was an average-class thug.

Vaidyaji suspected that there may be some politics behind his arrest. For some days, he had seen that the Sub-Inspector was behaving deferentially not only to himself but also to Ramadhin Bhikhmakhervi. At first he thought that Ramadhin had made him a partner in the illegal opium business, but now it seemed as if the Sub-Inspector was suffering from the illusion that, in the political game, Ramadhin Bhikhmakhervi could prove comparatively more useful than Vaidyaji. In any case, Vaidyaji felt that, in the present circumstances, if Jognath was arrested, then, to start with, things would go as the Sub-Inspector wanted, and what the Sub-Inspector wanted was what Ramadhin wanted.

Ruppan babu insisted that Jognath should be bailed out. So, against his better judgement, Vaidyaji prepared himself to speak to the Sub-Inspector.

The Sub-Inspector was no longer the vigilant officer of the morning whose very glance could cause blue bruises and scratches to form on a man's body. Now, his healthy figure was shown off to advantage by a silk kurta and a pair of khadi pyjamas. Betel juice was oozing from the corners of his mouth. Vaidyaji had heard the account of the whole incident from the Sub-Inspector's lips and was only surprised by the fact that the police had not recovered so much as a country pistol from Jognath's house. Having spent so many years in close association with the police, he had learnt that on such occasions a crudely shaped piece of iron—which was taken to be a pistol—was always found. Its crudeness immediately attested to the main reason for the defeat of the Indians by the British in the eighteenth and nineteenth centuries—an incontestable historical fact.

He felt it necessary to thank the Sub-Inspector for his courtesy.

To start the conversation, he asked, 'Only ornaments were recovered from Jognath's house? No hashish, bhang or opium?'

'I didn't search for opium. If I had, people would have said that the previous time I had caught one of the other party for opium dealing, so now this time I was catching one from this party.'

'Party?' asked Vaidyaji in surprise. 'What sort of party? What sort of language are you speaking?'

'Police language,' answered Ruppan babu.

The Sub-Inspector rubbed his eyes and tried to clear his head. He told himself that gin was the most deceptive of foreign liquors. It looked just like water but when it got into the stomach, it began to make your tongue turn the wrong way. What you should say and what it made you say! He opened his eyes and saw that Vaidyaji's face had assumed a serious expression. 'Now he's going to come up with some wickedness,' he thought, gazing at the lustre of the college manager's face.

'Your hesitation is reprehensible,' said Vaidyaji. 'There should be no pardon for those who smuggle opium. They are depraved; they are traitors to their country.'

The Sub-Inspector sat in silence. Inwardly, he took an oath not to make any more foolish remarks. Suddenly Vaidyaji asked, 'You didn't find even a pistol in Jognath's house. What sort of search do you call that?'

'You can call it a minor one,' said the Sub-Inspector humbly, 'Where can pistols be found nowadays that you can produce one every time you make a search?' Smiling, he thought that the gin was proving very helpful when it came to acting.

Ruppan babu's face was hidden behind a newspaper. He said, 'Where have all the pistols gone then? What happened to all the ones you had in stock? All finished?'

The Sub-Inspector said gravely, 'It's the result of the last speech Vaidyaji gave here at the police station. After that all the badmaashes went and got rid of their pistols outside the area. They sold most of them to people from Unnao.'

Badri Wrestler had gone to Unnao. He had not yet returned. Vaidyaji half closed his eyes and reflected for a moment. He said, 'The climate of Shivpalganj is excellent. It's very favourable for the advancement of the intellect.'

'I consider you to be the climate of the village.'

This time, the Sub-Inspector did not curse the gin; in fact, he laughed heartily. He kept on laughing and didn't realize that the gin had loosened not only his tongue but his throat as well.

Vaidyaji sat quietly. He had ignored the Sub-Inspector's last remark. The Sub-Inspector rose slowly to his feet to leave. When he was crossing the threshold of the sitting room, Vaidyaji said, as if he had suddenly remembered something he had forgotten, 'Perhaps the bail papers for Jognath have been made out in my name?'

The Sub-Inspector halted. 'If that had been the case I would certainly have requested you to sign them. But don't worry, the court will grant bail. Send someone there.'

Vaidyaji did not reply. Now Ruppan asked bluntly, 'What's the problem with granting bail here?'

'Theft is a non-bailable offence.'

'And murder?'

The Sub-Inspector said lightly, 'Perhaps you are referring to the Nevada-wallah case last year. But the accused there was a TB patient. Who was going to kill him by locking him up?'

Ruppan babu put down his newspaper and stood up. He said, 'Jognath is still in your custody. Have him examined there. He's sick, too, though it's another matter that he's got gonorrhoea, not TB.'

Vaidyaji said coolly, 'Ruppan, speak politely. The Sub-Inspector is one of us; whatever he does he will do in a considerate manner.'

The Sub-Inspector repeated, 'So, may I go?'

'Yes, of course,' said Ruppan babu, 'Ramadhin must be sitting waiting for you at the police station.'

The Sub-Inspector smiled and, referring to the most regrettable fact of any bureaucrat's life, he said, 'The country has gained freedom, so now things are different. Otherwise, Ruppan babu, there would be a lot of very important people having to sit and wait for me.'

After he left, Ruppan babu said to himself, 'We've mistaken quack medicine for elixir,' and to Vaidyaji, 'We've been badly disgraced.'

Vaidyaji was sitting peacefully. Seeing Rangnath coming out of an inner room he said, as if giving a speech, 'Profit and loss, victory and defeat, honour and dishonour—they should all be accepted with equanimity.'

'Father is talking of the Gita,' thought Ruppan babu. 'Now we'll see how far that Sub-Inspector will get!'

~

At Babu Ramadhin Bhikhmakhervi's door, bhang was being ground today. Opposite, underneath a thatched roof, cards were being played. Unconcerned with either activity, Babu Ramadhin was lying on a charpoy listening to Langar who was standing below the veranda.

Rangnath and Sanichar were passing by that way. Babu Ramadhin called them over, sat himself on a corner of the charpoy and invited them to sit at its head. He showed no formality towards Sanichar, but just said, 'Why are you standing? Sit down, pradhanji.'

This was only the second time Rangnath had come this way. The first time there had been no sign of gambling or bhang. The atmosphere was more congenial today. Rangnath looked towards Langar and asked Sanichar, 'How is he getting on?'

'He's a brave man. You can take it that this time he has milked the bullock.' Miming the action of milking, he indicated just how far your hands had to go to get milk out of a bullock.

Rangnath called out, 'What happened? Did you get the copy?'

Langar answered with the simplicity of a Vaishnavite saint, 'Yes, father, you can take it that I have. The application has come back from the headquarters. Many applications that are sent to the headquarters get lost there, but mine wasn't. It's thanks to the glory of the feet of people such as you.'

Sanichar said wisely, 'It's a very good sign. If the application has come back, he will get the copy.'

'When will you get it?' asked Rangnath.

This lack of patience somewhat displeased Langar but, to appease Rangnath, he said, 'The copy clerk told me that my turn was just about to come.'

Ramadhin said, 'Go, Langar! Go over there and get yourself some good milky bhang.'

Then he turned to Rangnath and asked with interest, 'I heard Jognath was arrested today?'

Rangnath had already prepared an answer to this question. He asked Ramadhin, 'Who is Jognath?'

Ramadhin stared at him in astonishment, and then requested Sanichar, 'Pradhanji, tell him who Jognath is.'

Sanichar replied, 'Please, Babu sahib, don't call me pradhan yet. Only when you give your valuable vote to Mangal Das, son of Dulare Lal, will I be able to become pradhan. It's pointless until then. Isn't that right, Babu Rangnath?'

A glass of bhang had been placed in front of Rangnath. He shook his head and said, 'I don't drink it.'

Babu Ramadhin felt the same degree of insult which had led ultimately to the Battle of Haldighati. He growled: 'How could you drink bhang, brother? It's a peasant's drink.'

A ganjaha was sitting opposite Ramadhin. From the start he had accepted Rangnath as his natural enemy because Rangnath was cleaner and better dressed than he. He spoke out, 'He's a town man—how could he drink bhang? You'll have to get out some bottled booze for him, Babu sahib!'

Ramadhin looked at Rangnath with great humour and said, 'He won't drink the bottled stuff. Don't you see, he's a Brahmin!' Then he said respectfully, 'But if you do drink it, just say the word, I'll send for it!'

Having been brought down to the level of a Brahmin, Rangnath found it difficult to reply, but Sanichar did not hesitate to say, 'Why should you send for a bottle? Let this beanpole send for one; after all, he's the one who raised the issue.' With this, he turned towards the ganjaha and said with contempt, 'Stupid oaf!' Then he quoted a local saying which translated into common speech as, 'You are running around inviting sixteen hundred pigs to a banquet, but you can't come up with even a drop of shit for them to eat.'

Rangnath thought it opportune to make a move as the conversation was getting more and more unsatisfactory. 'Now may we go, Babu Ramadhinji? I was going for a stroll, and it's getting late.'

'Strolling is work for a mare, not for the son of a man,' he replied intimately. 'Just do a quick five hundred squat jumps and you'll be able to digest anything.'

Rangnath and Sanichar set off, stopping for a while to watch the card players.

There were two groups of players. On one side, several men were sitting playing 'coat piece'. By observing them closely, they discovered that it was a game played with fifty-two cards. The cards should be old, worn and so tattered that a connoisseur could tell from the other side which card was which. By watching this group, they also learnt that coat piece is a game played by eight players. Four of them sit holding their cards, desperately anxious, their heads hanging down to their chests. Another four sit, one behind each of the players, giving a ball-by-ball commentary on the play, and sure to speak whenever silence is necessary. Not only this, they also rub chewing tobacco for the players, light their beedis, call for water and pick up the cards that the players lay down. At the end of a game, when the players work out their winnings and losses, it's also their responsibility to provide change, and to order betel nut paid for out of the winnings of the successful players. It is their job as well to indicate to the opposite player which card he should play, and also to make a commotion in protest when he is caught cheating.

To Rangnath this game seemed sluggish, just like the intoxication of bhang, but when he inspected the second group, his impression of gambling in Shivpalganj was completely transformed.

They were playing flush, which was called *fallas* here in accordance with the same principle which turns the English 'lantern' into the Hindi *lalten*.

The game was being played very fiercely. On one side, the automatic weapon of bluff was causing mayhem; on the other, a player was proceeding with pure native cunning. Suddenly the elephant of his intellect panicked, bolted, threw off its rider and stood with one leg raised ready to crush him. He threw down his cards and the other player immediately gathered together a fistful of money and secured it under his thigh. The loser whom, two days earlier, Rangnath had seen in Vaidyaji's home, working as a labourer for eight annas a day, lit a beedi without the slightest frown or complaint, and began uninterestedly to watch the cards being dealt for the next game. Inwardly, Rangnath praised his fortitude and courage.

These people had their own language. They called a pair *jar*, a flush *langri*, a run *daur*, a running flush *pakki*, and a trey a *tirrail*. Rangnath thought, 'This is the proper solution to the problem of translating English words into Hindi.'

Professional lexicographers and their committees had cast their net over the country and were inventing equivalents of English words in Hindi and other regional languages. This work was quite interesting because, on the one hand, a new language was being invented inside closed rooms; and on the other, so much time was being taken that the language builders would have a job until they could retire on full pension. It was also interesting because this newly created language was meaningless except for the fact that Indians could be told, 'Look, brothers, the very same thing that is in English is now in your language, too.' Not one expert was in the least bothered whether his brothers adopted the new words or not.

Occasionally, Rangnath considered this absurd problem, but he could see no way out of it. But today, repeatedly hearing the words, *pakki*, *tirrail* and *langri*, being used, he thought, 'Why shouldn't these four or five ganjahas form a committee and go and sit in Delhi? They would come up with words in their mother tongue for the most technical phrases, and if they couldn't, at any rate, they wouldn't take much time converting a trey into a *tirrail*.'

The two of them had wandered out into the fields, and Sanichar was taking leave of Rangnath to go off towards a small pond nearby. Rangnath said, 'I understand everything except why Chhote Wrestler is standing as a witness against Jognath. That isn't right.'

Sanichar was heading towards the pond like a rocket. He had begun to grope for the cord of his underpants, and there was no need to explain the reason for his haste. But as he went, he explained Chhote's action in thirteen words, 'Just wait and watch, Rangnath babu, these are the ways of the ganjahas.'

Then he pulled off his underpants as impetuously as if Miss World were waiting for him, threw them aside and, completely naked, in full

view of Rangnath, he suddenly squatted down on the bank of the pond
like a participant in a partridge fight.

22

In the country, small wayside culverts are put to the same use as
tea rooms, committee rooms, libraries and state assemblies are in
the cities—that is, people sit there and gossip. At about two o'clock
one Sunday afternoon, Rangnath and Ruppan babu were sitting
on a culvert sunning themselves and contemplating the state of
the world.

The state of the world—that is to say, the warm touch of two firm
breasts in the darkness. Rangnath had raised the subject. He hadn't
wanted to tell anyone about the events of that night, but after some
time had been spent discussing darkness, winter, ghosts and so on,
Rangnath realized that gradually, without intending to, he had
recounted the full story.

Ruppan listened very attentively and, by the time Rangnath had
finished speaking, he felt as if he were sitting in an oven. He sensed
within himself a strange heat and tension, as he always did when girls
were mentioned. He was certain that the girl on the roof had been
Bela and that the man to whom she had wanted to surrender herself
was himself. 'My love letter is working, and she is restless for me,' he
thought proudly, immediately beginning to feel restless himself. He
wished he had slept on the roof that night, and his regret brought to
mind a morose Hindi film song, but in front of Rangnath he had to
present himself as a sensible man, and so he sat as he was and looked,
superficially, like a sensible man. Seeing him silent, Rangnath repeated,
'I have no idea how she came and went. I only remember that she was
sitting bent over me and . . .'

Ruppan babu said with the voice of experience, 'It happens.
Sometimes you can make mistakes like that. Who knows who it
was, whether it was a man or not? There's no need to mention it
to anyone. These country rustics will start thinking about ghosts

and spirits, and how will you be able to explain it to them, brother Rangnath? Keep your mouth shut. It could be that you dreamt it, it really could.'

Rangnath objected to two points in this speech. Firstly, that Ruppan was trying to pass off his experience as a dream; and secondly, that he was using the masculine gender for the girl. He said, 'There is no way I could have been mistaken. I was fully awake. She came and sat on my charpoy and was bending over me.'

'All right, all right,' said Ruppan, fanning away some imaginary mosquitoes with one hand, 'I believe you. There really was some person there. But there is no need to do anything about it.'

Some person! Rangnath shut his eyes, made a summary examination of the beautiful goddesses of Konark, and repeated to himself twenty times, 'Not a person, a girl! Ruppan babu, will you ever be able to think of anything beyond "some person"?'

~

The next day.

They had run out of almonds and Rangnath had to go to buy some.

He had heard that two miles from Shivpalganj was a village where there were grocery shops which might keep good-quality almonds. For some distance, the way to the other village was just a narrow path, blocked in places by thorn branches. Ditches and irrigation channels had been dug across it and, here and there, it was also traversed by mud ridges marking field boundaries. With every step it became clearer that the farmers didn't want even a bird to be able to use this path. But Man who, today, is preparing to travel to Mars and the moon, had trampled over those obstacles and cleared a way for himself across fields and over ditches.

A man was walking down this path. Rangnath followed him. The man asked Rangnath whose son he was and Rangnath replied that he was Vaidyaji's nephew.

The man said respectfully that he had heard Rangnath's name and that, today, he had the good fortune of meeting him. He had also heard that Rangnath was highly educated and had passed his BA and MA. In reply, Rangnath told him that the path was in a dreadful state, and God only knew why people had stuck thorn branches here. The man responded by saying that nowadays no one questioned anyone, and whoever felt like it stuck thorn branches in the ground or built field boundary walls. Rangnath asked why the village council didn't stop them. He replied that all that the village council could do was impose fines. In the days of the big landowners, people used to be beaten with shoes. He explained that India was a country of bloody sheep, and nothing could be done here without shoe-beatings. The big landowners were broken, and their shoe-beatings had stopped, but you could see that now the government itself had to trade shoe-blows with the people. Every day, somewhere or the other, it had to resort to lathi charges or a firing. Even if you wanted to do something about it, what could you do? People worshipped kicks; they couldn't be persuaded with words.

The man was in a bad mood, and so Rangnath said no more. After proceeding a little farther, the man suddenly remarked, 'Is a BA more important, or a law degree?'

'How can I say which is more important? They are both the same.'

'That, I too know. In this tatty country, there's no difference left between great and small. But really, which is the greater thing—a BA or a law degree?'

To put an end to the subject, Rangnath said, 'A law degree.'

'Then you should know that my son is a lawyer.'

'Where does he live?'

The lawyer's father said proudly, 'Where do lawyers live? They don't go and live in villages. He's settled in the town and has been practising for three years.'

'Then he must be counted amongst the best lawyers.'

'Not just the best but the greatest. That man Jognath, from your village, he's representing him! Vaidyaji was completely helpless there. The Sub-Inspector didn't grant bail. But there, in the court, my son got him bail just like that. He's a real gentleman. I myself filled in the form appointing him Jognath's counsel, and he pushed five rupees into my hand for it, too.'

To encourage the lawyer's father, Rangnath said, 'That means he must be earning good money.'

The man was suddenly on his guard. He turned to look Rangnath in the face and said in a subdued tone, 'Good money? Well, if you like, I suppose you can just about say, it's all right. It's nothing very much, brother! Your uncle's the one who's doing well. What a splendid sight his sitting room is! Even if he just grinds a tamarind seed into powder, ties it up and gives it to a patient, he can charge a rupee. It's a matter of luck.' He made no attempt to conceal his jealousy, and in a purely peasant fashion began to lash out at Vaidyaji with the words, 'Suddenly he's become a great leader. Before, he was a simple, straightforward man. Now, there's as much of him below the ground as there is on top of it. And he profits from everything he does—even his piss can be used to light lamps.'

In conclusion he said, 'But the Sub-Inspector didn't listen to him when it came to Jognath. He sat Jognath in a cage like a monkey and had him sent to jail.'

He repeated, 'If my son hadn't bailed him out, he would be inside with the jailer's children in his lap.'

'When is the hearing?' Rangnath asked.

'For Jognath's case? In some honorary magistrate's court. There, you can get a hearing whenever you want one. My son is back home at the moment. In two or three days, he'll go back to town and then he'll fix a date for the hearing.'

They were walking over low-lying ground surrounded by bushes and shrubs. There was practically a forest of tall kans grass. It was dry and stiff and poked you as you went down the path.

At one point, tips of the grass were hanging across the path. Instead of pushing them out of the way and walking past, Rangnath grasped them and tied them into a large, fat knot. This, to some extent, cleared the path. He tied another knot in another clump of grass a little farther on.

The lawyer's father stood watching what Rangnath was doing. When Rangnath had finished tying the second fat knot, he asked, 'What's that?'

'What?'

'That knot you've tied.'

'That? That knot?' He was about to explain that it would stop the kans grass from spreading over the path but, seeing the expression on the lawyer's father's face, he paused. It seemed as if the lawyer's father wanted to uncover some great mystery. Rangnath thought to himself, 'If that's what he wants, that's what he'll get.' He said, 'Don't tell anyone. Uncle told me that on the way there was a forest of kans grass; tie a knot in the tips of the grass; Lord Hanuman will be pleased.'

The lawyer's father said doubtfully, 'I've never heard that before.'

'Nor had I,' replied Rangnath carelessly, as he walked on. The lawyer's father now fell in behind him and again began to talk about the legal profession. 'MAs and BAs mean nothing. Where I come from, there is a poem people used to repeat. How did it go? Let's see, it's on the tip of my tongue . . . yes, the last line was, "He's a middle-class pass, but he's still cutting grass." Now you can change it to, "Brother's a BA pass, but he's still cutting grass." Nowadays, MAs and BAs are two an anna. You should have taken a law degree too. As a lawyer, you can put your chair in the court and sit like a king. A man whose uncle is a ganjaha, an Ayurvedic doctor and, on top of that, a leader—when is he ever going to be short of cases? Your uncle must have a dozen or so cases of his own coming up every day.'

Rangnath expressed no opinion on this advice. He just stopped, tied a third knot in a clump of kans grass and said, 'Hail, Lord Hanuman!'

The lawyer's father also stopped. The moment he heard Hanuman's name coming from Rangnath's lips, he took hold of a clump of kans grass and busied himself tying a knot. He explained to Rangnath, 'I think I might as well tie a knot myself. It's not as if it's costing me anything.'

Rangnath said gravely, 'Victory to Lord Hanuman!'

The lawyer's father immediately joined his hands in reverence and repeated, 'Victory to Lord Hanuman!'

A very dark-skinned woman was walking behind them with a dirty bundle on her head. At first she was some way off, but when they stopped to tie the knots, she caught up with them. She was about forty-five, but looked an old woman. Two of her jacket buttons were undone, but she appeared to be in a state of trance-like absorption in God and certainly didn't know that her buttons were undone or that their being undone might cause her any loss or gain. At the first glance, Rangnath had observed this natural sight and then averted his eyes towards the lawyer's father. But the lawyer's father didn't see that Rangnath was looking at him because he himself was engrossed in the same natural sight which Rangnath had observed and from which he had turned away.

The woman bleated like a goat, 'What are you doing, brother?'

Rangnath didn't have to answer. The lawyer's father had already said, 'Can't you see? We're tying knots for Lord Hanuman.'

The woman took the bundle off her head and put it down, 'I'm a woman. Am I allowed to do it too?'

'In God's court all are equal—men and women!' said the lawyer's father with as much self-confidence as if he himself had just come straight back from God's court. The woman pushed her hands into a clump of kans grass and said with reverence, 'Victory to Lord Hanuman!'

~

Rangnath didn't get any almonds in the neighbouring village, but he did find Sanichar sitting in a barber's shop. Behind him, the barber was wielding a pair of clippers. The bush of hair around the side of his head had already been cut, and the hair on the crown of his head had been left long in such a way that, from a distance, it would look as if he were wearing a round hat. In short, Sanichar was having his hair cut in the English fashion.

He heard Rangnath's voice and, despite the powerful hands of the barber and the pressure of the clippers, managed to turn his head. Looking at Rangnath out of the corner of one eye, he said, 'All the barbers in Shivpalganj have gone for a funeral. So I thought I'd come and have my hair cut here for once.'

He said this as loftily as if he had his hair cut every other day. But the truth was—and Rangnath knew it—Sanichar's hairdressing habits were completely idiosyncratic. For a whole year, he would neither touch his hair nor let anyone else touch it; then, suddenly one day he would sit down in front of a razor. Rangnath couldn't understand the reasoning behind this haircut. He stood quietly.

Seeing Rangnath standing there, the barber stopped cutting Sanichar's hair and, pushing his head forward with two fingers, said, 'Get up! All done!' Sanichar immediately stood up.

Today, he was in a strange mood. He kept clenching his fists and sucking in his breath. He walked away very fast, as if he'd just been kicked by a stallion, muttering something to himself which brought froth to the corners of his mouth.

On the way back to Shivpalganj, he and Rangnath were walking through a huge mango grove. A kite gave a shrill cry. Sanichar made two remarks in one breath, 'That bloody bird too is making a fuss about nothing . . . Look out, Ramadhin, this time, I'm taking to the ring myself.'

Rangnath couldn't fathom the connection between the two statements. He asked, 'Which ring?'

Sanichar stared at him in surprise and avoided giving an answer. Shaking off some of the hair that had fallen on to his body, he said, 'He'll be cured—yes, he will. Just wait and see. Let the atom bomb explode.'

They passed the mango grove and came to the spot where the kans grass started. Rangnath went ahead so that no hairs would float off Sanichar on to him. Suddenly he stopped dead.

The clumps of kans were a peculiar sight. Along the edge of the path, for about a hundred yards, knots had been tied in the ends of the grass, looking like a line of puppet soldiers wearing turbans, standing to attention. A man was tying a new knot.

Sanichar bellowed like a bull, 'Eh, you idiot! What are you playing at?' He said to Rangnath, 'Have you seen what these peasants have done? They have ruined the whole forest. God knows which bastard went and tied these knots.'

Rangnath started and looked Sanichar in the face. Today, curses were flowing from his mouth somewhat faster than usual. Rangnath asked, 'Are these knots doing anyone any harm?'

'How aren't they? Don't you know that this land belongs to the Shivpalganj village council?' He added imposingly, 'Do you understand, Rangnath babu?' He raised his head like a camel to curse the man tying the knot. Telling him which part of a woman's body he had been born from, he asked, 'Is this kans your father's property?'

The man turned round and said, 'And if it's not, is it your father's?'

To prevent an argument, Rangnath stepped forward and said, 'Please don't swear, brother,' and then asked the man, 'What are you doing?'

'I'm just doing what the whole world is doing,' he said haughtily as if he were doing the most basic thing in the world.

Sanichar said, 'But do you realize that this land falls under the Shivpalganj village council? By tying knots in it you kill the kans hedge. Do you know that? If you're charged for it you'll be left running around in circles. Then this "world" of yours will be of no help to you.'

'Which bastard is going to charge me?'

'Not a bastard—the legitimate husband of your sister. I! The pradhan!'

Looking at Rangnath, he explained, 'Yes, Rangnath Babu, I! Today, I'm going to file my papers for the pradhan's election. In less than fifteen days, you wait and see, I'll be standing on Ramadhin's chest and seeing which bastard dares lay a finger on a straw of my council's property!'

So that was it! That was the reason for his English-style haircut and for his objection to the cry of a kite perched in a tree. That was the atom bomb that was about to explode. That was why he was being so dictatorial about the village council's land.

Rangnath understood the whole thing. 'You are going to file your nomination papers today?'

'Right away! This minute!' said Sanichar enthusiastically. 'I'll file my papers even before I take a bath.'

He glanced over at the man who had tied the knot to see whether he had impressed him or not. The answer was clear. The effect of Sanichar's awe-inspiring speech was limited only to himself—just as India's claims of leading Asia and Africa are taken seriously only in India. The man said with assurance, 'Jolly good, become the pradhan— after all someone has to!' Then he added with contempt, 'After all, what is the village council? Just a ruse of the government.'

Sanichar sensed that he'd been insulted. He said, 'It may be a ruse, but you'll see after fifteen days what happens to anyone who touches a blade of kans.'

The man said lightly, 'If it's like that, then I won't touch it. This "knot worship" started in Shivpalganj in the first place. It won't spread farther than that.'

Looking at the dozens of knots in front of him, Rangnath asked, 'What sort of ritual is this?'

'Who knows what sort it is? I've heard that Lord Hanuman appeared to someone in Shivpalganj in a dream. Following his orders, people have begun to tie knots here.'

Sanichar anxiously joined his hands and said, 'Then go ahead and tie as many knots as you like, brother, there's no restriction on matters of religion.' With this, he put to work whatever little brain he had and said to Rangnath, 'But, Rangnath babu, I've never heard of this. Who had this dream? When I came this way there were no knots here.'

'I don't know anything about it,' replied Rangnath. 'Uncle told me to tie a knot in the kans grass if I came this way. So I tied one. These are Hanuman's knots. Uncle said so.'

As soon as he heard this, Sanichar's mind became absorbed in Lord Hanuman. He leapt like a tailless monkey towards a tall clump of grass and began to tie a knot, at the same time raising three or four cries of 'Victory to Lord Hanuman!', cursing Ramadhin, and saying in conclusion, 'The truthful hold sway and enemies are disgraced today!'

Rangnath added, 'Ram's name is Truth. Speak the Truth for it is salvation.'

Sanichar didn't hear him. If he had, he would have objected, although, from the religious point of view, it was a very sound point and, being linked with Ram's name, the saying could be used on any occasion. After tying the knot, Sanichar took Hanuman's name once more and wiped both hands on the back of his underpants, unconcerned about his lack of a tail in that region. He quickly began to walk ahead.

Slowly, Rangnath's mind was filled with peace and self-esteem. Today, without realizing it, he had founded a new sect whose only philosophy, mythology and ritual was to tie knots in kans grass. He found himself standing in the same line as the Buddha, Mahavira and Shankaracharya, and in his heart he asked them, 'Masters, I know about myself, but you tell me your stories. How did you come to think about starting new sects?'

23

In some village, someone had murdered somebody. To settle scores with someone else's enemy, someone had some man's name mentioned as the murderer in the police report. Then, to settle scores with his own enemy, someone else agreed to give evidence against him. Then, someone else recommended his case to someone in power, and someone else bribed someone on his behalf. Someone threatened some witness, made someone look stupid, and someone made love to someone. So, by the time the matter came to court, it had completely changed its character, had ceased to be a murder case and become a drama titled *Blood for Blood*. The lawyers on both sides played their parts well, and the judge was confident that what was presented to him was an excellent piece of theatre and that the evidence presented was, in fact, fraudulent. Finally, the fraud theory influenced him so much that he not only believed that the defendant was innocent but also that there had never been a murder in the first place. The result was that the defendant, Hari Ram, was cleared of the charge of murder without a stain on his character.

The defendant Hari Ram didn't actually gain a stainless character just because the judge said so. He remained the hooligan he was, but, the moment he was released from jail, he invited all the local people, with the exception of those generally considered to be of good character—that is, women, Harijans and Muslims—to a feast. As a result, that day, all the leading citizens of Shivpalganj had gone to feast at Hari Ram's place in the neighbouring village, and Rangnath was left alone in Vaidyaji's house.

The whole day passed like a lacklustre, boring lecture. In the evening, he went out for a stroll and saw the Principal standing at a paan shop. He was chewing betel nut and attempting to pay the paan-wallah for it. The paan-wallah had already given him the betel nut and, as for the payment, he was telling the Principal that the shop was, after all, his. At this point, Rangnath appeared on the scene, and the Principal began to appraise seriously the items on display in the shop. From a multicoloured picture hanging on a door frame, Mahatma Gandhi was laughing a monstrous laugh. His political heir, Nehru, was standing with folded hands. The conclusion, written below, was that a certain brand of coloured oil was a sure cure for dry itch in children. Rangnath asked the Principal, 'Have you seen that?'

He replied with a saying in Awadhi, 'A harness t' suit the beast. The picture's suitable for a rural area.'

'There's no rural–urban divide on this issue!' said Rangnath. 'Everyone respects Gandhiji.' After studying the picture for a while, he criticized it passionately. 'I feel like beating the painter a hundred times with a shoe.'

The Principal laughed. From his laughter you could tell that he thought Rangnath was being foolish. 'A drink will be as sweet as the amount of sugar you put into it. What can an oil presser or a paan-wallah afford? No one's going to hang a Picasso in some tinpot shop.'

Rangnath interrupted him, saying emphatically, 'Stop it, Master sahib! Don't mention Picasso. Hearing a name like his coming from your mouth makes me want to faint.'

Both had made their way on to the road and were taking in the air among herds of cows and buffaloes, although there wasn't much air to take in—there was dust to inhale, cow's dung to smell and the horns of sacred cows to stab you in the back.

Rangnath's comment affected the Principal so badly that he became serious and began to talk like a really civilized human being. 'So, Rangnathji, you consider me completely unlettered? I too have an MA in history, and with 59 per cent marks. It's a matter of fate that now I am the principal here.'

This grave overture knocked the wind out of Rangnath. He felt that he had hurt the Principal by his remark about Picasso. He apologized. 'I already realized that. If you had passed in some low division you would never have been here.'

'That's true,' replied the Principal, 'I would have been a university lecturer. Several of my third-class-pass friends have got jobs in universities.'

For a short while, the Principal walked on in low spirits. He was attempting to be sentimental. Then he spoke, 'Rangnath babu, I know what you people think of me. You must think that, even though I'm a college principal, I'm a thorough peasant. That I simper in front of everyone. You're right. I listen very humbly to whatever anyone tells me—except for Khanna and his lot, those idiots are just boys. I specially support what my seniors say, always. Now you think I'm stupid, but there is a reason for what I do . . .

'The reason is . . .' he said, laughing and moving to the side of the road to make way for a buffalo, 'The reason is that stupidity, like wisdom, has its own value. Whether you agree with a stupid man or cut him short, he neither gains from it nor loses. He is stupid and remains stupid. So, it's my habit never to cross a stupid man . . .

'Sometimes, when people see me tolerating stupidity, they think I too am a fool, but they're fools themselves to think that, wouldn't you say, Rangnath babu?'

Rangnath was quite dazed hearing this all at once from the Principal sahib's mouth. That's why, when a calf butted him in the back, he felt no pain. The Principal caught him by the arm and pulled him over to the side of the road. It was an experience in itself just to witness this intelligent side of the Principal. Rangnath didn't even notice when he started grinning and simpering again. The next moment, Rangnath was almost apologizing: 'Yes, yes, I realize you know all there is to know about Picasso. It was only that you mentioned him here in Shivpalganj! If you think about it, can you ever imagine hearing Picasso's name mentioned here? That's why I was taken aback. It's neither your fault nor mine, nor Shivpalganj's nor the paan-wallah's. Sir, the fault is Picasso's.'

The Principal was watching Rangnath's personality crumbling and disintegrating before his eyes. In an even graver tone he said, 'Once I, too, was in the habit of talking about ability. At that time I was studying for my MA. In the town you must have seen young girls walking along the street. Some of them start putting on airs and showing off in front of any male they see—man or boy. I was just the same. I never noticed which professors were genuine and which were idiots; I used to show off my abilities in front of all of them. One professor was offended by this, and I was finished.'

They had now passed beyond the village market. The evening was drawing in. The smoke from the ovens where gram was being roasted, instead of rising, hung in the air before them. The sun had set. But there was still sufficient light for Rangnath to make out the daughter of the gram roaster sitting in her shop, and to have a quiet guess that she was worth looking at. They left the last of the village houses about fifty yards behind and reached the stretch of barren land which could be used only for writing poetry, committing highway robbery, or shitting. As a result, several children, who were incapable of the first two activities, were squatting on either side of the road, shitting and hurling lumps of earth at one another. And some way farther on, quite a few women were squatting in lines along the roadside for the same purpose.

Their unashamed behaviour was a blot on the builders of New India who definitely knew nothing about it because, at that time, they were probably sitting in lavatories—the smallest but cleanest rooms in their homes—pondering problems concerning newspapers, constipation and trips abroad.

When the women saw the Principal and Rangnath, they immediately ceased their crapping activities and stood up straight, forming a kind of guard of honour. The two men wandered on, unperturbed. The women remained standing, equally unbothered. A bleating goat pushed past Rangnath and the Principal, reached the edge of the road and, knocking over a lota of water on the ground, disappeared into a mango grove. Some of the children began to scream as well as throw clods of earth while attending to the call of nature. Some of them got up just as they were and started running after the goat. In this situation, Rangnath and the Principal sahib remained silent for some time.

When they had gone on another ten yards they turned to look and saw that the women had sat down by the roadside as before.

The Principal sahib continued, 'That's what happened, Rangnath babu! I had the temerity to correct a professor in class. He got offended and he stayed offended. He began finding fault with everything I did. Finally, he got me a degree one class lower than I deserved and fixed it so that I would never get a job in the university as long as he was there.

'If I hadn't upset that bastard I would be in his place now.'

The Principal sahib ended his story and fell silent. They walked on for a while. Then the Principal said, 'Afterwards I came to the conclusion that that is the way everything works. Let it be. If they're all crooks, then I'm not going to gain anything by pretending to be a big hero. And now I've reached the stage, Rangnath babu, when, if anyone says anything to me, I just say, "Yes, brother, you're very right." And if Vaidyaji says anything, then it's "Yes, maharaj! Very right!" And if Badri says anything, it's "Wrestler! Whatever you say goes!"'

Rangnath didn't have the courage to interrupt. The Principal went on, 'And that is the right thing to do, Rangnath babu! I have to get four sisters married off. And I don't have a rupee to my name. If Vaidyaji threw me out on my ear, no one would give me a paisa if I begged for it.

'Now tell me, should I go around treating that bastard Khanna and his tribe like my father, or Vaidyaji . . .?'

During this conversation, an altogether more human side of the Principal's character had come to the fore, but his last words began to reveal his familiar crudeness again, and the spell broke. Rangnath spoke lightly, as he had done at first. 'No, no. You are doing the right thing, and you're well off as you are. What's the point of being a university professor? Here, are you any less than a vice chancellor?'

For the first time, the Principal sahib laughed. He said, 'Well, that's true. I consider myself better than a vice chancellor. Even a vice chancellor's life is hell. From early morning, you have to drive around in your car paying your respects to the members of the executive. You have to appear before the chancellor or the minister or the Secretary. The Governor tells you off at least four times a year. Day and night, there's some commotion or the other. The boys march past in processions, hurling four-letter words at you. There's always the fear of being beaten up. You phone the police and the SSP laughs behind your back and says, "Look at this vice chancellor, he can't rest until he's had his students lathi charged a couple of dozen times a year." That is what it's like, Rangnath babu!'

Hawking and spitting, he continued, 'So far, I don't have this sort of problems as a principal. And when you have Vaidyaji as a manager, you can be assured that the principal is like a lion. I don't have to flatter anyone. I just hold on to Vaidyaji's coat-tails and speak to everyone else with the shoe. What do you say, Rangnath babu?'

'You are absolutely right.'

'And to tell the truth, I'm not at all unhappy about not being a university lecturer. Their life is even more like hell. Complete hell! Twenty-four-hour sycophancy! Some government board will give you a miserable ten-rupee grant and then twist your ear to make you write whichever thesis it likes. Wherever you look, people are grabbing some research project or the other. They say they're doing research, but what research? They just sing the praises of whoever's paying them. And what are they called? Let me see, what's the word? Yes, I remember . . . They are called "intellectuals". So the position is that they are intellectuals but, to get foreign trips, they'll disown even their parents. To get one trip to America they're prepared to undergo a public shoe-beating at a crossroads. That's intellectuals for you!'

He quoted another saying in his mother tongue, 'If tha' hast to eat dung, eat elephant dung. All I have to do is keep in with Vaidyaji, but I'm not prepared to kowtow to everyone. I don't have it in me to be a lecturer.'

The Principal shook his head as if refusing to become a lecturer and, thereby, spreading grief throughout the universities of the world.

'You're absolutely right,' said Rangnath.

The Principal looked hard at Rangnath and suddenly began to laugh lightly. He said softly, 'What's the matter, Rangnath babu? You're agreeing with everything I say?'

Rangnath replied, 'I was thinking that I should learn from your experience. What's the point of contradicting anyone? Whatever you say is right.'

The Principal roared with laughter. 'Then you, too, are absolutely right, Rangnath babu! When I mentioned Picasso, you must have nearly fainted, I think . . .'

~

They walked back. Darkness surrounded them and there was a nip in the air. Some *banjaras* were sitting by the roadside, warming themselves in front of fires and speaking to each other in a dialect which no educated person would ever understand. The Principal crossed the banjara camp with the same equanimity with which he had passed through the herds of cows and buffaloes on the outward journey. Rangnath turned to look back just once, and said merely, 'It's bitterly cold.'

The Principal was not prepared to comment on the weather. He turned the subject to Khanna Master. 'You people are still no judges of character. I've heard that Ruppan has been taken in by Khanna. But you should think carefully, Rangnath babu, about what sort of man he is.

'He's a very clever customer. You see how he caused a fight in the college that day? He lost nothing by it, but the name of the college has been disgraced.'

'But I heard,' said Rangnath, 'that the quarrel was on both sides.'

The Principal replied in the tone of an ascetic, 'How does it matter what you heard, Rangnath babu? Now the case is before the court. The magistrate will decide as he thinks fit.'

'But it's a very bad business.'

'Bad? It's enough to make you drown yourself in a mouthful of water, Rangnath babu! But this Khanna Master doesn't have even that much sense of shame. I myself would have to tie a rock round his neck before he drowned.'

He was speaking with the selflessness common to officials of the country's information departments—whether anyone was listening or not, he had to speak his lines. He went on, 'The police slapped a case of Section 107 on both sides. That's what you call police bloody-mindedness. Khanna caused the trouble, his companions were bent on having a fight, and then the police go and charge both his side and mine. But then, if the country is mad, the rulers will be lunatics.

'The hearing was only yesterday. I was told to make up with him. I asked why on earth I should, and why they didn't hang me straight away and put an end to the trouble. Then there would be only Khanna Master and his hooligans left in Shivpalganj, and no fights or quarrels.

'I came back quietly. He, on his part, had brought seventy boys and he got them to shout, "Down with the Principal!" in a town court, in the presence of a hundred respectable people. They asked who they were and so Khanna Master himself said, "They're boys from Changamal College . . ."

'If you want to be truly shameless, be like him.'

He quoted a third Awadhi saying to the effect that, 'A tree sprouted from the groin of a naked man, and the fool began to dance with joy and said, "Now I'll be able to enjoy the shade."

'Do you follow, Rangnath babu?' He continued, 'This is what Khanna Master is like! Let Ruppan babu know. Don't give him too much support or one day you'll regret it.'

They passed in front of the police station. A few constables were walking around with lanterns and shouting. Some boys were standing in the road singing some sort of chorus. Three trucks were standing near the station in front of the Sub-Inspector's quarters. Luggage was being loaded on to them. This was the real reason for the constables' activity and the commotion.

The Principal remarked, 'It looks as though the Sub-Inspector's loading up.'

The full implication of this statement dawned on him before it did on Rangnath. He shook Rangnath by the shoulder and chirped, 'That's what it is! This area was stinking; now it's clean.'

Rangnath said, 'I don't know how the orders could have come through so fast. Until lunchtime there was no news of it.'

The Principal sahib's joy at the sight in front of him was palpable. It seemed as if he might spread his arms, fly up to perch on the top of a tree and sing like a bulbul. He said, 'Rangnath babu, you still don't know your uncle after staying with him for so many days. He had the previous sub-inspector chased out of Shivpalganj in twelve hours. It looks as if this one's got twenty-four.'

He whispered, 'Can anyone afford to cross Vaidyaji?

'The day he refused bail to Jognath, I knew it was time for him to clear out. Then, on top of that, charging us under Section 107! You tell me yourself, where was the need to charge me? But who was going to tell him? Ramadhin had become his godfather. He had him wound around his little finger, and now you've seen that within ten days he's been packed off.'

The boys' chorus was continuing. 'The Sub-Inspector has packed up, the Sub-Inspector has packed up!'

They were standing there to watch the luggage being loaded.

On one truck were several huge bedsteads of solid shisham wood and, in the remaining space, a fine cow and her calf.

'I can't see the buffalo,' said the Principal. 'It's a first-class animal—a Murra.' He explained to Rangnath, 'The Thakurs of Tikaitganj gave him the cow. It was a matter of the illegitimate pregnancy of a widowed daughter-in-law. They were let off with the gift of a cow.'

There were more bedsteads lying next to the truck. Rangnath had heard that the Sub-Inspector was fond of beds; now he saw that, indeed, he was. In spite of the darkness, the boys singing a chorus on the street had formed a circle around the centre of activity and were watching the loading operations. One constable standing on a bedstead and holding a lantern was encouraging the men doing the loading with the words, 'Oh, well done! You've broken the joint, haven't you? I knew you wouldn't listen until you'd succeeded in breaking it.' From his tone it seemed as if a broken bedstead joint was the greatest mishap that could befall Indian democracy.

Rangnath too offered a few words of advice to the men loading the beds. 'Yes, brother,' he said reasonably, 'don't break any joints. Load them carefully.'

The Principal laughed rather loudly at Rangnath's words.

Without in any way preventing himself from attending to the bedsteads, a constable called out, 'Who is it? Principal sahib? Long live India, Principal sahib!'

'What's happening, brother? Long live India! Has he been transferred or what?'

'Yes, Principal sahib. The Sub-Inspector had applied to the SSP. It was a question of his daughter's education; he wanted a transfer to the town.'

'She could have studied in our college. Is there any place better than Shivpalganj?'

'Your college is a Hindustani school. Those people teach in the English medium. It's a convent school. Baby's already got her uniform. It's all blue and when she wears it she looks just like an English girl.'

'So he's being transferred to the town. That, in any case, is good. But where will he keep this cow? Isn't he going to sell it?'

The constable exerted all his strength to lift a bedstead. He said with a groan, 'No, the cow will stay on an army farm. The Sub-Inspector's brother works there. There was nothing for this poor cow here! She'll start getting a good diet now.'

Someone mentioned that Vaidyaji had just come to meet the Sub-Inspector. Vaidyaji had wondered how the Sub-Inspector could have been transferred while he was there to protect him and offered to have the transfer order cancelled.

The Principal said to Rangnath, 'If the Sub-Inspector has any shame, he'll be out of Shivpalganj before cockcrow tomorrow.' He occupied himself for a while, examining the Sub-Inspector's belongings. Then he remarked, 'He's fond of beds.'

'He's fond of everything he can get free,' he added and then addressed the constable in the back of the truck, 'Is the Sub-Inspector at home? And is Vaidyaji with him? Then let's go, too, Rangnath babu, and pay our respects to the Sub-Inspector. The poor soul is a good man, never did anyone any harm or asked for anything from anyone. Whatever God gave him, he accepted gracefully.'

'It's true. The poor soul was really a good man and now has passed away,' thought Rangnath.

24

On the outskirts of the village there was a small pond which showed that rural life was not as idyllic as it used to be. The pond was dirty, full of mud, stinking, and very small. Horses, donkeys, dogs and pigs were overjoyed at the sight of it. Worms and maggots, flies and mosquitoes—all oblivious to family planning—flourished there in billions, teaching us that if we learnt to live like them, the country's rising population would no longer be a problem.

To make up for any lack of filth, a couple of dozen boys, following the dictates of their stomachs, came regularly to the banks of the pond every morning and evening, and irregularly at any hour of the day, to surrender gases, liquids and solids—all three states of matter—and return home lighter.

In the same way that any developing country, despite its backwardness, has some economic and political importance, this pond, too, despite its filthiness, had its own value. Its economic aspect lay in the good doob grass which grew on its sloping banks and which solved the nutritional problems of the horses belonging to the *ikka*-wallahs of Shivpalganj. Politically, it was important because Sanichar was campaigning there among the grass cutters and asking them to vote for him.

When Sanichar reached the banks of the pond, he found two men cutting grass. They were not, in fact, full-time grass cutters but ikka-wallahs who, even after the proliferation of cycle rickshaws, were still surviving with their horses. The rapid growth of the cycle rickshaw–driving class in this country since Independence only goes to prove the success of our economic policies, and the poor quality of our horses. It also proves that, in the process of establishing a socialistic pattern of society, we have first stamped out discrimination between man and horse and will now consider wiping out discrimination between man and man.

Sanichar was worried about his election—elections being the sole means of interaction between the man who wants votes and the men who have them. Therefore, he told the ikka-wallahs without any preamble that he had filed his nomination papers for the position of pradhan and that they should vote for him if they knew what was good for them.

One ikka-wallah looked him up and down and soliloquized, '*This* man wants to be pradhan. Not a rag on his back but he'll still eat betel nut.'

Begging for votes humbles even the greatest leaders, and Sanichar was only Sanichar. At this remark his pride collapsed, and he began to grin ingratiatingly as he said, '*Arré*, brother, I'll be pradhan only in name. You can take it that Vaidya maharaj will be the real pradhan. Just think that you are voting for Vaidya maharaj. Take it that Vaidya maharaj himself is begging you for your vote.'

The ikka-wallahs exchanged glances without uttering a word.

Sanichar said, 'Well then, brothers, what do you say?'

'What is there to say?' said the second ikka-wallah. 'When Vaidyaji is asking me to vote for him, how can I turn him down? What am I going to do with my vote anyway? I can't make pickle out of it. So, take it. Let Vaidyaji have it.'

The first ikka-wallah said warmly, 'After all, it's not as if a vote is worth anything. Let anybody have it.'

The second ikka-wallah contradicted him, 'How can you give it away to anybody? This is the first time Vaidyaji has asked for anything from us, and so we should give it to Vaidyaji. Let him have it.'

Sanichar said, 'So, the decision is final?'

They both replied at the same time, the gist of their replies being that a man is always true to his word; that, though they were not really worthy of giving anything to anyone, when Vaidyaji asked for something it was very difficult to say no; and that they hoped that when Sanichar became pradhan, he would keep his feet on the ground and not think he could stick his bamboo in the sky.

After Sanichar left, for some time they cut grass and discussed its shortage. Suddenly they noticed a man approaching. He wrote his name on all official documents, but his name was known to only a very few people in Shivpalganj. In the village, he was known as Ramadhin's brother. He was, at this point, the real pradhan of the Shivpalganj village council. It was another matter that the people behaved as if Ramadhin Bhikhmakhervi himself was the pradhan.

In recent years, the fish from the village ponds had begun to fetch high prices at auctions. The village council's income had also increased by leasing out barren land. Quotas of sugar and flour were sometimes distributed through the village council, too, and for these reasons, the village council was becoming rich, and everyone in Shivpalganj knew that the wealth of the village council and the wealth of the pradhan were one and the same thing. Consequently, the position of pradhan was profitable and beneficial.

Not only this, it was also respected. Even if the Sub-Inspector and the tehsildar did summon the pradhan a few times and abuse him a bit, and even if one or two village hooligans did chuck a dozen or so clods of earth at him from time to time, it did not detract from the respectability of the position because, in Shivpalganj, as in the rest of the country, a man won respect simply by becoming rich, no matter what means he used to do so. And in Shivpalganj, too, as in the rest of the country, a man's reputation was not destroyed just because he pocketed the funds of any institution.

For these reasons, Ramadhin's brother was anxious to become pradhan again.

He had just pulled out some gram plants from a field next to his own and was on his way home, holding them under one arm, and swearing loudly so that people might think that gram plants were being stolen from his own field. He saw Sanichar by the pond talking to the ikka-wallahs and immediately changed his plans and headed in their direction. Seeing him approaching, and reassuring themselves that Sanichar had disappeared from sight, the ikka-wallahs greeted him and said, 'Brother, are you standing again for the post of pradhan?'

Referring to the impending theft of gram from the fields, Ramadhin's brother said that his year as pradhan was coming to an end; that was why the thieves were going back so confidently to their old ways; that as long as he had been running things, the thieves had held their breath and stayed in hiding. From this, he drew the conclusion that if the ganjahas loved peace and comfort, they would damn well make him pradhan again. To end, he said nonchalantly, 'What was old Sanichar saying?'

'He was asking for my vote.'

'What did you tell him?'

'I said, "Take it. It's not as if I can make pickle out of it."'

'If you vote for him, you'd better consider the pros and cons of it first.'

'That, I've done. If you want, you can have my vote,' said the first ikka-wallah, and repeated, 'After all, it's not as if I can make pickle out of it.'

'So then, you won't vote for old Sanichar?' asked Ramadhin's brother.

'If you like, we'll vote for him. We'll vote for whomever you say. Your word is our command,' said the ikka-wallah, beginning to repeat, 'After all, it's not as if . . .'

Ramadhin's brother interrupted him and ordered, 'You are not to vote for Sanichar.'

'Then we won't.'

'You have to vote for me.'

'We will. If you want, you can have the votes.'

Ramadhin's brother went off abusing the gram thieves as before. The virulence and volume of the abuse increased in proportion to the distance he covered, because he was approaching the village and he liked to impress upon the people there that he too, in his own way, was a thug and that today he was angry.

~

Today, instead of dogs barking, it was people talking on the Gandhi platform which stood between Chamrahi, where the houses of the Harijans were, and that part of the village where the upper castes lived. In view of the elections, Ramadhin's brother had improved the platform because, as perhaps is laid down in election law, or for goodness knows what reason, all big leaders have improvements made in their constituencies a few months before the elections. They may build a bridge or have a road laid or distribute grain and blankets to the poor. In the same way, Ramadhin had tried to give the area around the platform a facelift.

There was a neem tree there which—like many intellectuals—was completely hollow even though it kept its limbs outstretched to demonstrate its existence. Beneath it, Ramadhin's brother had a well dug. In fact, the well already existed, but he resurrected it and, according to current practice, had it registered officially as a 'well construction scheme'. It was a political ploy to extract a good-sized grant. Earlier, this well had collected rainwater which fell on the nearby hillside during the monsoon, thereby preventing floods in this area of the village. Now, a wall had been built around it, and it was clear that the work had been carried out in connection with a Five-Year Plan. To make this even clearer, two pillars had been erected, one on each side of the well. On one of them there was an inscription in stone which read, 'Third Five-Year Plan. Village Council, Shivpalganj. Foundation stone of this well laid by Dr Jhaulal, Veterinary Surgeon. Council Chairman Mr Jagadamba Prasad.'

Now that the wall had been built, water from outside had ceased to flow in and water from inside had begun to flow out. The water, when it first made its appearance, had been cool, soft and fragrant. Now, standing stagnant in a large gutter, it seemed to suggest to the villagers: 'Since you've already had plenty of experience with stomach worms, let them be and come and take away a little malaria and filaria, too, with you.'

At the same time that the well had been resurrected, the Gandhi platform had been raised. Some new bricks had been added to it, and the cement, despite the contractor, was so good that it hadn't disintegrated a whole two weeks later.

In this atmosphere of innovation, the platform had become comparatively more attractive and sometimes idle students from the college would sit on it and play cards. In the evening, the lads from Badri Wrestler's pit had begun to come there to scrape off the plaster of mud left on their necks from the wrestling pit.

Today was election day. A holiday had been declared at the college. The election was to be held at another location, definitely one that was nowhere near Chamrahi but, at the moment, there was a fair crowd at the Gandhi platform, and as Gandhiji would have wanted, all kinds of people were sitting there in unity. The card players had put their cards away in their pockets; the lads from the wrestling pit were spreading the fragrance of their renown all around without having fought a bout or without having been smeared with mud, but just with the aid of a mustard oil massage.

Ruppan babu was walking wearily and his face showed none of its usual alertness and intelligence.

Seeing him approaching the platform, one of the young wrestlers winked and asked, 'Well then, babu, how are you doing?'

In reply Ruppan babu neither winked back nor asked, 'You tell me, raja, how are you doing?' He merely shook his head to make it clear that the wrestler might joke, but he wouldn't because he was in a bad mood. He walked up in slow motion, dark glasses over his eyes, a silk scarf round his neck and sat down with a thud on the platform. For a short while, silence descended on the assembled multitude.

The boy wrestler idly stretched out an arm and flexed it upwards at the elbow. Above the elbow swelled a childish bicep the size of a mouse. Looking at it repeatedly with pride, the boy came up to Ruppan babu and sat beside him. He winked again and, rubbing Ruppan on the back, said, 'What's up, babu? Today you're looking a bit off colour.'

Ruppan babu paid not the least attention to his friend's presence. He sat in silence. A boy from the college said, 'Guru, you didn't tell us what to do, and there is not the same spirit in Sanichar's campaign as there is in Ramadhin's.'

Ruppan babu said in a voice pregnant with meaning, 'Now it no longer matters who has spirit and who hasn't. The election result has just been announced. Sanichar has won.'

The young wrestler and the college boys erupted in tumult. From all directions came shouts, 'How? How? How did Sanichar manage to win?'

Winking, Ruppan babu's companion asked, 'Tell us, babu, how did old Sanichar do it?'

'By the Mahipalpur Method,' replied Ruppan babu wearily.

~

There are three ways to win an election: the Ramnagar Method, the Nevada Method and the Mahipalpur Method.

Once, in Ramnagar, there were two candidates contesting the village council elections—Ripudman Singh and Shatrughan Singh. They were both from the same caste and so there was a problem with the natural caste break up of votes. The Thakurs were confused because both the candidates were Thakurs, and they couldn't work out for whom to vote. The non-Thakurs were in a muddle because, since neither of them belonged to their caste, it would make no difference for whom they voted. Some days later, it became obvious that Ripudman and Shatrughan were both Singhs (literally, lions) who devoured their enemies. When this became clear, the villagers reached the conclusion—in accordance with the traditions of democracy—that, regardless of who the pradhan was, it wouldn't harm them, and that the candidates should be allowed to eat each other.

When the candidates went out campaigning, people would generally tell them, 'It's not as if we can make pickle out of votes. Take as many as you like.'

The result of all this was that both the candidates realized that no one was going to vote for them. They began to appeal in the name of democracy and to tell people about the value of their vote. They said that if they gave their valuable vote to the wrong man, it would endanger democracy. Most people didn't understand this point; those who did, merely replied that democracy was not going to be endangered if they voted for the wrong man. Choosing the right man is a hit-and-miss affair; just look at what's happening in the rest of the country.

There were only one or two people who talked like this but they were enough to render democracy meaningless. So, both sides changed their propaganda methods and began to talk about the rights of the pradhan to give the village fallow land to others and to displace all those people who had grabbed the land against the rules.

Farmers dearly love land. Not only that, but they also love other people's land more than their own. So, as soon as the villagers realized that the village council had something to do with land deals and that their neighbour's fields may become their own, and that if such-and-such a farmer died without an heir they could be installed as his inheritors, they began to brim over with simple affection.

Before one's eyes, the whole village was divided into two parties— one which agreed to having the fallow land distributed by Ripudman, and the other which recognized Shatrughan as the more capable man for the job.

When there were only four days left for the elections, both sides could be seen making elaborate preparations. People were screaming out the slogan, 'Long live the Revolution!' They were abusing their opponents' mothers and sisters, oiling their lathis, sharpening their knives, and taking their lives into their own hands, together with a pipe of hashish. While all this was happening, Ripudman Singh called his younger brother, Sarvadaman Singh, and asked him affectionately what he would do if, in the coming battle, he and twenty-five of his men were killed.

Sarvadaman Singh had a degree in law, but had given up his practice four years earlier to leap into local politics just as, in the old days, great barristers had resigned theirs to join national politics. The only difference was that no one could ever find out how the barristers who took part in the freedom struggle had earned their income, but everyone knew very well how Sarvadaman Singh made his living, and was impressed by it. He had ten gas lamps which were rented out during the marriage season. He also had two rifles which were rented out to dacoits during the dacoity season. All in all, Sarvadaman Singh earned enough for him to be able to conduct village politics comfortably. His gas lamps and rifles travelled great distances, earning him goodness knows how many wide-ranging and deep social contacts, thanks to which he now spoke with a new self-confidence.

Sarvadaman answered his brother with appropriate self-assurance, 'Brother, if you and twenty-five of your men are killed in this battle, then, on the other side, Shatrughan and twenty-five of his men will also be killed. That would be the proportionate calculation. Beyond that, whatever you say, will be done.'

Ripudman Singh embraced Sarvadaman and tried to weep, but only a film star or a leader can weep at will and, due to lack of practice, Ripudman's attempt was unsuccessful. Sarvadaman slowly disengaged himself and said, 'Let it be, and tell me what's to be done after the 25–25 account is settled.'

Ripudman said, 'Imagine that the elections are held again and that you wanted to become pradhan; what would the position be?'

Sarvadaman brought out a pencil and paper, made a calculation and said, 'Brother, if you and Shatrughan die with twenty-five men each, then not only I but anyone from my side could also bring in fifty votes more than anyone from the opposition. Because, among the voters in the village, there are at the most only twenty-five men who are really ready to do or die for the other side, while on our side there are more than forty. If twenty-five men from their side die, you can say that their whole lot will be wiped out, but even if twenty-five of our men die, the field will be left in the hands of our remaining fifteen men.'

Three days before the election, Ripudman filed a petition in the sub-divisional magistrate's court against Shatrughan Singh and twenty-five of his men, saying that they were endangering his life and property, and that a disruption of the peaceful electoral process was feared. The police supported the petition.

In response, Shatrughan Singh filed a similar petition against Ripudman Singh and forty of his men. The police supported that, too, but calculated that it was applicable only to Ripudman and twenty-five of his men. On the day of the election, first, there was a hearing of both candidates and both sets of twenty-five men. The magistrate—as laid down by law—asked Shatrughan and his twenty-five men for a certain amount of bail and personal bonds, which they began to consider giving. Then the magistrate asked Ripudman Singh and his men for bail and personal bonds. Ripudman replied, 'Your Honour, we shall not give bail or personal bonds. Remember what I say—tomorrow, there will be a massacre in our village. Not even the highest amounts of bail will be able to stop Shatrughan Singh and his thugs from causing trouble. We people are simple farmers, and there's no way we can stand up to them. So please, sir, lock us up on the grounds that we're not able to pay the bail. If we are locked up, at least our lives will be safe.'

After this, Ripudman hugged the railings of the dock and attempted to weep.

The police supported this statement, too. Therefore, the magistrate decided that, as Ripudman Singh and his party would remain in jail during the elections, the bail for Shatrughan Singh and his party should not be accepted, and they, too, would have to stay in jail.

In this way, for the duration a few days, the candidates and fifty of their men died.

After that, the election took place in a very peaceful and civilized atmosphere. As for the efficiency of the two sides, Shatrughan's supporters proved completely useless—in fact, you couldn't tell whether he had any supporters left in the village or not. On the other side, Sarvadaman was present to fight for Ripudman since, thanks to police support and his law degree, he was considered a peace-loving man and was not locked up. He fought the election solidly, and the result that was declared was the one he had already calculated on paper.

This method of winning elections was patented under the name of Ramnagar.

The Nevada Method was somewhat more idealistic.

In Nevada, several people from different castes were standing for election, but there were two main contestants who were, respectively, according to the *Rig Veda*, the Mouth and the Feet of Brahma, the Cosmic Man. In today's terms, it was a struggle between Brahmins and Harijans, but in Nevada, the issue flourished in a highly cultural and practically Vedic manner.

The Brahmin candidate recited the 'Purush Sukta' of the *Rig Veda* several times to the upper castes, and explained that it was the Brahmins who were the Mouth of Brahma, the Cosmic Man. He also explained that the Shudras were his Feet. He cited several examples regarding the position of pradhan, showing that it was related to the intellect and the voice, neither of which is found in the feet. Therefore, Brahmins should naturally become pradhans and Shudras should not.

The Brahmin avoided using the customary abuse denigrating the Shudras; he just kept arguing on this cultural level. He did concede that any jobs which required a lot of running around, for which feet were essential—for instance, the post of chapraasi of the legal council—should definitely be given to the Shudras but maintained that it would be against the Vedas for them to become pradhans.

But, as generally happens, the voters did not accept the arguments made on a cultural level, and the Brahmin candidate was forced to alter the tone of his campaign. He began, in his position as the Mouth of the Cosmic Man, to make a somewhat more generous use of his mouth. Simultaneously, his supporters began to make more use of their mouths during the campaigning and, in a few days, the issue had descended to the time-honoured level of, 'Tell me this, Thakur Kisan Singh, are you going to desert me and vote for that untouchable?'

In a very short time, the Brahmin candidate's side had succeeded in creating a climate of violent abuse in the village and then, one day, the real meaning of the *Rig Veda*'s 'Purush Sukta' in which the Shudras are accepted as the Feet of the Cosmic Man, became apparent.

One of the supporters of the Brahmin was freely abusing the other candidate. He sat on a veranda and, through the stream of abuse issuing from his mouth, he asked the central question, 'Tell me, Thakur Kisan Singh, are you going to vote for that . . .?' Here followed a number of curses, and then the second half of the sentence, '. . . and desert us?'

Suddenly, he was stopped mid-sentence by such a sudden and intense pain in his midriff that he was unable to utter another word of protest. He just rolled down on to the ground where he was kicked ten more times. When he opened his eyes, he realized that the world was an illusion and that he had just renounced the slumber of worldly attachment. Several similar incidents occurred after this, and the

Brahmin candidate understood that the Mouth of the Cosmic Man was not too far from his Feet and that, when feet are used to reply to words, the latter cannot hold their ground for very long.

This piece of research stunned the Brahmin candidate. But on this occasion, he was helped by the advent of a babaji who was one of those many holy men who are easily able to gather disciples from among people, ranging from disaster-struck farmers to the most senior officials, leaders and businessmen.

One day, the Brahmin candidate, despite having made very limited use of his mouth, had been flattened by a kick from the Feet of the Cosmic Man and was thinking over the problem of how to save the pradhan's chair from being polluted by the untouchable and how to put it underneath a Brahmin. These deliberations took place by a well outside the village in the early evening under the soft, blue shade of a wood near a banyan tree. Suddenly, the candidate saw some bats flying out from beneath the branches of the banyan and, simultaneously, he heard a hoarse voice reciting several epithets of Shiva. The Brahmin candidate became convinced that there was some babaji beneath the tree.

And there was. The babaji was reciting Shiva's name and smoking hashish. Even if a man is not in distress, he will fall down prostrate before a babaji. In this case, the Brahmin was in distress, and the babaji appeared before him. Without thinking, the candidate fell at the holy man's feet and began to beg for help.

This sort of thing had happened to the babaji several times before in the course of his life. On the basis of his previous experience, he assured the Brahmin candidate that he would protect him and explained that there was no need to worry. If he had a problem of night emissions or premature ejaculation or was afflicted with impotency due to evil habits in childhood, he could be sure that, after trying the babaji's formula, he would be able to do justice to a thousand women.

But the Brahmin candidate shook his head and refused to take advantage of the babaji's generosity. Then the babaji told him that, with this extremely secret recipe, he would become a master of immense sexual potency and, if he were to use the recipe at the same time as a basis for medicines and were to start selling them, within a very short time, he would also be bound to become a millionaire. Despite this, the Brahmin candidate kept on crying and shaking his head, and when the babaji coaxed him a little, the candidate said, 'I don't want to do justice to a thousand women; I'll be happy if I can settle just one untouchable.'

The babaji consoled the Brahmin and when he had understood the whole problem, he set off towards the village to solve it, pushing his pipe into a fold of his dhoti and throwing a little dust on to his wig of matted locks. He pitched his camp in front of a temple and, the next day, began to recount the stories of saints from Kabir and Ramanand to Guru Gorakhnath, all of which reached the conclusion that no one should ask a man his caste and that any person who sings God's praises, belongs to God.

The very same day, people also began to understand just what God was. A lump of hashish was placed in a pipe, and glowing embers were stuffed on top of it. The hashish was lit by sucking in the cheeks and puffing them out an equal number of times, and then the smokers had to draw deeply on it. In between puffs, Shiva's name was recited in several ways and with different meanings. The pipe was passed around among the devotees either clockwise or anticlockwise. The devotees imagined that this was God.

Songs in praise of God were sung in the babaji's court for forty-eight hours at a stretch. Those who didn't smoke hashish were given a continuous supply of bhang and, as long as the hymns went on, the grinding stones kept grinding. The harmonium kept being played and Hindi film tunes with amended lyrics were sung to propitiate Radha and Krishna, and Sita and Ram.

Within two days, the babaji had been accepted as an incarnation of Krishna. It was another matter that, instead of drinking Yamuna water, he smoked hashish, and—like demons—seemed to be closer to Shiva than to Sri Krishna. All this time his pipe was constantly burning, proving that, whether hashish is obtained illegally or from a government shop, and whether Ganga water is taken from the source of the river or from its confluence with a dirty drain, its effectiveness under all conditions remains the same.

The babaji was a carefree individual. He not only listened to hymns, he also sang them. If he hadn't smoked hashish his voice would have been clearly audible, and if the harmonium hadn't been playing, you might have been able to make out some tune. But despite these natural impediments, the babaji managed to put the whole village under his spell in no time at all. He sang such bhajans of Kabir, Raidas and Ramanand that people began to raise slogans in their praise. Had these holy men been there themselves they would have cheered the babaji for creating such original poetry. Under his influence, casteism was completely removed from the entire village.

Then, one day, when, in a hazy atmosphere of hashish, bhang and song, he hinted that the pradhan of the village was a very religious man, people were amazed. One bhang drinker said that there was as yet no pradhan since they still had to hold the first elections for the post, upon which the babaji indicated that God had already held an election. In short, even before they sobered up, people realized that God himself had already chosen the Brahmin candidate as pradhan. On the basis of this piece of knowledge, practically all the villagers—even though still intoxicated—accepted him as such. In this way, the Feet were numbed and the Mouth triumphed.

The Nevada Method had proved extremely useful. In other villages, people adopted it with amendments and won many great contests.

Whenever they couldn't lay hands on a hashish-smoking holy man—or on sufficient hashish—they generally turned anyone available into a babaji and began to make arrangements to worship the goddess. At such places, they began to offer goat sacrifices and give liquor as prasad. This, too, led to the same result—the Feet were numbed and the Mouth triumphed.

The method patented in this way was entered in the election code as the Nevada Method.

The Mahipalpur Method was by far the simplest and was purely scientific. It owed its development to an electoral officer's error; and subsequently, this error was accorded recognition and repeated elsewhere. The error was connected with a wristwatch.

The election was to be held at twelve noon. Since the electoral officer's watch was set by the town clock, and the town clock was set by the household of the chairman of the town council, it was an hour and a quarter fast. Consequently, despite opposition from a number of candidates, the electoral officers held the election at a quarter to eleven with whichever voters and candidates were present and, there and then, announced the result. By the time the remaining voters and candidates arrived on the scene to fight the election, the electoral officers were at home having the meal that is eaten at quarter past one.

A petition was filed against this election, and in it, the entire debate hinged on watches. The case proved quite scientific, and the court had the opportunity to acquire a great deal of mechanical information about watches. In the end, the case carried on for three years, but neither was it likely to be proved nor was it due to any error by the electoral officers. The man whom they declared pradhan always kept his watch set an hour and a quarter fast and ruled the village according to that time. The other candidates—to quote Chhote Wrestler—sat there like fools with clocks instead of watches in the hope of catching him out the next time.

The Mahipalpur incident was purely accidental, but then the apple falling in front of Newton which led him to work out the principle of gravity was equally accidental. Later on, experts in the art of elections also worked out a principle based on the Mahipalpur incident. This principle stated that all watches do not show the same time at the same time, and not all voters arrive together at the same place.

After this principle had been established, it was used in several ways in village council elections on several occasions. With the example of Mahipalpur before them, electoral officers' watches would stray slightly, becoming half an hour slow or fast, and because watches were mechanical, no human being could be held guilty for their behaviour. The victorious candidate generally turned out to be the one whose watch told the same time as the watch of the electoral officer.

~

In geographical terms, Mahipalpur was farther away from Shivpalganj than Nevada, and so Ramadhin was quite familiar with the Nevada Method. He made good use of it. On the other side, on Sanichar's behalf, Vaidyaji relied more on history than geography. After contemplating all past methods, he gave the opinion that the Mahipalpur Method should be adopted by Sanichar's side.

As a result, they won, having incurred the sole expense of a cheap watch which, by mistake, the electoral officer took home strapped to his wrist.

Meanwhile the followers of the Nevada Method were defeated. They collapsed in a field under the influence of despair and alcohol. They got nothing out of the experiment except for some experience in drunkenness.

25

Come my sweetheart, my cruel beloved,

I miss you so, but how does the moon know that it is loved by a chakor? That poor chakor can look from afar but makes no sound. You do not know that you are my temple, you are my worship, you are my God, you are my God. Your thoughts rob me of sleep and I toss and turn all night long.

Now I have reached the point where I can endure no more, nor live any longer like this. Do you see how perverse my heart is? It saw you and it changed. And there you are, sometimes flying away, sometimes turning away, but, love, let me know the secret of your heart. I have this complaint against you, that you have the bad habit of hiding your love. Somewhere, there burns a lamp, somewhere, a heart, come and see, oh, moth!

I have many things to say to you when we meet. To whom can I present these smouldering emotions? I feel like squandering my love, but my innocent beloved knows not my heart. That's why I came to meet you that day. I had gone to meet my Beloved. But my moonlight has been torn from me, my house is lying in darkness. I wanted to tell you that I want nothing from you. Only be kind enough to let me rest in the shade of your eyelashes. But this is the ancient way of the world—to make some fall and to destroy others. I came to the roof but there was someone else lying on your bed. I died of shame. I returned, helpless. Whirlwind, laugh at me, laugh at my love.

I am being disgraced and you are silent. How long will you make me yearn for you? Even in my yearning I shall sing songs of you. I have to meet you soon. Will you come today? Because, today, without you the temple of my heart is desolate. I am alone, come to me wherever you may be. Embrace me, who knows if this fair night will come again? This is my desire, that at your doorstep, I should expire. Alas! I am sitting in hope, see that you don't break my heart.

Remembering you,
Someone mad with love

The grubby package, tied to a stone, which fell in the veranda outside the room on the roof, turned out to be a love letter concocted from the lyrics of Hindi film songs. Rangnath read the letter once, and then again and again, and it didn't take him long to realize that it was written by the same person whom he had felt leaning on his chest and who had reminded him that night of Konark and Khajuraho. It was also clear to Rangnath that the love letter was not intended for him but for someone else.

Who was that? Ruppan?

So, had Bela written the letter to Ruppan? If so, was the girl who came on the roof that night none other than Bela?

Putting the letter into his pocket, he left the house. Today was the date of Jognath's hearing in the town, and whoever counted in Shivpalganj was running there. Whenever a case is being heard against a hooligan, it is the natural inclination of village brethren to take a trip into town to see the court. They get deep satisfaction from seeing the hooligan humiliated. And the hooligan, too, gets heartfelt satisfaction from thinking that so many people have come from the village to support him.

In accordance with this tradition, several people had already left for town, and many more were just about to leave.

Rangnath saw Badri Wrestler approaching. He was at his most attractive, dressed in a muslin kurta beneath which he felt no necessity of an undervest. Despite its being cold for the month of Phalgun, his body was gleaming with perspiration. A loincloth was, of course, tied round his waist, but what was surprising was that he was wearing a lungi over it. On his feet were polished, black boots. His clean, closely shaven head shone with mustard oil, and above it—a long way above it—was the blue sky.

At first Rangnath had thought that he would present the love letter to Ruppan babu and, by making a few remarks on 'cinema's contribution to the degradation of Indian culture', prevent him from falling in love with Bela. He knew that it would be difficult to speak to Ruppan on this subject, but it didn't seem right to him to dismiss in an unimaginative way such an earth-shaking event as the receipt of a love letter. But the moment he saw Badri he changed his plan, just as, occasionally, we change our economic plans the moment we lay eyes on an American expert.

Badri Wrestler examined the love letter from a distance. To make it easy for him, Rangnath stood holding the letter up with both hands about one and a half feet away from him. Badri slowly read the whole letter through. Once, when he screwed up his eyes, Rangnath with the aim of assisting him, read out '. . . who knows if this fair night will come again,' and added, 'Fair. That means beautiful.'

Badri belched as if perhaps to say that there was no need to explain, since he understood such phrases very well. Having read the entire letter, he took it, folded it and put it into his pocket.

Rangnath said, 'Ruppan babu is heading down a very dangerous path. And that girl! God knows with what sort of rubbish she's filled that letter.'

Badri laughed heartily in reply. He said, 'That old hag of a village social worker must have written it. She's the only one around here who knows this kind of language.'

'So . . . So, has Ruppan fallen into the clutches of some social worker?'

The wrestler laughed as before, then, controlling himself, he said, 'No, no. You get everything the wrong way round. The poor old soul doesn't do that sort of thing; she just writes letters for other people.'

Badri Wrestler went his way. Seeing the confused expression on

Rangnath's face, he said as he walked off, 'Don't you worry about this piece of paper. I'll settle it.'

~

The court was in the town, but practically the whole of Shivpalganj had gathered there. The prosecution witnesses were giving their testimony against Jognath.

The atmosphere was rude and vulgar. Citizens were lying on the veranda like dogs. The festival of Holi was approaching, so the people had jokes and obscenities on their lips. They wore dirty but colourful clothes or rags. Grimy, unshaven plaintiffs, defendants and witnesses—either smoking beedis or chewing tobacco between discoloured teeth—were holding shrill conversations. One woman was lying on the floor, her baby suckling from the breast she had thrust into its mouth—a scene which several of the citizens present found of great interest.

A strong wind was picking up dust and leaves and spreading them over the whole veranda.

Two uniformed but bareheaded police constables, their legs wrapped in khaki puttees, were wandering around the veranda. The shoes of one constable, always ready to give anyone a hammering, were themselves being hammered into shape by a cobbler sitting under a nearby banyan tree. The other constable had taken his shoes off and left them by the courtroom door as they were still new and were pinching his big toe. The lawyers went repeatedly in and out of the courtroom, weighed down with work, even when they had none.

Stretching contentedly, the court's record-keepers came out every fifteen minutes or so, walked over to the paan shop opposite and then walked back, explaining to the litigants following behind and to the others hanging on their arms that, today, they had a lot of work and that the litigants should come the day after tomorrow. Then, with their mouths full of betel nut and lime, holding their necks high like camels, the record-keepers slipped back once more into the security of the courtroom.

Langar, too, was sitting in one corner of the veranda.

The presence of Sanichar, as pradhan, among those who had come to watch the spectacle was essential, as was that of Chhote Wrestler who, today, had come to testify for the police against Jognath. This was an event of historic importance because Chhote Wrestler was considered one of Vaidyaji's men, and Jognath, too, was one of Vaidyaji's men, and it had suddenly transpired that two men of the same man were to stand separately, one as the accused and the other as witness for the prosecution. As Ruppan babu put it in a style typical of folk theatre—two flowers blossomed together, but destiny tore them apart.

Sanichar, along with many other villagers, had entered the courtroom. Langar, whom Sanichar had brought along on his cycle rickshaw just for the fun of it, was sitting outside on the veranda, relating his life's experiences to his new audience. He had only one life and only one experience, and at that moment he was recounting it at some length.

'. . . so, father, after such a long time, after one year and three months have passed, the matter has now been settled. There is now nothing missing from the application for the copy, and the file, too, has come back from the headquarters to the tehsil office. When I went to the tehsil office yesterday, I found out that the copy clerk has my work in hand. He must be making a draft today. Then he'll compare it with the original.

'Now it's only a matter of waiting for two or three days more.'

A lawyer who was leaning against a pillar, smoking a cigarette, said, 'You've been running around from pillar to post for so long. If you'd first come to me or any other lawyer, the job would have been done in three days.'

These days, Langar had learnt to smile a sweet, saintly smile which, when it wreathed his face, made it seem as if the person he was talking to was being childish but that, due to his saintliness, he was enduring it. Making fairly generous use of this smile, Langar replied, 'There was no need for a lawyer, father. It was a battle for truth. If I'd given five rupees to the clerk, I could have got the copy in three hours, not three days. But he was not going to take it like that nor was I prepared to give it.'

The lawyer asked, 'Why wouldn't he take it? You gave him the money and he wouldn't take it?'

Langar was tired and was preparing to lie down. He said, 'It was a battle for truth, father; you're a lawyer, you wouldn't understand.'

People started laughing, but Langar just lay down and shut his eyes. Then he moaned softly.

Someone asked him, 'What's the matter, Langar? Are you feeling off colour?'

His eyes still shut, he shook his head and said nothing. A man sitting next to him touched him and said, 'It seems to be a fever.'

An old woman was sitting, silently regarding the world philosophically with her owlish eyes. She commented, 'It's a bad time. Two of my sons too are down with fever. The crop is ripe and there's no one to cut it. The rats are eating it.'

~

The court of the honorary magistrate.

Gayadin was giving his testimony. The cross-examination was coming to an end. Suddenly Jognath's lawyer asked, 'You have one daughter?'

'Yes.'

'Her name is Bela?'

'Yes.'

'She is about twenty years of age?'

'Yes.'

The magistrate looked at him sharply and with suspicion, as one should look at the father of a twenty-year-old girl.

'Does any other woman live in your house?'

'Yes. My widowed sister.'

'But she doesn't always live with you?'

'Yes, she always lives in my house.'

The lawyer thundered, 'You have taken an oath; if you lie you will be prosecuted. Is it not the case that your sister lives with her in-laws most of the time and that, during those periods, your daughter is left alone in the house?'

Gayadin stood in silence. The lawyer thundered again, 'Why don't you speak?'

'How can I? You're losing your temper so badly it's difficult to say anything.'

In the same tone as before, the lawyer said, 'I am not losing my temper.'

Gayadin said nothing. Then the lawyer said more softly, 'What is your reply?'

'My widowed sister lives with me all the time.'

'Is your daughter married?'

'No.'

'When do you intend to arrange her marriage?'

'That's in God's hands.'

Hearing the mention of God's name, the magistrate raised his head. Until now, he had been perusing some other papers which had nothing to do with this case. Now he told the lawyer, 'These questions have nothing to do with the case.'

'Your Honour, I shall establish the connection later,' replied the lawyer.

Seeing the magistrate held in check, the public prosecutor, too, became anxious to protect his witness. He objected, 'Your Honour, these questions are irrelevant.'

The magistrate answered his objection with a stern glance.

On the opposing side, Jognath's lawyer saw that the magistrate's mood was deteriorating and refrained from asking Gayadin any more questions about his daughter. The next witness was called.

This was the same witness who had appeared when Jognath's house was being searched and had run off the next moment, assuring the police that they could call him at any time to give evidence. His name was Baijnath and he was a disciple of Shivpalganj's Pandit Radhelal—the same Pandit Radhelal who had attained the highest degree of expertise in bearing false witness, and whom, up till now, not even the greatest lawyer had been able to shake in cross-examination. It was this ability to lie faultlessly which had won him unprecedented prestige among the litigants and the witnesses of the entire district. Recently, however, ever since his passion for his lady-love from an eastern district had rendered him somewhat housebound, he hadn't been able to find enough time for his private practice of giving testimony. As a result, in comparison with former times, he had practically given up appearing in court. Like senior lawyers and doctors, he now no longer ran a general practice but a specialist practice which was limited only to civil cases and, among those, only the ones to do with inheritance. With a view to maintaining the standard of false evidence in the criminal courts, he had trained several disciples over the past few years. Baijnath was the foremost among them.

Baijnath came from Bhikhmakhera but, for the purpose of giving evidence, he was accepted as already being present in any of the nearby villages. Consequently, his practice was well established not only in Bhikhmakhera but in several villages in the neighbourhood as well. It was also only by accident that he really was in Shivpalganj on the day of Jognath's arrest, since, for him to give evidence, it was irrelevant whether in fact he had been there or not.

Baijnath repeated the whole prosecution case. He said that Jognath's house had been searched in his presence; that the three ornaments in custody were recovered and sealed in front of him; that the report of their recovery was written in his presence; that his signature was also signed on the report in his presence, etc.

Jognath's lawyer began the cross-examination. 'You live in Bhikhmakhera?'

'Yes.'

'Bhikhmakhera is two miles from Shivpalganj?'

'I don't know.'

'Then how far is it?'

'If there's a *nautanki* show in Shivpalganj you can hear it in Bhikhmakhera.'

'It must be one mile?'

'I can't say.'

'Half a *kos*?'

'Don't know.'

'Twenty miles?'

'I don't know. I've never measured it.'

The magistrate stared at the witness and said, 'What is the distance between the two villages?'

'There are some fields between them.'

'How many?'

'There must be ten, twenty, perhaps fifty.'

'Give a proper estimate. How many must there be?'

'I don't know—I've never counted them.'

The magistrate turned his stare on to the public prosecutor, who said, 'Your Honour, the witness is correct. He hasn't counted the fields. But the two villages are close to one another. They're a mile apart—it was mentioned in the Sub-Inspector's testimony.'

The magistrate said to Jognath's lawyer, 'Then where is the need to cross-examine him about the distance? Are you challenging the Sub-Inspector's evidence?'

'I am not challenging it, Your Honour, but I do have to conduct a cross-examination.'

'Why?'

'To demonstrate the level of the witness's intelligence.'

'Or to demonstrate the level of your own intelligence?'

Hearing this from the mouth of the magistrate, the face of the defence lawyer began to turn red, but by then the magistrate had begun to laugh loudly, proving that his comment was not an insult but a jest. As soon as he laughed, one by one, as they realized it was a joke, other people, too, began to laugh. Ultimately Jognath's lawyer also joined in. It is an unwritten law of the courts that magistrates and lawyers should occasionally display a ready wit on the same scale as the humour of the Mughal emperor Akbar and his minister Birbal, and exchange repartees. After the completion of this unnecessary ritual, the magistrate expunged all the questions which had dealt with the distance between Bhikhmakhera and Shivpalganj. But the questions were expunged only after the answers had already been committed to paper.

Baijnath's cross-examination continued.

'Until now, in how many cases have you testified for the police?'

'I can't remember.'

'I am asking you: until now, in how many cases have you testified for the police?'

'You can ask as often as you like—I can't remember.'

'Before this, have you ever appeared as a police witness in any case?'

'What on earth is a "police witness"?'

'Don't answer a question with a question. Give a straight answer.'

'Don't start being rude to me. I'm not riff-raff.'

After this rebuke, the lawyer appealed to the magistrate for protection. The magistrate said, 'Answer the question in a proper manner.'

Baijnath bowed and said, 'The question too should be a proper one, O Protector of the Poor! He is asking me how many times I have been a police witness. What do I have to do with the police? I bear witness to the truth. I do not hesitate to say what I know, whether it is the police who call me or the defence.'

Before the magistrate had time to reply, Jognath's lawyer had become enraged. In fact, he was one of those lawyers who are celebrated for their displays of temper, and his agents used to catch hold of new litigants and bring them to the court simply to show them his wrath.

Rage alone was his discipline, his wisdom, his knowledge of law, his weapon and his armour. It was his signboard, his advertisement, his father-mother-helper-Lord-friend. When he lost his temper—whether or not other people trembled—he himself quivered like a leaf. Wise judges proceeded quietly with their work, unaffected by his anger and expressing no opinion on it, considering it a commonplace exercise in the same class as coughing and sneezing. If any magistrate did take objection to his anger, the lawyer would criticize him in a speech to the bar association, and the association would pass a resolution.

This magistrate was wise and so paid no heed to his temper. Below him, the lawyer roared, 'I have asked a simple question; do not try to be clever with me. Tell me, up till the present time, how many times have you given evidence for the prosecution in cases brought by the State?'

Baijnath replied, 'So, my question, too, is simple, Lawyer sahib! You tell me, up till the present time, in how many cases have you represented dacoits and murderers?'

The lawyer had seen people struck with terror by his anger or made intractable, but never had he seen anyone responding with such self-assured impudence. Faced with this response, his rage began to wag its tail and then lay down on its back and waved all its four legs in the air in front of the magistrate. The lawyer lifted his eyes to the magistrate and said, 'Your Honour, now you can see for yourself the behaviour of this witness. His vulgar remarks constitute contempt of court.'

Baijnath wagged his head craftily as if the lawyer had been running along and he had managed to kick his legs out from under him. He remarked, 'Lawyer sahib, you can say whatever you like, but if I ask something you go and complain to the magistrate.'

The magistrate was busy reading some urgent papers, and so the lawyer was forced to rely on his own genius to wriggle out of this hole. Clenching his teeth he said, 'You give evidence for the police for the most minuscule amounts, and then you turn around and start cross-questioning me!'

Baijnath looked around vaingloriously, gazed with pity upon the lawyer and said, in a voice that all could hear, 'Everybody has his own business to conduct.'

The magistrate had finished signing the urgent papers. Now he said in all innocence, 'It's not right to talk amongst yourselves. Lawyer sahib, please continue the cross-examination.'

The lawyer said, 'Your Honour, it is difficult to cross-examine this witness. He avoids answering any question. Please note this fact.'

The magistrate gave Baijnath a penetrating glance. Baijnath had begun to look towards the public prosecutor. The public prosecutor was looking at the magistrate.

The magistrate told the lawyer, 'Proceed.'

The lawyer changed legs like a crane, thereby ending one historic phase of cross-examination and entering another.

'Were you a prosecution witness in the case of the State versus Churrai under Section 379?'

'I can't remember.'

'You gave evidence just this month!'

Baijnath thought for a few moments, and said, 'I did give evidence once this month. I was leaving my mango grove, when a man ran past carrying a bundle . . .'

'It's not necessary for you to repeat what you said in court, just say whether or not you gave evidence during the past month.'

'I did give evidence but I can't remember the name of the case.'

At last, the magistrate lost his temper. He said, 'How can that be?'

'I'm a peasant, my Lord, not educated.'

The lawyer said, 'Your Honour, please also make a note of this duplicity.'

Baijnath remarked, 'How much will His Honour note down? Note it down yourself. Tell your clerk, he'll note everything down for you.'

This time, the magistrate reprimanded Baijnath. Very severely. So much so that, for a while, Baijnath was really frightened. His face turned pale while, above him, the magistrate's turned red. But when the reprimand entered its third minute, Baijnath recovered himself. He recalled his guru, Pandit Radhelal, who had explained to him, 'Son, when you're giving evidence, sometimes the lawyer or the judge will lose his temper. Don't be upset by it. The poor wretches are working with their brains all day every day. Their stomachs are delicate, and they generally suffer from indigestion, dyspepsia and piles. So they get cantankerous. You should not be upset when they tell you off. You should just remember that they aren't scolding you but their digestions. Not only this, you should also remember that they are all big men, educated people. They just cannot understand what you're about, so when they get cross, keep a clear head and work out how you can get the better of them.'

Finally, the magistrate instructed him to answer questions with a simple yes or no. The tank of cross-examination now began to rumble over level ground.

'Six months ago today, did you give evidence for the prosecution in the case of the State versus Bisesar?'

'No.' (This answer was correct because Baijnath had given this evidence seven months earlier.)

'A year ago, did you give evidence in the case of the State versus Chunnu?'

'No.' (This answer, too, was correct—Chunnu's case had been heard fourteen months earlier.)

'. . .?'

'No.'

'. . .?'

'No.'

'. . .?'

'No.'

'. . .?'

'Yes.'

'. . . ?'

'Yes.'

'In this way, you have, up till now, been a State witness in a number of cases.'

'You have only counted two such cases.'

'In a large number of cases, the police have found you as a witness. Is there any special reason for this?'

Baijnath looked towards the magistrate and said in a martyred tone, 'The reason is that I am a spirited young man.' He thrust out his chest. 'No one where I come from dares to testify against ruffians. I am a bold man, and vehemently opposed to troublemakers. Therefore, I do not hesitate to state in public what I see.'

The lawyer tried to interrupt him; the magistrate waved his hand and told him to stand down from the witness box, but Baijnath's speech did not end. He went on, 'I have sworn that I shall rest only when I have driven off all ruffians from my area. I am unshakable in my purpose. I will be happy to lay down my life for this cause if need be.'

~

'Your name?'

'Chhote Wrestler.'

Amending his statement, the public prosecutor said to the clerk of the court, 'Write Chhote Lal.'

Chhote Wrestler looked at him as if he had been belittled. He gulped with anger. The second question was, 'Father's name?'

'Kusahar.'

The public prosecutor amended this too, saying, 'Kusahar Prasad.'

This time, Chhote Wrestler looked at him as if he had insulted his father.

'Caste?'

'Brahmin.'

'Village?'

'We are ganjahas.'

'Fine, but what is the name of your village?'

'Ganj.'

'What ganj?'

Chhote said haughtily, 'It's not as if there are hundreds of ganjes!' He paused, then said, 'Shivpalganj.'

'Swear by God that you will speak the truth and nothing but the truth.'

'Take it as having been said.'

'No, we can't take it as having been said; it should come from your mouth that you will speak the truth and nothing but the truth.'

'It did come from my mouth.'

The orderly turned to the magistrate as the negotiations had reached a deadlock. The magistrate took a close look at Chhote Wrestler—bulging cheeks, a neck like a bullock, and in the words of Gayadin, 'an elephant without a trunk'. On the other hand, the magistrate was an intellectual character. He instructed the orderly, 'Tell the witness to go outside and empty his mouth.'

'First go outside and empty your mouth.'

Chhote Wrestler wiped some imaginary sweat off his face with a small towel, and then leant confidently on the side of the witness box, peering out like a person standing at the rail of a ship, watching marine creatures. The magistrate ordered, 'Get the witness to go and empty his mouth.'

The public prosecutor told Chhote Wrestler, 'Go outside and spit out your betel nut.'

At that moment, Chhote was, indeed, chewing betel nut with great aplomb. It seemed to him as if he were being told to go and spit out his aplomb. He ignored the instructions but gradually swallowed the betel nut and wiped his face once more with the towel.

The magistrate then instructed, 'Administer the oath to the witness.'

The orderly, looking askance on this compromise, told Chhote, 'Swear by God to tell the truth and nothing but the truth.'

Chhote glanced around him and, this time, took the oath effortlessly. 'I will tell the truth and nothing but the truth.'

'Swear by God.'

'I swear by God.'

The public prosecutor first asked Chhote Wrestler about the search of Jognath's house. Chhote answered up to the point where the Sub-Inspector had gone with Jognath into his house.

'Then, was the house searched?'

'Yes.'

'What was found?'

'Nothing.'

The public prosecutor's eyebrows shot up. Emphasizing his words, he repeated, 'I am asking you: what was found?'

'What do you think they found? A gong?'

Jognath and his lawyer both began to smile. From behind, Sanichar said, 'Well done! Keep it up, son!'

'Who said that? What incivility is this?' inquired the magistrate, but by then Sanichar had already left the courtroom.

The public prosecutor said, 'Three ornaments were recovered during the search. They are placed before you.'

Jognath's lawyer leapt to the fore and said to the magistrate, 'Your Honour, this is a cross-examination.'

The magistrate responded gravely, 'Proceed.'

Jognath's lawyer raised an objection, 'Your Honour, please note that the public prosecutor is accepting that the witness has turned hostile.'

'Very well, proceed with the cross-examination.'

The public prosecutor turned towards Chhote Wrestler and repeated his question, 'These three ornaments which are placed before you, were they or were they not recovered from Jognath's house during the search?'

Chhote Wrestler addressed the magistrate with the air of a man who doesn't want to indulge in any meaningless fuss, 'I have given whatever statement I have to give. Nothing was found during the search.'

The public prosecutor took a sheet of paper from his file and said, 'Was this list of recovered items written in your presence?'

'There was only a lot of swearing and abusing when I was there. They never came down to writing anything.'

'Did you sign this list? Look at it and reply.'

Chhote Wrestler didn't even glance at the list. He replied arrogantly, 'No.'

The public prosecutor pointed to the places on the paper where Chhote had signed and said, 'Look at this; look at it well. These signatures are yours.'

Chhote Wrestler told the magistrate, 'I have made my statement, my Lord, now why does he keep harping on the same old question?'

This time, the magistrate showed him no sympathy. He warned him, 'Look at the paper and then reply. If you make a false statement you will be sent to jail.'

Chhote was unaffected by this. He threw out his chest saying, 'This is all only a business of jails, Your Honour. When you set foot in a court, you already have one leg in jail and one out of it. But what can I see in any paper? Reading and writing is beyond me. I have nothing to do with it.'

The public prosecutor raised his voice, 'Then how can you sign anything? Are these not your signatures?'

For the first time in a while, Jognath's lawyer opened his mouth. Like a man lovingly caressing a calf, he said, 'Ask the witness gently, one question at a time. It's not as if he's going to run away.'

Paying him no attention, the public prosecutor asked, 'Then how can you sign?'

'Who is signing? Has anyone in my family for the past seven generations ever signed anything, that I should start signing? Go and see, I have five hundred papers. On each of them, there's a thumbprint. Each one.'

Chhote gazed proudly around the court. The public prosecutor repeated, 'I say you have signed this paper.'

'If you want to, you can go on squeaking like a partridge; who is stopping you?'

The magistrate interrupted, 'Be polite!'

Chhote Wrestler was coming to the boil. He said, 'Everyone has their own idea of politeness, my Lord. Why should I be forced by this bluster into saying something that's wrong?'

The public prosecutor gathered his papers together and said, 'I have nothing more to ask.'

Chhote gathered his lungi around him and began to leave the witness box, but then Jognath's lawyer spoke, 'I have some questions to ask, Your Honour!'

The magistrate made no objection. The lawyer asked, 'Do you know Gayadin's daughter, Bela?'

'Who doesn't?'

'Don't evade the question. Speak about yourself. Do you know her or not?'

'How can I not know her?'

'What is the girl like?'

'Immoral.'

The magistrate said, 'This line of questioning is irrelevant. It has no bearing on the case.'

'It certainly does, Your Honour! I will make the point clear just now,' replied the lawyer, snapping his fingers. He asked Chhote Wrestler sharply, 'How do you know that Bela is immoral?'

'I've seen it with my own eyes.'

'What have you seen?'

'That she had immoral relations with Jognath. That's why Gayadin has got him involved in this case.'

After this, the cross-examination returned to the old familiar pattern of proving a thousand times over that no one in this world is a thief; that, in fact, the man who is accused of being a thief is the lover of the wife or of the sister or of the daughter of the master of the house, who had been summoned to bed her in the loneliness of the night, but whom the master of the house does not refer to as his brother, brother-in-law or son-in-law. He is reduced to calling him a thief and, 'Your Honour, the result is that . . .'

~

The Sub-Inspector was no longer in Shivpalganj. He had arrived in the town with his broken bedstead, his milch cow and his convent-going daughter, and was living in a pokey rented house which he had located with great difficulty. He had been given some special assignment, which made it necessary for him to live like an ordinary citizen and since, for government officials, living like an ordinary citizen is a sign of being in a very sorry state, one felt sorry to see him in that state.

However, since he had investigated the robbery case brought against Jognath, he was forced to be in court and come into contact once more with ganjahas. When he heard Chhote's evidence, he at once muttered, 'Oh dear, oh dear,' and, before he caught the magistrate's attention, he grasped Gayadin by the hand and pulled him out of the courtroom. For a few moments, they were both silent.

Finally, the Sub-Inspector said, 'These ganjahas ... There is a limit to dishonesty. His tongue should have fallen off for saying such things about a girl like Bela!'

Gayadin was staring at the ground. A pin was lying between two bricks. It seemed as though he was wondering whether to pick it up or not.

The Sub-Inspector said in a tone full of censure, 'Anyone can say what they like about anyone. No one gives a damn about respectable people.'

Then Gayadin remarked in his familiar, world-weary tone, 'This had to happen, Sub-Inspector sahib! The day you caught Jognath, I realized that no one in my house would be left with their honour intact.'

'I am very sorry.'

'There's no need to be sorry. It's not your fault. The man whom you want to call a thief and send to jail is not going to leave any stone unturned to stop you.'

'I am burning with anger.'

'Don't burn yourself for my sake, Sub-Inspector sahib! This is the way our country works. When you see the inside of a courtroom, you have to endure everything. You can say that the man who has been forced to come here has been struck down by misfortune. What is the point of burning with anger, Sub-Inspector sahib?'

Jognath's lawyer shot outside like an arrow and ran off to another courtroom. To the clients running behind him, he said, 'Don't be in a hurry. Let Jognath be released. Then I'll deal with everyone involved—yes, even the police.'

The Sub-Inspector started and looked up, but there was no one left there for him to see.

26

The Principal sahib was considering the problems of the college in Vaidyaji's company—that is to say, he was abusing Khanna Master. The day before, when he had gone to court for the case registered under Section 107, he had seen it take a new turn as Khanna Master's lawyer had, in his argument, made remarks along the following lines:

'Your Honour, this is a case of the "haves" versus the "have-nots". On one side is the college manager, who is known as Vaidya maharaj and who, in fact, is less of a vaid and more of a maharaja. Backing him are hundreds of his henchmen and thugs, including the Principal of the college and a dozen or so masters who are either his relatives or the relatives of his relatives. They are all well off and, if they are not, the college fund makes good what they lack. Your Honour, on the other side are Khanna and his dozen or so masters, who are poor and who are continually oppressed by the plots of their opponents. This is the principal reason for the struggle between the two sides.'

The magistrate said in English, 'That is to say, it's a question of loaves and fishes.'

The lawyer edited, corrected, reduced and expanded his argument, and then, manoeuvring and evading the issue, said, 'No, Your Honour, that was not what I meant. I was just saying that the disagreement is over principles.'

'That's not what you said.'

'I was about to, Your Honour,' continued the lawyer. 'Khanna and his like-minded colleagues cannot bear to see public money being misspent in this way. Your Honour, they are all young men and are still not in the habit of compromising with honesty and resorting to deceit . . .'

The magistrate smiled and said, 'In that case, they should have no fear of lawsuits or jails.'

Without paying attention to this comment, the lawyer continued to argue, 'That is why they raise their voices—in a constitutional manner—about the continuing mismanagement of the college. Your Honour, only recently, an election was held for the post of college manager and, by force of arms, Vaidyaji was re-elected. A complaint about this has been made to the deputy director of education. Khanna and his colleagues objected to the election. Not only that, but they also met with the deputy director and now, very soon, an inquiry is to be held into the whole matter. Similarly, there was embezzlement in the same cooperative of which Vaidya maharaj is the managing director.

This fact was suppressed for six months. Khanna and his companions met with the registrar of cooperative societies and have had an inquiry started into that, too. If required, I can call both senior officials as witnesses.

'Your Honour, this case has been initiated in order to suppress Khanna and his companions, and to force them to keep their mouths shut during these inquiries. In a way this case, too, is a plot, Your Honour . . .'

What the Principal's lawyer said in court is not important. But that day, back in the village, the Principal told Vaidyaji that inquiries were about to be made both into the college election and the embezzlement in the cooperative.

Not a line of worry marked Vaidyaji's face. He bowed his head to dharma and, after saying, 'It's God's will,' fell silent.

But today, the Principal sahib had come with a definite plan and, being highly excited, said in Awadhi, 'Maharaj, 'tis my opinion that we should break every limb in that bastard Khanna's body and chuck him into some ravine. If that doesn't work, we grab them all by the ears and throw them out of the college and give them four *latai* kicks in the *chootar* back four times each.'

But this, too, had no effect on Vaidyaji. He simply said, 'I don't like talk of violence,' and belched. The Principal waited for him to say 'It's God's will' again, but he said nothing, perhaps being silently entangled in the problems of non-violence, the display of the pistol, the embezzlement, and the welfare of the country.

~

About a hundred yards beyond the liquor shop, there was a peepul tree inhabited by an evil spirit. The spirit was quite old and, despite hundreds of events like the winning of Independence, land reforms, the establishment of the village council and the opening of the college, he had not yet died. Whoever knew about his presence would never pass that way after sunset. If anyone did, he would hear all kinds of strange noises which would later bring on a fever of which he would probably die. If he didn't, people would say that Pandit Radhelal was excellent at exorcizing spirits.

One evening, a cyclist was riding on the road by whose side the peepul tree grew, and so he had to pass underneath it. The cyclist knew about the spirit and if a truck had not been driving along slowly in front of him, he may not have had the courage to pass by that way at that time. Guided by the red rear lights of the truck and taking the few remaining streaks of brightness in the west as signs of daylight, he cycled on right beneath the tree.

Then he heaved a sigh of relief. The wind of the month of Phalgun blew against his face and he took immense pleasure in it. Becoming a little more enthusiastic, he said *katilon-katilon* two or three times, imitating, for an imaginary audience, the call of a partridge; then began to hum a song called *He went off like a tiger after killing the hunter*, from Amarsingh Rathore's famous nautanki. Gradually, the volume of his voice increased.

Suddenly, the cyclist started. Just by the edge of the road, he heard a noise—*gon-gon-gon*. That was no human voice. Without even being told, the cyclist realized that this must be the voice of the spirit. He held his breath in the upper part of his body and expelled air from the lower end. It seemed that the spirit had changed his area of operation without informing anyone, had descended from the peepul tree and perhaps climbed a pakar tree.

He heard the *gon-gon-gon* noise again, this time slightly louder. At the same time, two kinds of voices could be heard. One man laughed loudly; another said, 'I told you not to drink too much but you wouldn't listen, would you? Drink some more, son!'

Then could be heard the sound of a man's voice singing. As he laughed, someone else started to sing *Don't make a fuss, chik-chik, I bow my head to everyone*, a song from the nautanki, *Hamid the Dacoit*.

At that point, there was some modulation in the *gon-gon-gon* noise. First, someone made an introductory *gon-gon*. Then, perhaps with the thought of showing some originality, he gave a throat-splitting cry for help and ended with the same old *gon-gon-gon*. But this time, there was no power in his voice; it was no more than a ritual. At the same time, the singer of the song from *Hamid the Dacoit* terminated his musical programme. Then, perhaps, it was he who said, 'I told you, son, don't drink too much. Except when the liquor's free.' Then the same laughter. And the same song from *Hamid the Dacoit*.

The cyclist's internal upset had been due to the ghost. He had no fear of men. Therefore, when he heard men's voices and smelled trouble, he jumped down from his bicycle and challenged, 'Don't you worry, wrestler! I've come! Look out, don't lay a finger on him!'

There was a bush on the far side of the pakar tree. Half a dozen men were moving around it in the twilight. Several voices could be heard.

'*Gon-gon-gon!*'

'Help!'

'Don't talk so much nonsense, son! I told you not to drink too much.'

'Don't make a fuss, chik-chik, I bow my head to everyone.'

The cyclist was looking around alertly and had raised his voice to save some unknown person from some unknown danger. Suddenly, a man came out from behind the bush and walked smartly up to the cyclist. His mouth smelled of country liquor as he said with authority, 'What's the matter, soldier? Why are you shouting? What's your problem?'

The cyclist pointed to the bush and said, 'Someone over there was screaming for help.'

'The fools are all merry with drink and want to talk nonsense. But what do you want?'

Another two cyclists came pedalling down the road. Seeing the two standing there, they slowed down and began to prepare to dismount. The voices from behind the bush had now become even louder, but no words were intelligible. The man said in a military style, 'There's no need for you to stop. This is a ganjaha matter. The bastards had a few and are well tanked. You fall in and get on your way.'

Hearing this discourse, both the cyclists increased their speed. The first cyclist, too, moved on, his nostrils pinched with anger. He left with the parting remark, 'They're all layabouts. The whole area stinks of these drunkards.'

The military-style man replied, 'You're absolutely right, soldier! Alcohol is a curse.'

Now the road was deserted. The man stood where he was and said, 'Let's go, boys, on the double! Forward march!'

A conversation was being held in a strange lisping tongue.

'Yesh, brother, letsh go now.'

'Shall we keep the gag in thish buggersh mouth or take it out?'

'Letsh keep it in.'

Five men came out from behind the bush on to the road. Not one of them was unsteady on his feet. They were all silent and, from their gait, seemed to be proceeding with the same preparedness as an ambush platoon entrusted with the task of recapturing border territory occupied by the Chinese. When they approached the haunted peepul tree, they got off the road. This could have been out of regard for the spirit and also because of the car heading towards them with dazzling headlights. As they descended from the road, they crossed into a field which had been surrounded by thorn branches. There was no crop in the field; the thorns were there just to protect the land.

One man let out a suppressed scream and said, 'Oh, my godfather! Thornsh!'

A second said, 'Whosh the bastard whosh put thornsh here?'

The first man replied, 'Ram Channa.'

'When?'

'After you'd been shent to jail.'

'Thatsh when! Well, now I'm back . . . Thish field ish mine. Did he think thish wash hish fathersh land that he went and planted thornsh on it?'

'Don't loosh your temper. Now you're back. Everything will be put to rightsh.'

'All right. But where did he get these thornsh from? Who gave them to him . . .?'

The detachment had climbed up from the field on to the road again. They were about fifty yards from the liquor shop. The men stopped speaking their lisping language and one said, 'Ram Channa doesn't have a single thorn tree of his own. Did he cut one down and bring it here?'

'Who's to know whose thorn tree it was?'

'Don't tell me then. I'll find out for myself, anyway.'

'If you're going to find out for yourself, why ask me?'

'To find out what kind of man you are.'

The second man laughed and, addressing society at large, said, 'In jail, Jognath has learnt how to cross-examine people.'

'Don't you worry, you idiot; I'll give you, too, a lesson.'

They disappeared into the liquor house. There were half a dozen or so people there already. One said enthusiastically, 'Jognath! When did you come out of jail?'

'This afternoon.'

'What was it like?' asked the same man with even more enthusiasm.

'Very good.'

'Did you meet anyone you know?'

'I got to know every one of them.'

'Bisesar must have been in there. Met him?'

'No, but all the people there turned out to be fathers of Bisesar.'

'Did you have to do hard labour?' asked a hoarse voice from a corner.

Jognath said angrily, 'Who's that? Son of a chicken . . .'

'It's a guest.'

'Tell him not to blow his trumpet. It's not appreciated in Shivpalganj.'

'Did you hear that, guest? This is Jognath. He's just come out of jail. He's telling you not to blow your trumpet.'

'Now listen to me. I'm telling you right from the start. I am a first-class bastard. Quietly drink up your liquor and throw up there in the corner. If you mention hard labour again, I'll damn well show you some.'

'Did you hear, guest?'

'Who's to hear? There's no one in the corner over here.'

'Arré, where's the guest? Has he slipped out?'

'Arré, well done, guest!'

Jognath took out a ten-rupee note, pushed it into the landlord's hand, and said, 'Give everyone a peg each. No one should be left out; I've returned to my land after a long time.'

'You've brought a lot of money with you.'

'Sanichar's become the pradhan. It's his orders that everyone should drink deeply today.'

'But where has Sanichar got any money?'

'Now Sanichar is no longer the old Sanichar; he's the pradhan. Do you follow?'

Everyone sat down with a peg each on the veranda of the shop, which was separated from the road by a wooden fence. The shop itself was in the small room inside. A hurricane lamp was burning on the veranda by the light of which you could make out the faces of the drinkers. A small earthenware oil lamp was burning inside the shop, by the light of which you couldn't make out their faces. Two men were sitting on a bench on the veranda. Jognath, too, sat down there. The other people were sitting on a piece of jute sacking on the floor, and a few on the mud floor itself. The shop was Shivpalganj's answer to Omar Khayyam's wine bearer, flask and cup. The smell of country liquor spread quite a distance down the road, revealing to people far and wide that country liquor was being sold here. Where we come from, the smell of country liquor is its advertisement. So, while you find advertisements for English liquor in the major newspapers, there's no mention of country liquor. It needs no such publicity.

After taking two or three gulps, Jognath looked around and said, 'It's been watered.'

'What?'

'Water! The liquor's watered down.'

'I think so too.'

'Me too.'

'Me too. I've been thinking so for a long time. In fact, now I've got so used to it that it tastes the same to me as the real stuff.'

The landlord rose from his seat and came over to Jognath. He said coolly, 'Enjoy your drink. You're getting high just on your first peg. If you want to drink a quarter bottle or so on the house, just say so and I'll give it you. But it's cheats who water down liquor. It doesn't happen here.'

This had the necessary effect on Jognath. He pulled several five-rupee notes from his pocket and said, 'If I had to drink free, I certainly would. But don't you fret, take a look at this! Have you ever seen so much?'

The landlord was a scrawny man but didn't lack courage. He walked back boldly and replied, 'My days of looking at money are over. If you've just discovered what it looks like, go ahead and look at it.'

The second round was served. One man asked, 'So what are you going to do now, Jognath?'

'I'm short of money,' remarked Jognath in a tone which indicated that no one should believe it, 'Right now, I have to settle scores with the Sub-Inspector. What's it to me if he's been transferred? I'm not going to leave him alone. Even before I came here, I put in a claim against him in the town. A dozen hearings will loosen up his plaster.'

'What sort of case?'

'Civil. Don't you know he filed a false case of robbery against me? I had to stay in the lock-up for two or three months.'

'Didn't Vaidyaji bail you out?'

'He would have, but my mind was made up. I said I'd stay right there as the Sub-Inspector's prisoner. After all, it wasn't as if I had to pay rent to stay there.'

'Then?'

'Then what? I was disgraced; my crops were damaged. Ram Channa grabbed one of my fields. For all these losses, I've lodged a claim for damages of eight thousand rupees. When the decree comes, the Sub-Inspector will have to sell himself.'

'But what about the legal fees? Civil cases are very expensive!'

'All that, God will give.'

'Now look here, brother Jognath, you were born in a Brahmin home, so don't start making up stories. Who's going to pay the legal fees?'

'I told you—God is.'

'Now he's annoyed, he won't say. Don't tell us then, let it pass. So, are you going to stick in the claim or have you stuck it in already?'

'I've stuck it in.'

'When did you stick it in?'

'Today.'

~

A man staggered out from behind a bush and, moaning, began to walk along the road. The meaning of those words of his which filtered through to the liquor house was that, just a short while earlier, he had been attacked by the roadside, beyond the haunted peepul tree, and some men had robbed him. He was on his way to file a report at the police station to get his own back on every single one of the robbers.

A little later, when the group staggered out from the liquor shop, there was no one on the street but a couple of scrawny dogs.

The man who had gone past earlier, moaning about being robbed, now walked straight back past the group without any of them even noticing him. His sins had been washed away, and his faith in religion strengthened because, before he had even reached the police station, a knowledgeable gentleman had advised him, 'What will you get from writing a report? Whatever is gone is gone. Does the year that has passed ever return?

'Tell me, are you a Hindu or a Muslim? If you are a Hindu, you believe in karma, don't you? Those forty-five rupees were not written in your karma. Now, running from pillar to post will serve no purpose. God had ordained that you should lose the money . . .

'Go home; your life is safe, that is enough. Last year, at the very same place, a man was butchered like a goat.

'Take the name of Lord Ram, go home and get a priest to recite the glorious deeds of Satyanarayan. Spend the money you would have spent on court cases on religious works.

'Drink warm milk with turmeric and turn over before you go to sleep. By tomorrow morning, you'll have forgotten all about it.'

27

There was a time when philosophers used to argue about the existence of God. Now they argue about wheat. One group is of the opinion that the country has sufficient wheat but that mischievous traders prevent it from reaching the bazaars. The second group is of the opinion that there is no such thing as wheat, and even if there is, at any rate there's none in India. Recently, this stage of the discussion had also reached Shivpalganj, and people there had begun to exhibit a lack of belief in milk, curds and ghee as well.

How could the wrestling pit manage to keep going in the prevailing atmosphere of starvation? A few years earlier, when the boys came back home worn out with exercise and wrestling, at least they could rely on getting some soaked gram and buttermilk. Now they couldn't even do that. This, together with several other facts of a similar nature, was creating an environment which left the village boys with no option but to become layabouts. They covered their skinny legs in old, torn, but colourful trousers or pyjamas; and whether there was any flesh on their chests or not, their hearts swelled with the desire to sleep with Saira Banu. They roamed aimlessly, distributing their red betel-juice spittle all over the alleys and by-lanes. Many of them occasionally took a round of the fields, workshops and jails, too. The ones who baulked at this went to local colleges to obtain a rustic education. These colleges were generally founded at the inspiration of a local leader for spreading education and, even more so, for preparing his ground for the next State Assembly or parliamentary polls, and their main achievement was exploiting teachers and government grants. The colleges were run entirely according to the current fashion—that is, without any manner of foresight or hindsight—and it was a certainty that the boys studying in them would never cease to be servile and would never try to assert themselves. Therefore, the people who controlled the senior bureaucracy and professions didn't find their monopoly in the least bit threatened by these colleges.

Howsoever that may be, amidst this clamour over food, the wrestling pits were closing down, and the physical development of the village youth had now reached the same level as their mental development. From this point of view, it was significant that Shivpalganj had a wrestling pit and that several boys attended it regularly. It goes without saying that this was due to Badri Wrestler. For several years, he had been going to the pit, exercising, making his disciples wrestle with each other, throwing them, injuring them and then accepting them as full-fledged wrestlers. When any pupil came home groaning after several days of exercise and wrestling, it was proof that he had returned after having received his degree at his convocation.

Two wrestlers came swaying from the wrestling pit. One was Badri, the other Chhote. Both had shaven heads, and their bodies were plastered with sweat and earth. On the backs of their necks, there were rhinoceros-like folds of skin. Both had let the front ends of their loincloths dangle down like elephants' trunks. On both sides of the narrow strips of cloth, a limited part of their testicles was displayed to the world. But just as, in the name of art, Henry Miller and D.H. Lawrence are forgiven their obscenities, both these wrestlers, in the name of physical exercise, had been given licence to expose themselves.

Chhote Wrestler had attended his convocation ceremony several years earlier, but had now perhaps received a postgraduate degree, which would explain why he was groaning very softly and intermittently. Out of self-respect, he groaned not with an 'Ow!' but a sigh and an 'Oh!' Badri Wrestler was walking along with him as if he had nothing whatsoever to do with all this.

Today, Badri had flattened Chhote with the dhobi-slab throw. A wrestler using this move has to work like a high-class poet. He has to see the wrestling pit as an attractive lake, himself as a dhobi, and his opponent as a petticoat. Then, grabbing hold of his opponent's hands, he pulls them behind him, and—just as a dhobi beats clothes clean on a stone slab—he throws his opponent over his shoulder and down on to the floor in the middle of the pit. As he makes the throw, he has to be careful that the petticoat falls with its front uppermost—that is, his opponent must land on his back. After that it is, 'Victory! Victory! Glorious victory! The enemy lies speechless, astounded, with bent knee and bowed head . . .'

Badri Wrestler had been rather too imaginative when he threw Chhote today. He had imagined the wall around the wrestling pit to be a dhobi's slab. The result was that when Chhote had been flattened on his back, sparks had seemed to fly before his eyes. The lower part of his body was outside the pit and the upper part inside, and it was just his shamelessness which prevented his back from breaking.

If Badri Wrestler had not been his guru, Chhote would, at this point, have showered him with thousands of curses, with tears in his eyes and froth falling from his mouth. But, out of regard for his guru, he was quiet, and when it became difficult for him to walk in silence, he let out an 'Oh!'

But his affliction was not going to end there. As they walked on, Badri Wrestler asked, 'Well then, what did you go and say in evidence for Jognath that day?'

'Which bastard was witness for Jognath? I went to give evidence for the police,' replied Chhote carelessly, suppressing the pain in his back.

Badri remarked peaceably, 'When you're asked a straight question, give a straight answer . . . What did you say about Bela in your testimony?'

'What did I have to say? I just said what came into my mouth.'

Badri spoke very gently. He held Chhote's hand and asked, 'Is she carrying on with Jognath?'

Chhote slowly withdrew his hand. When you hold on to a man's fingers, you can catch hold of his wrists, and when you've caught hold of his wrists you can flatten him with a dhobi-slab throw—all this he had just seen. To avoid the issue, he said, 'How would I know who is carrying on with whom? There are fields of arhar all round the village. Do you expect me to go peeking into all of them to see who's hugging whom?'

Badri continued in the same gentle tone. 'But you said that you had seen Bela and Jognath all over one another.'

'Just saying something doesn't mean anything.'

Suddenly, Badri stood still. In a harsh tone he said, 'Why doesn't it? Did you say it or not? Speak up!'

Chhote Wrestler now became apprehensive. The ring of self-assurance in his voice disappeared. In the same way that the greatest and most visionary authors stammer when faced by radio interviewers, Chhote was suddenly overawed by Badri Wrestler.

He said apologetically, 'Why shouldn't I have said it, guru? You can say I said a great deal. It was a court matter. I said whatever came into my mouth. It's not as if I had to tell the truth.'

Badri Wrestler stood silently in the darkness for a while. He was doing what no wrestler can do with ease—he was thinking.

Chhote was now even more overawed. Hesitantly, he asked, 'Guru, what are you thinking about? Thinking is for cheats and bird-catchers. Tell me what the matter is.'

Badri said slowly, 'I'm wondering whether I should kick you or give you a shoe-beating. You bastard, puppies' piss on your youth! I spit on you!' With this, he spat on the ground with venom.

Chhote stood dumbfounded. Haltingly he said, 'Don't say that, guru! Tell me where I've been at fault.'

'How can you understand, you bastard? You've dirtied the name of a girl from a good family in front of the whole world. And as far as you're concerned, you've done nothing!'

So that was all it was! Chhote Wrestler heaved a sigh of relief. He remarked carelessly, 'Guru, whatever I said, I said in a full courtroom under oath. Everyone knows that you can never rely on anything said in court. How has it done anyone any harm?'

Badri's silence somewhat encouraged Chhote. In his natural style—that is, as if regarding the whole of humanity as maggots—he completed his point. 'That is what you want to give me a shoe-beating for, guru? Great! Even you make such a fuss over things sometimes! I just couldn't think what the matter was.'

Badri Wrestler rubbed his neck with both hands and slapped it two or three times. In this way, he knocked off the mud plaster sticking there and threw off the thoughts which had up to now been assailing him. Then suddenly he laughed, 'You're a born fool. Can't you see what's going on around you? This Bela is about to become your mother. Now you can call her a slut or whatever you like. The insult will rebound on you.'

'What did you say, guru?'

'What is there to say? Within a month, Bela will be married to Badri Wrestler! And you will blow a trumpet! Do you follow, son?'

Circus clowns talk nonsense and perform acrobatics. Drummers at nautanki shows take a stick from under their arm and start beating an irregular rhythm. In the wrestling pit, two or three wrestlers stand on their hands and walk with their legs curved back like the tails of scorpions. When calves come home in the evening, they lower their heads, run from side to side, rush off in the opposite direction and jump into the pond. Without any reason, Sanichar would suddenly say, 'Arrrrrrrrrr!'

Listening to Badri Wrestler, it seemed to Chhote almost as if there were a pile of such absurd things before him and as if someone had just thrown him down on his back on top of it. From his mouth came the words, 'What are you saying, guru?'

'Aren't you listening to what I'm telling you?' replied Badri Wrestler lightly, as if making a joke. 'What's the matter? Are your ears full of dirt? Here it is again—I am marrying Bela. I've already promised her. That day, when you defamed her in court, every hair on my body was burning. I felt like thumping you and bashing your head down into your stomach. But you are my disciple. As my own foster child, you are forgiven.'

With a deep sigh he concluded, 'Anyway, whatever's done is done. Keep a rein on your tongue from now on.'

Chhote still felt as if he were lying on his back on a pile of absurdities and that whatever Badri Wrestler was saying was a dream. He said, 'Guru, you're a Brahmin; she's a Bania. Think twice before you speak. If Vaidya maharaj objects, your plan will fall to pieces.'

Badri Wrestler replied, 'Elephants go their own way; dogs just keep barking.'

Chhote was practically imploring him when he said, 'You're talking in riddles. But that's never going to make Vaidyaji accept it!'

It seemed as though Badri Wrestler felt lighter for having revealed his heart's secret. He gave no reply but just began to whistle.

After walking on for a while, the matter penetrated Chhote's brain with all its weight. Only recently, there had been a rumour about Ruppan babu writing a letter to Bela. The story floating around about some girl coming on to Vaidyaji's roof at night, running into Rangnath and running back again had also reached Chhote's ears. The roof of Gayadin's house was one of the roofs which could be reached from the roof of Vaidyaji's house. Ruppan babu had also told him one day that Rangnath had laid his hands on a letter written by some girl but that Rangnath was saying nothing about it. Chhote Wrestler had suspected that, for some time, Ruppan babu had been out to ensnare Bela and had now succeeded in doing so. In this state of mind, the sudden revelation that Badri Wrestler was involved with Bela and that it had gone so far, unsteadied him.

He asked, 'But, guru, I've heard that Ruppan babu wrote something to Bela.'

'Yes, he did. He's a boy. They do daft things.'

'And I hear that some letter also came from her side?'

Badri growled, 'Who told you?'

'No one at all, guru!'

'Then how do you know?'

'I heard it, guru!'

'From whom?'

'I can't remember, guru, but there was a rumour about it.'

Badri Wrestler fell silent. When, in the course of conversation, anyone adopts the expression of a professional witness facing a cross-examination under oath, it's pointless to question him further.

After an interval of silence, Badri Wrestler said clearly, 'Yes, there was a letter. It was for me. But it wasn't a letter—the pranks of girls these days!—it was all about songs and music.'

Chhote said, flattering him, 'So, guru, this affair must have been going on for some years? On the roof itself . . .'

Badri replied, 'You are the first person I've told about this important matter. That's enough. Now don't try to look into it too deeply. And see here—don't tell anyone else about it yet.'

In the dusk, Chhote Wrestler collided with the corner of a platform which, according to local custom, someone had built with the intention of grabbing more land. Swearing once and then uttering an 'Oh!' out of consideration for the pain in his back, he vowed, 'I shan't tell anyone, guru.'

'In a few days the news will in any case spread, but for the time being, keep it to yourself.'

'I've given my word, guru. I won't tell anyone.'

A little while later, Badri Wrestler began to laugh. He said, 'But what a great match you made, young Chhote! Bela involved with Jognath! Huh! The bastard's like a paisa's worth of jaggery! If Bela were to take his hand he'd start whimpering, and *he* is the one *you* linked with Bela! You really are a complete idiot.'

Chhote felt a sudden smarting pain in his back, as if after the dhobi-slab throw, someone had thrown him down again.

Before they parted, Badri again cautioned Chhote against mentioning anything to anyone about his relationship with Bela just yet. Chhote faithfully took the oath of secrecy, but his oath was like all the oaths of secrecy which are taken in governors' residencies by members of state governments and, as a result, the very next day, Badri Wrestler met several people who looked at him with new eyes.

28

There was an unhappy lad in the village and his name was Ruppan babu. Up to a few days ago, his influence had spread far and wide and he had a high status because his father's name was Vaidyaji and, on top of that, he had made a name for himself, too. He had been studying in the tenth class for several years and was a student leader. The tehsildar was his companion, the Sub-Inspector of police his courtier, and the Principal his subordinate. At home, his status was that of a bright, skittish calf, and it seemed certain that he would learn the art of grazing the political pastures like other capable progeny and that, on Vaidyaji's death, he would spend between six months and a year wandering on various roads and then one day, be seen ruminating on his father's old patch.

Five months ago, a young man by the name of Rangnath had come to the village. People recognized his greatness because his uncle's name was Vaidyaji and, apart from that, he had greatness of his own. He had an MA in history. He looked like a good and straightforward man but he could make some wry remarks when he wanted to. He was among the 95 per cent of intellectuals whose intellect makes them deliver speeches on what others should and should not do and keeps them miles removed from the vulgar thought that they, too, have some responsibility for all the things which are left undone.

The young man whose name was Ruppan babu had become sad because, for some days, his personal preferences had been at odds with his political likes and dislikes, and the evil in the latter which had never been visible to him before had now begun to hang from his eyelashes like a football. Earlier, Ruppan had considered the Principal merely his father's slave, but now it seemed to him that he was extremely foolish and stubborn and that, in his malice against some teachers, he was drawing Ruppan's father into factionalism. Earlier, some masters had seemed to Ruppan to be fools and idiots, but recently he had begun to feel that even though they were idiots they were not ruffians and should be protected. Just a few days ago, Badri Wrestler had looked the ultimate in strength, and Ruppan had been proud of it, but now he had begun to notice the ruffians from neighbouring districts who sometimes came to Shivpalganj, talked to Badri and went back. That is to say, Ruppan's heart had begun to feel the restlessness which turns a man into a Vibhishan, a Trotsky or a Subhash Chandra Bose, and makes him want to achieve something, and which finally culminates on the gallows, in jail, or in a belief in the asceticism of Jayaprakash Narayan or Achyut Patwardhan.

The other young man, Rangnath, was in rather low spirits because, in these five months, he had seen people begin to get their arms and legs broken in games that had started only in jest, and that the dust which had been laughingly thrown into people's eyes had blinded them. When the matter of Sanichar's becoming pradhan was raised, or when Chhote Wrestler had gone to give evidence against Jognath, everything had seemed a joke. But when Rangnath saw that Sanichar really did become pradhan, and Chhote came back laughing after getting Jognath released from jail, he had received something of a jolt. The day Sanichar won, Rangnath had thought a great deal. He visualized goodness knows how many Sanichars in state capitals, slipping into a line of innumerable Vaidyajis, ministers and chief ministers.

Another incident occurred while the restlessness of the young man called Ruppan babu was stirring, but it had nothing to do with that particular restlessness. He had wanted a girl for a very long time, and while recognizing this fact, he had mistakenly come to believe that he needed only Bela, he loved Bela and, not being in possession of the full facts, he also imagined that Bela must love him, too. He had written a love letter to her, to which she had not replied but for which he himself had had to answer in several places and on several occasions. He had defended himself stoutly but in his heart he was ashamed. Then, the day he heard from Khanna Master that Bela and Badri were involved with one another and that Badri was going to marry her, he felt an immense disquiet in his heart and, for some reason, this disquiet compelled him to think insulting thoughts about the Principal, Vaidyaji, Badri Wrestler and Sanichar.

At the same time, Rangnath realized that it was not enough to learn by rote, stories of oppression and exploitation, and that even loading a donkey with the weight of the Vedas, the Upanishads and the Puranas, and making it chairman of an international scholars' council, doesn't make it human. To be human, one has to do more than just carry the load of scholarship.

Before he told Ruppan babu about Badri's love story, Khanna Master also told him something else. This meeting had taken place three days after Holi, as the moon was rising, on a small roadside culvert—the same culvert where, a few days earlier, Rangnath and Ruppan babu had sat and Rangnath had told Ruppan about his experience of sleeping alone on the roof.

Khanna Master had Malaviya with him. They were both sitting on the wall of the culvert. Ruppan babu was exhausted from drinking bhang continuously through the Holi festival. In order to rid himself of his weariness, he started imbibing bhang all over again and then set out for a stroll with Rangnath. Seeing two men sitting on the culvert, he said naturally, 'Who's there, then?'

'Who is it? Ruppan babu? Good evening, Rangnathji, I'm Khanna here.'

'Who's that with you?'

'It's Malaviya. Good evening, Ruppan babu, please come and sit down.'

Giving a curt reply to his teacher's greetings, Ruppan babu sat down on the culvert. The Big Four Summit began.

It was about nine o'clock in the evening, but there was no peace anywhere. The battery-powered radio in the paan shop opposite the tehsil office was still blaring away. Near at hand, jackals were calling. But the most powerful noise—which drowned out all the others—was from the trucks which were racing towards the town at seventy miles an hour, their horns blaring. Night had already fallen. 'In some cheap bar in the town, rum bottles must be emptying; in some wayside restaurant, meat and hot tandoori rotis must be ready; and somewhere, some girl must be puffing on a beedi and waiting for me'—such thoughts were enough to rouse longing in the truck drivers coming in from hundreds of miles away, making them push their feet down on the accelerator as hard as they could.

As a result, every five minutes, a truck would roar past down the road, and as it passed, the four great men seated on the bridge would hold their breath. Then, once it had gone, they would assure themselves that they had survived and could complete their unfinished sentences.

Despite this inconvenience, the talks were progressing. Khanna Master was appealing in an aggrieved tone to Ruppan and Rangnath for help. He took a piece of paper from his pocket and said to Ruppan, 'Please read this. See what your Principal has written.'

Ruppan babu replied, 'I can't read in the dark. If you can, read it out.'

Then Khanna Master recited a summary of the letter. It was about Malaviya's conduct. If the summary was to be believed, one would have to accept that Malaviya loved his students and that his love for some students was on a purely physical level. The handbill described several occasions when Malaviya had taken a boy into the town to the cinema, spent the night with him, and after giving him the math paper for the coming examinations, returned to Shivpalganj. The handbill had not been written with any literary purpose in mind, but to inform the general public of these incidents. Its descriptive style was therefore clear, simple and occasionally obscene. The paper appealed to the Principal and the manager to throw such masters out of the college by their ears.

After reciting the summary, Khanna Master asked Ruppan babu, 'Do you still want us to keep quiet after this? To say nothing against the Principal?'

Ruppan babu, well under the influence of bhang, asked, 'Then what do we do?'

'We have incontrovertible evidence. This handbill was published by the Principal. We will file a defamation case against him.'

'It's a shameful matter,' observed Rangnath.

Ruppan babu said carelessly, 'See here, it is true that at one time things like this were being said against Malaviya. One boy had told me himself that Malaviya had asked him to go to the cinema with him . . .'

A rather strange noise interrupted him. Malaviya was blowing his nose very forcefully. Then the others remembered that he was there.

Khanna Master became enraged, and said, 'This . . . This is character assassination. A decent man is being disgraced. We hoped for some sympathy from you, and then you go and make the same kind of comments.'

Ruppan babu replied unkindly, 'I am just saying what I've heard. You masters are always getting up to such things. Even if this complaint is true, it's nothing new. But I oppose this sort of publicity campaign. Rest assured, I shall oppose it openly.'

Khanna became even angrier. 'Ruppan babu, you are going on repeating the same thing. I disagree with you. This is false propaganda against Malaviya. It is character assassination. Anyone can say anything they like about anyone—is that in any way right?' He continued, 'Look, people have also begun to say things about Badri Wrestler. God knows what nonsense they're talking, but I don't believe any of it.'

It was Rangnath who asked first. 'What nonsense are they talking about brother Badri?'

Then, after a rambling introduction, Khanna Master related the story of Badri's love affair, which he had heard from a student, and which the student had heard from a wrestler at the wrestling pit, and which the wrestler had heard from God knew whom. In the report which Khanna Master gave Ruppan and Rangnath, he also added the point that even without getting his daughter married, Gayadin was going to become a grandfather in seven or eight months' time and Ruppan babu was about to get a nephew as a gift.

The news was so earth-shattering that Ruppan babu almost fell off the culvert and Rangnath had to try to cover it up by blaming it on the effect of bhang. But it was clear that Ruppan babu had been shaken. A little later on, when he'd regained his composure, many things of which he had never taken any notice before became significant. He remembered that recently Badri had been staying on the roof doing his exercises for rather a long time, and that he would shut the door at the top of the stairs when he was doing them. It also became clear who the girl who had come to Rangnath's charpoy was.

Now Ruppan babu really felt the warmth of the bhang, and he began to look around uneasily. Simultaneously, he also began to feel pity for these masters and for himself. He started to rant abuse against the Principal and when Rangnath tried to calm him down, and to tell the masters—as he had earlier—that it was nothing, just the effect of the bhang, Ruppan babu shut him up with a growl.

~

In one corner of the town, there was a large, spacious bungalow surrounded by a high wall, which seemed from its appearance to belong to an old landowning family. After land reforms, it had been rented out to a member of the aristocracy of the new age.

In a corner room of the bungalow was the office of the district inspector of schools; the rest of the bungalow was his residence. The government paid the full rent for the portion which formed his residence, believing it to be his office. The district school inspector paid the full rent for his office as rent for his residence. This amicable arrangement gave the inspector what is known in English as an 'office-cum-residence' and, in Hindi, as an 'office-*kum*, residence-*zyada*'—less of an office and more of a residence.

Vaidyaji, the Principal and Ruppan babu came out of the office, that is to say, the corner room. To anyone observing them, they would have looked like three thieves who had just pulled off a robbery. After taking a dozen or so steps they slowed down and began to look around, inspecting the extent of the lawn and the beauty of the flower beds. Looking up at the portico, Ruppan babu said, 'The Inspector sahib's car is turning to scrap.'

The Principal glanced at it and said, 'He's had some restrictions placed on his travelling allowance.'

'That explains it!' Ruppan babu looked around the lawn, gardens and building, and said, 'Whatever else you may say, this is style! And everything is free!' A chapraasi appeared at the gate. Seeing the Principal sahib, he made a face. The Principal pulled a different face and rolled his head stupidly. Then he took an eight-anna coin from his pocket and gave it to the chapraasi saying, 'Now, brother, are you going to ask for a tip every day?'

The chapraasi said in a civilized tone, 'I live only on what you gentlemen give me.'

Ruppan babu said, 'Can we doubt it?'

Vaidyaji gave him a sharp glance and walked off in silence to the road. This did not affect Ruppan's good humour. He told the Principal lightly, 'On such occasions it's not right to give more than two annas. You can buy two paans for that much. It's more than enough to give as a tip . . .'

This was the part of town which the British had named Civil Lines and had left to their heirs and spiritual progeny. There was very little traffic here. Occasionally, some sleek automobile—either paid for by the government or by a loan or provided free—zoomed past leaving pedestrians cowering on the roadside, happy that by God and good fortune they had survived; occasionally, some rusty hulk of a car would rumble past—a genuinely private car, appearing emaciated and anaemic for lack of sufficient allowances.

It was four o'clock in the afternoon. Class Four government servants were pedalling down the street, their whirring cycles loaded down with the children of senior officials. The children were on their way back from their English-medium schools. All of them had some important message to deliver at home. Two children were discussing the statement, 'If your mummy doesn't buy you another sketchbook, you will be punished for it tomorrow.' One was sitting on the crossbar; the other on the carrier. Between them, on the seat, was a uniformed chapraasi.

Eventually, Vaidyaji spoke, and when he spoke his voice was thick with emotion, 'Look at the education these children are getting! What a world of difference!'

The Principal sahib stuffed both hands into his pockets, thereby preparing himself to make a very important statement. 'I think that whatever happens, next July onwards we should get the boys in our college to wear uniforms too.'

'It's a lofty thought,' said Vaidyaji.

Ruppan babu's voice came from behind the Principal sahib, 'What sort of uniform will you introduce—one like the chapraasi's or one like the children's?'

The Principal replied, 'Ruppan babu, I am a thorough socialist. I look on them as equals.'

They walked on in silence. Then the Principal sahib said to Vaidyaji, 'We didn't get the barrel back from the Inspector sahib's house.'

Vaidyaji walked on gravely. Pondering the matter, he remarked, 'It must have been at least ten kilograms. When you've given so much ghee, why worry about the barrel?'

The Principal laughed, 'All right. Let it pass. When the cow is gone, why regret the loss of its tether?'

'Quite.' Vaidyaji became even more serious and began to relate a story: 'When you have given away an elephant, why argue over the goad? When Ram anointed Vibhishan king, Jambvant said, "Maharaj, you could have kept one golden palace for yourself." At this, Lord Ram Chandraji—that very image of the most righteous conduct, the most exalted of men—replied, "O Jambvant, when you have sold an elephant, there is no profit in arguing over the goad."'

It seemed as if a thorn had been removed from the Principal's heart. He nodded like a first-class fatalist and said bravely, 'Then it's all right. Let it pass. What's in a barrel, anyway?'

'But this is fundamentally wrong,' objected Ruppan babu. 'He should have returned the barrel. From where are we going to get a new barrel every time? If you are afraid to say anything, tell me and I'll ask for it.'

But no one told him.

They had reached the bazaar. Even today, there are two types of bazaars in Indian towns: one built for the blacks or 'natives', and the other for the white rulers. This one belonged to the latter kind. Here, there were cinemas showing English films; English liquor stores; hotels and glittering shops. Flashing neon signs advertised cigarettes and alcoholic drinks. Here, it seemed that, even though you might not get bread in India, there was cake to be had in abundance, and that if your throat was dry for lack of water, you could always refresh yourself with beer. In short, here, it seemed that your problems with food, drink and clothing would last only as long as you were one of the masses; and if you wanted to rid yourself of these problems, you should stop being one of them and work out some way of joining the upper classes.

On the footpath, there was a group of about half a dozen men in dhoti–kurtas and Gandhi caps, strolling along and gossiping, all very pleased with themselves. Occasionally, in an excess of pleasure, they would spit out long streams of betel juice near one another's feet. Ruppan babu, who had been born after the slogan 'Quit India' was raised, said with great conviction, 'God is feeding jalebis to his donkeys. Idiotic owls are sitting on every branch.'

This expression was very much in vogue and well known to the general public. By repeating it, Ruppan babu was not displaying any originality, but from the tone in which he said it, he seemed to be growing serious. The Principal called out to him and said to Vaidyaji, 'Let's go, maharaj, and have a snack and something to drink. The boy is losing his spirits.'

First they thought they would look for a paan shop. This is not a difficult task for Indians. Had an Indian been shipwrecked on a desert island instead of Robinson Crusoe, he would have discovered a paan-wallah instead of Man Friday. In fact, the definition of a true Indian is a person who, wherever he is, can make arrangements for paan and find a place to piss. But in this bazaar there was no need to look for paan shops; the paan shops themselves came looking for customers. There were paan shops in front of you and paan shops behind you, paan shops to the left and paan shops to the right. These three men went up to the paan shop right in front of them. Vaidyaji adjusted the angle of his turban, looking at his reflection in a large shop window; Ruppan babu half closed his eyes and attempted to smile; and the Principal sahib began talking to the paan-wallah.

He said softly, 'Three glasses, a rather thick mixture.'

Vaidyaji pretended ignorance and said, 'What's that? What's that?'

The Principal sahib replied, 'Nothing, just making arrangements to drink some water before the paan.'

The paan-wallah mixed the bhang and poured it into three glasses. The Principal said, 'There should be just a touch of black pepper and almonds.'

All around was the delightful prospect of English culture. The names of the shops were solely in English. There were clerks with dirty collars; children of businessmen, in flashy clothes; a large number of political riff-raff wandering around like vagabonds; and satiated, pampered officials, their chins in the air—all of them speaking in English. People in Western dress came and went, exuding pomposity. In a poster for an English film, a European woman, practically naked, half supine on a bed, was being kissed. A few black-skinned, dirty children were standing nearby examining it. A record of Western pop music was playing in a gramophone shop, and some young lads—oblivious to the fact that their country had had to display the leprosy of its poverty to import the wheat they ate—were engrossed in throwing their arms and legs around in some form of dance. Turning Rudyard Kipling on his head, the twain cultures of the East and West were meeting on an enormous scale.

Two girls with wildly abundant hair, and dressed in tight churidar/pyjamas and kurtas which showed off their bodies to good effect, were walking along, talking in English.

It occurred to Ruppan babu that he might pounce on them both and carry them off, but all he said was, 'Do you see? It looks as if they have all come from Europe, that they were born of European urine.'

The Principal sahib refrained from joining this sociological debate. He said, so that Vaidyaji might hear, 'It's the influence of that Khanna Master's company on you that is speaking, Ruppan babu! You too have begun to speak in obscenities!'

Ruppan babu banged down his glass on the counter and asked, 'Is urine obscene?'

'It's not a matter of urine; it's a matter of mixing with Khanna Master.'

Ruppan babu addressed his father, 'Please could you restrain this Principal sahib from raising the matter of Khanna Master here? If he does, and I do some plain speaking, he'll not be able to escape even if he runs for it.'

Vaidyaji fluttered his wings like a messenger of peace and forgiveness from the gods—that is to say, he wiped away the bhang from both sides of his moustache and said, 'Don't bring me into this, Ruppan! The Principal deeply regrets that you've started speaking up for Khanna. Talk to him yourself and settle the matter.'

They were heading towards the rickshaw stand. At this remark, Ruppan babu stopped dead. Putting his bag down on the footpath, he said, 'Come on then, Principal sahib, first let's settle the matter of Khanna Master.'

The Principal sahib turned away and said, without stopping, 'Some other time.'

Ruppan babu lost his temper. 'The bird-catcher-cheats who put off today's work till tomorrow live somewhere else, not here. This matter will be settled now. If you ever let a bird fly, you'll never get it back again.'

Vaidyaji had noticed a Shiv lingam standing beneath a peepul tree. Around it a small shrine had been built. The moment he saw the Shiv lingam Vaidyaji became gripped with devotion. This was the bazaar of the white rulers where the name of God should be taken only furtively. But, oblivious to this, he went and stood beneath the peepul tree and began to recite the praises of Lord Shiva.

Back on the footpath, the Principal sahib and Ruppan babu were standing ready to perform tomorrow's work today.

Vaidyaji closed his eyes. Behind him, motor cars drove past, and the English-stained voices of girls made the air throb.

Toy sellers, in imitation of a tune which some female toy seller had played in some film, were creating an ear-splitting racket. But, in the same detached way in which a true minister accepts as illusory the shouts, screams, imprecations and abuses of the opposition, and continues to walk straight along the road to nepotism, Vaidyaji too ignored all the noise around him and prayed to Shankarji.

He ground the herbs of thousands of hymns, the sifted powder of his prayer being as follows:

'O Shankar, strike down my enemies!

'You are Rudra. You are Wrathful. You infuse the whole world with the spirit of destruction. In the village, Ramadhin Bhikhmakhervi has lost the election for the post of college manager. He has sent a petition to the deputy director of education saying that the election was won at gunpoint. He has also complained to the district inspector of police. You imbibe bhang and thorn apple. O Shankar! Pour your bhang and thorn apple into the rotten minds of these officials, and make them a little more rotten. Inspire them to write in our favour. O Lord of Ghosts, strike down Ramadhin Bhikhmakhervi!

'O Triambak, Fragrant One, Source of the Energy of Creation, tear me from the company of death, just as a cucumber is broken from the stem; but do not tear me from immortality. And, O Shiva, tear my enemies from the vine of immortality and thrust them into the blind well of death. Accept the obstacles of your servants as obstacles to you. Remove the obstacles of Sanichar, the servant of myself, your servant. Against him, enemies have produced a petition on the subject of his election as pradhan. Give Sanichar victory in this. If the enemies do not withdraw the petition, strike them down.

'O Spouse of Uma, Inceptor of the World, Shiva adorned with Snakes! Raising the question of Ram Swarup, the cooperative supervisor, my enemies are speaking of embezzlement in the union. They are screaming that I, too, had a hand in it. The cooperative inspector is a low rascal but honest, and is not raising his hand. Last time, alone with me, he tried to scare me. Strike down that cooperative inspector.

'O Rudra! In the heavens, your weapon is rain; in space, your weapon is the wind; on earth, your weapon is food. By lightning, by whirlwind or by cholera or gastroenteritis, by whichever means that pleases you, strike down my enemies!

'O Shiva, O Mahesh, I meditate upon you. You are full of celestial bliss, your effulgence lights the Nine Heavens; you are the Sleepless, the Ineffable, the Eternal, the Origin, Without Equal, Without Attachment.

'For this reason, Shiva, strike down my enemies.'

Vaidyaji worshipped Shiva with great humility. In less than five minutes, standing by the roadside, he laid before Shankarji more humility than could be produced by hundreds of government servants put together, sitting for up to five hours in their puja rooms in the early morning, all afflicted with the desire for promotion and profit in this big town.

But a glut of humility had caused its market price to fall, and this may have been the reason that the highest quality and measure of humility had no apparent effect on Shankarji. The Shiv lingam stood firmly just as before. It didn't even emit a spark. Not so much as a single garland fell off it.

When Vaidyaji opened his eyes, he saw that the material world was just as it had been before he had closed them. The only difference was that ten yards away, Ruppan was screaming at the Principal.

'You are pretending to be a big hero. You tell me I'm Khanna's boy? I'm not in any bugger's faction. I only support the side of truth. Do you understand, Principal sahib?'

The Principal sahib replied with the laugh of an elder statesman, 'That's enough, Ruppan, calm down now.'

'So far nothing has happened, Principal sahib! I am telling you the case you brought under Section 107 should be settled out of court tomorrow. If there's any hearing after tomorrow, you can rest assured that all the students will be raising slogans of revolution, and all your politicking will be of no use.'

'Ruppan!' cried Vaidyaji sternly as he approached them, but the student leader was unperturbed by his presence. He said, 'Father, I didn't speak then, but I was present at the fight between Khanna Master and the Principal sahib. Moreover, I separated them. This 107 case is entirely false. It's being done to trap Khanna Master. The student community will never support it.'

Vaidyaji said coolly, 'It's nothing to get upset over. We'll go home and consider it.'

Heaven knows what got into the Principal sahib at this point. All of a sudden he shrieked, 'You can consider it by all means, maharaj, but Ruppan has disgraced me in public, right in the middle of a bazaar. God knows what Khanna has not led him on to say against me! Now, how can I tell you how Mrs Khanna has corrupted his mind? How can I tell you here about what's going on behind the curtain?'

Vaidyaji said gravely, 'There is no need to tell me. I know everything.'

He began to move on, but Ruppan babu stopped him with the words, 'No, father, this should be settled on the spot. Tell me, what do you know? Tell me! Speak! Why are you dragging Mrs Khanna into this conversation?'

Vaidyaji paused, and then looked dramatically at the Principal. The Principal was crushed by that glance. Then Vaidyaji turned it on

Ruppan babu. If Ruppan had been a weaker type of man he would have collapsed before such a look, but in such things he was master of his own father.

Ruppan said aggressively, 'Speak up, why have you stopped?'

Vaidyaji drew in his breath and replied, 'Ruppan, I know why you have suddenly turned against your guru and why you have joined forces with Khanna Master. One thing is clear—your frequent vists to his house seem to me to be inappropriate.'

Ruppan babu stood for a while without uttering a word. Then he tightened the scarf around his neck and, swinging his bag from one hand, said, 'I understand. You are casting aspersions on my character. I understand it all.' He lifted his finger and stood in an oracle-like pose. 'This Principal sahib has filled your ears, I know! But no good will come of it.'

Suddenly he turned and remarked, 'And brother Badri? The whole village is condemning him. He's bringing Bela to sit in our house. Don't you have the courage to say anything to him? His character is being . . .'

The Principal realized that lightning was about to strike. Before Vaidyaji could fall on to the footpath in a faint at hearing a complaint against his elder son's misconduct, he interrupted Ruppan, saying, 'What are you talking about, Ruppan babu? Come to your senses.'

He told Vaidyaji, 'Please let it pass, maharaj, Ruppan babu's still a boy. He must have heard something somewhere and is going around shouting about it.'

But Vaidyaji was in no need of being shielded or consoled by the Principal. He was bearing Ruppan's charge with serene gravity. Apart from one or two flutterings of his moustache, his face betrayed no sign of uneasiness. Ruppan babu began heatedly to denounce Badri's love affair. First, he went into its history; then, he put forward some facts and figures about the immediate circumstances of the problem; finally, he criticized Vaidyaji's habit of pretending not to see what he did see, as a cowardly and partisan policy. He also tried to prove that Vaidyaji was applying double standards to himself and Badri, which was against the fundamental principles of democracy. As he concluded his speech, his face turned red, his lips became wet with froth, and he began to screw up his eyes.

The Principal realized that his words of consolation were of no use. He gathered them up and put them back into his bag like a piqued dried-fruit merchant.

Seeing no sign of a reaction in Vaidyaji, Ruppan babu, too, fell silent and began to think up some method of slipping away. Vaidyaji had listened to the whole speech as if, instead of Ruppan's frenzied jabbering, the essence of the detached philosophy of the Gita were being lovingly fed to him on the footpath. He said to the Principal sahib, 'Let's go back to the station. It must be time for the train.'

Ruppan babu was shaken to see his father unperturbed. He blurted out in astonishment, 'I am staying here. I'll come by the night train.'

His words were ignored. To reduce the tension, the Principal tried to make a reasoned comment on the subject. 'About Badri Wrestler . . .'

Vaidyaji silenced him with a gesture of his hand, and then stated simply, 'There is no need to say anything. I have already made up my mind.'

Ruppan was torn apart with curiosity but, to display his indifference, he stood a short distance away, watching the traffic. Vaidyaji said in such a loud voice that even those who were not interested could hear, 'I am not so conservative. Gandhiji was in favour of inter-caste marriages. So am I. Badri's marriage to Bela will be accepted as a model in every way. But I've no idea what Gayadin's reaction will be. We shall see.'

With this, he turned to Ruppan babu, who didn't have the courage to look him in the eye, and muttered, 'I'm off . . .'

The Principal sahib wasn't prepared to see such a simple end to the love story, either. In his dismay, he began to speak in Awadhi, 'Maharaj, I knew from the very start what tha'dst say. Such a great reformer as thou . . .'

With this, he hailed a cycle rickshaw.

29

It was approaching late afternoon on the day after Vaidyaji, Ruppan and the Principal had returned from the town. There was no one on the veranda except Vaidyaji and Badri Wrestler. This part of the house was reserved for men, and women seldom ventured here. It was quite still. Ruppan babu was lying down quietly in a room off the veranda. It was a college holiday that day and he had lain awake till quite late the previous night. Hence, even after having had sufficient sleep, he was attempting to go back to sleep. It was then that he heard his father's priestly tones: 'I had no conception that you could fall so low!'

Any ears which did not prick up immediately on hearing such a remark would be worse than even a dog's tail. Ruppan's ears pricked up, and he quietly peeped out of the door. Vaidyaji was sitting cross-legged on a charpoy, and Badri Wrestler was squatting on the platform just nearby.

Without announcing it, the two of them were quarrelling informally. The atmosphere was so homely that, if Ruppan babu had not heard that remark of Vaidyaji's, he would have imagined that his elder brother and father were holding preliminary consultations on some subject of importance to the community, such as the immediate necessity of a further embezzlement in the cooperative union.

However, Ruppan had heard Vaidyaji's remark and then he heard him say something more in the same tone, 'You are a fool too—I would never have imagined it.'

Badri Wrestler said carelessly, with a yawn, 'What's the point of cursing and abusing each other at home? It's not a good thing.'

Perhaps this comment about behaviour had the necessary effect on Vaidyaji. He dropped his melodramatic tone and said, as if it were a normal conversation, 'And what you have done, is that a good thing? Do you have even an idea of what the result will be? How much anguish it will cause me? Do you know?'

Perhaps Badri Wrestler had not drunk bhang that morning. It is a fact that people who are unaccustomed to bhang yawn when they drink it, and that people accustomed to drinking bhang yawn when they don't. So, a second edition of the yawn appeared on his face. He chased away a mosquito sitting on his shoulder with a gentle slap, but the mosquito was the kind that preferred to die rather than fly off. Then, he replied to Vaidyaji's comments, 'What is there to be upset about, tell me? Whatever trouble there is will pass.'

Vaidyaji lowered his voice, 'You're so sensible—how on earth did you get trapped by Gayadin's daughter?'

Badri Wrestler sat for some moments without speaking, and said, 'It's pointless talking to you.' He pulled down a kurta from a peg, threw it over his shoulder and headed for the door. Vaidyaji said, 'Now, where are you running off to?'

'Who's running? If you have anything sensible to say, say it. But if people begin to talk nonsense even at home, I'm not staying to listen to it.'

Vaidyaji changed gear. 'But this matter will have to be discussed at some point.'

Badri braked, and remarked from where he stood, 'At the moment, your tongue is saying some very odd things. This is not right. We'll talk again some other time.'

'When? When my nose has been cut off in disgrace?'

Badri Wrestler was compelled to return. Still with his kurta over one shoulder, he went back and squatted down on the platform. 'Don't talk about things like having your nose cut off. Where is your nose in the first place? It was cut off in the days of Pandit Ajudhya Prasad.'

Vaidyaji replied, 'You are still making low remarks.'

Badri Wrestler began to rock back and forth on the balls of his feet. He said in a thick voice, 'If I am, then for now, just let me do it. You say that I have been trapped by Bela. You are my father; how can I make you understand? Trapping is the work of cheats and bird-catchers. In your family, a great saint like your grandfather Ajudhya Prasad was trapped by a sweeper woman. That's what you call trapped? Yes? And if not, then what *do* you call it?' After a pause he said at great speed, 'Anyway, now we can end this conversation.'

Vaidyaji put his foot down on the accelerator. '*Your* family! *Your* grandfather! You're using such language! This family is ours! Isn't it yours? Aren't these forefathers yours too?'

Badri's car jerked to a halt as if faced with a red light at a crossroads. He said with self-control, 'Isn't it happening again? I tell you one home truth and you get irritated. Anyway, let it pass.'

Vaidyaji said in a voice that sounded like a car engine when a learner is trying to drive with both the clutch and the accelerator pushed down together, 'No, Badri, I will not let it pass. Today, I won't let matters stop here. We are Brahmins, she is a Vaishya. But it's not just a matter of caste, it's also a matter of principle! A girl of such morals . . . What did Chhote say in court?'

Badri Wrestler leapt to his feet. 'Enough! The matter is closed! And I have just one more thing to say and then I'll shut up, too. I can't behave like Baba Ajudhya Prasad. What I do, I do properly. I don't like any mucking around.'

He walked towards the door. Suddenly, Vaidyaji got up from his charpoy and, despite lacking matted locks, beard and begging bowl, he struck a pose like a Hindu ascetic delivering a curse, and bellowed like a double-powered motor horn, 'You low creature! Then hear what I, too, have to say . . .'

Ruppan babu was listening to this conversation in amazement. In the town, the day before, it had seemed from Vaidyaji's remarks as if he would allow Bela and Badri to marry, and that if there were any obstacle it would come from Gayadin, but he could be brought round. But from this conversation, he realized that what he had thought to be the end of the struggle was in fact just the beginning.

He could restrain himself no longer. Springing nimbly out of the room, he began to play peacemaker.

'Father,' he said, 'what can be gained from arguing now? Why not say exactly what you said yesterday in front of the Principal? Just keep on repeating that. We will say that we don't accept casteism. When brother Badri has already been trapped by Bela, then . . .'

Ruppan was unable to finish his sentence. It seemed as if his neck were breaking. It was a routine occurrence. Every day, Badri Wrestler laid hands on somebody's neck. Today, he had grabbed Ruppan's. In one second, Ruppan's eyes saw the courtyard whirling by, ten times, and then turned upwards until only their whites were visible.

Badri was grinding his teeth and saying, 'You want to play leader even in this house? You're saying that I've been trapped by her? And that, too, to my face! You *chimirkhi* ass!'

Giving Ruppan's neck a violent jerk, he shoved him over to the far side of the courtyard in an unusual fashion. Ruppan was so unnerved that he couldn't even decide whether to accept or return the title of 'chimirkhi ass' which he had just received.

On the other side of the courtyard, Badri Wrestler was saying to Vaidyaji, 'This is what you call a real leader! He himself wrote a two-page letter to her! God knows what nonsense he put into it! He himself was trapped, and he turns round and tells me that I've been trapped!'

Ruppan babu had recovered himself before he could fall. He said in an offended tone, 'I am not so low as to talk to you on that matter.' He said to Vaidyaji, 'Father, it's useless saying anything at all to him now. Let him do whatever he likes.'

But at this time, Vaidyaji was eager to give, not take, advice. He said in a stern voice, 'Whatever the case, Ruppan, this is not a subject for you to speak on. I have complaints against you both. I am also well aware of your own behaviour.'

Ruppan babu lost his temper completely. 'So that's it!' he replied, holding his head high and pushing his chest out. 'Then I too am well aware of your behaviour.'

That was the last scene of the battle. Badri said sarcastically to his father, 'See that?' Ruppan babu rushed out of the house, and Vaidyaji stood in silence next to the charpoy. He didn't even do the easiest thing for a man of his profession—he didn't even appeal to God.

~

It was late afternoon. In a sweet shop, there sat a vendor who looked like a vendor of sweets, even from a distance. On the road below his shop stood a local political leader who looked like a leader, even from a distance. There, too, holding the handlebars of his bicycle, stood a police constable who looked like a police constable, even from a distance. The sweets on display at the shop looked stale and prepared from adulterated ingredients—which they were—and the milk looked watery and thickened with arrowroot—which it was. This was a corner of heaven on earth where the whole truth was apparent before your eyes. Nothing was hidden nor was there any need to hide anything.

On sale were jalebis, *pera* and *gatta*. Next to them, in small glass jars, there were some dry, rather wood-like things, which were local substances baked in the European tradition of biscuits, cake, rusks and so on. As in the town, here, too, these substances gave the message that East is East and West is West and both meet in Shivpalganj's sweets.

Here, too, Ruppan babu met Langar.

Ruppan babu regarded Langar rather as a first-class passenger regards a third-class passenger who is suspected of travelling without a ticket. But today, Ruppan babu was in such a depressed mood that he could easily act upon all the principles of Panchsheel. So he asked in a subdued tone, 'What's happening about your copy, then?'

'Today's a holiday, father! I couldn't find out. But anyway the copy must have been made by now.' He began to recount the progress made in recent days. 'It had been made already, but I couldn't go and collect it. I had a fever for a long time. That day when I fell down at the district courts, I couldn't get up again. Then I thought that if I have to die, I'll go and die in my own village. A Thakur from my village had in fact come to the court. He took me back with him. There, people told me it was typhoid.

'But one day, some people came to the village in a motor car. Goodness knows what they wrote in English with ochre paint on the walls of the entire village. After that, father, they took my blood, poured it into a machine and looked at it. Now look at this, father, what a wonder it is in this Kali Yug—here I am, an Indian, and I go and catch an English disease. The people who came in the motor car said, "Langar is a big man—he's got malaria."

'How can I tell you, father? After that, the motor-wallahs did a lot of work in the village. Two or three of them, with a machine each, went all around to the wells, ponds and ditches, making a kirr-kirr noise. Two men went to every single house and wrote on the front of each one, prayers to Goddess Malaria with ochre paint in English letters. It was the influence of those letters, father, which chased away the mosquitoes. I, too, father, suffered for a whole month before I could stand on my feet again to have the privilege of a sight of you.'

The political leader said, 'What a tale that is, Langar, old fellow!'

They've written in English letters, look,
And the malarial mosquitoes have us forsook.

The vendor of sweets praised the leader, 'What a poem it is you have recited! It calls for a jalebi.'

The leader waved away the flies with familiarity, took four or five jalebis from the tray and began to eat them.

The constable opposite said to Langar, 'So you can say that you were saved from the brink of death.'

'That is indeed right, father, but I knew that I wouldn't die. In God's court there can be no such injustice. Until I have got the copy from the tehsil office I cannot die.'

The leader suggested, 'Go and build your hut there; you'll save yourself a lot of running around.'

Ruppan babu sat on the bench stretching his legs for a few moments before saying to the vendor of sweets, 'Give me a bowl of milk.' After consideration, he added, 'Give Langar one too.'

Ruppan babu drank his milk and was about to get up, when the leader said, 'So, how would that be, Langar? Shall we have your hut built just there in front of the tehsil office?'

By his saintly laugh Langar made it clear that the leader was a fool and that he himself was humble.

The leader said, 'In a few days' time, go on a hunger strike. It'll be good. Your name will come in the papers. Whether you get the copy or not, you'll be famous. Think about it, Langar, old fellow.'

Langar's laugh this time was not merely the gentle, contented one of a Vaishnavite saint. It obviously bore the stamp of the Kabir school, the Gandhian school and the school of social service, and there was also some influence of the local Lucknow school. Faced with it, a man's only response could be to grin and try to chuckle. The leader did precisely that. At the same time, he clapped his hands and said, 'Well done, Langar, old fellow!'

The mood Ruppan babu was in made him disapprove of the leader's jokes. He felt he was making fun of Langar by calling him 'Langar, old fellow'. 'We too call him Langar,' he thought, 'but what sort of a name is that—the Lame One? What is his real name?'

The moment this occurred to him, the floodgates of his mind opened. Suddenly he remembered several such names. A lame man was called Langar; a blind man used to come to their door and people used to call him Soore—the Blind One; anyone whose ears were pulverized by too much wrestling was given the honourable title of 'Tutte'—Broken Ear.

There was an old man whom everyone honoured with the name
Deaf Grandpa. A man whose face bore the scars of smallpox was called,
in Shivpalganj, 'Honeycomb' Prasad. 'Changu' or 'Six-Fingered' Ram
naturally had to have six fingers.

This is how we traditionally show our love for cripples and
amputees. Thus thought Ruppan babu, adding to himself, 'If this man
calls him "Langar, old fellow" once more I'll give him a shoe-beating.'
Aloud, he said angrily, 'Eh, Squint-Eyed Prasad, why are you calling
him Langar?'

Ruppan babu had thought that the leader would be thoroughly
upset at being called Squint-Eyed Prasad. However, the epithet had
no effect on him, since, in his own village, he was known simply as
Squint-Eye. The leader felt gratified at receiving the blessing of 'Prasad'
from Ruppan babu, in the same way that a menial employee called
'Booby', after spending his days working in dirt and dust, being cursed
and abused, feels gratified when he is about to appear in court and
hears himself being addressed as 'Mr Booby'.

The leader remarked to Ruppan babu, 'What else should I call
him? He is lame and so he's called Langar.'

Ruppan babu threw his empty bowl into the middle of the street
in front of him, as people do after drinking milk in a shop. Tens of
millions of flies descended eagerly upon it but had no proper words
to thank Ruppan babu. Two pedestrians, near whose feet the bowl
fell and shattered, jumped over to the side of the road but didn't have
the courage to abuse Ruppan or object to his action. Ruppan paid
them no attention. He said to Squint-Eyed Prasad, 'You shouldn't
mock anyone by calling them nicknames. You should address him by
his real name.'

The leader turned to Langar and asked, 'What is your real name?'

'Now everyone just calls me Langar, father,' said Langar, after
some consideration, 'but my real name, given to me by my parents, is
Langar Prasad.'

~

Walking along the edges of the fields, Ruppan came to the end of
the village which has already been mentioned under the name of

Chamrahi. It was deemed an event for Vaidyaji or any member of his family to walk through Chamrahi. Once upon a time, if any Brahmin or Thakur passed by, the people there would hastily put their hookahs on the ground or throw down their pipes and stand in their doorways. The men would join their hands and raise the slogan, 'We touch your feet, maharaj!' Women would pull their children's hands away from their necks and sometimes, in their confusion, begin to rain punches on their babies' backs. The maharaj would hand out blessings in all directions and note whose daughters had begun to look more womanly in the last four months, which girl had come back from her in-laws' house, and would pass on, his chariot taking to the skies as chariots used to in the Treta Yug of Raja Ram Chandra.

The abolition of landlordism had resulted neither in Chamrahi's being absorbed into the rest of the village nor in any properly constructed wells and houses being built, but at least what had happened was that visiting Brahmins were no longer afforded the guard of honour they once were. And so, to escape the feeling of nostalgia and regret for the good old days, Brahmins—and especially Vaidyaji—had given up taking this route as far as possible.

Ruppan babu only realized that he was in Chamrahi when, once or twice, he heard the words, 'I touch your feet, maharaj.'

A man was sitting at ease on the platform outside his door, as men can be seen doing throughout our country. At the sight of Ruppan babu, he stood up. Ruppan said, 'Sit down, Churaiya, the old days have gone.'

Churaiya, whose real name was Churai, and in the meaninglessness of whose name lay its beauty, replied, 'I touch your feet, Ruppan babu.'

'Nowadays, no one touches anyone's feet. It has come to the point where they just hit them with a stick.'

A boy—a bundle of dust, lampblack, saliva, mud and spit—was standing in front of Churai. Churai gave him a shove—like Rahul being offered for initiation to the Buddha—and said, 'Go on, lad, touch brother Ruppan's feet.'

Ruppan babu blessed him. 'What's the boy's name?'

'Chand Parkas.' That is to say, in correct Hindi, Chandra Prakash, Light of the Moon.

Ruppan babu smiled. 'Chand Parkas, son of Churai the Chamar. You've managed to find a very powerful name.'

He walked on. Churaiya said, 'How did you manage to stray here today, Ruppan babu?'

'Is there a ban on walking through here?'

'The village council election is over. Now what election is in the offing, brother?'

For a few seconds Ruppan babu stood astonished by Churaiya's impudence. Then he laughed for the first time that day and said, 'Bastard, showing off to me!' He passed down an alley. Its speciality was that, despite not having been constructed as an integrated development scheme, it had become a part of our integrated development programme. It was an alley. At the same time, it was a drain which carried away thousands of streams of water from smaller drains. It was a depot where the filth flowing in the drains was rotted into manure. Besides all this, due to the fact that there was no street light in the vicinity, after dark, it also functioned as a community meeting place for couples eager for love. In short, simply by being there, it was really a rather good scheme for village improvement.

Ruppan babu made his way out of the far end of the alley without pinching his nostrils. Beyond it, there was an open field; then the tehsil office and the police station came into view. A little farther on, the thatched roofs of the Changamal Vidyalaya Intermediate College were visible. In one corner of the alley, a man was trying to buy a chicken from an old woman. The old woman was saying, 'I have prayed for a boon from the tomb of Pathan Baba, and I am rearing this chicken to offer to him.'

The man trying to buy the chicken was extremely anxious to get hold of it, and was prepared to deal with all kinds of obstacles. He began to explain to the old woman that Pathan Baba's only interest lay in getting a chicken and that he wouldn't mind whether it was this one or not. He also explained that there are two ways of selling a chicken—one straightforward and one where you get a kick in the backside.

He very kindly granted the old woman the liberty to sell the chicken in whichever way she chose. He also said that he wouldn't only buy the chicken, but he'd also give her money for it.

Ruppan babu remarked in passing, 'Is some official coming or what?'

In reply, the man abused someone roundly with a dozen or so different expletives, adding, in between, the autobiographical detail that he had been searching for a chicken since early morning and the geographical observation that Shivpalganj was an absolutely one-horse village, and that, from the way people talked it would seem as if there were chickens all over the place, but if you tried to buy just one, they all disappeared back into their coops.

Ruppan babu gathered from this that the man's superior officer was about to arrive from the town. As he walked on, he said, 'You've got the chicken all right, but what about the other thing?'

'What other thing?'

Ruppan babu made a gesture but to the man it was just like abstract art. He wasn't prepared to understand it. Putting his head on one side, he asked again, 'What other thing?'

Ruppan babu replied, 'Ram Channa's daughter has gone to her in-laws' house. Now, what will you do?'

'Heaven forbid! How can you suggest such a thing, panditji?' reprimanded the man.

~

Outside the police station, wearing a vest and underpants, and with his sacred thread looped over one ear, sat a healthy-looking constable. Village watchmen were lying under trees, sprawled out like dogs. Around them were broken earthenware bowls, dirty leaf plates buzzing with flies, and sweet and tea shops with small, smoking oil lamps. Greasy stools. Caravans of murderous trucks in the hands of drunken drivers roared down the road. Petty revenue officials with papers loaded on the carriers of their cycles like piles of grass. The tehsildar's foul-mouthed orderly. Pandit Ram Ghar's licentious son who drank and picked fights at the barber's shop and whom the local postman beat with a shoe seven times a week, after having drunk an even greater quantity of liquor. Students, singing as if in chorus, were walking from the college, their arms around one another's waists.

Ruppan met the Principal and Rangnath coming down this road.

The Principal said, 'Have you seen what Khanna Master's come up with now, Ruppan babu?'

Ruppan replied, 'I don't want to hear anything against Khanna Master. If you want to tell someone, go and tell my father.'

Before the Principal could say more, Ruppan asked Rangnath, 'Will you come with me, brother? To celebrate his victory, old Sanichar is inviting people for a good time at the local still. If you want to see a film for free, come along; we'll go off from there.'

Ruppan babu's heart was lighter for having snubbed the Principal. Rangnath said, 'I'm going home.'

'Fine, go ahead. I'm going to see the film.'

30

About a hundred yards from Vaidyaji's sitting room, there was a small square in which stood a couple of neem trees on which perched hundreds of screeching parakeets, and beneath which hundreds of dogs played tag. Recently, an enthusiastic primary schoolteacher had begun assembling boys there, drilling them and getting them to play kabaddi. Vaidyaji believed that there was some politics behind this. But since the teacher belonged to Ramadhin Bhikhmakhervi's faction, Vaidyaji had taken the matter no further than mentioning it in his own sitting room. A local market was also held there once a week, where spinach and other vegetables were sold and, occasionally, a rare sack of wheat like a freak baby could be seen laid open and on sale.

After becoming pradhan, Sanichar had put up a wooden cabin in one corner of the square and opened a general store. He had no comment to make on why he hadn't been able to do this before becoming pradhan.

Sanichar had decorated the shop a good deal according to his likes. On one side of the wooden wall, there was an advertisement for herbal sweets to treat backache in women; on the other was stuck one of the 'Grow More Grain' posters which have already been mentioned. In the remaining space were advertisements for a lampblack invented by some old woman; medicines to treat ringworm, coughs, asthma; a special sort of battery; vegetable ghee and so on. The items advertised were mostly not on sale at the shop, and the items on sale at the shop were generally not advertised.

The shop stocked everything from betel nut and beedis to wheat flour, lentils, rice and spices. All these could be bought and consumed in broad daylight. This was the equivalent of that side of politics which is written down in manifestos. Then there was the other side which is revealed in secret counsel during party meetings, and which is known only to reliable sources. In shop terms, this comprised items which could not be bought openly but which could be consumed. Under this category of goods came a large number of allopathic medicines which originated from the storeroom of the local hospital. The goods also included tins of American milk powder, whose origin was the local primary school. In this category were some items which could be bought only under the counter, and be consumed only in secret. They included cannabis, bhang and charas. Sanichar had shown no enthusiasm for opium because, in the village, Ramadhin Bhikhmakhervi controlled the underground opium monopoly.

As Holi approached, Sanichar's shop gained official recognition; he began to sell sugar, which was well known to be available on the production of a government ration card. However, it was not well known how to get hold of a government ration card.

On Holi day, Sanichar also began to sell country liquor at the shop. The special feature of the liquor he sold—not shared by the liquor available at the government-licensed shop—was that it was undiluted.

The shop was built on top of a wooden platform and, inside, there was just enough room for Sanichar to sit. Higher above it, to enhance its status, were inscribed the words 'Pls don't Enter'. This phrase had been borrowed from the signboard hanging on the door of the local post office. In protest against there being such an unoriginal sign in Shivpalganj, a young boy had amended it. The amendment was only minor. He'd changed the 'Pls' to 'Piss'.

If there was anyone who had opposed the setting up of the shop, it was Rangnath. The very day it was opened, he saw Sanichar sitting at the counter and said, 'It doesn't look good.'

'Just you wait and see, Rangnath babu. In a few days it will start looking good. The old days belonged to the rajas, maharajas and big landowners. Now, wait and see, the shopkeepers will hold sway. They do already.'

Without getting involved in this economic debate, Rangnath replied, 'I was referring to the way things are done in the town. Lying around here in Shivpalganj, you think you're very clever, but where I come from there are people who would make you look a fool.

'Don't you know that the custom is that the man in office doesn't do business himself? He sets up brothers and nephews in business. They wear long faces, and get on with their work. They don't waste their time with the political game. The man who gets into office keeps apart from them and quietly looks after his own position.

'Even then, the poor nephews and brothers have enemies. Someone will go and say that the man in office had got their firm so many contracts, and that his nephew had made so much money from them. If you read the papers you'll see that they reek of this sort of stories. Then the man in office puts on airs and says, "How would I know? What's it got to do with me? Someone must have given a backhander somewhere. I was just quietly serving the country. If you people want to take action against anyone, why are you bothering me?"'

Rangnath continued, 'I'm just telling you what I read in the newspapers. That's why I'm trying to persuade you not to get mixed up in a shop. Put some nephew here. Let him run it. When the time comes, you'll still be able to say that it's nothing to do with you.'

Sanichar pondered a while and then said, 'I don't have any brothers or nephews. You people are all I have.'

'Then where was the need for you to become pradhan? You could have filled your stomach just as you were.'

'Which bastard really becomes pradhan himself?' interjected Sanichar with some force. 'I accept only Vaidyaji as pradhan. Consider this shop as his. I am only sitting in it. Look on me as tenant.'

He had enunciated the last sentence with great devotion. Rangnath was convinced that what he said was true. This is our tradition. Bharat had worshipped Ram's sandals and ruled in his name for fourteen years. Rangnath suggested, 'In the town, tenants have begun to sublet after renting a place. If you want to live in peace, find a subtenant.'

~

'There are boys all over the place. They drive you up the wall and prevent you from sleeping at night.

'Just look at your village. See how many boys there are, lying screaming in the dirt. They're raising enough dust to destroy the world. They're all filthy. They all squint. They've got trachoma. Their ribs are sticking out. The only part of them that's growing is their stomachs and that is because their livers are enlarged. They all whine. The moment you hear their voices, you feel like slapping them.

'Think it over, pradhanji! Can any country educate so many boys? Keep them healthy? Make men of them?

'How long will they be looked after properly? Up to what point can anything be done for them? It's been done for so long! What do you think? That not enough has been done? A lot has been done, but the problem remains the same—there are boys wherever you look. What can anyone do?

'That is why no economic plan can work and why every scheme is unsuccessful. If you make a scheme for a crore, by the following year, an army of a crore and a half is on its feet to take it.

'So, what's to be done?

'This is what should be done—the spring should be cut off at the source. If there is no bamboo, there can be no bamboo flute to play. The problem of boys and children will be wiped out. Even if you want to produce them, produce only as many as you need. There are several ways of controlling the birth of boys . . .'

A shy young man, about twenty-four or twenty-five years old, had been sitting at Sanichar's shop for about an hour, delivering something of a speech. Four or five people were listening to him with curiosity. Ruppan babu was among them. The young man's speech was highly civilized and rational, but only a summary of what the listeners understood of it has been given above.

The sensible people did not have difficulty in accepting that boys are a cause of anxiety and trouble but, to explain this point, the young man had given an example—if a quarter kilo of *kheer* is made in a home and there's only a man and his wife to eat it, they get half a quarter kilo each. If they have one son, they still get nearly one hundred grams apiece. If there are five sons, the amount drops from nearly one hundred to only thirty grams. There's not enough of the pudding to enjoy it . . .

Ruppan babu asked, 'Brother, I don't have any sons, and I don't know what it's like to have them. But tell me one thing. I accept that you shouldn't have five sons—two or three are plenty. But why make only a quarter kilo of kheer? Why not make a kilo?'

The young man hesitated and then said, 'How many people can afford to make a whole kilo of kheer?'

'Then talk about improving their finances. Why are you running after their sons with a stick?'

Sanichar raised his hand and said with the authority of a pradhan, 'There's no harm in castrating a man. But shall I tell you what ought to be done? Some years ago, we had a plague of monkeys in Shivpalganj. The whole harvest was ruined. There was a huge number of monkeys, greater than the number of boys now. Every morning, the ganjahas would set out with a net shouting, '*Leho! Leho! Shoo!*' in the fields and drive the monkeys into one house. But they couldn't save the crops. Then we called some men from the western districts. They were expert monkey catchers. In just a few days, all the monkeys were caught and taken away from here.

'You should do the same. Catch as many boys as you can find and shut them up. There's no need to shoot them or anything. I hear that the monkeys were sent to America. Put the boys in a boat and send them there. They can go and live there and raise families.'

Ruppan babu was standing a little way off. He suggested, 'It won't cost anything to send them to America. I hear that ships come here from abroad, loaded with wheat. When they go back, they can take a full load of boys. The whole thing will be done free of cost.'

The shy young man thought about these suggestions for a moment, and then blushed and said, '*Arré*, no! You people are pulling my leg.' He stood up and joined his hands in supplication before democracy which, at that point, was visible in the form of Sanichar, and said, 'I will come and present myself to you tomorrow.'

Sanichar said in a pradhan-like tone, 'Don't take us wrong, brother, these are the ways of ganjahas. If you come tomorrow, we'll have a meeting at Vaidyaji's door. If everyone agrees, we'll start vasectomies. I'm a celibate man myself; I don't have any wife or family, but if you give the word I'll have one, too. Then I'll be free to do anything I feel like.'

The villagers gave the young man a joyful farewell, but he returned home with a heavy heart.

It was about three o'clock in the afternoon and the roads and doorways were deserted. Crops were being harvested, and a fairly large proportion of the inhabitants had gone to the fields and threshing floors.

The young man—with the air of a messiah roaming through an empty country whose population has been decimated by plague—was looking and walking straight ahead. He wore a shimmering Terylene bush shirt and the emblem of an official: trousers. Some way from the edge of the village, he suddenly gained the impression that a dog had become infatuated with his bush shirt. The dog was barking and advancing towards his ankles. The young man bounded off towards the opposite house and stood on the veranda beneath the tin roof. He picked up a switch of arhar plants and stood erect, like Abhimanyu with the broken wheel of his chariot, prepared to face a *chakravyuh* of dogs.

Heaven knows what magic there was in the bark of the dog which had pounced but, in the blink of an eye, the young man was surrounded by dogs on all sides. Nearly all were barking. Those that weren't able to were wagging their tails in excitement and flexing their spines. Innumerable puppies were splitting the heavens with their sharp yapping.

The door of the house opened and out came Gayadin. He remarked calmly, 'They're making a big row.'

Then, noticing a man from the town waving a thin cane of arhar at his door, he made a dash towards the dogs. An enthusiastic young boy came out of a neighbouring house and began to run repeatedly at them and pelt them with clods of earth. The enemies lost their footing. The dogs began to scatter. Their barking resounded but was diffused.

Gayadin asked the shy young man, 'Who are you, brother?'

Every Indian has just one easy answer to this question and that is to give promptly the name of his caste. So he said, 'I'm an Aggarwal.'

Throwing down a charpoy which had been standing on its side against a wall, Gayadin invited the young man to sit down, and asked him what he did for a living.

The young man sat down, wiped away the perspiration which was a result of the episode with the dogs, not the heat, and replied, 'I'm in government service.'

Gayadin observed his face closely. He looked embarrassed but, all in all, handsome. Gayadin inquired, 'How did you happen to come here?'

In reply, the young man began hesitantly to speak about the boys being born in the country day in and day out. After a while, it struck Gayadin that people were continuously producing children and that this young man's job was to stop them from doing so. He asked a question about the young man's salary and was dumbfounded to know that anyone could make a living merely by delivering speeches on birth control.

Suddenly he asked, 'How many children do you have?'

'Not one. I'm not married.'

Gayadin now looked the young man up and down with interest. He asked, 'You're a Vaishya Aggarwal?'

The young man nodded in confirmation of this honourable piece of information.

Gayadin leant forward and happily moved up closer to him on the charpoy. He asked the young man's address, which was in the nearby town. Then he asked his father's name, and he turned out to be a well-known businessman of his acquaintance. He inquired after the young man's father and discovered that, like many other small businessmen, he had become something of a local leader, as a result of which, his son had been posted not far from his home—in fact, only fifteen miles away. Then, when Gayadin asked about the young man's brothers and sisters, he found out that his sister had married a rich businessman, a high-class man from Calcutta, and his younger brother was in business there with his brother-in-law. After some further inquiries, Gayadin found that this was the rich businessman's third marriage. Then, when Gayadin asked in a roundabout way whether the young man was going to get married or not, he replied that his father had decided that he should get married this year.

Finally, Gayadin put the point, 'Brother, you are a well-educated person. You would only dream of marrying a girl with a BA or an MA.'

This time the young man said, like average young men who fall in love with the girls with whom they study, and marry the girls whom their fathers bring down from the ladder of dowry, 'I don't know anything about it. I'll do what my father tells me to.'

At these words, before the young man could get up from the charpoy, Gayadin said, 'You're one of my caste, and have come to my house, so you must have a glass of sherbet before you go. If not sherbet, then milk. All right, if you don't like milk either, then have some tea.'

With this, he called out to Bela.

~

On one side of the ridge of earth on which Sanichar was sitting, there was a field where the crops had already been cut and which was being irrigated with water from the canal. In the field on the other side of the ridge, there was a crop of ripe wheat in no danger from birds as the ears were devoid of grain.

The farmer had sown this field on the advice of a progressive man and so the plants had grown equidistant from one another, in perfectly straight lines. When the seedlings sprouted, this field was highly spoken of and was presented as a model of progressive farming to officials who knew not only how to walk with their feet on the ground but also along field boundary ridges. When the seedlings in the field grew to be a span high, the whole scene became immensely charming and poetic. It completely overwhelmed the inspecting officials. For two or three months, they came there regularly and gazed like birds at the wheat, standing line upon line. The rows of wheat could be seen. However, since the quality of the seeds, the quantity of fertilizer and the irrigation arrangements were not all visible at first glance, the farmer, his adviser and the inspecting officials never thought about them. When the time came for the crop to ripen, the sole significant feature of the field which remained was the lines of plants.

Lines. The people of Shivpalganj had been taught that lines mean progress. Real progress is doing everything in lines. Plant trees in lines and let them die in lines. Stand in a line for bus tickets and when the bus has come and gone its way, stand in line for ten hours for the next one, twiddling your thumbs. Tether your cattle in lines and pile up your rubbish in lines. Put up lines of flags at public meetings, stand boys in lines to sing songs of welcome, stand in lines to throw garlands around the necks of leaders.

Do everything in lines because they are visible, and progress is whatever can be perceived by the eye. There's no need for you to look or think beyond this, because there are other people to do that.

A man could be seen approaching from some way off. Sanichar was at an angle to him. At first, the man walked along the boundary ridges of the fields. Then, perhaps because he had studied geometry and knew that two sides of a triangle put together are longer than the third side, he climbed down from the ridge and, leaping across a field of young sugar cane, took the route which a man who is scaring away crows would take, and began to head straight for Sanichar. Once he stiffened and looked to his right, causing a small towel to fall from his shoulder down to the ground. He strode forward decisively for seven or eight paces, then turned and saw the towel on the ground. Glancing at it, he walked on as before. He shouted in a loud voice, 'O Girdhariya, Girdhariya, Girdhariya, ré!' A herdsman standing about one hundred and fifty yards away, holding a staff as weighty as a mountain, answered this call. The man said, 'I've dropped my towel; pick it up and give it to me. I'll be standing there by Sanichar.'

Then Sanichar realized that this was Chhote Wrestler and that he was heading for him.

The moment he arrived, Chhote said, 'What are you digging up, sitting around here? Back there, Vaidyaji has been watching the road for you for a whole hour.'

Sanichar yawned and said, 'How can I tell you what I've been doing? This pradhan business seems a waste of time to me. I've been running from pillar to post since early morning.'

Chhote Wrestler was not impressed by Sanichar's statement. But, just as some bureaucrats get into the habit of repeating stories of their honesty without the least concern about whether they have any effect or not, Sanichar, too, continued describing the trials and tribulations of being a pradhan.

Chhote Wrestler suddenly interrupted, 'Let's be off—you've added enough colour. Now go straight to Vaidyaji's door and try out your act there.'

Sanichar said somewhat hesitantly, 'I was sitting here irrigating my field with canal water. I've got sugar cane to sow. I was planning to go after a while.'

The field, in fact, belonged to Vaidyaji who had given Sanichar permission to farm it that year.

Chhote raised his head and tried to focus on something in the middle distance. He said, 'It wasn't your turn for the canal water today. Last night, it was flowing into Churaiya's fields.'

Sanichar said, 'Wrestler, will you make me—the pradhan— wait for my turn? At least give me leave to water my fields when I need to.' Then he decided confidently, 'I'll water it. I'll see that Churaiya's fields, too, are watered. Waiting for one day will not kill anybody.'

Chhote Wrester sat down on a boundary ridge. He shoved Sanichar in the back with one hand and did something which made the pradhan leap hastily to his feet. Chhote said, 'Now trot off straight to Vaidyaji's house and if you want to take canal water don't do it by taking Churaiya's turn. If you're a true son of your father, take the water from Ramadhin's fields one of these days.'

Sanichar replied as he walked away, 'I'll do that, too. Just wait a bit and you'll see what happens!'

'Nothing's going to happen. Ramadhin's already watered his fields once,' said the wrestler disrespectfully. '*Arré*, Sanichar, don't show off so much. Here, you need a blow from a lathi, not one from an election. You couldn't pull out a radish on your own even if you tried.'

~

The news had spread through Shivpalganj that day that the former Sub-Inspector, who was transferred because he had incurred Vaidyaji's wrath, had come to apologize to Jognath and was present in Vaidyaji's sitting room. This news was, to a large extent, correct.

He was indeed in Vaidyaji's sitting room, dressed in a Terylene bush shirt and wearing gold-rimmed glasses, the ends of his moustache curling.

Ruppan babu had now become an open opponent of the Principal's and he generally sat in Khanna Master's house. Rangnath had begun talking every other day about going back to the town, and occasionally he, too, went over to Khanna Master's. Three days earlier, Badri Wrestler had gone off on a tour of the neighbouring districts as, in their simplicity, two or three of his disciples had been arrested—for highway robbery and dacoity. At this point, only Vaidyaji, the Sub-Inspector, Jognath and Kusahar Prasad were present.

After his transfer from the Shivpalganj police station, the Sub-Inspector had faced several hardships. One was that the new sub-inspector had instituted a number of inquiries against him. The initiation of the inquiries was a painful occurrence, like an operation without anaesthetic, even if in the end they were to result in nothing—like coffee house discussions. The second difficulty concerned his cow. When he arrived in the town, he discovered that there was an anti-corruption campaign going on at the military farm where his brother worked and he didn't dare to take up the burden of looking after it. Living in a house down a narrow alley, every day the Sub-Inspector had to think about how to care for the cow. The third major problem had been caused by Jognath's claim.

Jognath had staked a claim for eight thousand rupees in damages in a civil court, the final words of the argument going something like this: 'That the defendant had charged the plaintiff falsely with the crime of robbery and, with the intention of causing him harm, conducted a false case against him. That the plaintiff had been kept in detention for approximately two months which caused him to be thoroughly disgraced in society and brought his work to a standstill. That damage of several lakhs of rupees has been caused by all this, but the defendant does not have the ability to pay so much. Therefore, a symbolic claim of a mere eight thousand rupees is being entered against him.'

The Sub-Inspector was unruffled by Jognath's diminishing of his status, or by the amount at which he had fixed it. He was bothered by the interest taken in the whole matter by the general public. About half a dozen Hindi and Urdu rags, known as weekly papers, were published in the town. Floating these rags were some semi-educated people who called themselves journalists and whom journalists called rascals. These rags generally published court notices and reports of road accidents. At the same time, every rag would, without fail, carry an account of an event in the life of some official in which the official himself featured as one character, and a bottle of liquor, a girl, a bundle of notes, gambling or a pimp, as the other. These rags were read with enormous interest in the legal and bureaucratic world and, in those circles, were presented as proof of the dangers posed by Hindi and Urdu journalism.

On occasion, the denial of a report on the life of an official would also suddenly be published. From this, one would gather that the editor himself had investigated the incident described in the rag of such-and-such a date, and had found that there was no truth in it; that he regretted having published the news; and that he was enraged with his special correspondent, who had now been sacked and was reduced to selling peanuts. The official in whose favour this sort of denial appeared would smile at his companions and say, 'There you are!' Behind his back, his colleagues would say that the Editor sahib would not have agreed to do it without milking him first, and in this way, the contact between literature and the administration was growing deeper.

In a similar way, one rag had dragged up the news of Jognath's claim against the Sub-Inspector and stuck it on the front page. The other rags had published the story several times in different ways, making some interesting additions so that the news might not seem stale. At the very same time that the Sub-Inspector came to the town, he also became a famous man.

So far, the case hadn't even had its first hearing but he saw that the interest of the men of his department in him had increased, just as that of the journalists had. When he went to his club, his companions made speeches, the conclusions of which were that times were bad; worthless characters were making themselves out to be big heroes; this was no longer the time to be in government service; and, despite being such a sensible chap, how had he got mixed up in this business? He received such a lot of sympathy from his colleagues that it became difficult for him to walk on the streets. When they all began to chorus, 'Don't worry, we'll stick together and fight the case up to the Supreme Court. It is written in the scriptures that the truth shall prevail,' his heart began to sink.

One day, a venerable well-wisher expressed the opinion that he was a funny sort of man. Was he going to keep on trailing all round the place after this case? Why didn't he go and find some way to bury the matter?

After that, the Sub-Inspector took refuge in Vaidyaji.

They were sitting in silence. What had to be said had perhaps been said. The Sub-Inspector was at his most captivating. To break the silence, he said to Kusahar Prasad, 'Well then, are you and Chhote still fighting each other?'

Kusahar Prasad replied, 'No, Inspector sahib, now I'm out of shape. I don't have that wrestler's strength any more.'

'So, are you suffering your son's blows in silence?'

'I've told you. I'm not up to it any more.' Kusahar Prasad addressed Vaidyaji, 'You know it in any case. Before Holi he abused me, and I hit him with a cane. Then what he did was lift me up and swing me as if he was going to throw me into the courtyard on my back. But goodness knows why, he put me down. I just collapsed on to a charpoy. Around midday, he told me, "Look here, your body is weak. It doesn't have a wrestler's strength any more. When I picked you up to throw you on your back it was like lifting paddy straw. That's why I didn't throw you into the courtyard."

'From that day, we don't take liberties with each other. Chhote says, "If you want to die, die your own death; don't rely on me to help you. I've nothing to do with your living or dying."'

Vaidyaji listened to the whole story and said, 'Don't even take that sinner's name in front of me. The base fellow raises his hand to his father!'

Speaking as one elder to another, Kusahar remarked without the least hesitation, 'Well done, maharaj, all this time while you were listening to the story you said nothing. After you found out how things stood you tell me not even to mention Chhote's name. Well done! You're a real leader.'

Vaidyaji laughed in such a way that the Sub-Inspector might realize that Kusahar Prasad had his leave to insult him. As he laughed, he looked towards Jognath. Jognath saw that Vaidyaji's moustache ends were laughing but not his eyes. He cleared his throat and said, 'Eh, Pandit Kusahar Prasad, even if Chhote has stopped giving you shoe-beatings, don't lose all control over your tongue. Speak politely to Vaidyaji. If you roam around making that sort of crooked remarks, someone's going to give you more than you bargained for.'

Vaidyaji continued to laugh in the same way, which made it clear that Kusahar too was being insulted with his permission. Kusahar

Prasad just said, 'You've learnt a good deal in jail. But keep company with boys your own age. This is a matter between me and Vaidyaji; why are you squealing about it?'

Suddenly the Sub-Inspector said, 'Vaidyaji, it's nearly time for my bus.'

'I'll do as you say,' said Vaidyaji. 'You're the defendant. Jognath's the plaintiff. At the moment, you're face-to-face. The matter can be sorted out only if you talk to each other. How can I interfere in young men's affairs?'

Jognath replied, 'Maharaj, this is not a personal matter. It's a question of the honour of Shivpalganj. That's why the village council is paying my legal fees from its own pocket, and there will be a settlement only if the village council proposes one. I was junior to the Sub-Inspector when this happened, and I'm junior to him now. Officers remain officers. But I have nothing to say; whatever you decide will be final.'

The Sub-Inspector felt as limp as a portulaca flower at sundown. He sensed that his moustache was drooping, but the wax was preventing it from going up and down with his emotions. He said nothing.

Vaidyaji said to Jognath, 'So leave it up to the council then. Talk to Sanichar. Such an important officer has rushed down here from the town. The matter should be settled.'

The Sub-Inspector frowned, 'Sanichar? Who's that?'

'You won't know him. His name is Mangal Prasad. He's our pradhan. That's his shop over there. Go and have a word with him,' said Vaidyaji respectfully.

Kusahar remarked, 'Became a yogi yesterday and already has matted locks down to his buttocks. Just look at Sanichar—in a few moments, he has become "Mangal Prasad". Well done, Guru maharaj! If you want them to make up, why don't you call Sanichar here?'

Vaidyaji said gravely, 'The dignity of the office should be maintained. Look how much respect Gandhiji gave Nehruji after he became prime minister! Our personal relationship is another matter, but in public, one must maintain the dignity of the office.'

To encourage the Sub-Inspector he repeated, 'Please go over there to his shop. The pradhanji must have come.'

~

Sanichar was sitting in the cabin of his shop waiting for the Sub-Inspector and Jognath. As he was returning from the fields he had found out through ganjaha means that Jognath's claim had knocked the wind out of the Sub-Inspector; that he had come whimpering for peace; and that he should be given a hard time so that people would learn that in Shivpalganj the most senior police officers had owned defeat—a fact that would prove useful in times to come. Sanichar had sold four or five packets of bhang while waiting for the Sub-Inspector. Then he gave one away free to a passer-by who was a member of the village council. The member asked, 'What am I supposed to do with this?'

'Keep it. The Sub-Inspector is about to come and beg for mercy. When he does, let's celebrate with bhang. The bhang is on me; you provide all the almonds, pistachios, sugar and milk.'

The council member shoved the packet into the fold of his dhoti and said with a smile, 'Pradhanji, you are pulling a fast one. What's in an anna's worth of bhang? The real expense lies in the almonds and pistachios.'

Sanichar pulled a face as if he had taken strong objection to this allegation against his generosity. He said, 'Keep the packet; what's eating you? Let the Sub-Inspector come and beg for mercy, and if there's no bhang ready, I'll order a bhang feast at the council's expense.'

The council member said, 'That'll set us back twenty-five rupees.'

'Let it.'

'The secretary will raise an objection to the expenditure.'

Sanichar tried hastily to lose his temper, and succeeded. 'Every evening here, for the last ten years, there have been bhang sessions in the cooperative union, and no whore's son has ever objected, so who's going to object to a bhang session by the village council?'

The council member left the path of reason and took the straight but illogical path of principle. 'But this is not right. I can't swallow it.'

Sanichar looked at him sideways and said, 'You are all idiots. Do you know anything about the outside world at all? Big councils give banquets worth thousands. You think I'm talking nonsense? Just go and ask him—Rangnath babu. Then you'll understand how much expense official work entails.

'Here you are going soft over just one bhang session in the village council. When a mahua flower falls on a squirrel's head, he thinks the sky has fallen.'

The Sub-Inspector and Jognath could be seen approaching. Sanichar first picked up his shirt to put it on. He'd had it stitched after the election and wore it only on special occasions under instructions from Vaidyaji. Then, for some unknown reason, he put it down on a basket of rice. He stroked his naked torso once, dispersed his long topknot well over his scalp and hitched his underpants up to the very top of his thighs. He prepared himself to meet the Sub-Inspector like a half-naked Avdhut sadhu and started weighing out some goods on a pair of scales for an imaginary customer.

The moment he arrived, Jognath said, 'Pradhanji, the Sub-Inspector has come.'

Sanichar threw a glance over the top of the Sub-Inspector's head and asked, 'Where is he?'

'This is he.'

Sanichar gestured towards the opposite bench and said coldly, 'Sit down, Sub-Inspector. You're not in uniform. It was difficult to recognize you.'

The Sub-Inspector sat down on the bench. He thought it impolite to dust it first. Jognath sat down beside him.

The Sub-Inspector began to say that Shivpalganj would make a lot of progress in the hands of a man like Sanichar. He expressed regret that, during his posting, he had not been able to make his acquaintance. He said, 'Jognath was under some misapprehension, which is why he lodged a claim . . .'

Sanichar interrupted. 'Misapprehension! What does that mean when it's at home? Forget English and speak in a local language. I'm a rustic man. Speak so that I can understand.'

The Sub-Inspector's honour was saved by the wax on his moustache ends. Under the protection of his curled-up whiskers, he explained in a tone of immense sweetness, 'Jognath got the mistaken idea that . . .'

Sanichar said, 'If he got the wrong idea, this case will clear it up. After four hearings we'll see who had the wrong idea.'

On the bench, the Sub-Inspector showed no sign of internal conflict.

He looked at his watch and said, 'Look, pradhanji, you can take it that I was the one with the wrong idea. It was my mistake. I shouldn't have touched the case without looking at the whole evidence. Now I'm ready to make a settlement. Whatever you think is right will be done.'

Jognath smiled, but Sanichar asked gravely, 'What do you say, Jognath?'

'What is there for me to say? I was a hooligan then, and I'm a hooligan now. It's your job to do the talking and the listening. But still, if you want my opinion, here it is. The Sub-Inspector should put down in writing what he has just said, and that'll be the end of the whole matter.'

The Sub-Inspector made no comment. Sanichar thought for a while and then suggested, 'I'll tell you what, Sub-Inspector. Let's go and have a word with Vaidyaji.'

The Sub-Inspector replied, 'I've already spoken to him. He says that the matter is in the village council's hands. The village council is fighting Jognath's case. He says that you're the one to decide whether to withdraw it. Vaidyaji's not even a member of the village council.'

'Yes, that's true,' Sanichar admitted pompously but then paused and added, 'But still, we should have a word with him.'

He slapped his shirt down hard on the basket of rice. Dust flew up, but the Sub-Inspector didn't even pinch his nostrils. Putting on his shirt, Sanichar said, 'Let's go there. That is the court in which we have to appear.'

~

As evening fell, there was a bhang feast, courtesy the village council. Several grinding stones clicked together on the Gandhi platform. The bhang was ground amidst dust and confusion. To remove all possibility of its refusing to intoxicate, some thorn apple seeds were added as well. Almonds, pistachios, black pepper, cardamom and a dozen or so things which couldn't be recognized were ground and dropped into it. The mixture was dissolved in milk and water, and before one's very eyes several buckets began to froth. Leaping like a monkey, Sanichar first took a glass of bhang and poured it over a Shiv lingam standing underneath a nearby tree, at the same time reciting by heart hundreds of maxims and prayers relating to bhang. People began nodding their heads in appreciation of the fact that even uneducated men of the old school knew so much more than the educated men of today. Then the bhang was distributed.

Goodness knows how many boys were gathered round the Gandhi platform. Mud was streaming from their eyes; froth was dripping from their mouths. The stomachs of practically all of them were enlarged, proving, perhaps, that there was no shortage of food in their homes. Their voices sounded squeaky—sometimes hoarse—and even more unnatural was the happiness suffusing their faces. The bhang was distributed first among those boys. Even if they didn't know how milk tastes, they were familiar with the taste of bhang, and they began to describe it with words like 'very fine' and 'first class', and drank it up with happy hearts.

~

That same night, Jognath invited select people to imbibe alcoholic refreshments. The chief guest had returned several days ago, having been acquitted of a murder in a nearby village. In his presence, the atmosphere at first remained quiet and respectful, but later on, when a man said in a military style, To slaughter a man like a goat while he's asleep is not something to be proud of, soldier. It's the act of a butcher,' the peaceful atmosphere put its tail between its legs and slipped into a hole.

'Have you ever slaughtered a goat?' asked the chief guest.

'I'm not a butcher.'

'I'm asking a straight question,' repeated the chief guest. 'Have you ever slaughtered a goat?'

He was speaking in a very soft and simple tone, his eyes fixed on his bottle. When he repeated his question, people began to feel nervous and slipped up to him. Someone touched his hand and said, 'Let it pass.'

The guest jerked his hand away and said for the third time, 'Have you ever . . .?'

'Let it pass, let it pass, brother,' they coaxed, but the man speaking military language had also reached the stage where he imagined every object to be made of straw and every man a maggot. Addressing the general public, he said, 'The drink has gone to this soldier's head. Lay him down over there in the corner and pour some cold water over him.'

That was the start. It didn't take long for the flasks and bottles to start breaking. Then the drinkers went out into the street to trade curses for a while. At one o'clock, they began to indulge in kicks, punches and lathi blows.

In the neighbouring houses, people were awake, and in the police station, people were asleep.

Rangnath was lying in the veranda of the room on the roof. He lay for a while in silence, listening to the screams and howls coming from one corner of the village. Then he said to Ruppan, 'I hate it here. I'll go back tomorrow.'

Ruppan babu had not taken part in the day's feast, but bhang had been sent to the house for his consumption. He said sleepily, 'What's the point, brother? There is this sort of bastards there as well.'

Rangnath said hotly, 'I hate it there too.'

Ruppan babu turned over, yawned and said, 'Who are you to hate anyone? Are you any different from them or what?'

As he said this, he sat up on his charpoy. He continued, 'You've been making this sort of remarks for some days now. You talk as if you have come from England and the rest of us are black men shitting in the open. If you want to sleep, keep quiet and sleep. If not, then sit up all night hating people.'

31

The moment he returned home, Badri Wrestler saw that Vaidyaji was troubled. When troubled, his turban would become somewhat looser, his moustache would appear disarrayed and after every third sentence, he would comment, 'What can I say? Do whatever you think best.'

A friend of Badri's had been sentenced in a neighbouring district for the illegal possession of weapons. A Sten gun, some hand grenades, a rifle and a shotgun had been found in this friend's house and it had been proved that this armoury belonged to him. In court, he had stated that neither the house nor the armoury was his as the house, in fact, belonged to his wife. But it was said that the judge's heart was terror-stricken by the sight of so many weapons and the moment he could, he sentenced Badri's friend to two years in jail.

Badri Wrestler had no interest in guns but he considered it necessary to go to express his condolences. By then, his friend had lodged an appeal in the high court and was out on bail. He told Badri repeatedly that if he lost in the high court he would go to the Supreme Court and all this would cost a lot of money, which he would have to bear personally as, nowadays, no one gave a damn for anyone else. Badri took this to mean that the legal expenses would have to be borne by the wayfarers who ventured on to the local roads after sunset. Since he regarded highway robbery with contempt, he assured his friend that he shouldn't worry about the money and that God would provide whatever was lacking.

But his friend smiled and, explaining that whatever he already had was God-given, extracted a cloth bundle from some thatch. In the bundle, there were wads of folded notes. The friend took out two thousand rupees, insisted on handing them to Badri, and instructed him to keep them with him. What, after all, did they mean to him? The yogi wanders, the river flows, and he had one foot in jail and one foot out. If his appeal was rejected by the high court, his bail would be cancelled then and there. That was the time these rupees were to be used to make arrangements for the Supreme Court appeal. If God gave him another two or three thousand in the meantime, he'd have that sent to Badri as well. He was going through hard times and had only God and Badri to rely on . . .

After finishing the discussion on the Almighty in this fashion, Badri returned home with two thousand rupees in his pocket, even if it was to be held in trust. When he arrived, he told Vaidyaji about his friend's afflictions and explained that they might have to take the case to the Supreme Court, and if that happened, he himself would have a lot of running around to do. Vaidyaji said in a subdued voice, 'What can I say? Do whatever you think . . .'

Badri started, and then examined his father. He was not wearing a turban, but his moustache was untidy. Badri became worried. He realized that Vaidyaji was troubled. He raked through the happenings of the past few days to investigate the cause of his unhappiness and discovered that several people had done a number of bad things.

The Principal had gone to the town and had shown the college committee's annual report to the deputy director of education. The report described Vaidyaji as a 'lion among men' and clearly proved that he had been happily elected as the manager by a unanimous vote. It did not mention that some committee members had been threatened at gunpoint outside the college and had not been allowed to enter it. In spite of this written proof, the deputy director intended to inquire into Ramadhin Bhikhmakhervi's allegation that the election for the post of manager had been held in an atmosphere of terror at pistol-point. He had given the Principal notice that he would conduct an inquiry in person and had set a date for it.

Khanna Master had filed a complaint and, amongst several other allegations, he had also claimed that teachers were made to sign for twice the amount they received as salary. That was the practice in 70 per cent of colleges, and no attention should have been paid to it, but the deputy director had promised to inquire into that, too. There is a hard and fast rule throughout the world that the amount written on a receipt is to be accepted as the amount for which the receipt has been made. Despite the written evidence of the receipts, the deputy director was all set to hold an inquiry.

Someone had printed an anonymous handbill against Malaviya's bad conduct. Whether or not the allegation was true, it was a cowardly act to make an anonymous complaint. It was also a cowardly act to bugger a child, and if he had done so he ought to be openly condemned. But Vaidyaji had heard that Khanna Master had managed to get some boys to give evidence to prove that this handbill had been printed by the poor old Principal sahib. Ruppan wasn't saying anything, but Vaidyaji had heard that he had helped Khanna get proof of this. Several students had been egged on to make a complaint that everything except education took place in the college. They alleged that poor Master Motiram taught how to run a flour mill and not science. There was no written evidence in support of these allegations but, still, there was going to be an inquiry into them, too.

And if that weren't enough, Rangnath had begun talking to Khanna from time to time as well. On the one hand his health had improved, but on the other his mind had become polluted.

The cooperative inspector was trying to one up even Yudhisthira. He had put in a report saying that the supervisor, Ram Swarup, had embezzled upwards of two thousand rupees and that this had been done with Vaidyaji's cognizance. He had proposed that the sum be recovered from Vaidyaji. Despite it being put down in black and white, no action had been taken on the report which Vaidyaji, in his capacity as managing director, had sent in against the inspector whom, in spite of repeated efforts, he had not been able to get transferred. Moreover, Vaidyaji had written that the inspector drank but, so far, this hadn't caused even a tremor, let alone a volcanic eruption, at the cooperative department.

Badri Wrestler placed one foot next to where his father was sitting on the wooden bed, put his elbow on his knee and his chin on his hand.

As Vaidyaji concluded, he said, 'Is that all?'

Vaidyaji replied, 'You call this "all"? When this is the reward I get for my services?'

Badri Wrestler ignored the remark about a reward and said, 'These matters can be settled in ten minutes. Beat the cooperative inspector ten times with a shoe and he'll come round. If the deputy director doesn't listen to reason and comes here for an inquiry, we'll arrange to give him, too, a warm welcome. To sort out Khanna Master, we'll order him and his party not to set foot in the college from tomorrow. We'll mark them absent and sack them after fifteen days . . .'

Vaidyaji interrupted with, 'How can we do that?'

'The Principal will do it. How did we get rid of Tripathiji last year? Was he or wasn't he kept absent for a month?'

Catching a glimpse of confidence in Vaidyaji's expression, Badri Wrestler continued, 'You just leave things as they are; the Principal will set them right. Chhote has trained a couple of disciples over here. We'll put them on duty outside the college. They'll thrash Khanna if he tries to go in.

'Why worry about what nonsense Rangnath gets up to? He's a town man—like pig shit, no good for plastering the floor or burning.

Don't even bother looking in his direction; he'll just get upset and run away.

'That leaves Ruppan. I'll have to give him a bit of a beating. Whenever you give the word, I'll thrash him.'

Vaidyaji sat serenely for a while after listening to Badri's defence strategy. Then he suddenly said, 'What's happened to Ramdayal Tiwari's appeal? Has any date been set by the high court?'

Badri planted his foot even more firmly on the wooden bed and said, 'We'll talk about that, too. First of all, we're dealing with what's going on here, so let's finish that. Tell me, is there anything left to worry about?'

Vaidyaji thought and said, 'Here, things will be sorted out all right, but there's something very wrong with politics on top. That's why these petty officials are getting so uppish. I can't even get the cooperative inspector transferred and there's some very high-level politics behind that. That is what we have to worry about.'

Badri Wrestler said, with some irritation, 'Politics is your business. I've had my say. The inspector should be beaten with a shoe ten times—no more, no less.'

Something occurred to him and he amended his statement, 'If he should proceed on leave, then I can't promise I'll do even that. I'll let him go.'

Vaidyaji drew a deep breath. His body relaxed; his hands went to his head, but since he wasn't wearing a turban at that moment, he couldn't tighten it and, instead, he began to pat his scalp, as if pouring blessings down upon his own head.

Then he asked, 'What will you do about Ramdayal Tiwari?'

Badri Wrestler replied in the same tone, 'Let these things be settled first.'

He took out the money from the pocket of his kurta. Handing it to Vaidyaji he said, 'Here's one thousand three hundred rupees. I hear the Sub-Inspector has left some peace money as well. Put it together to make a full two thousand rupees. If the cooperative puts on the pressure, go and deposit the money straight away.'

Vaidyaji said gravely, 'Some of the cash the Sub-Inspector left has been given to Jognath. There's four or five hundred left. That belongs to the people.'

'The cooperative also belongs to the people.'

Vaidyaji returned the notes to Badri and said, 'So keep it for the time being; we'll see what happens.'

After this, Badri didn't stop to discuss his friend's case. He turned around once towards his father who was on his way into the house, and said in an odd kind of voice, 'Bapu, have a word with Gayadin as well.'

Badri Wrestler had not addressed his father by any name for several years. As a child he had called him Bapu, or Daddy, but as soon as he grew up and took to wrestling he had given up this childish habit. Vaidyaji heard Badri's remark, and for some reason closed his eyes.

~

Every child in Shivpalganj knew one law of nature—that a clever crow sticks only its beak into refuse. The same thing was true of Vaidyaji and corrupt officials.

The cooperative inspector had caused a great deal of difficulty. The old inspector used to work in a democratic way. That is to say, when arrangements were made to grind bhang at the union, he would arrive even before the other members—the moment the first grinding stone hit the slab—and take part in the programme as one of the common people. The new inspector was implacably opposed to bhang and, according to information obtained by Vaidyaji and the letter written by Vaidyaji to the inspector's superiors, fond of the bottle. At the same time as he had become addicted to drink, he had also become addicted to honesty and, instead of cooperating with the members of the union, he had begun to oppose them. At first, Vaidyaji had been convinced that the inspector would be transferred but when, after several days, he had received no answer to his letter, he grew worried. On inquiring, he discovered that the whole thing was a political game and, in the same way that civil servants can be transferred by politics, high-level politics can also stop their transfers.

Then he realized that the inspector didn't hold only a bottle and a pen in his hands, he also held the strings of power.

One day, Vaidyaji went out alone on a friendship mission. When he arrived in the town early in the morning, he did the rounds of dozens of bungalows. With the exception of a few where it was not considered demeaning to wait outside for an hour or so, he received an enthusiastic welcome, and his wounded self-confidence again fluttered and arose within him. At many bungalows, people were thrilled by gifts of his virility-enhancing pills. To many, he had, in addition, given the information that he had recently met an astrologer of very high standing, and if 'sir' would give his horoscope, he could have it re-interpreted. To rouse some people's enthusiasm, the pills and the introduction to the astrologer were not enough. He had to tell them that a certain mahatma of Rishikesh was due in town on a certain date—yes, the same mahatma whose blessings had shown all the allegations against a certain police officer to be false and, on top of that, had brought him immediate promotion—and that it would be most convenient to meet him at night after ten o'clock, and if 'sir' liked, Vaidyaji, too, would come that day to introduce him.

Vanquishing in this way several senior politicians and bureaucrats, he finally arrived at the bungalow from which the order for the cooperative inspector's protection had been issued. There, he discovered that word had come of a new thinking in the cooperative movement which rolled nepotism, casteism, socialism and other elevated principles together, and which would be the source of inspiration for future office holders. The thinking went along these lines: if you hold power, don't use it in an obvious manner to strengthen your position. Use it to create new and conflicting forces, and give them sufficient strength to keep fighting one another. In this way, your own power would remain safe and supreme. If you just keep trying to increase your own power and do not control the creation, preservation and annihilation of other mutually opposing forces, after a short while, some other power would rise from an unexpected direction, attack you and break your strength.

One result of giving shape to this thinking was that, in this bungalow, requests from opposing factions—as well as from one's own faction—were given a hearing. Since the request for stopping the cooperative inspector's transfer had come at that moment from the leader of another faction, and since that faction leader's strength was to be used to harass the leader of a third faction, the transfer wouldn't have been possible even if Vaidyaji had decided to fast unto death for it.

No one told Vaidyaji any of this, but many things at such bungalows can only be sensed through sight and smell, and that's why, the moment he arrived there, he understood all. Still, he didn't lose courage. He tried a great deal of persuasion but the matter became more and more entangled. Vaidyaji said that no embezzlement worth the name had taken place, and even if it had, the man who did it was missing and, due to the incompetence of the administration, had not yet been apprehended. Vaidyaji himself had nothing to do with this dispute, and if it were ever proved that he did, he would donate to the union whatever sum was set. But before this, the inspector should be transferred. He was prepared to do whatever was asked of him; his only condition was . . .

Then Vaidyaji was told that they had to set a good example to the community. If they didn't, public behaviour would degenerate. If that happened, the present and the future would both be the worse for it. What had Ram done? Hadn't he renounced Sita? That's the reason they still remembered Ram's rule. One should find one's enjoyment in renunciation—that should be our model. This had also been said in the Upanishads. That's what all reputed leaders did to this day. They enjoyed the fruits of power, renounced them, and then enjoyed the fruits of renunciation.

What had a certain finance minister done? Had he or hadn't he resigned? That rail minister had done the same, too, as had a certain minister of information. At present, the country, the state, the district, the cooperative union—all needed such renunciation. In order to hold an open inquiry into the allegations, it would be best if Vaidyaji were to set an example to the people. As soon as the building of an example was erected, all the allegations would be crushed beneath its foundations. Therefore, Vaidyaji should resign from the post of managing director. This would be the reply to the reports against him. If he so wished, he could resign in protest against something—either the low character of a colleague or in defence of some principle. If he were prepared to resign, he would have total liberty to choose the grounds for his resignation. But there should be nothing indecisive about it; it should be an unconditional resignation. Otherwise, there should be none at all. If it were conditional, a great deal could also happen which would certainly prove very unpleasant for Vaidyaji.

It seemed to Vaidyaji as if there were some things about him which people on a senior level found difficult to swallow.

He reached a decision. He said, 'I will resign. Possibly it will be seen as weakness on my part. Still, on your suggestion, I shall resign in protest against this baseless campaign. However, when the question arises of selecting candidates for the state cooperative federation . . .'

He was assured that he could hand in his resignation with the same confidence with which all great men did, when the occasion came for them to set an example to the people. There was a shortage of capable men. So, capable men never lacked for anything. They left from one direction and were brought back from another.

Today, apart from potency pills, information and broadcasting on the subject of astrologers, and meditation with saints, Vaidyaji also had a fourth subject on offer. Before taking his leave from the bungalow, he broached this, too. 'You will be happy to know,' he said, 'that I am considering arranging an inter-caste marriage for my elder son. The wedding is not yet fixed but I hope very soon to dispatch invitations to you. Your valued presence will be sought. I may not be able to request you personally at the time, so I am informing you now. At such exemplary marriages, your cooperation and blessings are absolutely essential. You will also be happy to learn . . .'

He was happy to learn. He would certainly be present.

'In the village environment it is being opposed also, but . . .'

He was bound to be happy, whatever Vaidyaji said, and he was. Over and over again.

~

The annual meeting of the cooperative union passed off very successfully because, this year, the sweets had been ordered from the town. Bunting was strung from the cooperative building and the flower garlands piled up. The official who had recently inaugurated the cooperative farm had been called to take part in the meeting. He had acquired a taste for public speaking and garlands a long time ago, and the moment he smelt them, he would pull on his trousers, call for a car belonging to a local businessman and chug along to the meeting.

Without anyone having read it, the annual report had been taken as read. It had been a profitable year and the members were to receive their dividends. They received them without the money being distributed. Many things happened without happening, and then, finally, the one thing that was bound to happen, did. The speeches started.

The reality of a speech lies in the giving, not the receiving. So, the speakers kept on speaking, and the audience kept on working out other matters amongst themselves. For example, the official from the town said that Vaidyaji was the embodiment of the cooperative and people began remarking that Badri Wrestler had been trapped by Gayadin's girl.

Then the official said that it would be difficult for the cooperative movement to progress until such embodiments were produced in every village. The people said that this matter wasn't going to die down however much a lid was put on it, and so he was going to marry her. Despite all this whispering, no one voiced any such comment out loud, because if there was absolute rule anywhere, it was in the union, and if anyone was an absolute ruler, it was Vaidyaji.

Still, even during the rule of Lord Ram, a dhobi had come forth to make a painful comment, and here, too, a man stood up and said with great fervour that he wanted to make a speech.

The people sitting next to him caught hold of his dhoti and began to tug at it. They wanted to make him sit down again, if only to retain his garment. But the man belonged to Ramadhin Bhikhmakhervi's faction and had come prepared to do everything according to instructions. So he paid no heed to his descending dhoti. In fact, it doubled his zeal and, above all the other speeches, he delivered a powerful speech to the effect that he, too, was going to make a speech.

His shouting had the same effect as shouting generally does. The opposition began to quiet down. The official from the town said, 'Go ahead. Certainly give a speech. Who's stopping you?'

To maintain his fervour, he didn't commence with the words, 'Respected Chairman' or 'Brothers and Sisters'. He took off with, 'In this report there's no mention of—what's-his-name—Ram Swarup.

That bastard—what's-his-name—committed the fraud; he took two loads of wheat to the town and ran for it. He was a drunk and used to whore, too. He used to have secret talks with Vaidyaji. One night, two—what're-their-names—trucks came and loaded up all through the night. No one had any idea. What's-his-name—that bastard—talked very sweetly. The moment he saw me in the distance, whatshisname would say, "I touch your feet". He got on very well with Vaidyaji. Now don't take me amiss; whether I say it or not the whole world knows it. He—what's-his-name—got away with two thousand flaming rupees. So, who is to be held responsible? Vaidyaji is a great embodiment of the cooperative, and so we should take him and cart him around the place. Nobody ever asks Vaidyaji what anyone is up to. Eat the sweets, have a drink of water and go home. But that's not going to do anything for the—what's-its-name—uplift of the country. In our country, customs should apply. However, the embezzlement took place; there should be an inquiry. I'm not educated, so don't mind what I say. It's Holi!'

The man's fervour was increasing and when he raised the cry 'It's Holi!' it became quite apparent that he was about to raise his hand and recite poetry. If fervour and poetry ever combined in Shivpalganj, they could cause fights of an epic proportion. That was why people attempted to stop the speech with the words, 'Yes, yes, pipe down now, calm down.' But the speech was running on at full speed. Even with people in pursuit it wouldn't stop. That's when Vaidyaji rose to his feet and came to stand at the front. At the sight of him, the speech jumped a little from its place, wagged its tail and began to sniff the floor.

Vaidyaji stood for a while, smiling, as if it had been proved that he had no connection with the embezzlement. Then he said in the manner of a sage, 'It is worth paying attention to how embezzlement takes place. If you have one thousand rupees, you cannot embezzle them. They are yours. You can spend them improperly but not embezzle them. The only person who can embezzle them is the man to whom they do not belong.

'In the cooperative no one has his own property. It is held jointly. The property of several individuals is collected in one place. It is protected by someone to whom it does not belong. Pay attention, gentlemen: if you use your own property wrongfully it is not embezzlement; if someone else does, then it is. Embezzlement is the fate of all cooperative property. There's no need to be surprised by this. Nor should one be distressed to see the word "embezzlement" linked with cooperative property.

'On occasion, embezzlements are concealed. One should not conceal one's faults, else they take root. This is the principle I follow. One should look with suspicion on any cooperative where no embezzlement has been detected. Generally, embezzlements there are disguised with figures. Here, nothing at all was hidden. There has been the best management. At the end of the year, the union hasn't suffered a loss—in fact, it has declared a profit. Whether it's a profit of a paisa or a crore, profit is profit.

'In this situation, the topic of embezzlement is devoid of meaning. To raise the question here is to insult the cooperative—to insult the cooperative movement.

'However, allegations have been made against me personally. It is improper to level allegations. It is even more unseemly to make personal ones. No individual can function in such an atmosphere. Certainly a man of decency cannot. I oppose this sort of allegations. But please note that I oppose the allegations and not the man making them. The person making them is Shri Ram Charan. I respect him. I revere him deeply in my heart.

'But I oppose his charges. I oppose them strongly and, in protest, I resign my post as managing director.'

With this, Vaidyaji sat down serenely in his place.

Things began happening fast. There was an awful rumpus, as if a member of the State Assembly was being dragged out of the House. Then the rumpus began to subside and the serious tones of the official from the town could be heard. 'Vaidyaji stands firmly by his decision. So my advice is that his resignation be accepted. As it is, today, the election for the coming year was to be held. The resignation means that Vaidyaji does not wish to be managing director in the future.'

Vaidyaji said from where he sat, 'I don't even want to remain a member. I have fulfilled my duty. Now young men should come in. They should run the movement.'

The town official advised, 'I don't think you should withdraw your hand completely, or the union will collapse. You're talking of young men. Where can you find them nowadays?'

But Vaidyaji wouldn't listen. He stubbornly stuck to his opinion that, even nowadays, there must be young men somewhere, and that they should run the movement. Finally, the town official said, 'So, let a new managing director be elected . . .'

With this, he began to speak without giving anyone else an opportunity to say anything. He began with tradition. 'Brothers, it has been the tradition of this union that all elections here are unanimous. Not only do I hope, but I am also fully confident that today, too, the task will be completed in accordance with that tradition. You people choose one name . . .'

Suddenly, Chhote Wrestler stood up, complete with lungi. He interrupted, 'What's there in any election-felection? This union is a small set-up and you want to start election fighting in it, too?'

After this, he grumbled a saying at which a lot of people sitting nearby began to laugh. The official understood that Chhote Wrestler had made some obscene comment about him. He said agitatedly, 'Wrestler, you misunderstand . . .'

Chhote Wrestler cut in defiantly, 'Of course I won't be able to understand. You, sahib, you're the one with the trousers. You're the one who'll understand rightly.'

The official said almost beseechingly, 'Please try to understand, wrestlerji! I was speaking against an election, saying that there's no tradition of holding elections here. Here, every decision is taken by consensus. An election . . .'

Chhote's chest swelled. He challenged, 'You're again carrying on about an election. There's no need for one. If Vaidyaji doesn't want to stay on, then he doesn't have to. Just because there's no cock does it mean the day won't break . . . ?'

It must have been four o'clock in the afternoon. A strong wind was blowing, whipping up dust. Chhote Wrestler was swaying as he stood, rubbing his eyes against the dust, and he began to yell with fervour. There was no apparent reason for this shouting and emotion, but he was becoming more and more roused, and his voice louder. The audience was growing proportionately more excited, and the official, more agitated. Finally, Chhote, who was now inspiring an imaginary platoon to advance farther into the field of battle, shouted, 'Vaidyaji has stepped down. Not to worry! We'll replace him right away. We'll see how there's an election! You think you can hold one? That sort of swindling can go on in the town! It won't work here! Here, we can put whomever we choose in Vaidyaji's seat. On your feet, Badri ustad! If Vaidyaji's not there, you sit in his place. Stand up, stand up ustad, take over!'

Amidst the chaos, arose great cries of, 'Say, "Victory to Mother India!"' Then the same old sequence of '. . . Pandit Jawaharlal Nehru!' '. . . Vaidya maharaj!' '. . . Badri Wrestler!' '. . . Idris sahib!'

Idris sahib, that is, the official from the town, was stunned; stars shot before his eyes. When he regained his senses, he saw that Vaidyaji had disappeared somewhere; someone was dragging his opponent, Ram Charan, by his arms, out of the gate; and Badri Wrestler was sitting next to him on the platform, garlanded with flowers, his face suffused with the lustre of the managing directorship.

32

That year, the winter crop in Shivpalganj was good. It had rained during the cold weather. The senior canal official, who considered the public grass and refuse and democracy a plague, had been transferred. The official who had replaced him used the canal water like water and tried to see that everyone got his share. The westerlies of the season of basant didn't blow hard. There were no plagues of rats or locusts. Of the two celebrated thugs who used to wield lathis to persuade people to let them graze their animals on unripe crops, one was run over and killed by a truck and the other was in the police lock-up. No one set fire to any threshing floor to settle a feud.

Some banjaras had come and settled on the scrubland near the village. Their girls were young and alluring. They brewed country liquor and sold it cheap. They would capture any young men who passed that way and tether them in their huts like rams. At a time when the young men needed to be in the fields hoeing, they were bleating away in the huts. This year, the police interfered, first with the girls, then with the country liquor business and finally, with the banjaras' whole way of life, and cleared them out of the area. So, apart from the gambling in the mango groves, there remained no obstacle between the young men and the fields, and they laboured hard.

The harvest was good, but it didn't happen out of the blue, as some people thought. These circumstances, or rather the lack of them, lay behind it.

The farmers paid scant attention to the good harvest because they never paid attention even to a bad one. But a good many other sections of society began to clap their hands and dance for joy. The leaders said that it was the effect of their speeches; the development officials began to say, with the help of statistics, that it was all thanks to their efforts. In official circles, people began congratulating each other.

One other result of the good harvest was that Gayadin was afforded some relief from litigation. He had initiated a number of claims for recovering loans. The defendants in these cases now came to him with money and settled out of court. Many farmers began to bring him money and, despite the proximity of the marriage season, repayments increased and the cash outflow decreased.

One day, he was busy with his bookkeeping, surrounded by a ring of seven or eight farmers, when he saw Vaidyaji heading for his house.

Gayadin welcomed Vaidyaji much in the way that one great man greets another, and they went and sat apart from the others. Vaidyaji said, 'I have come to speak to you about a very important matter.'

Gayadin said nothing. He knew that Vaidyaji would say what he had come to say even if he kept quiet. After a few moments of silence, Vaidyaji said, 'What are your feelings about casteism?'

An expression of confusion spread over Gayadin's face. He replied, 'It's a gift from God. He made you a Brahmin and me a Bania.'

'I don't agree,' said a smiling Vaidyaji. 'It's because of casteism that our country is in such a bad state. That's why I want to arrange inter-caste marriages for my sons. Someone has to step forward in that direction, too. The Mahatma used to say . . .'

Gayadin raised his hand to prevent him from taking the argument further and said, 'If you want to marry off your sons outside your community, Vaidyaji, please do so! But, as a sensible man, don't drag the Mahatma in among all these girls and boys.'

Vaidyaji faltered, and then said, 'I was making a point.'

'So was I,' replied Gayadin.

For a while, neither spoke. Opposite, a buffalo tethered to a peg in the ground was walking round in circles and emitting various sounds. It was in immediate need of a mate. If any human being could have understood the animal's language, he would have sensed in the buffalo's bellowing the yearning expressed in the sort of song that is sung in the middle of a bazaar by a heroine pining for her hero in a Hindi film.

After some time, Vaidyaji said, 'So, what is your opinion on inter-caste marriages?'

Gayadin was sitting with his head bowed. At this, he slowly raised his head and watched the restless buffalo for a few moments with indifference. Still looking in its direction, he replied, 'Maharaj, these are the domestic matters of Brahmins and Thakurs. How can we Banias and traders advise you about them?'

Vaidyaji smiled as he said, 'What are you saying, Gayadinji? This is a question of our two families. If you don't speak about it, then, who will?'

Gayadin now turned his face slowly towards Vaidyaji. When Vaidyaji's face came into focus, he centred his dismal and dejected glance on it, devoid of any sense of a deal to be made. He asked, 'What has it to do with my family, maharaj?'

Vaidyaji raised his eyebrows in astonishment, 'So you know nothing?'

Gayadin was unmoved. His silence revealed that he knew nothing.

Vaidyaji now began to talk at great speed, 'This is what pleases Badri. When a son grows to be sixteen, you have to treat him like a friend, too. That's why I made no objection. Naturally, he has found out the girl's feelings. And so now, you shouldn't have any objection, either.'

This time, the buffalo took such a big leap that it almost pulled out the peg from the ground and flew skyward. Gayadin frowned, looking with disapproval at his whole environment. But, without expressing his annoyance, he said, 'Why should I object? Your sons can marry wherever they like. Why are you dragging me into it, maharaj?'

Vaidyaji was finding this tedious. He said, 'I am not dragging you into it. The girl is your daughter. That's why I'm talking to you, but you are purposely feigning ignorance. A sleeping man can be woken, but if anyone is pretending to be asleep how can he be . . . ?'

Gayadin raised his hand to interrupt, but Vaidyaji continued, 'When Badri has already made up his mind and news has spread all through society, it is your duty to accept this proposal gracefully. It will be considered a model marriage. They'll both live happily. I'm drawing Badri into politics. I've made him managing director of the cooperative already. After some time, I'll also get the girl involved in some social work. There's the women's board; I'll get her on to that. She'll get a car, and a chapraasi to accompany her. Later on, I'll even manage an MLA's ticket. Husband and wife will work contentedly in the service of the nation. What more can we want?'

In his enthusiasm, Vaidyaji hadn't noticed that his listener had begun to look as if he were going to burst into tears.

Gayadin implored him with folded hands, 'Maharaj, don't ruin my plans. As it is, my daughter has no shortage of misfortunes! Her mother died when she was a child. I've managed to bring her up somehow or the other. There's a family of Aggarwal Vaishyas in the town. They are prepared to accept her. The boy is educated and has a government job. The marriage date is just fifteen days away. In the meantime, if you great men start spreading lies and blackening her name, what will happen to her, maharaj? Just think about it. If you disgrace my daughter, then it will not matter how big a leader you are; you'll be dragged to hell like a worm. Don't force me to say more.'

Vaidyaji was stunned. Gayadin then said, 'Those bulls of yours—what are their names, Chhote, Ruppan, Sanichar-Fatichar—have spread God knows what rumours about my daughter. Even a wise man like you has begun talking like those boys and loafers. Maharaj, I beg of you to keep your own mouth shut and call off these young bulls of yours. Just keep quiet until, somehow or the other, the wedding is over. This age belongs to you, everyone is rolling at your feet, but don't forget yourself to this extent. Let decent men continue to live in Shivpalganj.'

Vaidyaji sat listening in silence, but there is a limit even to how long one can dispassionately watch a jumping buffalo. Reaching this limit, he rose to his feet while regarding the beast's new but unsuccessful attempt to leap into the sky. As he left, he remarked, 'Marry your daughter according to your decision, and let me know if I can be of any service to you. Forget what I said. I have been misinformed, and I regret it.'

But he did not regret hearing what he had heard about Bela's future. He returned joyfully with a lightened heart.

~

After Vaidyaji left, Gayadin remained sitting as he was for some time. His face did not appear like that of a clever man. At first glance, he seemed confused and worried by the rutting buffalo. But history is witness to the fact that, up till now, buffaloes have never caused deep disquiet to mankind. Gayadin's confusion at this time was not due to the buffalo, but due to Bela's future.

He had told Vaidyaji a half-truth. Bela's marriage had not yet been fixed. Gayadin had thought of purchasing as a son-in-law the young man who had recently started coming to Shivpalganj to explain the advantages of not producing children. The very day after he met the young man, he had gone to town to see the young man's father, who had a draper's shop which had been running well, but was going downhill for two years since the arrival of a Punjabi shopkeeper in the locality.

After explaining the reasons for his declining business to Gayadin at some length, the boy's father reached the conclusion that, 'The boy is yours. Arrange his marriage whenever you wish, but nowadays, I'm going through hard times and so I'm not prepared to part with him cheaply.'

Gayadin was sympathetic to the father's point and said that, as he had set out to buy a son-in-law, he was prepared to give a good price. With that, the marriage was settled without any difficulty, only the price for the boy remained to be fixed. His father, calculating his losses from the day the Punjabi had arrived until the present moment, asked Gayadin for fifteen thousand rupees. Gayadin replied, in praise of his caste, that the request was reasonable since, even the dung of an elephant weighed a quintal, and even a bankrupt shopkeeper was justified in assessing the worth of his son at fifteen thousand rupees. He remarked in conclusion that he was a man of a much lower status than the boy's father and could not give more than seven thousand rupees.

After this, the conversation continued in the same way that similar conversations have, tens of millions of times before. The young man's father said that seven thousand was very little since, even before Gayadin's arrival, the price had been set at fourteen thousand. Gayadin said he was not capable of paying such an amount and had just explained what he had the means to pay with. Then the young man's father said he'd speak to the boy's paternal uncle, who was the assistant sales tax officer at such-and-such a place; and to the boy's maternal uncle's cousin's wife's sister's husband, who was the district and sessions judge in such-and-such a place, and who loved the boy like his own son; and to his cousin's brother-in-law who had an ironmonger's business in Calcutta; as well as to the boy's mother, maternal and paternal aunts, grandmother and great-grandmother.

He assured Gayadin that he would consult with all of them and give him a final figure on the boy's worth within ten days and that, if God willed it, they would soon be related. He refused to make any inquiries about Bela, merely commenting that if the girl was educated, then good; if not, so much the better because it wasn't as if he wanted to turn her into a schoolmistress; and if the girl was pretty, then good; if not, so much the better as he wasn't planning to set her up as a courtesan.

So, when Vaidyaji had started discussing the beauty of inter-caste marriages, Gayadin's first reaction was to get up, run away to the town and slap fifteen thousand rupees into the hand of the young man's father. As soon as Vaidyaji walked away, he prepared to leave for the town.

A little while later, when he came out of his house, he caught sight of Khanna Master, Malaviya and Rangnath coming towards him. 'These people can't be sent off within an hour,' he thought. Then he remembered that, anyway, the bus into town didn't leave for another two hours.

~

After mentioning a few items of local news, Khanna Master noticed the buffalo. It was jumping around the peg in circles as if taking turns at kabaddi with some imaginary male buffalo. It was bellowing continuously and letting flow a stream of urine.

Khanna Master remarked, showing the familiarity of a family man, 'The buffalo's on heat. Make some arrangements for it.'

'What arrangements can I make? All the male buffaloes in the area have been castrated. I've sent a man to look at Ramjani Ghosi's buffalo. He's been gone two hours and still hasn't come back . . .'

Khanna Master interrupted, 'Have it AI-ed, AI-ed. If you have any problem, ask me; the vet's a friend of mine. My father and his father were . . .'

Rangnath interrupted him to ask the meaning of AI and Khanna was happy to have found something which he knew and Rangnath didn't. He said, 'Artificial Insemination. See—what do you call it in Hindi?—it's a very simple thing. When the buffalo comes on heat you take it to the AI centre and have it AI-ed.'

Rangnath looked to Gayadin in the hope that he would get some more help in understanding the meaning of AI from that direction, but Gayadin was staring at the buffalo with a worried expression. This time, the buffalo moved back and forth, putting on such a display of rock 'n' roll that it seemed they'd better send for Elvis Presley instead of a male buffalo. Gayadin said, 'I've sent this buffalo to the centre twice already. But God knows what sort of syringe they use. It won't get pregnant.'

Khanna Master said, 'Who knows whether fake and adulterated goods aren't used there, too? I'll speak to the vet about it.'

Gayadin shook his head in disagreement. 'No, it's not the fault of the goods; it's my luck. If three buffaloes are syringed, on one or the other, it doesn't work. The trouble is, that particular buffalo is always mine.'

Through this conversation, Rangnath had learned the meaning of Artificial Insemination, and he began blushing needlessly. To overcome this, he joined in, 'You're always talking as if you're completely helpless.'

'If you don't get helplessness in a village, what do you get?' Gayadin said morosely. He sat down slowly. The charpoy creaked but today he showed it no consideration. He coughed and said, 'Rangnath babu, you're a town man. In the town there's an answer to everything. Say someone gets run over, he's taken to the hospital. If the doctor in the hospital is a scoundrel, a complaint is made against him. If the man hearing the complaint takes no action, there is always a dozen or so loafers to take out a procession. If the police lathi charge them, there's an inquiry. So there, everything is easily countered. That's why, there, one doesn't feel the blows of helplessness and compulsion. And if, by any chance, someone does, then there's an answer to that, too. He can easily hang himself, and the next day, his name is in the newspapers. People come to know that he felt he had no choice but to kill himself and then, for some days, the papers write about why he felt compelled to do it. And, you see, even this is a reply to helplessness.'

Looking compassionately towards Rangnath, Gayadin said, 'I know everything about the towns. I lived in Calcutta as a young man.'

Khanna Master opened his mouth to say something but Gayadin cut in, 'And what happens here in the village? If anyone is run over, the motorist disappears. The man who's been run over is left lying like a dog. If there is a hospital anywhere near, he's brought there, dying, after three or four days. If there is actually a doctor in the hospital, all he does is put a bottle of water into the patient's hands and tell him to drink it and pray to Lord Ram. The doctors will certainly take the name of Lord Ram, as they won't have any drugs to give. Even if there had been drugs, they will have been stolen or put on one side to be sold. That's why it's said that, in the towns, there's a way out of every difficulty while, in the villages, there's a difficulty blocking every way.'

Rangnath said, 'There are lots of difficulties in the town, but there's no point in telling you.'

A man came up, naked but for a small cloth covering that part of his body which proved he was a man. He brought the news that Ramjani Ghosi was prepared to let loose his buffalo for two rupees. Gayadin sighed and said, 'Every dog has its day.' He nodded to the man.

The moment the man got the signal, he untethered the buffalo from the peg. As they watched, the buffalo's bellows faded out like the sound of a radio drama. The almost naked man moved out of view with his loincloth and the beast.

~

The atmosphere became less heated after the buffalo had gone. Gayadin, who had had to raise his voice because of its bellowing, regained his natural lifeless tone. He said, 'It may seem vulgar to mention it, but if this buffalo gets pregnant, then I can relax. Ramjani is ready to let his buffalo loose, but supposing my animal refuses?'

At this, he smiled. This was something of an event: no one in Shivpalganj had ever seen him smile. Rangnath realized that he had had to smile to stop himself from crying.

Suddenly Khanna Master asked, 'How is Bela? I hear she's been unwell.'

Malaviya stared at him. Rangnath thought, 'Masters are like that. The moment they get out of the classroom they say something stupid.'

Gayadin showed no reaction to this question. He just turned a direct and innocent gaze on Khanna Master and kept it on him silently for one minute. For that minute—which seemed like an age—Khanna Master couldn't think where to look. Then Gayadin asked, 'Tell me how you are, Master sahib. What's happening about your case under Section 107?'

'That's what we've come to tell you. Now, only you can save us. We've got trouble on all sides. The Principal is out to have us beaten up and, in court, the magistrate is annoyed with us even before the full case has been heard.'

Gayadin turned to Rangnath. He said nothing. Malaviya explained, 'In this matter, Rangnathji is on our side. We can talk freely in front of him.'

Since every intellectual writhes with discomfort when openly accused of belonging to a faction even if he does belong to it, Rangnath shook his head and said, 'I'm not on anyone's side. I am with them on this issue because they are facing injustice and that's why I sympathize with them.'

Gayadin said, 'Then why do you say that you're not on their side?'

Malaviya continued, 'The Principal sahib has incited Chhote Wrestler against us. The day before yesterday, as I was walking down the road he told me, "Master sahib, nothing has happened to you yet, so quietly get out of Shivpalganj; if you don't, and something unfortunate happens, your family will suffer." Other people, too, are giving this sort of advice. Perhaps the Principal wants to have us thrashed. We don't know what to do.'

'What can you do? Keep quiet and get beaten. You're a teacher, after all, how long can you afford to be scared of a beating?' inquired Gayadin gently, looking at the ground.

Khanna Master's hackles rose. 'We are not the sort of people to take a beating quietly. We'll reply to bricks with rocks.'

Gayadin didn't comment, and so Khanna went on, 'These are not the days of the nawabs, that anyone can go and beat up whomever he likes.'

'No, things are worse than that,' said Gayadin. 'I've been watching things for four or five years now. Wasn't the headmaster at Rangapur murdered? And what happened? The murderers are still wandering around freely with their spears, stroking their moustaches.' He nodded consolingly. 'No, Master sahib, don't you go throwing any rocks in reply to bricks. You'll be finished. God knows how many teachers are beaten up by their students every year at exam time, and what can they do about it? They rub their skulls and slowly make their way home and drink the glass of water their wife brings to them. Some file a report at the police station and earn another beating. That's the way things are now and, being a teacher, you shouldn't worry about being beaten up.'

Khanna Master's temper had cooled. He asked, 'Then what should I do?'

'Do what they say. Either settle the case of 107 or run away from Shivpalganj.'

'That's what I'm crying about,' said Khanna, screwing up his face as if to weep. 'I'd sent a message to the Principal to settle. He says he'll only do it on condition that I leave Shivpalganj. Whatever happens, he says, I have to leave. Tell me, after this, what do I do?'

Gayadin thought. He thought for a quite a while and then, smoothing away the lines on his brow to prove that he had finished, he said, 'What can you do after that, Master sahib? Spread out a map of the country in front of you and start looking at it. Perhaps you'll find some other place beyond Shivpalganj.'

For a few moments they sat in dejected silence; then, like some worm writhing around, creating and erasing lines in wet mud, Khanna Master began to describe in detail the last hearing of the case.

~

The first group in the case under Section 107—the people about whose pugnacious nature the police had warned—were Khanna Master, Malaviya and three novice masters who were considered to be opposed to the Principal's group because they didn't belong to it. In the second group were those whom Khanna had denounced, before the magistrate, as being a danger to his life and property. One lawyer had even jokingly asked what property a teacher had and what his life was worth. But the magistrate paid no attention to that and issued a summons against the second group, too. In this group, besides the Principal, were four of his nephews. They had been teaching in the college for the last three years, but people had grown accustomed to looking at them as the Principal's nephews and refused to recognize them as masters.

Khanna Master had had to face one great difficulty in court. All the researchers, historians and creative artists of the police department had contrived to prove that Khanna Master and his group had been about to cause trouble. On the other side, he himself had not managed to concoct any convincing story due to lack of suitable evidence from Shivpalganj. Therefore, when Khanna Master's lawyer was making a powerful argument against the Principal with the aid of a few facts and an excess of contention, the judge turned his head, looked severely at Khanna Master and asked, 'You people are teachers?'

'Yes.'

'Aren't you ashamed of yourselves?'

They were always ashamed to be teachers but, at this moment, Malaviyaji hesitated to admit it. He said, 'What is there to be ashamed about in being a teacher, Your Honour?'

'Despite being teachers, you're fighting like hooligans. You've even got involved in a case of 107. Don't you feel ashamed of that?'

Khanna's lawyer said to the judge, 'Your Honour, you should say this to the other group as well.'

The judge was already angry. He growled—naturally, in English—'I certainly shall. But I still say to these people, aren't you ashamed, as teachers, to be fighting a case like this? I am ashamed to hear it. I wonder what effect it must have on the students.'

Eventually, Khanna's lawyer had to say that, in principle, he accepted that they should be ashamed of themselves, but both sides should be equally ashamed.

Then the judge began to lambaste the Principal. The purport of his speech was that the Principal should be ashamed of the way he was running the college. 'If I were principal, I wouldn't tolerate this kind of teachers in the college even for a day. If there's a quarrel between teachers, why should the police station and the courts get involved? A wise principal would never allow these elements into the college in the first place and, if they did manage to get in, would not waste a minute in throwing them out. The future of the students is at stake. There can be no compromises. But just see to what a pretty pass principals have come! In my days . . .!'

Now, the Principal sahib's lawyer had to say that, in principle, he accepted that the Principal had shown weakness towards the masters; that, until now, he had not taken any tough action against them; and that he felt ashamed that he had not done so.

At this point, the judge told Khanna Master that they had made enough of a spectacle of themselves, and they should either settle their quarrel or leave the college. If they didn't, he would be forced to give a judgment at the next hearing.

Upon this, the Sub-Inspector delivered a short speech on the judge's large-heartedness and appealed to him not to give a judgment as it would be disastrous for the teachers. Whatever else he may say, after all, they were only poor teachers. They had been instigated. If His Honour passed judgment they would be in a complete mess. It was enough that the judge had cautioned them. He had explained the matter thoroughly, and they must have understood. The Sub-Inspector was now convinced they would reach a settlement. If they were just given time until the next hearing, everything would be agreed upon and His Honour would not have to pronounce judgment.

~

Rangnath said, 'So that means that . . .'

Khanna Master said, 'It means that the moment he got back from the hearing, the Principal set Master Motiram on to us. Until now he's kept quiet, taught science and looked after his flour mill. Now, since the day before yesterday, he's been telling us that there's more profit in opening a flour mill than in teaching. When he talks about profit, he also brings up the subject of a saw mill. Yesterday evening, he told Malaviya about the advantages of running a paan shop. You tell me, what's the answer to all this?'

Gayadin yawned. 'Settle the matter.'

'But that means . . .?'

'You've already said what that means, Master sahib. If a settlement means you have to leave Shivpalganj, then go. What's the point of cribbing about it night and day? You're going to lose your job anyway, and unemployment isn't such a bad thing. Tens of millions of people are unemployed. The real problem is the cribbing. You should steer clear of that.'

Rangnath had been in Shivpalganj for six months now. His health had improved but his tongue had taken a turn for the worse. He had begun to get into the bad habit of keeping quiet when it was right to speak and of displaying his excitement at the wrong moments. The sense of being excluded from the current conflicts had begun to give him an inferiority complex. He, too, felt naturally enraged at the circumstances but, like the rage of most Indians, his rage expended itself in argument and discussion, whatever was left afterwards being suppressed by a good meal. But, today, goodness knows what possessed him. His sense of inferiority and his anger together made him read the riot act. He began and ended with a dressing-down, the purport of his argument being that the present situation should be vigorously opposed. 'Khanna Master should not retreat; he should not compromise with injustice,' he said, feeling as he did so like an English-educated Indian, brokenly reciting a Hindu religious text. He fell silent.

The masters said, 'We can't do anything.'

Rangnath asked, 'And you, Gayadinji?'

In reply, Gayadin began haltingly to tell a story. 'A long time ago, there was a man in our area called Mata Parshad. He was the first leader of this area. People listened to him with great affection. When necessary, he would also go to jail, and then people would remember him with even more affection. When he came back from jail, people would generally talk to him in a way that would excite him and make him go back to jail again. Once he spent several years without going to jail. The result of this was that people began to be bored by his speeches. Abolition of landlordism; women's education; the boycott of foreign goods and liquor shops—people became so familiar with his speeches on these subjects that when he stood up to speak, even before he opened his mouth, schoolchildren would begin reciting extracts from them. He had nothing left to say. When he came to collect contributions, people thought he was begging. When he shouted, "Victory to Mother India!" it seemed to people that he was promoting his own family. When he talked about the abolition of landlordism they realized that he wanted to get through the year without having to pay his land tax.

'What I mean to say is that Mata Parshad's leadership worked well for five years and then it seemed to him that it wasn't doing well any more. I had to tell him, "Brother Mata Parshad, you don't have the qualities of a leader. A leader needs to know every vein in his people's body, but the people shouldn't know anything about the leader. Here, everything is the wrong way round. You yourself have no idea of the condition of the people, but the people know you backwards. That's why the leadership of this area does not suit you. Either go from here to a different area or have another spell in jail." Mata Parshad accepted my advice and went to jail. A full year after that, your uncle Vaidyaji arrived. No one knew anything about him; they only knew that he had a black moustache, a strong body and that his potency pills were a wonder. He founded the cooperative society, opened a middle school and his own Ayurvedic dispensary, and by the time the people worked out what he was all about, he'd already become the local leader.

'Mata Parshad came out of jail with a government pension and began to look after his stomach in the town, and here, Babu Rangnath, there's only one tall man in the whole area, and that's your uncle.

'Babu Rangnath, leadership is a seed which can take root only in soil far away from its native place. That's why I can't be a leader here.

People know me too well. They won't follow me. If I try to speak up, they'll just say, "Look at Gayadin, he's trying to be a leader."

'And in any case, I wouldn't try to be a leader for this Khanna Master. How far can you defend someone who has no sense?

'To befriend such boys is to court trouble.'

Rangnath listened quietly to this speech and then asked, 'But, Gayadinji, you know my uncle well. You're the only one who can influence him. You will have to help Khanna.'

Gayadin wondered at their brazenness. For months he'd been telling them not to rely on him. They would go off, fretting, and then come right back to him again. The judge was right—they ought to be ashamed of themselves.

He said, 'I cannot help Khanna Master, but you can. You've started speaking out openly against your uncle now. You've no hesitation left. You too are an outsider. People don't really know you, and you're just like Khanna Master. Now you show some leadership.'

Rangnath said angrily, 'So be it. What do you say?'

'To befriend such boys is to court trouble,' said Gayadin, but only to himself. He watched uninterestedly as they all hurried off. It occurred to him that it was time to take the bus to town. Fifteen thousand rupees was a very large sum but, for Bela, at that moment, it was nothing at all. The buffalo hadn't yet returned, and now it had become a matter of disgrace to live in the village.

33

In our ancient books of logic it's written that, wherever there is smoke, there is fire. To this should be added that, wherever there's a bus stand, there's filth.

The filth at the Shivpalganj bus stand was extremely well planned. Some natural means already existed for promoting the Filth Propagation Programme. Behind the bus stand was a small pond. In the mornings and evenings, it provided people with open air, and it was also used as an open-air toilet. When dawn broke, you could see people concealed modestly behind every blade of grass growing there, all following the principle that 'the twig of a broom is sufficient shield for a virtuous person.' All the domestic pigs of Shivpalganj used to arrive there in the morning to take advantage of this situation. They assimilated the human filth and scattered it around. The breeze blowing across the pond towards the village centre forced the passengers sitting at the bus stand to keep their noses covered. Over in the town sat eminent scholars of village uplift, deep in thought about the problem of lavatories for villages. They had, in fact, been thinking—only thinking—from 1947 to the present day. Here at the bus stand, the passengers with cloth wrapped over their noses sometimes appeared about to embrace the Jain religion; and at other times, listening to the grunting of the pigs, seemed lost in contemplation of the 'boar incarnation' of Lord Vishnu. The atmosphere was thick with stench and religious possibilities.

Whenever the herd of pigs took to the streets, they imitated man. They could be seen walking along immediately in front of every vehicle, paying not the least attention to left or right, and were better than even students at jostling one another. The wall surrounding the bus stand was broken down at one place. Taking advantage of it, the pigs would slip straight from the road into the bus stand and head for the banks of the pond. Their revelry there created an impression of a porcine picnic or a youth festival.

These natural amenities must have been taken into consideration by the Filth Propagation Programme when the bus stand was constructed. In fact, other filth supply agencies were already in existence there. Among them, situated on one side, was a temple, the greasy steps of which made it a great fly-breeding centre. The scattered, fading flowers, the leaf cups which had held sweets, and the broken earthenware bowls lying all around, also attracted ants. On the other side was a dharamshala, to the rear of which, one always suspected, lay a drying ocean of urine.

In perfect coordination with these programmes, other means were used to make up for any minor inadequacies. The chief among these was spittle which, one feels, should be made the national symbol as it is so universally apparent. Just as the most important element in our planning is paper, so the most important element in filth is spit. A dozen or two paan shops—some stationary and some mobile—worked at spit production, like government-approved private sector companies. The level of spit production was high. To spread spit, several spittoons had been sunk into the ground, the very sight of which made a man expectorate in any direction—except upwards—and so beautifully that it all landed outside the spittoon. As a result, on all sides up to a height of four feet on the walls, and here and there on the ground, rivers of spittle had begun to flow as, we are told, rivers of ghee and milk once did.

Then there were the limping, whining beggars who, even though few in number, seemed, through perseverance, to appear simultaneously on all sides. At tea shops were drains full of old tea leaves and dirty water. There was dust from arriving and departing buses. Resting sickly dogs. And the all-India institutions that offered the greatest encouragement to the Filth Propagation Programme—sweet and puri shops, together with the pot bellies of the sweet makers and the filthy clothes of their boy workers.

~

The deputy director of education was coming to investigate the problems at the college. There were now only four days left before his visit. Ruppan babu and Rangnath thought that they would go to Khanna Master's house and ask how his preparations were getting on. When they set off along the path between the temple and the bus stand, they saw a sight.

A head was sticking up above the wall on the far side of the bus stand. The body was hidden. The chin was resting on the wall, and the head was staring unmovingly at the temple. On its face was a wide but unnatural smile. From a distance it looked as if someone had been suddenly decapitated mid-grin and the head had been placed on the wall.

Ruppan pointed to the head to attract Rangnath's attention and for a while they stood gazing at it. Suddenly they realized it was Langar's.

Ruppan babu called out to him and his neck, too, appeared. They both went up to him and began to talk over the wall. Ruppan asked, 'What are you doing, hanging around the bus stand?' Langar's smile disappeared and he began to look normal. He replied, 'What do people do here, father? Only people who have to go somewhere come here.'

'You're going back? That means you got the copy. When did you get it?'

He punched his forehead four or five times using his left fist like a hammer. The two young men watched him in silence.

'You treated me so well when we met last time at the shop, father. The very next day I had to go back to my village. I got news that there'd been a death in my community. The moment I reached the village, the fever struck me again.

'I lay on my bed for a full fifteen days. I returned yesterday, father! When I went to inquire from the tehsil office, I found that the birds had pecked the field clean.

'There, they told me that my copy had been prepared several days earlier and information about it had been posted on the noticeboard. But no one came to collect it for fifteen days. Then they tore it up and threw it away.

'When a copy is made, they keep it for fifteen days. If no one collects it, they tear it up. I didn't know that.'

Saying this, he attempted to laugh, but Ruppan and Rangnath saw that he was crying.

Rangnath began to explain, 'Look here, Langar, it's nothing to do with your not knowing the rules and regulations. The thing to know is that you're a member of the public and the public doesn't win that easily.'

Langar stopped crying, rested his chin on the wall as before and gazed at them unblinkingly.

'It doesn't matter that you lost. Go back to your village and do some farming. After a while, these wounds will heal by themselves.'

'How can I farm, father? It's my land that the whole case is about.'

'Then rob and steal,' said Ruppan suddenly and severely.

Langar stood in dejected silence for a few moments and then he said, as if it had just occurred to him, 'Should I put in another application for the copy?'

Rangnath sighed heavily, 'Go ahead. But this time, engage a lawyer. Even if you get away without giving a bribe, if you're fighting a case you can't get away without a lawyer.'

They went back to the path. Ruppan babu kicked a dog lying in his way but, besides opening its eyes once, it didn't react. He said, 'It's better if Langar stays away from Shivpalganj. When he comes here he rubs you up the wrong way. The moment you see him you feel like slapping him.'

'Then why don't you?' snarled Rangnath, and thought, 'Today, for the first time, I am snarling.'

34

They were sitting in Khanna Master's house, that is to say, one room in an old building to the rear of which there were a courtyard, a veranda and a closet. Cooking was done on the veranda; a drain in the courtyard, next to which people squatted to bathe, served as a urinal. As in 95 per cent of the houses in Shivpalganj, there was no bathroom or toilet.

Those seated were Khanna Master, Malaviyaji, two other masters from their faction and Rangnath. Besides them, there were two boys who were well known throughout the whole area for hitting first and asking questions later, and who came to study at the college when they felt so inclined. Two subjects were presented for consideration:

1. The obscene handbill published against Malaviyaji, and the situation arising from the maltreatment of Khanna Master by the Principal the previous week; and

2. The preparations for the impending inquiry by the deputy director of education.

There was also a third subject: should the Principal's nose be chopped off, or should he just be let off with a shoe-beating. But due to Rangnath's presence this could not be included in the agenda.

These days, the boys' annual exams were in progress, and Khanna had caught one of them copying. The boy had refused to be apprehended on the grounds that he was being victimized because he was a sympathizer of the Principal and that Khanna Master had given several boys whom he favoured complete freedom to copy. At this point, Malaviyaji had arrived on the scene and tried to say something in Khanna Master's defence, but before he could, the boy had said, 'Eh,

Master sahib, why are you getting all upset? You let the boys who go with you to the cinema in town copy the whole exam book, and here I am just taking a line here and there and you take it worse than anyone else.' At this, Malaviya had blushed and fallen silent, but Khanna had begun to issue threats. Then the boy had said with great gravity, 'I don't want to disgrace you, so go off quietly to another room. If you don't, I'll throw you out of the window, and if your legs and arms break, it won't be any responsibility of mine.'

Khanna went and reported the incident to the Principal. The Principal remarked, 'Wherever this Khanna turns up, there's some disaster or the other.' He refused to take cognizance of the report.

And the battle commenced. Four or five masters from Khanna's faction landed up at the Principal's office. In the examination rooms they abandoned, boys began to copy at will. In the Principal's room, insults were the only weapons and the masters began hurling abuse. Drowning out this clamour, the Principal ordered that Khanna should leave the college and shouldn't come anywhere near it until the examinations were over. If he did, shoes, not tongues, would do the talking. Khanna Master remonstrated against this. The Principal responded by replacing words with shoes and beating Khanna Master with them. Khanna Master remonstrated even harder but, although in international politics, an argument may stop bombs from being dropped, there's no argument that can prevent a shoe-beating.

One master called the police. He didn't have to go far. There were close links between the annual exams and law and order. The police were on duty at the gate. They arrived the moment they were called. There was no murder or dacoity going on and, therefore, they arrived on the scene as soon as they were thought of, without even waiting for the incident to be over. They decided that, in accordance with the Principal's order, Khanna should leave at once.

Khanna Master left the college. As he left, he heard the Principal's final warning. In Awadhi, he shrieked, 'If I lay eyes on thee again, I'll beat thy brains out! Tha'd best know it, Master sahib! Tha' shouldst know me for what I am. For a good man I'm a good man, and for a thug a damn great thug.'

The boys were not affected much by all this. They went on quietly with their exams, copying in their usual fashion.

This incident had been described as the maltreatment of Khanna Master, and it was being discussed here in the meeting. Khanna Master told Rangnath, 'Last year, they did the same with Tripathiji. They told him, "Right, don't come to college from tomorrow." The next day, he did go and was surrounded by three or four of Badri Wrestler's disciples at the gate. Poor old Tripathiji just managed to get away with his self-respect intact. By the time he complained anywhere, they had suspended him for being absent for so many days. After that he was thrown out.

'He filed a case. It's still going on. He's paying *his* expenses and the college is paying the Principal's. The Principal is not frightened of lawsuits.'

Rangnath said, 'Then you'd better do something quickly.'

'What that something is, that is what we have to think about.'

They sat racking their brains for some time. The two boys flipped through some cheap novels belonging to Khanna Master. They knew that their role in this drama did not include thinking.

Malaviya said, 'File a report with the police that when you were going to college they surrounded you and blocked your way.'

Khanna Master laughed with contempt, as if asking how he was going to run a faction with brains like that. He said, 'What guarantee is there that they will not just surround me and block my path? Who knows, they might let me into the college and then suddenly disgrace me. Before I can file a report I'll have been insulted.'

Malaviya paid close attention to this statement. Then he gave his interpretation, 'So that means that you are scared to go there.'

Khanna Master said rebelliously, 'Yes. Yes, I *am* scared. Do you have any objection?'

Malaviya explained, 'It's not a matter of objection, but until you go there and they stop you from working, how can you file a complaint against them?'

Rangnath said, 'Draw up a first-rate application in English. When the deputy director comes here for the inquiry, place it before him. Our Principal sahib will go up in smoke.'

Khanna laughed long. 'You, too, Rangnath . . . ? What can I say? I have no faith in these deputy directors. Whenever you look under anyone's tail, they turn out to be a bitch.'

One of the masters chuckled. Hearing the word 'bitch' the boys stopped reading the novels. They began to look attentively at the pictures of women on the covers and to listen to the conversation with interest. Malaviyaji said, 'Anyway, this deputy director is new. We may have some faith in him. I've heard he's very tough; he doesn't offer a chair even to important leaders. The moment anyone makes a wrong suggestion, he threatens to throw them out of the room.'

'You keep on listening to such things, Malaviyaji, but I know better,' said Khanna despondently. 'He's tough only with the leaders of the opposite faction. He's a very smooth character—half leader, half official. He's managed to get around a few leaders for his own purposes. He goes and wags his tail at them at night and acts tough with others during the daytime with their support.'

Malaviyaji said, 'Whatever you may say, he's a thousand times better than the last deputy director.' He told Rangnath, 'The first deputy director was as meek as a cow. He was well known for it. Two or three of us masters went on deputation to meet him, and explained everything. He listened very attentively, and when he spoke, he sounded exactly like Gayadinji.

'He said, "Your college is very fine. You say that only factionalism goes on there; that the boys don't get proper education; the accounts are fiddled; copying goes on during exams; the Principal mistreats you—is this anything to complain about, brother? All this goes on in every single college. What is one to do if the boys don't get a proper education? If the boys themselves don't want to study, how can you make them? In my days, boys from good families went to college and they concentrated on their work. Now, the children of sweepers and Chamars are coming to study, so what sort of education can there be? You tell me, brother!

'"If truth be told, your college is very well thought of. Vaidyaji is the manager—he's a man of great virtue. He doesn't eat even onions, let alone meat and fish. And look, your college doesn't run at a loss—you people get your salaries every month. There's never any embezzlement there nor any strike. No one has ever set fire to the building. There has never been a theft or a murder. Everything goes on peacefully. Yours is a model college."

'Rangnath babu, the deputy director kept on talking to us about peace and order, as if he were a police inspector and not an inspector of education.

'When we left, he told us, "This business of complaining isn't proper. If you have any problem, go straight to Vaidyaji and tell him; he'll put everything right."

'Rangnath babu, we wanted to tell him, "You bastard, you're such a big bloody cow you should be tethered in a dairy, eat hay and give milk. Why on earth are you here?"'

The audience began to laugh, the boys especially. Then they became engrossed in the women's pictures again. Malaviya concluded, 'But I'm satisfied with this deputy director. When we were leaving after complaining to him this time, he said, "You go back and get on quietly with your work. I shall come and investigate personally."'

Khanna Master shook his head in despair, 'Uh. I'm not satisfied. This is an election year. I've heard that they're going to double the college budget. This year, everyone has been given the freedom to do what they like. The inquiry will take place the day after tomorrow, but nothing will come of it; what are we to do?'

Until now, the boys had said nothing. Now one of them opened his mouth to speak. He was wearing the common costume of Shivpalganj—striped pyjamas and a muslin kurta with no vest beneath. His head was clean-shaven and he looked like a thug. When he spoke, it became clear that he was exactly what he looked. He said, 'Master sahib, nothing's going to come of any inquiry. The only way is this: You give the order and one day, right here, at nightfall, we'll give the Principal sahib a right royal welcome.'

The second boy explained, 'We'll just cut his nose off—there's no need to kill him.'

Rangnath was in a bad way. For some time he had been taking an interest in Khanna's afflictions. He felt sympathy for this faction of masters, and he was especially angry because Khanna had been prevented from attending college, not by any written order but simply by force. When the Principal and Vaidyaji had seen Rangnath going around with the masters, they had begun to smile. Rangnath had tried to make them understand that, by listening to Khanna's point of view, he was attempting to bring about peace. Vaidyaji heard him out but said nothing in reply.

Now Rangnath was distressed by the self-confidence with which the boys talked of cutting off the Principal's nose as a 'royal welcome'. He remembered the royal welcome that Bharat had given his brother Ram in the Ramayan and thought that if, after this royal welcome, the Principal was crowned—as had happened in the epic—within two or three days, he may find himself in the lock-up with these boys and masters, facing a murder charge. And though the climate of Shivpalganj was healthy, the same could not be said for its lock-up.

He stood up, but before he could leave, a sound of footsteps came from outside. Ruppan babu opened the door and came in. Today he was in full armour. The end of his dhoti was placed properly on one shoulder, a silk scarf was wrapped around his throat, a lock of hair waved over his forehead and his face glowed with the after-effects of a bath and of the oil which oozed down from his hair. Betel juice was dripping from his lips. As he entered he said, 'Don't get up. I still have a lot of work to do. I won't stop.'

He looked all around him like a tiger. But to the others he didn't seem like one. His was the face of an innocent, thin, handsome young man, whose eyes were somewhat moist and whose lips appeared softer than usual.

Rangnath said, 'Sit down, Ruppan; I, too, shall be leaving in a minute.'

'No, brother, I can't stop even for a minute. I've just come to say that I've fixed up everything properly in all the neighbouring villages. The people of this whole area are determined to tell the truth about the college. The people are all with us.'

He was excited. 'This is what father wanted, so this is what he's getting. He'll see, too, that "truth can never be concealed behind false principles."'

Khanna Master interrupted this poetry recital. 'Sit down, Ruppan babu. Tell us what you've done.'

'Try and take it in quickly,' said Ruppan. 'The whole thing will become clear tomorrow. Right here, in Shivpalganj, the deputy director will beat the Principal one hundred times with a shoe in front of five hundred people. If he doesn't, you can beat me a hundred times, instead.'

Raising his voice, he went on, 'Now you can sleep in peace. Leave tomorrow until the morrow. Let's go, brother Rangnath; let's allow Master sahib to take some rest.' He raised his hand as if administering a blessing, and, as though inspiring a unit of the army at the Battle of Panipat, said, 'Keep fighting, sons!'

They left the room. Rangnath followed in Ruppan's wake. They both walked for a while in silence. Once on the road, Rangnath touched Ruppan's shoulder. Ruppan started and looked at him, then turned away.

Rangnath put his hand on Ruppan's shoulder and asked softly, 'Ruppan, have you been drinking?'

Ruppan was walking as if intoxicated, but he wasn't stumbling. Continuing to look in the opposite direction, he replied, 'If you want, I'll say yes, and if you want, I'll say no.'

'Say what's true.'

'What on earth is this bird called truth? In which nest does it live? In which jungle is it found?' Ruppan roared with laughter. 'Brother, this is Shivpalganj. Here, it's hard to tell what's true and what's not.'

Rangnath switched direction; they were no longer heading for home. He held Ruppan by the elbow and steered him along. 'Let's go this way; this too is all right. We'll sit down and take the air on a culvert up ahead.'

Slowly they walked along the road towards empty land. After a few moments, Ruppan himself said, 'Sooner or later, you have to start somewhere. If you're going to live in Shivpalganj, you have to live like that.' He continued somewhat haltingly and angrily for no apparent reason, 'You can't get anywhere here by being a Mahatma Gandhi.'

They sat down by the side of a road on a small bridge. They were sitting close together and, apart from the fact that Ruppan had put his hand affectionately on Rangnath's shoulder, there was nothing new or drunken about his behaviour. Rangnath interrupted him and said in the tone of a senior, 'Don't talk nonsense, Ruppan. It's not a good thing to lower your standards because of Shivpalganj. It's not as if Shivpalganj is the only place on earth. The whole country is open to you and me.'

Ruppan sat with a long face, and grumbled, 'It seems to me that Shivpalganj has spread through the whole country.'

~

The Principal sahib was being forced to endure many afflictions. The day after the next, the deputy director of education was coming, and he had to make all the arrangements at the dak bungalow. The Principal stood in the doorway giving instructions to the college clerk who sat on a chair drinking sherbet made from unripe mangoes. After listening to all that the Principal had to say, he commented, 'Such bird-catchers are always coming here. How much can I be expected to run around for them?' The Principal sahib informed the clerk in a friendly manner that if the deputy director was kept happy he might not manage to do anything for them, but if he was upset he could do them a great deal of harm.

The Principal's short talk on this subject had no effect on the clerk. He quietly emptied his glass of sherbet, gave a loud belch of contentment—behind which lay years of parasitic living and indigestion—and said, 'As long as uncle is there, no one can harm us.'

'Uncle,' that is, Vaidyaji. The Principal realized that, today, the clerk was determined to be of no use, and if he tried to force him to work he would just lie down on a bench and start complaining about his old stomach pain. In that state he wouldn't work the next day, either. 'Yes, it's he on whom we rely,' said the Principal, departing with a few unnecessary flattering remarks about Vaidyaji. Outside, he called for one of his trusted masters to give him instructions. But he discovered that the master had taken a boy into town to the cinema. 'Up till now we just had one Malaviya, and now this one has gone and picked up the same line too,' said the Principal with some force. As he considered to whom he could entrust the next day's arrangements, he began freely cursing some unnamed person and unknown circumstance in Awadhi. At this, his chapraasi, his brow smeared with sandalwood, walked past throwing him a look of loathing and creating an unholy clatter with his wooden sandals.

As the Principal was on his way to Vaidyaji's house, he was overtaken by the first squall of the year. Dust filled his eyes. The thatch of a roadside paan shop flew off, hit him on the shoulder and fell into the road. In the dust and wind, he stepped into a cowpat. The Principal cursed Khanna Master. Then, amidst thunder and lightning, hail began to fall. He cursed Khanna Master again and, pushing past two or three people and stepping on a dog's tail, he slipped into a tea shop.

After the squall and hail stopped, he slowly made his way to Vaidyaji's house. The farmers he passed were discussing the fact that any crops which had not been brought home from the threshing floor would be ruined, but he paid them no special attention. For him, the greatest misfortune in the world was that his foot was covered with cow's dung. Every time he saw a farmer he thought he would laugh at his foot, but not one of them did. The Principal reached Vaidyaji's house.

The door to the sitting room was closed. He banged the latch chain against the door to be let in. It had perhaps been shut to keep out the dust. The moment the door opened, he saw Vaidyaji, Badri Wrestler, Sanichar and Chhote sitting on the wooden bed. They looked serious. Vaidyaji gestured to the Principal to enter. In reply, the Principal said in his familiar high-spirited tone, 'Call for a pot of water, please. I want to wash my feet before I come in as I put my foot in a job of Our Mother the Cow.'

No one laughed at his joke. Sanichar got up and silently handed him a pot of water. The Principal entered, grinning with embarrassment, touched Vaidyaji's feet and sat down beside him.

Badri Wrestler asked, 'How are things with you, Principal sahib?'

'Things with me are always good,' he said and bravely attempted to joke a second time. 'How are things with you? When will we be joining the marriage procession?'

In reply, Badri looked at him questioningly, as if he didn't know the meaning of 'marriage procession'. Vaidyaji said, 'Whose marriage procession, Principal sahib?'

'Our new managing director's. What does it matter even if it only has to go from one side of the village to the other? A marriage procession is a marriage procession. I've just had myself measured for a silk kurta. The price will be paid from your pocket, isn't that so, Managing Director sahib?' he asked Badri, laughing. After so much irritation and vexation, he was suddenly becoming light-hearted.

Badri began to discuss some other matter with Chhote; he didn't consider it necessary to listen to the Principal. Vaidyaji said, 'Badri will not be getting married this year. So, whose marriage are you talking about?'

'Why? Gayadin's . . .'

Vaidyaji raised his hand and prevented the Principal from completing his sentence. He said, 'Even you have been taken in by our enemies. It's a great pity.'

The Principal was astonished. The whole village was talking of Badri and Bela's marriage . . .

'Our enemies have spread these rumours just to disgrace Gayadin's daughter's name. You yourself know that Bela is the embodiment of virtue, and Badri's character is stainless. That day, when I returned from the town, I inquired into this and discovered that it was a plot by our enemies. I said that now the girl's welfare lies in forgetting the whole episode. Poor Gayadinji has fled to the town to escape this calumny. He is arranging his daughter's marriage with someone there.'

'Good God! What an amazing place this village is!'

Badri Wrestler rose and went out. Chhote began rubbing his open thigh with his right hand and said, 'If I speak now, you're not going to like it, maharaj.'

'You are a fool. You impress only as long as you don't open your mouth,' said Vaidyaji severely. 'You are one of the people who behaved childishly and spread these irresponsible rumours, disgracing Gayadin. Now shut up. Let his daughter have a happy marriage. Enough of this business. The subject should not be raised again.' Saying this, he leaned back on a cushion like a Mughal emperor who had just exiled some slave and wished to hear no more of the matter.

The silence in the sitting room was becoming unnatural. The Principal, who was always high-spirited, thought, 'I have a duty to perform here.' As if nothing had happened, he brushed aside all that had been said and turned to Sanichar with the words, 'And how are things with you, pradhanji?'

'Bad,' he replied. 'That was what we were talking about before you came. Jognath went into town yesterday. We heard the police have locked him up under Section 109. The poor man was drunk and lying on a bench at the station . . .

'They wrote a mountain of things in the report against him. The moment we got the news, Badri and I rushed there. That is the trouble with being pradhan. You don't get a chance to open your shop two days in a row.

'Today was a holiday, so we came back. We'll have to go again tomorrow—for the bond. I'm thinking that if I have to do this every day, I might as well close my shop down.'

The Principal sahib noted that Sanichar was making repeated references to his shop. He deliberately ignored them and said to Vaidyaji, 'If Badri is going to town tomorrow, he'll be back by evening. The day after tomorrow is the inquiry into the Khanna matter.'

Vaidyaji nodded and said, 'I've told him.'

35

In the days when white men ruled India, dak bungalows were built on river banks, or in valleys, forests and mango groves—that is, wherever the poetry of Wordsworth, Rabindranath Tagore or Sumitranandan Pant came naturally to mind. Such things, as dust and bustle, cholera, smallpox and plague, starvation and poverty, ugliness, bad manners and unpleasantness, found it very difficult to reach them. Sahibs of both races—white and brown—would stay there when on tour.

In those days, while staying in a dak bungalow, one could easily make an official tour appear to be a picnic—just as a picnic can easily be turned into an official tour these days. The sahibs would sit there reinforcing the problems; sometimes researching into trees and plants, animals, birds, worms, insects and maggots; sometimes wonderstruck by the good health of the local female goatherds; sometimes convincing the loose women of the area that, despite a conspiracy by clothes and tailors, there was no real difference between the men of the East and the West; sometimes opening gift baskets of Scotch whisky; sometimes laughing, sometimes angry, sometimes silent; and sometimes behaving like a mountain or a desert or a pile of cow's dung or a river or a bridge between the people and the government. That was how things were in former times.

Now, the influence of the countryside is strong in the towns. There are primary schools and council buildings in the villages, and the plague—until and unless a man himself becomes one—is no more. It is no longer believed to be an act of hara-kiri for an educated man (that is, someone who knows English) to go from a town into a village. And a picnic can easily be turned into an official tour.

There have been hundreds of experiments in which brown sahibs have gone from a town to the country, stayed in a village for a few days, drunk the local water and returned alive and kicking, without contracting a contagion or disease. After these experiments, people have changed their minds about the country, although it is still difficult for them to give a final decision on the water. However, by means of jeeps—which stir up typhoons of dust, day and night—one thing has been settled: India which, until now, had been located only in the towns, is spreading into the villages.

There are still some rare specimens of brown sahibs who are bound to the dak bungalows by ties of affection despite the fact that the baskets of Scotch have been emptied long ago, the goat grazing in the compound has been eaten, and the female goatherd has grown old.

The deputy director of education, who was due to arrive for the inquiry into the Changamal Vidyalaya Intermediate College, was such a specimen. He wanted to stay in one dak bungalow so that his devout wife could descend the steps at the back and bathe in the Ganga; in another, to write an epic poem on Maharana Pratap which would then become a course book for intermediate classes; in another, to visit Fitkariha Baba's hut once a year; and in another, to study the Gita and relieve his aching heart of the memory of all his foolishly missed opportunities; and in yet another . . .

And he wanted to run away to the Shivpalganj dak bungalow to escape the tumult, uproar and strife of city life; to suck sugar cane pieces, eat water chestnuts, chew corn on the cob; and get through five hundred files a day.

~

Chhote Wrestler was standing outside the dak bungalow thundering, 'The British have gone back to England and left their progeny here. If he were to come straight to the village, the matter could be settled at once. But his horse has to come straight to the dak bungalow and stop there. The whole village has to traipse two miles to get there and then has to sit doing bugger all.

'We came at nine in the morning, and now it's one o'clock. Over a hundred people are just hanging around with nothing to do. Now he will come chugging along in the evening in his motor car and say, "Hee-hee-hee, brothers, I'm late." You people are completely shameless. You'll just grin and titter back at him.

'Every hair on my body burns at the thought of it.'

In front of the bungalow was a green and pleasant lawn. Even if the wheat in the neighbouring fields withered for lack of water, the grass here always remained green. On four sides, along the compound wall, stood a line of mango trees whose fruit was consumed by the gardeners, the watchmen, three or four local thugs and an engineer who lived in the town. But the people had rights over the shade cast by these trees, just as they had over the air and so, at this moment, both parties of villagers were making the best use of it.

On either side of the bungalow, adjoining the trees, two small shamianas had been erected. Rugs and carpets were spread on the ground. One camp belonged to the Principal sahib and his companions, the other to Khanna Master's faction. At that moment there were, in the Principal's camp, besides the Principal himself and Badri Wrestler, about sixty people, including Chhote Wrestler, who was leaning elegantly against the trunk of a tree, and making known his views about the deputy director's conduct. Under the shamiana on the other side were Khanna Master, Ruppan babu, some masters of their group, and a few disciples and followers of Ramadhin Bhikhmakhervi. Ramadhin himself, as expected, was not present despite having promised to do so.

A stream of music flowed through the resounding roars of Chhote Wrestler, through the incessant chatter, eating and drinking, attempts to sleep, yawns, tobacco chewing, pipe, beedi and cigarette smoking.

It began with transistor radios. Also present in both camps were dandies with a cloth over their shoulders, each with a ball of lime behind one ear, a rifle strapped to their backs, a cage of partridges in one hand and a transistor in the other. In just a few moments, the transistors of both camps started blaring out songs from commercial radio, full of words like 'beloved', 'betrayer', 'liar', 'deceiver'. At eleven o'clock, a gramophone arrived in Khanna Master's camp from goodness knows where, complete with records and an amplifier, and by eleven-fifteen it had blasted out of memory the songs about 'liars' and 'deceivers', and had begun broadcasting music about coexistence and universal love—*Embrace me, O my companion of the road!*

It was clear that white doves were flying from, and olive branches were waving in, every word of this song. But in the Principal sahib's camp it was taken as a battle cry and, in a matter of minutes, a gramophone appeared there too, with records and an amplifier, and began to scream out the song, *Ooooooooooooh, hold me tight!*

As happens at village weddings, after this declaration, there was a clash of film songs from both sides.

Who could be angry in such an atmosphere? No one, except Chhote Wrestler but, in a way, there was good cause for his anger. Some people had, in fact, been there since eight, as the deputy director was expected at nine. Even the simplest and most straightforward cow of an official can be two or three hours late, but after five hours of waiting, Chote's irritation was fully justified.

'What can he do? He's beset with meetings, day and night. The moment he's ready to go anywhere, some meeting or the other comes and pounces on him,' said the Principal sahib good-humouredly.

It was two o'clock and the day was turning out to be quite hot. People began to suspect that the same gramophone records were being played over and over again. They kept getting up and disappearing hastily behind the bushes, and the leaders of both sides began to fear that they might be going to piss and then get pissed off. By this time,

Chhote Wrestler had slipped from beneath the tree into the shamiana and begun discussing Ruppan babu.

'Ruppan's gone and joined the enemy. He couldn't find anyone but his father to go against. I have badly beaten up my own father, but I'd like to see any outsider try to take liberties with him. Here is this bastard Khanna giving his father a shoe-beating and he is running along behind him yapping.

'Yesterday, Vaidyaji started beating his head over Ruppan's behaviour. I have given my father a beating with my lathi hundreds of times but I've never seen him look so unhappy. Ruppan's a perfect example of a worthless son . . .'

Badri had monopolized the corner of the shamiana where he was lying. Without waiting to hear Chhote complete his remark, he realized that Chhote was trying to make Ruppan look even smaller than himself. He said in the tone of a senior ustad, 'Enough, enough . . . Put a rein on your tongue.'

Chhote shut up. Then he said in a fit of sudden anger, 'This bird-killer looks as if he won't turn up till midnight.'

This is what is called mud-slinging. The deputy director had never so much as harmed an ant, let alone a bird!

~

At about four o'clock, Vaidyaji could be seen approaching the gates of the dak bungalow along with Sanichar. The gramophone-wallahs from the town played a film song to match the occasion, the first line of which ran, 'My eyes are fixed on your bungalow, Raja!' The moment it started, Chhote Wrestler gave such a sharp rebuke that the gramophones stopped by themselves. Some people sat down in an orderly way; others stood up.

Badri Wrestler alone lay as he was, in his corner, like a fallen tree trunk. Vaidyaji came and sat down confidently on the carpet. A cushion slipped itself automatically behind him, and Sanichar and the Principal sahib stood to one side as if intending to fan him with yak-tail fly whisks. When Vaidyaji sat down, it seemed as if the emperor of the whole world was ascending his throne. In comparison, Khanna Master, Ruppan babu and the others in the opposing camp looked like complete loafers and layabouts. Vaidyaji asked the Principal, 'What news?'

The Principal sahib began in high spirits, 'All our men are around here. Those on the other side are pissing themselves continuously.'

Sanichar remarked with relish, 'So, what do you say, shall we call Ruppan babu over and ask him? If he's in too much discomfort, we can bring some *jamalgote* from maharaj's dispensary and hand them one each.'

The happy expression faded from Vaidyaji's face. He said, 'Don't take that low fellow's name in front of me.' He paused and recovered himself. 'There's still no sign of the deputy director? It won't be long now before it is sunset.'

The Principal said, as if he were a dog wagging his tail—perhaps in the hope that his words would somehow reach the ears of the official—'He's such an important officer. He must have got stuck in some meeting. He should be coming now.'

'You should have sent someone.'

'That I did,' the Principal informed him. 'Master Motiram went there in the morning. He's neither in this group nor in that one. He only cares about his flour mill. That's why I told him, "Master Motiram, *you* go, you're a senior man. Ride back with the DD sahib in his car. No one's going to say to you that you'd gone to fill the DD sahib's ears on our behalf."'

Vaidyaji began telling a story to entertain the public:

'At that time, Pantji was in power in our state and the national government was very new. There was an election meeting, and Pantji was due to come at ten. The district magistrate, the police superintendent . . . they were all standing wearing their badges of office. It got to be eleven, then one, then two . . .'

Sanichar interrupted to say, 'After that, maharaj, it must have been three.'

Vaidyaji magnanimously accepted this piece of information. He said, 'That's what happened. At three-thirty, Pantji's motor car suddenly arrived at the meeting. Such an important national leader was present, but all the district officials were missing. It turned out they had gone to have lunch . . .'

The story went on. It was nearly five o'clock. By then, it had become apparent to the Principal sahib that people from his shamiana, too, had begun to get up and go off into the bushes, and the urinary problem had become so acute that some of them hadn't returned. He said to Chhote, 'Member sahib, this is not good.'

Chhote Wrestler had become bored. He said, 'So what should I do? Stop people from pissing and shitting?'

Now the songs from the gramophone were practically exhausted, and people had broken up into small groups to talk. The time had come for the sun to set. The Principal sahib was staring in the direction of a mango tree on the side of the road some distance from the dak bungalow. On the part of the tree at which he was staring, there was a dry branch. A bamboo cane was attached to the sickle which was caught up in the branch. The lower end of the cane was in the hands of a girl, who was about twenty. Her sari was dirty but her blouse was bright, and was pulling apart beneath her neck with the exertions of her tight body. As has been described, the Principal was just watching the branch. Suddenly he started, looked up the road in the opposite direction and said, 'Why is that bus coming along here so slowly?'

People began to rush towards the gate. A bus really had come and stopped in front of the dak bungalow.

Master Motiram climbed down carrying a huge bag. People surrounded him. After a short while, he made his way into Vaidyaji's presence and said, 'The deputy director isn't coming today.'

This fact had already been announced informally, as was evinced by the uproar all around and by the fact that even those who did not have urinary problems had begun to disperse in all directions. The Principal sahib asked, 'Then on which date has he said he would come?'

'I can't say. He wasn't even in the town today. He's been out on tour for three or four days and hasn't come back.'

'When will he come back?'

'How can I tell? No one knows anything. One man told me that he'd be back in four days, someone else told me five. I think that it'll be a week or so before he returns.'

Vaidyaji closed his eyes to relieve his tiredness. He asked, 'Then why didn't you come back in the morning? The people have had to endure such discomfort.'

Master Motiram humbly bowed his head. He said even more humbly, 'How could I come, maharaj? I had to buy this.' He pointed to the bag. 'It's an old flour mill. The parts keep on breaking. God knows how much I searched, then in the scrap market I found . . .'

Among the many people listening to Master Motiram's conversation was Rangnath. Perhaps he had come from the enemy side to discover the full details of the matter. When he tried to slip away, Vaidyaji called out to him. Rangnath came and sat down beside him.

Vaidyaji smiled at him and kept smiling. Rangnath was taken aback. Then he regained his courage and said, 'What can I do for you, uncle?'

'Nothing at all,' replied Vaidyaji sweetly. 'This is a war between right and wrong. You feel that these few teachers are on the right path, and therefore you're showing them kindness. But, sooner or later, you will learn which path is the path of virtue and which is not. When you do, you will return to your original place.'

He drew in his breath and continued, 'You are educated and intelligent, and I don't worry for you. I'm worried about Ruppan.'

To bring some lightness into the conversation, the Principal laughed loudly and said, 'Arré, no, maharaj, you don't know Rangnath babu. He's a big politician. He has already understood the situation on the other side; there's no need to explain it to him.'

Vaidyaji, too, smiled. 'In a righteous battle, faith, not understanding, is needed. When you are convinced that we are at fault, don't worry about it; fight us hard. Tell me the day you have need of my life. Like Bhishma Pitamah I myself will set the day of my death.'

Rangnath couldn't reply. He said, 'You misunderstand me.'

Vaidyaji's face was red, and he said emphatically, 'No, those people misunderstand me. I work in a democratic manner. I give everyone the freedom to speak their mind. That's why these teachers—who are my slaves—are roaming around opposing me. But there is a limit to this, too, isn't there, Principal sahib?'

The Principal lowered his eyes and said, 'How can I speak in front of you? One thing I do say—but for you, I would have resigned and left a long time ago.'

'Why should you go? No. The time has come to put an end to this chapter. Wait, I shall reach a decision just now.'

He called out to Chhote: 'Chhote, go over to the other shamiana and call Khanna Master and Malaviya. Bring Ruppan too. If they don't come, we will go to them. And tell the people to go home and rest. Principal sahib, go over there and thank the people.'

In a short while, both shamianas were almost deserted. Khanna Master's had emptied a little earlier because, on his side, there were no personalities of the calibre of Badri and Chhote Wrestler to prevent people from getting urinary trouble; and the moment they got the news that the deputy director had let them down, many people simply vanished. Now the few who remained around that camp were mainly those whose jobs were to look after the gramophone records or to hand around earthenware bowls of water. In Vaidyaji's shamiana were Badri Wrestler, Chhote, Sanichar, the Principal sahib, Vaidyaji, two or three respectable people and a few of Badri's hooligans from the wrestling pit.

Upon receiving Vaidyaji's message, Khanna, Malaviya, two masters of their faction and Ruppan babu came over, chatting carelessly among themselves, and sat down in front of him. Khanna Master said, 'You remembered us?'

It was growing dark. In the last sinking rays of light was this forest of garden, tents, carpets—all creating a magical atmosphere. It was as if some emperor of Delhi had reached the Deccan and was in council with his courtiers at eventide on the summit of a hill, about some captured rebel nobles who were being presented to him.

Then Vaidyaji's speech began:

'Khannaji and Malaviyaji, I have called you here considering you as my own kin.

'The mutual opposition between you and the Principal has increased. Legal cases are going on. Abuses and insults are exchanged in public, and preparations are being made for violent confrontation.

I do not blame you. The blame can be anybody's. I myself am guilty.
How can I apportion blame? But I do know one thing and that is that
the situation is unpleasant. It should be resolved.'

Khanna said, 'Please give me the chance to have my say, too.'

'No,' replied Vaidyaji solemnly shaking his head, 'No! No! No! You
have already had your say on several occasions, in various places. Only
one man has not had his say up to now, and that man is me. Today,
only I will speak.

'I made this college: I watered it with my blood. Both factions
consist of wage-earners. If not here, you'll go somewhere else and
be teachers. You can become teachers anywhere and draw a good
salary. But I shall remain here. If this college runs successfully I will
consider myself successful, and if it is destroyed by factionalism, I will
consider myself destroyed. I am troubled. Immensely troubled. Deeply
anguished. You people cannot comprehend my anguish.'

He paused. The shamiana was engulfed in silence. Then he
bounded on, 'I see only one way forward now. I have decided. It is my
humble request to you that you accept my decision. This is the only
way open to you. You will have to tread it.

'Khannaji and Malaviyaji, I am not saying this to anyone else, but
just to you—you will have to resign.'

At this, Khanna interrupted and said, 'But . . .'

'No,' repeated Vaidyaji kindly but firmly, 'no, I have already told
you—today only I will speak. So, as I was saying, you will have to resign.
Today, now, right here and this very moment, you will have to resign! I
am not saying this in anger but after careful consideration. I am saying
it for your benefit, for the benefit of the college and for the benefit of
the whole society.

'This is my humble supplication. Don't reject my request. Hand
in your resignations this moment. After that, you will have complete
freedom to do as you wish. You can, if you like, say that your
resignations were extracted by force. You will remain free to file a case
against us on those grounds. But it is my request that, at this time, as
well-wishers of the college, you quietly hand in your resignations of
your own free will.

'You have asked me for many things, and you have received them. I have never asked you for anything. Today, for the sake of the college, I am asking for your resignations. My request . . .'

Ruppan babu had leapt to his feet. His voice was trembling. He was so excited that when he spoke one word tumbled out after another. He said, 'This cannot happen. You cannot force them to write their resignations. They will not resign.'

Vaidyaji ignored him and said to the Principal, 'You have the papers already typed, don't you? You have? Then take them over there. Chhote, you take Khannaji and Malaviyaji over there. They are wise. They will understand everything. Go on, Badri, you go too.'

Then he exploded. The explosion was so sudden and unusual that Badri leapt towards him and other people also came running. He thundered, 'And, this Ruppan! This fool! Low! Animal! Depraved! Traitor!'

He kept on speaking in this way, proving through his elevated vocabulary that Sanskrit is not at all a weak language when it comes to abuse. Something in his thundering voice, something in the ire of his Sanskrit, made the audience listen in awed silence. Today was the first time people had seen Vaidyaji so enraged.

He was sitting on the carpet pumping his knees up and down like steel pistons, and screaming from a trembling throat, 'You're trying to be a leader! You want to become a leader by opposing me? I'll show you just now!'

His voice began to tremble even more. He said, 'I had hoped to pass my old age in peace and quietness. I have brought an end to the fight in the village council. There was the cooperative union—that, I've already given to Badri. I had thought to hand over the burden of this college to you. What else do I have left to give you now? But you low creature! You turned traitor! Go! Now you will get nothing.'

There was a strange catch in his voice. He proclaimed, 'Go. I cut you off from your inheritance. Let everyone hear it. After I am gone, only Badri will be the manager of the college. This is my final decision. Ruppan will get nothing.'

As he said this, he choked. Tears of anger and frustration filled his eyes. Rangnath felt that everyone was looking at him. He lowered his glance.

When Ruppan babu headed for the gate, people regained their wits. Vaidyaji was wiping his eyes. People suddenly began to move again. They began to disperse. A lantern was burning on the veranda of the dak bungalow, and there, Malaviya began raising his voice. Chhote called out to him, 'Take it easy, Master!'

The Principal grasped Khanna's hand and said, 'Come, Master sahib, we'll go over there. Our fight is over. From today, we're friends again.'

~

It wasn't to be hoped for, but even so, there was a morning after the night before.

Rangnath had neither been able to sleep well nor think straight. But the moment he awoke he did have one thought about himself. Some months previously, after a long illness, he had come here for the sole purpose of recovering his health. Now he suddenly realized that he had recovered.

Ruppan babu's charpoy, next to his, was empty. He didn't know where Ruppan could have spent the night. In some ways, he had complete confidence in Ruppan. He knew that when he seemed stupid it was because he wanted to. He wasn't compelled to be stupid; it was something he enjoyed, almost a self-indulgent luxury. Therefore, he was confident that Vaidyaji's outburst would not send him running to the liquor shop. He wouldn't have gone off to the temple either, because he didn't have the look of a person who depends on the temple in times of trouble.

Then where was he? Was he at that moment gathering his followers for a strike at the college? Was he organizing a revolutionary party to burn down the building, beat up the Principal or purposelessly loot the bazaar? Or was he, in accordance with the celebrated formula of the teaching profession, in some other village anointing Khanna Master principal and setting up a new college comparable to the Changamal Vidyalaya Intermediate College for him? Rangnath thought, 'He must be doing something like that because, when he left after Vaidyaji's display of anger, Ruppan was angry, not subdued.'

Vaidyaji used to go for a fairly long morning walk, and he had still not returned. Rangnath knew that now it would be difficult to talk to him naturally, and he wasn't prepared to talk unnaturally. He told himself that he had collapsed with his first attempt at opposition and that now he should see himself for what he was. He should leave this place even before his uncle returned.

As the song went, 'Don't tarry here, it's an alien land.'

Sanichar had opened his shop and two men were fighting very dramatically in front of it. The struggle was verbal, logical and, so far, non-violent. One of them had diverted canal water from the other's fields to his own. They had come to the head of the village council to have their argument settled and to argue before it got settled.

The life around which, over the last few months, Rangnath had hovered, which he had penetrated, but to which he still remained very much an outsider, appeared to him a disgrace. The strings of his soul—always supposing the soul is in the shape of a sarangi—began to reverberate with escapist music.

He stood in the doorway watching silently. Chhote Wrestler passed by, scratching his ringworm as usual and not looking at Rangnath. There was a loud rumbling from the street. This would be the cooperative dairy truck from the town which came to collect milk. A man with a pot hanging from his hand could be seen going towards Sanichar's shop. Rangnath realized that this was the oil seller who bought oil from a mechanical press in the town and passed it off in the village as pure mustard oil from a genuine bullock-powered press. A clean soldierly man in underpants and a vest appeared on his way back from buying meat. As he did every day, the man said, 'Long live India, sahib!'

He went off swinging his bundle of meat. Rangnath felt like embracing him and saying, 'Well, at least for some reason, someone here has mentioned India.'

From far off came the sound of a magic man's drum. The exchange of insults at Sanichar's shop was reaching a new peak. Rangnath felt sick and tired. The strings of his soul now began to resound with the full melody of escapism.

The Music of Escapism

You are an average human being and are stuck in the mud of humanity. You are surrounded by mud and mud alone.

Don't extol mud. Don't be under the illusion that lotuses grow in it. Only mud flourishes in mud. Mud spreads mud and throws up mud.

Save yourself from the mud. Leave this place. Escape.

Go and hide yourself in the places you have seen in the colour photographs of *Look* and *Life* magazines, in places where crowns of flowers, guitars and girls constantly beckon your soul to new explorations, where the air is thinner than thin, where you will find the eternal dreaminess of Ravi Shankar's brand of music and Maharishi Yogi's brand of meditation . . .

Escape from here. Leave.

Escape like young doctors, engineers and scientists, like thinkers who pine for international fame, and whose constant lament is that not all the people here could make them happy. Don't get trapped in the mess here.

If you are unfortunate and are forced to stay here, create a separate, make-believe world for yourself. Live in that world, where many intellectuals lie with their eyes closed. In hotels and clubs. Bars and teahouses. In the new buildings of Chandigarh, Bhopal and Bangalore. In hill station retreats where endless seminars are held. In brand new research institutes funded by foreign aid, where the image of Indian intellect is being shaped. In cigar smoke, books with shiny covers, and universities enveloped in a fog of incorrect but compulsory English. Go and stay there, and hold fast.

If you can't do that, go and hide in the past; in the philosophy of Kanada, Patanjali and Gautam; in the temples of Ajanta, Ellora, Konark and Khajuraho; in the heavy breasts of the sculpted female figures of Shalabhanjika, Surasundari and Alasa Kanya; in prayers and mantras; in saints, astrologers and palmists—hide wherever you can find a place.

Run, run, run! You're being pursued by reality.

Rangnath was about to get up when he saw the Principal coming from the direction of the college. Today, he was wearing shoes and socks as well as a shirt and shorts. In his hand was the cane he always carried. From a distance, he laughed and joined his hands in greeting. In a matter of moments he came on to the veranda and sat down on a chair there, quite confident that he was the only thing that had been missing from the scene. He asked, 'Maharaj still hasn't come back from his walk?' and began to take off his shoes and socks so that he could sit comfortably.

In a little while, he had settled himself in the chair like a frog. He said, 'Yesterday, maharaj was very hurt, but, still, that matter is over now.'

He became more enthusiastic, 'I had already told him that you were sitting back and watching the spectacle. You were never really against us. You used to go over to them just to see what was going on. I've convinced maharaj of this.'

Both sat for a few moments in silence. The sound of the magic man's drum was drawing closer. The Principal said, 'Your health looks to be really *tichinn.*'

'Tichinn?'

'Yes, you're looking completely fit.'

Rangnath said with great civility, 'It's due to your blessings.'

'So what do you intend to do now?'

'I'm going back. I've not done any research for so long, and I have to complete it this summer.'

The Principal made a few absurd remarks, the meaning of which was that Rangnath was a great scholar of history, but that, generally, people were the sons of asses, and universities were no better than stables, and even the biggest professors were just hacks. Rangnath showed no interest in these comments, so the Principal asked, 'What are your chances? Is there any hope of your becoming a lecturer this year?'

'So far, there's no question of it.'

The Principal pulled his chair two inches forward and said, 'You know that Khanna Master has resigned. The post of history lecturer in our college is vacant. Why don't you take it? You can live like a king in your uncle's house, teach a couple of hours a day in college and use the rest of your time for research.'

Rangnath felt as if all the blood in his body had rushed to his brow, making it swell like a cobra's hood. He said sharply, 'You want me to work for you? And that, too, in Khanna's place!'

Not a trace of a frown crossed the Principal's face. He said, 'I've spoken to Vaid maharaj about it.'

Rangnath went on with the same asperity, 'I saw it with my own eyes. I know how Khanna was thrown out from here . . .'

The Principal said sadly, 'What can I say? Even you are repeating such things. This smacks of factionalism.'

A man in a torn loincloth and a dirty black kurta, beating a small hand-drum, went up to Sanichar's shop. With him were a male and a female monkey, dressed in costumes for dancing. Behind them came a number of small boys shrieking with laughter. There were also some dogs in the crowd and, to frighten them, the man would bring his drum down over their heads with a sudden bang.

Because of the drum the Principal had to raise his voice. He went on, 'What does it matter whether the post is vacant because Khanna has left or Malaviya is dead? It's your own mango grove, so eat the fruit. Why are you counting the trees?'

Finding that Rangnath had no answer, the Principal began to speak tenderly. He descended from the formal *aap*, Hindi 'you', to the more intimate *tum*. 'I am saying this to you because I consider you as one of my own kith and kin. In the end, what are you going to do? You have to get a job somewhere or the other, don't you? Here, Khanna has resigned of his own free will. In another place, how will you be able to tell whether some other Khanna hasn't really been thrown out on his ear?

'How long can you go on escaping from this fact, Rangnath babu? Wherever you go, you will be taking some Khanna's place.'

With this, he addressed the magic man standing some way away from the veranda, and with a forceful gesture of his hand, advised him to go to hell.

Rangnath flushed. Raising his voice as if, with it, he were raising the flag of truth, he said, 'Principal sahib, I am revolted by what you are saying. Please shut up.'

The Principal listened in surprise, and then said despondently, 'Rangnath babu, your ideas are very elevated. But all in all, they only prove that you're a fool.'

~

After this, there was a break in the conversation. The magic man, instead of going to hell, began to sing at the top of his voice where he stood and beat a different rhythm on his drum. A little way off, two dogs were arching their spines and barking. The boys had surrounded him. Both monkeys were sitting in front of the magic man with their cheeks puffed out, looking as if, when they got up, they would perform nothing less than Bharatanatyam.

NOTES AND GLOSSARY

Abhimanyu	A character from the Mahabharat who penetrated a circular battle formation and, when trapped in the middle, his weapons rendered useless, whirled a chariot wheel about his head to ward off attackers
ADO	Assistant Development Officer
Arhar	A type of lentil which grows into a tall bush
Arjun	A hero of the Mahabharat who, once, could not stop the abduction of some women
Avdhut	An ascetic devoted to Shiva
Babaji	A Hindu ascetic
Bajrangbali	A name for Hanuman, the monkey god
Banjaras	A nomadic tribe
Bharat	The devoted brother of the great king Lord Ram who refused the throne and, instead, ruled in his brother Ram's name until he returned from exile
Bhishma Pitamah	An elder in the Mahabharat who could not die unless he himself chose to lay down his life
Chakor	The Himalayan partridge, often mentioned in poetry as being in love with the moon
Dada ganjaha	An elder brother; also the dominant thug of an area, meaning 'inhabitant of Shivpalganj' in the local Shivpalganj dialect
Girdhariya	Under this name, Lord Krishna used a mountain to shield humans from a storm
Harishen	The fourth-century Sanskrit poet who wrote a panegyric extolling the virtues of Emperor Samudra Gupta

Ikka-wallah	The driver of an ikka (horse cart)
Jamalgote	A purgative nut
Kabirpanthi	An ascetic belonging to a rather austere and protestant sect
Kali Yug	The present age in the Hindu cycle of time; the last age of the universe before its destruction and rebirth
Kalkin Avatar	An incarnation of Lord Vishnu yet to come; it is believed that he will come to destroy evil at the end of our present era, riding a white horse and carrying a blazing sword
Kos	A distance of about two miles
Kukrahao	Encouraging one another in a fight (ganjaha dialect)
Lasebaz/bazi	A trickster/trickery (ganjaha dialect)
Mahishasur-mardini	Durga, the brave goddess who killed the buffalo demon
Maya–Manohar	The Hindi equivalent of Mills & Boon love stories
Nautanki	A type of popular folk theatre
Paan	Betel leaf
Panch	One of five (panch) elders; title of a member of a village law council
Panchsheel	Jawaharlal Nehru's five principles for peaceful coexistence among nations
Phalgun	A month in the Hindu calendar, around February
Phuttpheri	Wandering like a vagabond (ganjaha dialect)
Pindaris	A tribe of hereditary thieves and plunderers
Portulaca	A flower which closes at sundown
'Purush Sukta'	A hymn of the Rig Veda which says that the highest caste came from the head of the Cosmic Man, and the lowest caste from the feet
Pus	A month in the Hindu calendar, around December
Rahul	The Buddha's son who was accepted into the Buddhist order when he demanded his inheritance from his father

Ramlila	The enactment of the ancient epic, the Ramayan, performed during every Dussehra festival
Rana Sanga	The Rajput king who was defeated at the Battle of Panipat by the first Mughal emperor, and who bore innumerable wounds
Sarangi	A string instrument, generally thought to sound rather melancholy
Section 107	A section of the Indian Criminal Procedure Code which provides for action to prevent a breach of peace
Section 109	A section of the Indian Criminal Procedure Code; when a person moves in suspicious circumstances, fails to explain his presence satisfactorily or conceals his presence, and there is reason to believe that he is doing so with a view to committing a cognizable offence, a magistrate can ask him to execute a bond for good behaviour
Tehsil	Smaller administrative areas into which districts are divided
Tehsildar	The chief land revenue official of a tehsil
Thakur	A title given to members of the Rajput caste
Treta Yug	The second age in the Hindu cycle of time, a much better age than the present, which is Kali Yug, the fourth age
Ustad	The Urdu equivalent of guru—a teacher, master of an art held in immense respect by his pupils
Vedanta	A school of Indian philosophy
Vibhishan	The brother of the demon king Ravan; he joined the forces of Lord Ram against his own brother because he wished to be on the side of right
Vishwamitra	An Indian sage whose meditation was broken by the celestial nymph, Menaka
Yudhishthira	The eldest of the Pandava heroes in the Mahabharat; he embodies truth and justice